A WORLD APART

Gretta Curran Browne

88
Eighty-Eight Publications

Although this work was originally published as a lengthy major book under one title, *Fire On The Hill* : it is now published in eBook edition under two separate titles:- *Fire On The Hill* and *A World Apart*

———————

`Here is a real blockbuster, magnificent, passionate, poignant.' – *Books Ireland.*

`A powerful historical novel.' – *Guernsey Evening Press*

`Powerful! A love story which endures more than half a century and spans two continents.' – *Brecon and Radnor Express*

`Browne has a talent for drawing us into her characters and situations.' – *Irish News*

British Library Cataloguing in Publication Data
Browne, Gretta Curran
813.54 [F]

ISBN: 978-0-9927374-2-9

Cover Design: Asha Hossain Design, Inc.

Eighty-Eight Publications
2 Spencer Avenue
London N13

Dedicated with love to my son

SÉAN

Prologue

They thought they had killed him – on the same winter night his friend Sam McAllister had been shot dead on the hillside of Derrynamuck – they had chased Michael and seen a trail of his blood in the snow. Oh yes, the young rebel captain was dead and gone, and would cause no further trouble to them – the hated militia who raped and burned houses at will and treated the people of Wicklow like some dirt that kept getting under their boots.

Desperate for his protection from the militia's brutality, only the people refused to believe that Michael Dwyer was dead. To them he was like a prince – `aye, a prince, same as a king's son' – and if Michael had been killed, all his friends would have been in mourning, but they were not. Too many times they had seen the small, secret smiles of Michael's friends when the militia gloated over his death.

And then there was Mary – his beautiful Mary who had adored him – why was she not looking in any way heart-broken? Why was she just carrying on with her life as normal?

No, the people concluded, Michael was not dead – injured maybe, a whole lot of bullets had flown towards him that night at Derrynamuck – but he had been dodging bullets for years and not one had ever reached him. No, only the stupid militia would believe that Michael had been defeated – the whole dumb pack of them.

PART ONE

CHAPTER ONE

In the shadowy stillness of the small green wood, rich with the fragrance of pines, a young man stood as motionless as a hawk marking its prey. In his hands he held a gaming-rifle in readiness, his face shadowed by the brim of a black hat pulled low on his brow.

Slowly he raised the gun almost level with his cheek, the barrel angled downwards, his eyes fixed unwavering on the tawny hare. He gently pulled back the flintlock mechanism, making only a slight click, and prepared to fire. Then – a chaos of noise erupted behind him. The hare dashed for cover. A black cloud of cawing rooks screamed into the air.

He turned abruptly towards the noise, then ran swiftly to the edge of the wood, where he spied a small hunting party some way off. His eyes fell on the barking dog galloping wildly across the field, a red setter, half-mad with panic, pursued by a shouting man on horseback.

The setter frantically skidded right, then left, then plunged forward again.

`You unmanageable hound!' the horseman shouted, then spotting the young man by the trees, `Catch him! Don't just stand there, man! Catch him!'

He hesitated, not used to taking orders, but he could see something had badly upset the dog. He stepped out a few paces, whistling in a long and low way. The setter's ears pricked uncertainly, he skidded to a trot, looked around and bounded over to him, eyes wide and tongue hanging.

`There's a good boy,' the young man said softly, rubbing the russet head. `Calm down now, calm down. Nothing to be frightened of. Nothing at all.'

The setter shuddered and shook himself, his animal instinct telling him he would suffer no harm from this human. Panting with relief, he shook himself again and moved his head to lick the back of the hand gently stroking him – and it was then that the bloody wound on his flappy ear came into view.

The young man glanced up as the horseman drew rein.

An elegantly dressed man only a few years older than himself. He recognised him instantly as William Hume, the son of the late Mr Hume of Humewood. He quickly turned his face back to the setter.

`Setters are an unpredictable breed,' Hume exclaimed angrily. `This one keeps turning a bit mad. He's spoiled a good day's sporting for me.'

`He's been hit – either with a whip or the graze of a bullet – on the ear.'

`What?'

`Aye, just a small nick. But enough to make him think he was maybe for the kill and not the fox.'

`Damn the bloody blockhead who did that!' Hume cried, looking over his shoulder in the direction of the hunting party. `Whoever it was should be horsewhipped. That setter is a very valuable dog – my late father's favourite.'

`Well, he seems calm enough now.'

`Yes, thanks to you.'

Hume's eyes raked over the young man kneeling and petting the dog, taking in every detail of him from head to foot. A tall fellow, strong-made but light-limbed. He wore shoes, black wool stockings and leather breeches. His upper body was clothed in a black knitted jersey of the type fishermen wore. But he was not a fisherman, for bathe as often as they may, fishermen always carried the smell of the fish with them.

There was something else about this fellow, something that made Hume uneasy as his eyes moved over the black hat to the black hair curling around his neck. Then Hume realised what it was that bothered him – the hat! The insolent fellow had not thought to remove it in the presence of a gentleman! Not even briefly to touch his forelock.

'Oolaloo `For'ard away!'

Hume jerked round in the saddle. `Sounds as if they've spotted the varmint again,' he said, excitement in his voice. `A big one he is too; an old dog-fox with a greying brush, so he must have eluded many a hunt. But we'll catch the clever old thing this time.'

The young man glanced up at Hume's turned back, then

in the direction the noise came from, the noise of the hunt in full cry, yelping hounds baying with blood lust. `Sounds as if they are near the river,' he said. `Horses and hounds are likely to get bogged down in the banks there, I reckon. And if the fox once slides into the water, as the clever old thing surely intends, then his scent will be lost.'

He again bent to smooth the dog, the smile on his face hidden under the low brim of his black hat.

Hume turned back. `Yes, I fear you may be right there,' he said sourly. `You are obviously experienced in hunting the fox?'

`Only if he has asked for it by attacking the hens in the yard. I've never hunted him for pleasure. I prefer to hunt game that will provide a good breakfast or supper.'

Hume laughed. `And old Reynard could never do that! You are a farmer?'

`A farmer's son, sir.'

Hume smiled, warmed by the fellow remembering his manners and rightly addressing him as `sir'. And that black hat would soon be whipped off when he disclosed who he himself was.

`Well, I am William Hume of Humewood, the new Member of Parliament for Wicklow, and a captain of the Humewood Cavalry Corps.'

`An honour to meet you, sir,' the young man replied, his lips smiling as he touched a finger to the brim of his hat, but did not remove it.

`Your own name?' Hume demanded.

`Byrne, sir.'

Hume frowned. There were hundreds of Byrnes in Wicklow. He was about to ask which Byrne of which district, when the young man said quietly: `I was very sorry to hear about your father, Mr Hume, about the way he was killed at the end of last year.'

Hume was taken aback at the sincerity in the voice, for he had not expected any tenant's son, undoubtedly a papist, to be sorry about the death of one of the Protestant landed gentry.

`Why are you sorry?' he demanded.

`Because Mr Hume senior was a fair man,' came the reply. `And from what I have heard, it was a deliberate murder, provoked through a personal and bitter enmity between two men, and nothing to do with the cause of the rebellion.'

Mr Hume's young face clouded at the memory of his father. `A terrible, terrible business,' he said sadly. `Shot in cold blood while out sporting one morning. It was Michael Dwyer who did it.'

`Michael Dwyer?' The noise of the hunt filled the pause. `Then why did they hang Moore of Killalish for the deed? And it's said Moore confessed at the gallows that he did it.'

`True, but the militia still insist it was Michael Dwyer.'

The young man shrugged. `The militia would blame the Crucifixion on Michael Dwyer if they could. But I doubt if a condemned man would tell a lie on the threshold of eternity. If Moore said he killed your father, then I would imagine he did, and not Dwyer.'

`Maybe so, maybe so.' Hume said with a sigh. `Moore of Killalish even confessed to me, at the end, that it was him who did it. But the militia still insist he was lying. Did you know Dwyer?'

`I never did come face to face with him myself,' the young man said. `Did you ever see him, sir?'

`Once or twice, as a boy, but not since I left Wicklow for school in England. A very quiet lad as I remember. Very respectful and quite well-educated.' Hume sighed. `Turned into a wild and vicious character by all accounts.'

`So they say, sir.'

`Well, at least Wicklow is rid of him. They say he died in a cave somewhere up in the mountains near Corragh. The eagles and hawks will have done for him by now.'

`One would imagine so, sir.'

Impetuously, Hume decided he liked this young man who had tamed his dead father's beloved mad setter into tranquil contentment, lying on its belly, front paws out.

`Look here, you must allow me to reward you for your trouble,' Hume said benevolently, `for assisting me in catching the dog.' He withdrew some silver from his pocket.

14

`No, no, I want nothing!'

The smile disappeared from William Hume's face at the young man's sharp tone. `But you did me a service! The dog had turned mad and would have disappeared for weeks, or even altogether, if you had not caught and calmed him.'

`Just being neighbourly,' the young man answered over his shoulder as he turned and strolled away. `Good hunting to you, Mr Hume.'

The dog rose to his feet and slunk after him, as if hoping the man on horseback wouldn't notice, but after a pat on the head, he was ordered back to his master.

The dog did not obey, just stood there watching the young man until he had disappeared into the shadows of the wood from which he had first emerged.

*

Leaning on the window ledge of the tavern in the small square of Donard, the young red-coated captain stood watching the girl as she moved from stall to stall down the busy square. It was market-day, the square crowded with hawkers selling everything from dairy produce and small pigs, to wool and sewing-threads.

It was not just the girl's stunning beauty that drew the soldier's attention, made him pick her out from the crowd. It was the way the people responded to her, every single one of them, in a way bordering on absolute homage.

She seemed unaware of it, her manner modest and restrained, her expression preoccupied as she sorted through the various coloured cards of sewing threads while the old hag sitting behind the wooden box smiled up at her lovingly.

She was young, no more than nineteen or twenty. She wore a long blue cloak that hid her figure, but from the angles of her smooth face and delicate nose and chin, and the tall way she carried herself, he guessed that the body hidden beneath the cloak was slender. Her black hair hung long and straight in a simple style to her waist. And when she turned her head, and her eyes lingered for a thoughtful moment on the tavern, he saw they were large and dark.

He was fascinated by her, wondering who she was, and why the people treated her with such deference as if she were some Celtic queen who had graced their shabby square. She might be lovely, but she was still a peasant girl, probably the daughter of an Imaal farmer.

Still, he could not take his eyes off her. If she had betrayed some signs of being a doxie, given some hint in her manner, by look or laugh, that she was the type who would not mind enjoying a night or two of a soldier's pay, he might have even considered approaching her, striking up an acquaintance.

But she was clearly no doxie. She had the look of a gentle madonna, but also with a look of that dark Celtic pride that could be withering and hostile. He was the wrong man, in the wrong place, for a girl like her. Even without speaking to her, he instinctively knew there would be an infinite gulf between them.

And the realisation of that made him suddenly resent the girl.

There were two or three other redcoats in the tavern, a number of the hated militia too, but the eyes of the tavern keeper were fixed on Captain Woollard of the 38th Regiment, standing by the window. He watched carefully as the captain turned, and beckoned with an authoritative hand to a yeoman named Hawkins sitting near the fire.

Sergeant Hawkins was of the Humewood (Upper Talbotstown) Yeoman Cavalry. He had been born in the Glen of Imaal, the son of a farming family who rented a hundred and twenty acres of land from the Humes of Humewood, and he knew all the inhabitants of this part of County Wicklow. He joined Woollard at the window.

`Who is that girl?' Woollard asked.

Hawkins bent and peered. `Mary Doyle,' he said. `The daughter of William Doyle of Knockandarragh.'

`A farmer?'

`Aye.'

`Does he hold a special position in the community?'

`Who, Doyle?' Sergeant Hawkins laughed. `Only when he's had a good few drinks and starts his singing.' Hawkins laughed again. `And can that man drink!'

Captain Woollard looked perplexed.`So why do the people treat her as they do, as if she were someone special.'

Sergeant Hawkins gave the question a little thought. He leaned an elbow on the ledge and stared at the girl.

`Ask any other yeoman that question,' he said, `and they would not be able to tell you. But I think I can. She was the sweetheart of Michael Dwyer, before he was killed. And because the people adored him, they now adore her. She reminds them of him.'

`Michael Dwyer!' Woollard spat the name. So that was her claim to fame. He was disappointed, for he felt nothing but contempt for these people and their heroes. And Michael Dwyer was a local hero that Woollard was sick to the bowels hearing about.

Most of the tales were embellished with hatred and vindictiveness, because Dwyer had always beaten the militia who were poor soldiers, sloppy and cowardly in the extreme.

`He was a savage and against the law,' Woollard said. `He would have been caught and hanged eventually, if the Eighty-ninth had not shot him while running away.'

Sergeant Hawkins was not a fast-talking man. He was also extremely fair and honest. He said slowly: `With all respect to you, sir, but Michael Dwyer was no savage. No man knew him as well as I did, for our families grew up alongside each other in Imaal, and I never knew him to do a mean or unmanly act. And even after the rebellion when he carried on his mountain warfare, I could not censure him for that. He was hunted and hounded mercilessly by certain factions of the militia, bent on murdering him. What else had he to do but fight back.'

`I was not aware you had sympathy for the rebel,' Woollard responded sourly.

`Is it Michael Dwyer you are talking about, Sergeant Hawkins? Oh, it's an ill wind that whispers his name!'

Captain Woollard spun round. He saw that the man addressing them was not tall, but thickset and strong, getting on in years, leaning on a blackthorn stick. His hair, eyebrows and side-whiskers were white and bushy, his eyes a very clear shade of blue. He wore the breeches and gaiters of a mountain shepherd, a rug-cloak slung across his shoulders. Woollard wondered how long he had been standing behind them, listening. He was about to tell him to be off, when the man said:

`A right bastard he was – Dwyer! And any yeoman who felt sympathy for him is a fool of the first order. Some ignorant folk around here may try and let on that he was fighting against injustice and in defence of the people of Wicklow against the brutality of the militia, but the truth is, the bastard was nothing more than a disgrace to humanity. Aye, aye: I could tell you a tale or two about Michael Dwyer that would cure your sympathy in no time.'

Despite himself, Captain Woollard was interested. He knew the man was probably only looking for a free drink, but, he decided why not? He called over to the surly tavern keeper for a bottle, and when he came with it, Woollard did not miss the look of hatred he fired at the white-haired old man.

`Oh yes, sir,' said the old man, sitting down on a stool nearby and sipping his drink, `I knew Dwyer well – before he died, that is. And let me tell you, it was him, and him alone, that turned this here hair of mine white! Persecuted me he did, persecuted me something sinful, until one day I could take no more, and at Baltinglass Fair I lifted this here stick and hit him such a cracking larrup on the head it nearly left him a corpse; troth, it did.' The old man sniffed proudly at the memory.

Woollard looked at Hawkins, who nodded. He had seen the old man do it. And the enmity between him and Michael Dwyer had been legend ever since.

`Who is he?' Woollard asked when the white-haired old man had stepped unsteadily out of the tavern, after consuming a good portion of the bottle of whiskey. `He never stopped talking long enough for me to ask his name.'

`John Cullen,' Hawkins replied. `An old shepherd that lives way up in the wilderness of the sheep hills. He has only his dog and goat for company and very few humans venture up there, so he has little else to think about while sitting by his hearth or tending his sheep on the hills, but his brooding hatred of Dwyer.'

A sudden commotion outside abruptly diverted both men's attention back to the window. The girl was now standing by the wooden box of a woman selling balls of wool. The white-haired old man was shouting at her, waving his stick in the air.

`Good Lord!' said Woollard. `Looks like he might hit her!' He rushed out of the tavern followed by Sergeant Hawkins who clutched his arm.

`Don't intervene,' Hawkins warned quietly,`unless he strikes her. Otherwise the people will be glad to turn on you. The old man too if you attempt to take her side.'

Both men paused a little way back from the group of people who had moved closer to the old man and the girl, listening with expressions of horrified fascination.

`You're a fool, a fool,' the old man shouted, `to be wasting your youth mourning that bastard. And you may as well know the truth of it – for I *knows* the truth of it, and the truth is – Dwyer was making a fool of you – using you like a common doxie. The lass he really loved was the daughter of Reilly of Coolamaddra. Aye! And rumour has it that he would have married her if he hadn't been shot.'

The girl made no answer, but her pale cheeks had stained with a red flush, her dark eyes flickering.

`And serves you right!' the old man cried. `You and Reilly's daughter along with you. Sluts, the both of you, *sluts!*'

Within seconds the old man was converged upon and seized by two young men who unceremoniously lifted him off his feet and carried him bodily away from the girl while the furious women jeered and booed him.

`Let me go, you gouts!' the old man screamed. `Let me go!'

The girl had turned and stood looking after the two men who dumped the old man at the end of the square and ordered him to be off – 'or else! And when she turned back, Woollard saw her face contained no anger, but a strange look of disbelief.

He felt a pang of sympathy for her, but then his head overruled all his other instincts and he found himself agreeing with the old man. Serves her right, for getting mixed up with a rebel.

For a moment, by the way she clutched at her stomach and breathed deeply, he feared she was going to faint. But then she noticed him looking at her, and instantly she seemed to collect herself, her chin lifting slightly, before she turned to speak to the plump rosy-faced woman behind the box of wools.

`Do you have any other colours?' she asked. `Any *light* colours?'

`Ah no,' the woman replied apologetically. `Only the black and the brown. It's the dye, d'ye see. The dyes for other colours are more costly than the black and the brown. But I may have them next time.'

`I bought too much black last time,' the girl said. `Will you take back what I have not used?'

Woollard waited for the woman to scowl a refusal, for there were no people more shrewder than these market dealers. But the woman smiled rosily and cried, `Sure I will, me lovey!'

And when the girl took out three balls of black wool from the goatskin bag under her cloak, the woman happily counted the money into the girl's hand in refund.

`I'll likely have some blue next time,' the woman said brightly. `Or maybe even white or yella.'

The girl nodded and walked on, and Captain Woollard watched the woman's eyes following her lovingly as she moved through the crowded square, the people parting and smiling at her, with the same attitude of absolute homage as before.

Whatever the vicious old shepherd had said about Michael Dwyer being in love with the other girl, these people seemed to think different.

*

From the shadows of the trees the young man watched the

hunting party that had failed to catch the clever old fox. He watched them as their horses formed a procession and made its way uphill before breaking into a free trot on the open meadows beyond.

He turned to go, moving out of the shadows, then mused away the time as he strolled along the wild and hilly paths that would lead him home. The gaming bag on his back contained two pheasant and a rabbit.

He breathed deep into his lungs and gazed over the deserted hills. He had been out since the chilly dew of morning and now the afternoon was fresh and warm with the smell of May-blossom in the air.

He sprang down from a ridge onto another path below, and then stopped abruptly, his attention attracted by the distant screams of a female.

He moved in the direction of the screams, towards an old sand quarry which bordered the beaten pathway.

When he reached the edge he saw a young peasant girl struggling with two of the militia, the bodice of her dress torn in two. One laughed savagely, then bent his head as if biting her. As slight as she was, the girl struggled wildly until one of them began to punch her mercilessly in the stomach.

For a moment he stood stunned as he watched them fling her violently to the ground, one of them holding her down, kneeling at her head and clamping a hand over her screaming mouth while the other tugged at the belt around his waist and prepared to mount her.

As the leather tongue of the belt came free of its buckle, and the soldier yanked at the buttons on his breeches, a bullet hit him straight between the shoulder blades.

The second militiaman looked up, eyes flashing wide with shock. He reached for the pistol in the holster at his waist, hand flaying wide as he careened backwards from the bullet in his chest.

That was the last of his ammunition – two bullets – but it had been enough.

He jumped down into the quarry and ran to the girl, kicking the body of the militiamen aside and knelt down beside her. `Are you badly hurt?' he asked.

At first she was speechless from terror, but as her panic died and her pain struck sharp, she rolled on to her side and clutched on her stomach, moaning.

It took some minutes for her to stop moaning, but when her gulping breathing eased, and thick fair lashes fluttered, she lifted her eyes to him, eyes as blue as the cornflower.

`What happened?' she whispered.

`They're both dead,' he told her.

She breathed out a long quivering sigh of relief, and, as if unaware of her torn bodice, lay back and closed her eyes. He found nothing provocative in the way she lay back. He could see she was in deep shock, and also startlingly pretty. She looked like a fair young angel, only fifteen or so, sweet and delicate and lily-pale.

He bit on his lip as he knelt on one knee looking down at her. He dared not touch her. His eyes moved over her torn bodice and bare young bosom, there were teeth marks and blood above her left breast. She put him in mind of a new spring flower, crushed and bruised by a careless boot.

He was glad he had killed them.

But he could not delay here much longer.

`Do you think you can walk?' he asked softly.

`Yes,' she whispered, but did not move.

He laid down his gun and put his hands under her shoulders, lifting her to a sitting position, one hand on her back while the other reached for the shawl that lay in a heap a few feet away. He draped it around her and covered her bodice, then said firmly: `Come now. Stand up, and I'll take you home.'

She was so dazed it took him some time to discover where she lived. She staggered and fell continually until he caught his arm around her waist to support her, talking to her quietly about everyday things but getting no response. She felt very small and fragile against him, like a shaking young fawn.

They stopped at a stream and he made her drink a few handfuls of the cool water, then wash her face. She seemed to get better then.

`Can we rest here awhile?' she asked.

He was reluctant, but agreed. `A short while,' he said.

He remained crouched by the stream while she sat a few feet away, her back against a tree. Silence fell, broken only by the sound of birdsong. From the branch above her head a wren sang loudly. He turned his head and listened, wondering as he always did, how such powerful notes could come from a bird as tiny as the wren.

`Why?' she said in a small voice. `Why did they treat me like that? As if I was some filly in a field they could just beat and jump on.'

He didn't answer her at first, his interest seemingly caught by the antics of the wren above her head, but he could feel her eyes on him.

`Because they are animals themselves,' he said quietly. `Bulls – dressed as men.' He lowered his eyes and looked at her. `And because ... you are very pretty.'

She looked away with a crimson flush, shrugged, and then looked back at him. `Would they have done it if I was ugly?'

He took off his hat and shook loose his black hair. `How can I answer that? You are not the first, you know. The best thing you can do now is to try and forget it. But never walk so far abroad alone.'

She sat staring at him with her pink mouth slightly open, her brow furrowed as if something about him puzzled her.

`What's the matter?' he asked warily.

She tilted her golden head to the side as she scrutinised him, then her entire face lightened as it came to her.

`I know you,' she said. `You're Michael Dwyer.'

`Who me?' He laughed. `Of course I'm not. Do I look like a ghost?'

`Not a bit, but you are him,' she insisted. `I know it for sure. I used to see you when I was a little girl, a few years ago, when you used to play in the Hurley matches with the other lads.'

`Ach, you're confusing me with some childhood memory.'

`And then I saw you playing in the ball-kicking match against the Carlow boys. Do you remember that? Wicklow won handsomely.' Her smile was wide, her voice excited. `You didn't die then? But what was the trail of blood you left in the snow?'

Now that she smiled he saw her dimples, and again thought how pretty she was, in a baby-faced way. But give her another year or so and she would be breathtaking. His eyes moved over the gloss of her sunny hair, long and pale as the primrose. She had that moon-like, quiet beauty of the blue-eyed and fair. Aye, another year or so and she would no doubt be running up these hills after sunset where some love-struck lad would be waiting for her.

Through the haze of his thoughts he had been looking at her, and she dimpled in a smile again. `Is it true that Sam McAllister walked out and took all the bullets himself to help you escape?'

His eyes shadowed as he remembered his friend, Sam McAllister, a young Protestant from Antrim who had left his militia regiment in disgust and joined the rebels. Sam Sam McAllister was a memory and a heartache that would never leave him.

`Where have you been these last few months?' she asked.

`So many questions ..!' He returned the hat to his head. `Come now, it's time we left.'

`Michael Dwyer, who would believe it?' she mused as they walked on.

When he made no answer she looked at him thoughtfully, he was older than she remembered, about twenty-five years old now.

`Would you like to know my name?' she asked.

`If you'd like to tell me.'

`It's Etty ... Esther.'

`That's nice. I have a sister called Etty ... Esther.'

`Will you be playing in any more of the Hurley matches?'

`Oh, I doubt it.' He smiled sidelong at her. `I'm supposed to be dead.'

`Is it true what they say ... you got married in secret at Green's River?'

`Aye, I did.'

`Is *she* pretty?'

`She's beautiful. She's expecting a baby. Though you never would know it to look at her.'

He halted as four white cottages came into view. He looked down the hill. `Is that it? Is that where you live?'

`Aye, the last house but one.'

`I'll leave you here so. Will you be able to make the rest of your way on your own?'

She nodded, then of a sudden she clutched at her stomach, her mouth twisting in pain.

What's wrong?'

`They ... they punched me. It's hurting.'

He closed his eyes briefly, reluctant to go any closer to the houses with her. But then he sighed, and took her arm in a resigned manner.

`I'll see you down to that tree by the first house,' he said.

He held her elbow as they moved downhill, listening silently as she told him bits and pieces about her family. As she spoke, he realised that he knew her father and brothers well, but he had never met any of the females, woman or child.

At the tree he stopped and looked at her carefully. Her pain and shock was gone. She was breathing and speaking normally.

`Are you all right now?'

`Aye, just a bit sore where they punched me, but I'll be fine.' She held out a small hand to him and smiled into his face. `Goodbye, Michael Dwyer, and thanks.'

`You're welcome,' he said lightly, turning to go.

His eyes scanned the surrounding land as he walked away. There was nothing left in his gaming-gun or pistol and he had no more ammunition on him. If any further trouble presented itself, he would have to rely on his wits to get him out of it.

He glanced over his shoulder and saw the girl still standing by the tree, her primrose hair shining in the sunlight. She lifted a hand and waved.

Smiling, he waved back, but as he moved on quickly he thought of the two militiamen and found himself hoping that his coming child would not be a girl. It had not really mattered to him before today, but now he realised what a terrible worry it would be if he had a daughter, and fervently hoped that Mary would birth a boy.

But if it was a girl, he decided, he would teach her to defend herself, right well!

*

Up in the wilderness of Knockgorrah, old man Cullen plodded up the path to his cottage. Inside the house was neat and clean, with those certain touches that only a woman can bring to a house, a bowl of dried flowers here, a lace circle on the table there, a warm cosiness everywhere.

But it was empty.

He leaned his stick against the wall, threw off his rug cloak and hung it on a hook in the corner, then sat down on his chair to the right of the fire. He lifted the poker and stirred the smoored turf into flames, then lit his long-pipe and sat gazing into the fire, recalling every word of his conversation with Hawkins and the officer, not to mention the fine whiskey he had drunk, before the lads had dumped him at the edge of the square.

He hunched his shoulders and chuckled. Musha, it had been a great day!

Only the militia had no knowledge of the fact that John Cullen was not simply a lonely old bachelor, but he was also a distant uncle to Michael, and down the years the two had been great friends, man and boy, travelling over the hills or going salmon fishing together. Now that boy was a strong young man, but Cullen still treasured him with all the affection of a precious son.

Cullen was still chuckling when Michael came in some minutes later and looked at him curiously. `What has you so happy?'

`Ah, treasure, I've had a jewel of a time in Donard, telling the soldiers what a bastard you were. If you could have just heard me! Have you had a good day?'

`I've had better,' Michael said grimly.

`Then take off your bag and hat and come and sit down,' Cullen said gently. `Will I put the kettle on to boil?'

Michael nodded, and Cullen smiled. And if Captain Woollard had seen the gentle face and heard the kindly tone of the white-haired old man at that moment, he would never have believed it was the same man who had drunk his whiskey that morning.

'Did you meet up with Mary?' Michael asked.

Cullen lost his smile, a worried frown moving onto his brow. 'I did, but I'm not sure if I didn't get a bit carried away with all the play-acting by the time I seen her. I'd had a few drinks, d'you see. I hope I didn't upset her. She looked a bit shocked when I'd finished.'

Michael glanced round sharply as he pulled the game bag from his back. 'What did you say to her?'

'Well,' Cullen looked at him a bit sheepish. 'I told her that the lass you truly loved was the daughter of Reilly of Coolamaddra. And it was her you might have married if you hadn't been killed.'

Michael smiled. 'I shouldn't worry about that. Mary knows only too well where my heart lies.'

'But that's not all ... I called her a slut.'

Michael frowned at him from under his lashes. 'Now that was going too far,' he said coldly.

'I know, treasure, I know.' Cullen rubbed a hand over his white hair and shook himself unhappily. 'But they were listening, d'you see, the militia! And I wanted to make a good display of it – and I did too! No one in that square today would ever believe that Mary has been living here with me for the past few months. Ever since you were killed.'

'Will you stop saying that!' Michael could not help smiling at the way Cullen spoke with utter conviction. No wonder people really thought he was dead – those that were supposed to think it, anyway.

'I think I'll go down the hillside and watch for her,' he said suddenly. 'You can make yourself useful by taking the rabbit out of that bag and preparing it for cooking.'

'Did no nice pheasant stroll across your path today?' Cullen queried. 'I have a fancy for a bit of roasted pheasant. We had rabbit last night.'

`And grateful you should be that you did,' Michael said reprovingly. `There's many a poor family in Wicklow that would be thankful for a taste of any kind of meat to go with their potatoes.'

Cullen knew he was right, but a person couldn't help having fancies, and his fancy tonight was not rabbit!

When Michael had gone out the door, the old man shrugged his shoulders and sighed, then moved to his feet and sidled over to prepare the rabbit. Still, Mary would do wonders with it when it came to the cooking. She had a knack with the herbs that was magical. A twist of this herb, a shake of that, a handful of another, and by the time it was cooked, the smell alone would have his mouth watering.

And then he unstrapped the bag and saw the flash of feathers on the two pheasants. Oho! He chuckled in delight and rubbed his hands together. Boys-oh-boys, but it was true! Unlike many another poor family in Wicklow, he and Mary ate as richly as royalty with the food that Michael brought back to them.

*

Carefully scanning the surrounding land as he went, Michael had only gone a short distance from the house when he saw her, the dark girl in the blue cloak just a few feet away on the hilly path below. He stood for a moment watching her, and as he did, even the fair loveliness of young Esther paled into insignificance.

He gave the whistle of a song thrush, soft and melodious. She looked up, and they smiled together.

He jumped down, anxious to know if Cullen had really upset her, but when he reached her she dropped her bag and clung to him in a tight embrace and a flurry of kisses that left him smiling.

`What brought this on?' he murmured.

`Absence,' she said. `I feel as if I've been away from you for a lot longer than a day.'

He lifted her bag in one hand and took her hand in his other and led her on up the path.

`And was it a good day or a bad day?' he asked quietly.

`A good one. I still have some of the money you gave me in the purse left over, but ...I treated myself to some more lavender water.'

`Ach, Mary, the bedroom reeks of that stuff whenever you've had a bath in there. Why can't you use carbolic soap like everyone else?'

`Carbolic soap is not very romantic,' she said sullenly. `And anyway,' she added with a smile. `I also bought yourself and Cullen a twist of tobacco each.'

He looked at her. `You're not angry with him then? He's worried you might be.'

`No! He played his part well. For a minute he even had me believing him. But 'tis how it should be, Michael, him convincing everyone that he would shoot you on sight if you ever came near him – if you were still alive.'

They both laughed at that; then a worried frown came on Mary's face. `Did you meet anyone today? Anyone who might recognise you?'

`No,' he lied, deciding to make no mention of either the meeting with William Hume or the incident with the girl. If Mary knew he had shot two men, even militiamen, she would be very upset for days. But perhaps if she had been there, and seen what he had seen, she might have understood. As it was, he decided to spare her and say nothing.

*

Three evenings later, Cullen came bursting into the cottage in a fury. He stared redly at Michael.

`You never told us what happened with you and young Esther Costello the other day!'

`Etty?'

`Aye, Etty Costello. As purty as a primrose.'

Michael threw a glance at Mary who had paused in the act of stirring the cooking-pot on the crane above the fire.

`Nothing happened!' Michael snapped at Cullen, turning his back on his wife and making eyes at the old man, attempting to warn him off mentioning any dead militiamen in front of Mary.

29

But Cullen was too upset and angry to notice. He blurted out the whole story, in every detail, as told by Etty to her father, who had now told Cullen.

`You did right to shoot them!' Cullen cried angrily. `But it's a pity you didn't come along a few minutes earlier! The bla'guards roughed the poor child up something cruel, something cruel! Her daddy said her whole stomach was black from the punches they gave her.'

`Oh, the poor girl,' Mary cried in a distressed tone. `The brutes! To treat a young girl like that.'

`It's a pity you didn't come along a few minutes earlier,' Cullen cried again. `Oh, sorra that you didn't. Sorra, sorra, sorra ... '

`I went as soon as I heard her,' Michael said. `I stopped them as quickly and in the only way I could.'

Cullen nodded his head up and down several times, and then he looked cloudily at Michael.

`Aye, she said you treated her very kindly. She said it over and over to her mother and father, that you treated her very kindly. But prepare yourself for this, treasure. Young Etty had a haemorrhage in her stomach the same night and died from it. She was buried in her grave this afternoon.'

Chapter Two

Mary had spent the afternoon collecting herbs; her basket was full of young sorrel leaves which grew profusely in Imaal. She walked easily up the hilly path towards Cullen's cottage without any sign of breathlessness, although she was almost six months with child.

She gazed about her in the vast silence of the wilderness, an immense green silence that stretched for miles around these hills, disturbed only by the warbling of birds and intermittent calls of animals. It was a solitude that reassured her, lulled her into a sense of peacefulness as her eyes scanned the undulating landscape dappled white with hawthorn blossom. Down below she could see fields of oats still as green as grass stalks. She put a hand to her breast and inhaled the sweet air, suddenly exhalted at the joy of her life up here in the wilderness.

As she drew near to the top of the path and the house came into view, she saw Michael sitting on a stool outside it, reading a book in the sunshine, his back propped against the wall, his legs stretched and crossed at the ankles, his head bowed. She smiled as she looked at the key to her happiness. Up here she enjoyed peace, pleasure, and companionship. What more could she ask for?

A sparrowhawk rose up from a pine tree with a fierce shrilling cry and startled her, but worse was the stillness that followed the cry, as if all the world had paused in its breathing; and then she heard the rhythmic sounds, drawing closer and closer.

Her heart beat wildly and she looked at her beloved, his head bent over his book, calm and motionless, as the redcoated soldiers appeared on the ridge above him. Her blood raced around her brain, and she wondered if it was all a mirage of her imagination. They seemed afar off, outlined against the sky.

She watched the mirage of a detachment of soldiers moving in double column down towards the steep path that ran a few yards from the house. Amidst the feverishness of her brain she found herself thinking that they could not have come from the old mountain road above her head, but must have come across the mountains from the right.

Michael's dark head was still lowered over his book. At times she was sure he went deaf with the engrossment of his reading. She felt her legs weakening under her and reached for the support of a tree, hidden by the branches as she watched, her head and heart pounding as she saw Michael lift his head and glance at the soldiers marching only a few yards away from him, and calmly returned to his book.

Some of the soldiers turned their heads towards the cottage and the man sitting outside it, but the column marched on along the path without hesitating, continuing down the far hillside in the direction of Leitrim, becoming smaller and smaller until they eventually drifted away.

And then she knew it had all been a mirage of her imagination, and suddenly she did not feel so happy with her life up here anymore.

`Life in the lush stillness of the wilderness,' Cullen had once told her, `can be as full of fanciful notions as life in a vast desert of sand, full of dream-like images and voices that exist only in the mind.'

Michael looked up again as she slowly approached him, concern tightening his face as he noted the paleness of hers. He sprang to his feet and in an instant was beside her.

`Are you all right, Mary?'

`The soldiers,' she managed. `Did you see any soldiers, Michael?'

`Aye, I heard them before I spied them on the ridge. I knew from their perfectly ordered tramp they were an English regiment. And so they were.'

`What? Did you truly see them? Are you sure they were real?'

`Only a fool doubts what he sees with his own eyes,' he said.

`Then why,' she said weakly,`why did they just pass on? Why did they not search the house?'

`Well, they most definitely would have searched the house if it had been deserted. But they obviously saw no reason to suspect a house where the occupant was not frightened or start away on their appearance.'

`Oh, is that why,' she whispered, then fainted.

*

Later that night, old man Cullen sat in his favourite chair to the right of the inglenook, smoking a long-pipe as he studied the fire. These past few months had been a time of great companionship for him. Every morning setting off to his sheep at Leoh after breakfast, returning in the afternoons to a warm house and the smell of bacon or a roasting pheasant, or whatever game Michael had managed to shoot.

Aye, his little house had become a home. And he too was beginning to wish that things would stay as they were forever, and let reality and the rest of the world go to hell or high water.

He turned his eyes to the girl sitting opposite him at the fireside, her head bent industriously over the fine Irish linen she was carefully stitching.

She too, he thought, had been very contented these past few months, delighted at having Michael all to herself and secretly living with him up here instead of lodging in harbourers' houses. Bustling around the house as busy as a bee, keeping it as clean and nice as his darling mother had always done. And Michael had not been idle either.

He had rethatched the roof, strip by strip, ensuring the house would have no dampness in its walls when the baby came. He had even managed to plant the potato garden before St Patrick's Day. The seeds had to be down before the 17th if the potatoes were to have St Pat's blessing and flour in the taste. He had even managed to get over to Eadstown and help his father with the spring sowing. And how he had managed that still made the old man and many another laugh.

He had dirtied his face with earth and whitened his hair with flour, then covered it with a large scarecrow's hat, dressing himself in the tattered old cloak and clothes of a beggar, leaning on a stick and smoking a long-pipe as he took to the road; touching his hat with a wheezy `Top of the mornin'' to the militia as they passed.

Cullen puffed happily on his long-pipe, smiling to himself. The tragedy at Derrynamuck had not damaged his nerves a bit, not a fray, they were as cool and steady as ever.

`Heck, sure I don't know,' Cullen muttered, as if in reply to a question.

`What don't you know,' said Mary in a low gentle voice, her head still bent over her stitching.

`What? Oh, nothing, treasure,' Cullen murmured, as if waking from a dark study.

He glanced at her, at her bent head with its smoothly combed length of black hair gleaming in the candlelight, then turned his eyes back to the fire, watching the flames and glowing embers and smiled subtly to himself. Sure wouldn't you think it was the Virgin herself sitting there sewing. Looking like butter wouldn't melt in her mouth.

Huh! Over these past few months he had come to learn that Mary was not entirely the gentle creature of perfection he had first thought her. She could be a very frivolous person, adorning her hair in tortoise-shell combs, and at times laughing much too merrily for a girl in her condition.

He glanced at Mary with grave disapproval.

Mary's head came up from her sewing, but her eyes were turned towards Michael sitting at the table, frowning as he read a newspaper by the glow of a candle. She was very proud to have a husband that could read and write. Very few of the older men in Wicklow could. And only a small number of Michael's comrades had come from families comfortable enough to send them to the barn-school and later a scholastic priest. Neither John Mernagh nor Martin Burke could write their name, depending always on Hugh Vesty or Michael to read and explain things to them.

And Michael would read anything, books, pamphlets, anything that told him of the world outside the Wicklow Mountains. But his favourite was the newspapers which carried the latest about Napoleon and Nelson, and the unrest and talk of revolution amongst the workers in England who were presently incensed by the latest extravagance of the Prince of Wales.

Michael had explained it to herself and Cullen –England was almost bankrupt due to the cost of the war with France, but Parliament still had to find the money to meet the cost of the Prince's wine and clothes bills, which every year were enormous. Poverty was rife in the rural areas, and half of London was homeless. And now the dandy Prince had commissioned the building of an elaborate dome in a place called Brighton, to the cost of *seventy thousand pounds*. And for what? – to house his horses! The English people were very angry.

Mary's eyes were still on Michael, wondering why he was frowning so sharply, looking at the newspaper as if he could not quite believe what he had just read.

`Is it something else about the Prince of Wales?' she asked quietly.

Michael slowly looked up.

`They've agreed to sell us,' he said incredulously. `The British government has agreed to sell us off!'

`Eh?' Cullen removed the pipe from his mouth and turned round in his chair. `What are you saying?'

So Michael explained it to them. The aftermath of the rebellion had left the Irish prisons overcrowded, despite the fact that great numbers had been despatched to serve as seamen in the British Fleet. But now the rumour was fact – Britain and her administrators in Ireland had made a deal with the King of Prussia – agreeing to the disposal of prisoners by sentencing them to serve in his army, and those males who were too old, or too young, or simply did not fit the cut of a soldier, were sold at so much per head to work in Prussia's coal mines.

`They have agreed to *sell* us!' Michael said again incredulously. `The British government are blatantly, and without any shame, *selling* the Irish in boatloads to the King of Prussia!

He threw the paper down and moved over to the fireplace, standing with feet apart and arms folded, eyes blazing with anger as he stared into space, looking tall and strong and every bit the rebel captain again.

Cullen stared at him in mute horror, but Mary dipped her head and silently resumed her stitching, tears of anguish moistening her eyes. First young Esther Costello, now this. What next? Things always happened in threes, and the third would be the one that did it, ended her peace and the wedded idyll she had enjoyed for only three months.

Cullen finally found his voice. `Ach, pay no heed to what you read in the newspapers, 'tis all lies!' but Michael had moved across to the bedroom, kicking the door shut behind him.

Chapter Three

At his Lodge in the Phoenix Park, the Viceroy, Lord Cornwallis was still suffering a hail of public abuse from the high-ranking gentry for being altogether too harsh on the militia. Cornwallis defended himself stoutly in a letter to London.

> On my arrival in this country I put a stop to the burning of houses and murder of the inhabitants by the militia, or any other person who delighted in the amusement. I also stopped flogging for the purpose of extorting confessions; and to the free quarters of soldiers which comprehended universal rape and robbery throughout the country. I stopped all this, and if this be a crime I freely acknowledge my guilt.

Although he sincerely believed he had, the Viceroy had stopped nothing. In Wicklow the house-burning season started a few days later. The militia marched through the villages in search of rebels, setting fire to hillside dwellings and occasionally shooting any man who stood out against them.

Once again young men were being forced back up the mountains in droves, only this time they had no captain to command them or organise their systems of defence. And as the days moved on, many became angry and confused.

`Where is Dwyer?' they demanded. `It's hard to know which tales to believe anymore. Is he dead or alive or what?'

They looked at Michael's cousin, Hugh Vesty Byrne, pleading the question.

But neither Hugh Vesty nor any of Michael's principal men would give them the satisfaction of a straight answer.

`He must be dead!' some decided.

`He's alive!' others insisted. `Wasn't it he who answered the cries of the girl and dealt with her persecutors?'

And so it went on; while Hugh Vesty and the others maintained their silence, not sure if the captain would ever be willing to come out again, leave his little paradise with Mary and enter the fight again, even if it was in defence of his own people, his own friends.

*

It was usual for many of the farmers to send their sheep up to the grazing lands of Wicklow under the care of shepherds. But now the militia had begun to kill sheep at whim again, deciding a good meal of lamb or mutton tasted better if it didn't have to be paid for.

Two yeomen had just completed this venture and were on their way back down the hills when they came across a twelve-year-old boy with a haversack on his back.

One of the two men was Ned Valentine. `What have you got in the bag?' he demanded.

`A loaf of bread,' said the boy, `and a flask of buttermilk.'

`Where are you taking it?'

`To my daddy at Aughavannagh. Himself and some other men are cutting turf there.

`Liar!' Valentine snapped. `You're taking it to feed rebels. Come now, admit it!'

The boy stared at him in white horror. `No!' he cried. `It's for my daddy cutting the turf.'

Valentine narrowed his eyes in sudden cunning as he looked at the boy. `Tell me, is it true what some are whispering ... that Dwyer is alive?'

`Ach no, sir! He's as dead as Moses.'

`How can you be so sure?'

The boy shrugged. `Well I can't be truly sure, seeing as nobody's found his bones, but everyone says he is dead. Even my daddy. He says some are pretending the Reb-captain is alive just to worry the militia.'

Valentine's eyes were sparkling, his face bright. The boy was not ready for his instantaneous response, almost falling over as the bag was ripped from his back. `We'll have to confiscate this,' Valentine said. `It's evidence that you were endeavouring to supply rebels with food. You're under arrest.'

Two Protestant gentleman came riding along the road; a

Mr Henry Evebank and Mr Goodwin. They muttered a few words amongst themselves, and then challenged Valentine.

`What are you doing with that boy?' Mr Evebank demanded.

`What is it to do with you, sir?' Valentine snapped.

`He's but a child. What crime could he possibly have committed?'

`He's a damned rebel caught in the act of taking supplies to his friends.'

`I wasn't! I was taking it to my daddy cutting turf at Aughavannagh.'

`Let the child go on his way,' Mr Goodwin ordered. `You know very well who the boy's father is and where he lives.'

`And there is an easy way to find out if he is lying,' Mr Evebank suggested. `Go along to the bog at Aughavannagh and see if his father is cutting turf there. If not, you can find the boy at his home later and call him to account.'

After a moment's hesitation, Valentine nodded. `All right, we'll go – but we'll take him with us!'

`You will not harm him,' Mr Evebank said sternly.

`Why should we harm him if he's telling the truth? But if he's lying ... he'll be on the next prison ship learning the ropes.'

The boy looked relieved, knowing his daddy was cutting the turf. The two gentlemen rode on, their eyes occasionally straying to the yeomen; one dragging a dead sheep and the other pushing the young boy in front of him, in the direction of Aughavannagh.

The following morning the boy's father and a group of searchers found him under a hawthorn bush, shot through the head. The bag of bread beside him.

*

Mary was not sure what had awakened her. For a brief moment, eyes blinking, she wondered if she had been dreaming. Then she heard the sound again.

The *tap-tap-tap* against the window glass.

The bedroom was in darkness, she was alone in the bed, but she could hear his movements as he quietly and swiftly dressed; the snap of his belt-buckle, the shrugging on of his jacket. It was only when he moved to the window that she saw him clearly, his face calm but unreadable as he looked out and examined the sky. Outside the night was bright and calm, but she could feel the storm of tension in the air.

The third thing had happened.

He paused for a moment to check the pistol in his belt; then the latch on the bedroom door clicked. He slipped quietly out of the house like a lover slipping out to meet a maid.

The old man was still asleep in his settle-bed in the corner of the living room when she entered and moved quickly to the front door, opened it and ran down to the low stone wall.

The entire land was drenched in moonlight, but she could see no sign of him. She stood like a silent ghost in her nightgown, trembling. Then she saw him some distance down the hilly path below. Hugh Vesty Byrne beside him.

They were running.

She saw them again a short time later, as they crossed a moonlight meadow below.

They were running more swiftly now. In the direction of Aughavannagh.

She turned and walked back to the house. The old man was sitting up in his bed when she entered. `Has Michael gone out?'

`Aye.'

`To his men?'

She nodded. `Hugh Vesty came for him.'

The two were silent for a time, glooming in harmony. They had been a good threesome, like the eagle and the dove and the old happy thrush living together in peace. But now they knew the eagle of the mountains was about to leave the nest.

`Go back to sleep,' Mary whispered, bolting and chaining the door. `He'll not be returning tonight.'

*

The dark fields around the house in Fearbreaga, some miles

before Aughavannagh, was well manned with armed picquets. Two of Michael's lieutenants, John Mernagh and Martin Burke, jerked alert at the sound of footsteps, then rushed to give a hard grasp of the hand to their captain.

A large group of neighbours were gathered outside the house. They fell silent abruptly when the four men approached, staring in astonishment at the captain who walked through them as if they were not there, and entered the house.

The kitchen was empty but for two people. By the fireside sat a youngish woman with a face as pale as a ghost, her hands in her lap, staring into the fire in a vacant tearless trance. According to Hugh Vesty, she had been like that since the hour they brought her dead boy home.

Behind her stood another woman, a generation older, quietly murmuring prayers as she sprinkled holy water over her daughter.

`Where is Dary?' Michael whispered.

The older woman glanced up. She was silent for some time before answering. `My son-in-law is in the bedroom,' she finally said. `You'd better go on in yourself. He'll not believe me if I tell him it's you. He's not up to believing much any more.'

Hugh Vesty and the others remained near the front door while Michael retired to the bedroom. He was in there a long time. When he came out he looked at the older woman still murmuring her prayers, then his eyes moved to the white-faced woman sitting in the chair ... she was stirring out of her vacant trance ... a puzzled frown on her face as she began to look slowly around the room, as if searching for something she had lost.

Michael froze where he stood. For she brought back a memory to him. A memory he had not had in a long time. He had been sixteen, alone on the farm when the cow gave premature birth to her calf. His father was in yonder fields with his younger brothers, his mother at market with the girls.

Cumbersomely, still in pain from the birth, the cow had bent over her calf, smelling and licking it. Then suddenly she lowed and moved away to the corner of the field and stayed there. The calf was dead, stillborn. He had stood looking sadly across at the cow, flicking her tail against her flanks wearily, still in pain, and thought the best thing he could for her was to bury the calf as quickly as possible.

When he returned from the nearby meadow the cow was lowing loudly, looking searchingly around the field. On the corner ground where she had moved to, was the afterbirth bag. And now it had been delivered, she was looking for her calf.

She began stumbling round the field, smelling the ground where her calf had lain, putting her head over the hedge here and there, lowing madly, searching and not finding until she became as wild as a bull. He offered her a drink of warm milk, but she ran away in fury, attempting to break through the hedge, sniffing in the direction of the meadow; she knew her calf was there.

In the end he took his spade and led her out through the gate and up to the meadow. And there he lifted the newly dug earth and let her see. The long lashes on her big old face moved up and down, and then she jiggled with delight at the sight of her calf, straining down her neck to lick him lovingly.

After that she had looked so stupid, that great bulk of a lovely cow, just standing and staring at her calf for a long time, and then her dull old brain grasped why he had not responded to her love. Suddenly she fell down on her four knees, her big body covering the hole containing her calf, and she had raised her head and cried and cried in such a terrible and mournful way it had echoed over the hills for hours.

And now this white-faced woman was looking searchingly around the room for her offspring, lying dead in the bedroom.

`Let's go,' Michael whispered urgently to the others and they all silently left the house. The door swung back on its hinges and stood open behind them, but none of the neighbours dared enter without permission.

A buzz of chattering rose up when they came out and

moved quickly through the crowd of gaping neighbours. They had reached the edge of the field when a group of men ran after them. One caught Michael's arm. He spoke breathlessly, urgently: `None of us know where you've been. But we do know it won't be easy for you if you come out again. So it's been suggested that a subscription be levied amongst the people to help you buy ammunition, and any other rations of food and drink will be supplied to you and your men as before, as regular as the soldiers in the barracks.'

Before Michael could answer, another man grabbed roughly on his arm. `Do you know what we're saying to you, Dwyer? Do you know?'

`I'm not a fool,' Michael answered, shrugging the man's hand away. Once again he was being asked to lead his small army of men and take up the role of defenders of the local population against the yeomanry and militia.

The man grabbed his arm again. `Can't you see? It's them or us! They've made that penny plain. Only this time they've started on the children. Two down already.'

`Look,' Michael said irritably, `will you just leave me be and let me move on.'

`Listen, brother, you and Dary were good friends. And now his boy – '

`Get out of my way!' Michael snapped.

The man remained where he was, utterly perplexed as Michael walked on. The huddle of neighbours stared after the four rebels in bewildered silence. They had only walked a few yards when a scream rose up from the house behind. A woman's scream.

`*Oh, mercy, Jesus!*'

`Keep walking,' Michael said urgently. `She's reached the bedroom and come back to her senses and I don't want to be around for it.'

The armed picquets fell silently into pairs and followed at a distance in irregular intervals. It was not until the leading four reached the vicinity of the Lugnaquilla Mountain that anyone spoke.

`What did Dary say to you?' Hugh Vesty murmured.

43

`Very little,' Michael answered. `He was too choked over the boy to say much. But the last thing he said to me was ... *"as surely as God hears me, I'm asking you to come out, stay out, and make them pay."'*

`Those were his very words?'

`Those were his very words.'

`And what did you say?'

Michael looked up at the sky for a moment. The stars had long grown dim, and now the dawn was spreading its light over the land. It was going to be a warm June day. He looked at his three companions and asked: `Do you know what day this is?'

`Aye, Thursday.'

`Oh, it's more than just Thursday,' Michael said. `It's the first day of summer horseracing at Davidstown. And not only that. It's the day of the Blue Ribbon.'

`The Blue Ribbon?' Hugh Vesty slowly smiled. `Sure now, isn't it just typical of you to remember a thing like that.'

*

Daylight streaked into the bedroom. Mary threw back the covers and prepared her mind for the day. She could hear old man Cullen bustling about in the living-room.

`Is that you up, Mary?' he called.

`There's only me in here,' she reminded him.

`Do you want your bowl of warm water?'

`Aye.'

Five minutes later the door opened a few inches, and Cullen's hands placed a bowl of water on the floor before the door closed again. Mary cleansed herself and dressed, then moved out to the kitchen where, to her surprise, Cullen had already prepared the breakfast.

`You were right then,' Cullen said as they sat down to bowls of hot milk and oatmeal. `About him not coming back last night.'

`Aye, I may as well go over to Bushfield this very day,' she said tiredly.

`And what business have you over at Bushfield?'

44

`Business with the bootmaker. I slipped over there one day and ordered Michael a new pair of mountain boots to replace the pair he lost at Derrynamuck.'

Cullen was astonished. `And have you the money to pay for the boots?'

`Aye, I saved it from the money he gave me – his share of the farm's quarter-profits.'

`Musha, but you're a grand and thrifty woman altogether,' Cullen declared. `And who did you say the boots were for?'

`My brother, who else?'

Mary laid down her spoon and looked sad. `It will be so hard to leave here,' she murmured, `so hard to go back to the unsettled life of harbourers' houses.'

`Aye, lass, aye. But we chose our man and we chose our side and now we must face it and look bravely. And listen, won't you be able to come back here now and again for your little trysts, just like before.'

`Even when the baby arrives?'

`And why not? Isn't there plenty of room in the bedroom for three? Oh, hear me, Mary, when that little lad arrives, he'll always find a hundred thousand joyful welcomes waiting for him in *this* house.'

`And if the little lad turns out to be a little lass?' Mary queried.

`Ach, Mary, this is no time or place for a girl to be born. A lad has more chance, he can fight back.'

`But if it *is* a girl – what then?'

`Then ... then ... the same waits for her too. A hundred thousand joyful welcomes.'

Mary smiled. `Do you mean that?'

`Oh I do, treasure, I surely do,' Cullen insisted, then sat scowling sourly as if he had just eaten a bowl of last year's rhubarb.

*

The evening sun was far down in the west. The Blue Ribbon had been won by a gelding trained in Kildare and sired by the famous Green Dancer.

45

The races were over, most of the people gone, only a few hucksters remained, packing up what was left of their wares and preparing to leave. One girl, a gypsy type selling little brass bells and charms, nodded and chatted as Michael questioned her. Soon the other remaining hucksters had formed a group beside her, grinning and slapping the latecomer on the back, then raising their arms to point northwest.

`Just as I predicted,' Michael said on returning to his principal men on the hillside. `Some mules will always choose the same old watering-hole.'

*

From the open window of Plant's tavern at Castleruddery the uproarious laughter of the revellers inside could be heard.

Michael strolled up to the window, stood for a moment looking inside, then moved along and entered the tavern. Around the fireplace sat a group of locals drinking and talking. He strode quickly past them towards a table near the rear of the taproom and sat down on an empty stool amidst a group of yeomen playing cards.

`Any room for another player, avics? What is it? Fifteen or Twenty-five?'

The yeomen all looked up and stared at him.

`Hell's flames,' one said. `Is it you, Dwyer?'

`Aye. Who were you expecting to join you in your games ... the Devil?'

`Ach, no,' said Hugh Vesty, sliding up behind him, `it's not cards they use when they play their little games with the devil ... it's children.'

The yeomen's stampede to the back door was sudden and noisy. Michael darted back to the front of the tavern where his men were waiting.

`Catch them at the rear,' he commanded.

House by house the inhabitants of Castleruddery and the surrounding neighbourhood rushed out to watch the sport as the yeomen ran over the fields like hares and the rebels chased like hounds.

Ned Valentine was running the fastest. He looked wildly over his shoulder and saw two rebels swiftly closing in on him.

`Hell's flames!' he cried again.

Angrily, Michael pushed Hugh Vesty out of his way. `Go your own trail and find your own fox,' he cried. `Valentine is mine.'

Chapter Four

John Cullen was still up when Michael came in later that night. Mary was in bed but not asleep. She could hear him talking urgently to Cullen in the living room, and instantly knew that he had already gone back to that life on the mountains which he would not allow her to share.

Life on the run.

`If that's how it must be!' Cullen was saying fretfully, `If that's how it must be! Musha, no place will be safe for you now awhile ... Have you eaten at all? Mary left some food simmering here in the pot for you in case you came back. Shall I lift it up for you?'

`Yes, and quickly,' she heard him answer as he reached the bedroom door.

`Aye, and I'll have some more myself, there's plenty left. Arrah ...' Cullen added gloomily, `God knows when I'll eat such fine cooking again.'

She sat up as he entered the room, which was in darkness except for the light from the fire. `Where have you been?' she demanded.

`Mary, it's been a long night and a long day and it's a long story,' he said by way of explanation. `Now you must get up and dress. I'm moving you out of here tonight.'

`Tonight?'

`I'm afraid so.'

`Why?'

`By dawn every redcoat and militiaman will be back on the hunt for me. I want you to stay at the old couple's house in the wilderness for a few days. Then I'll move you on.'

`Why can't I just go home to Mammy?'

He paused then sat down on the bed. `Best not to. In case they have any suspicion of you being associated with me. Best to hide where they would not think of looking for you.'

`They wouldn't think of looking for me here. You neither.'

`No, but Cullen hating me as he does, they may come and ask him to give them the wink if he spies me.'

`My,' she snipped, `but you think of everything, don't you?'

`Well I do try,' he answered, sensing the rising misery behind her sulky face and sharp tone. `When did you say the baby is due?'

`The end of August.'

`Then at the beginning of August I will take you home to your mother. I promise I will. By then the heat may have cooled.'

She looked at him darkly. `You might have given me a little warning that this was going to happen so sudden.'

`I didn't know it was.'

`Yes you did,' she whispered harshly, flaring into a passion and pushing her tears away. `Last night you knew. But you just slipped out without even a nudge or a word.'

`Ah, Mary, all I knew last night was that – '

He could say no more, for she had pulled his face down to kiss his mouth fiercely.

Cullen sat at the table frowning as he stared at Michael's untouched plate. His own second helping had long been eaten. `Quickly,' he muttered in a tone as sulky as Mary's had been. `That's what he said when I asked if I should serve it up. Do it quickly.' And now it was cold.

Abruptly he stood up and walked boldly to the bedroom door. `Will I put this food back in the pot for you or what?' he shouted. `'Tis cold. Will I heat it up again or no? Answer me.'

But nobody did. So he grunted over to the table and put the food back in the pot, then sat crouched over the fire scowling, his humour as black as the soot in the chimney at the certain news that his birds were migrating.

All in all, he grumbled in thought, it had been a divil of a day and the two in there had treated him very badly. One threatening him with a girl and now the other ignoring him. And if himself had so much time to spend in delay he could have spent some of it talking with him awhile, not locked in there with her.

When the bedroom door finally opened it was Mary who crept into the living room. She had a shawl over her nightgown and her hair as wild as brambles.

`What ails you?' Cullen cried angrily. `Keeping him in there all this time. He told me he had to be away within the hour.'

`Hush!' she whispered. `Michael is sleeping.'

Cullen gaped at her in astonishment. `God forgive you, woman of no sense, but you'll get him killed yet. And why is he sleeping when he should be away.'

`He's only human, you know.' She took down a plate and moved over to ladle herself a plate of the reheated lamb and turnip stew. `He's had no sleep since the night before last.'

`He's had no food either,' Cullen declared, `and now you're sitting down to eat his supper!'

`He's too tired to eat it,' she explained. `And I'm very hungry. I'm eating for two.'

`Well, could you not let him eat it himself,' Cullen pouted. `You don't have to do everything for him. And that lad has suffered great deprivation and hunger in his time.'

`Has he?' Mary's spoon halted in mid-air over the plate of steaming food. She frowned at the old man. `In what way?'

`Down in Wexford, during the rebellion; he told me he once went five days with nothing inside him but goat's milk. Small wonder they were defeated.'

`Five days? Why did he not shoot something?'

`With all that war and gunfire and marching going on? Don't be docile! Any game within miles would have long run for cover.'

Mary put down the spoon and gazed at Cullen with a forlorn and guilty expression on her face. Then she stood up and lifted the plate and spoon. `You're right,' she said in a determined voice. `I'll wake him and make him eat it.'

When they were both ready to leave a short time later, Mary put her arms around Cullen impulsively and kissed him on the cheek.

`Huh!' he said. `None of your female games with me.' But his tone was soft and sad.

Michael did not say goodbye, for he would be back off and on and would continue to keep an eye on the old man. `I'll see you in a few days or so,' he said, lifting Mary's bag in one hand and leading her out with the other.

'God spare you,' Cullen said, and then glumly watched them slip away into the darkness.

*

The white-haired old couple who lived deep in the fastness of the glen were delighted to have Mary back with them, but Michael was very stern with the old woman. She patted his arm and gushed apologies in a singsong voice, and assured him that she knew right well who Mary was. No, she would not fall into the wishful haze of imagining she was her dead daughter.

'Tis the flickering of the fire's flames in the shadow of evening when she sits across from me sewing,' the old woman whispered. 'Then I like to pretend the three of us are together again as we used to be. But I won't do it again. Aye, I promise! I promise to God. Now off you go and let us settle in awhile longer.'

Then holding her skirt she dipped a creaky knee and bobbed her white head and sang, 'Top o' the morning to you.'

'And the rest of the day to you,' he answered in kind, although it was not yet morning. The stars still glittered in the distance of the sky.

She stood at the door and watched him with her rheumy blue eyes as he walked away. She would liked to have told him the truth of it, but God willing, he would one day learn it himself, when he too was old, left sitting in the corner, left sitting on the edge of life.

She would have liked to have told him that there was great loneliness amongst the old, great loneliness. The young and even the not so young could look to the future, but the old could only look back; and sometimes, sometimes the memories became confused.

She shook her head and looked up at the stars, shining like the wings of so many angels who stood in distant groups watching the earth. She sighed. Still, heaven was waiting; the Land of the Ever Young.

'Praise be to God!' she whispered, then turned and

creaked indoors, her arms opening wide to the dark silent girl who smiled nervously at her.

`Welcome, child,' she crooned. `*Cead mile failte*. You will not be lonely here, for I will comfort you, and talk long with you. And maybe you will learn something that I would have liked to tell that young man of yours. Aye, and many another young person too.'

`What is that?' Mary asked.

The woman's old blue eyes smiled, her voice became as soft as candleglow. `That there is truly great wisdom among the old,' she said.

*

He had walked only two miles but he felt very tired. Every few steps his eyelids drooped heavily. He had had less than an hour's sleep, lying between clean warm sheets, before she had woken him with her usual lilting little phrases of love, then rammed a spoonful of food into his mouth.

He would miss those clean warm sheets. He would miss that solid old four-poster that even the movements of their lovemaking could not creak. He would miss his darling girl. He suddenly realised that he was no longer tired, he was exhausted. He wanted to lie down where he stood.

He looked about him and decided he would do just that. The men up on Lugnaquilla could wait. Another hour or two of sleep would have him fit again. He had never needed much sleep, but he did need more than one hour in two nights. Wearily, he bent his steps up towards a deep crevice on a stone crag, hidden by overhanging purple heather.

There was still a mattress of old straw on the floor, for he had once spent a long summer night up here with Sam McAllister, a night when the two had talked and laughed and hardly slept at all, so mighty and witty had their humour been.

Late last summer that was. Long enough for some creature of nature to have made a home in the straw. He struck his flint and peered around, then stamped with his feet all over the straw, but there was nothing to see and nothing to hear and nothing scampered away. It was as empty as purgatory.

He sank down on the straw, stretched his tired limbs and closed his eyes. Instantly he was asleep, for long ago he had taught himself how to sleep immediately. But as he slept, a vision came to him, a vision of a young man from Antrim, wearing a green cravat.

Sam McAllister was calling him, bending over him and calling him. `Wake up, Michael, wake up.'

He opened his eyes and stared all around, but there was no one there. He gave a superstitious shudder and closed his eyes again. `Ah, Sam,' he whispered, `you've never haunted me yet. Don't start now.'

Within minutes he was asleep again, and Sam McAllister was still bending over him. `Wake up, Michael, wake up.'

It was definitely Sam McAllister, same face, fresh and young, but no bullet wounds. Same voice, crystal clear. He looked at McAllister's arm, the left arm that had been smashed by a hail of bullets ... it was undamaged. And then he said something that only Sam McAllister could say.

`Michael, wake up! Don't die in your shoes like a trooper's horse.'

His eyes flashed open, and then looked from left to right. The deep crevice was empty of all but himself, and it was light outside. He lay blinking a few seconds, then in one swift movement he rolled forward on to his heels, his head bent low as he crept outside and peeped over the brow of the crag, and saw the redcoats.

An entire company, about a hundred strong. They were moving upwards – only another ten minutes or so and they would have reached his bed. He moved on to his stomach and slithered noiselessly around to the side of the crag where he was hidden from view to anyone below. But he could not stay there, the risk was too great. Neither could he move upwards, the climb was steep and a man had to be standing to do it.

Looking down to the land, he saw a possible way out, and moved to his feet to take it. He bent slightly, every muscle in his body held tight as he jumped the twelve-foot drop to the land below, landing as lightly as a robin on a rosebush.

Moving flat on his stomach, he slithered through the long fern and furze until he reached the high cover of an old whitethorn bush, and there he crouched hidden as the soldiers moved up, passing only inches from him. So close they might have heard his breathing, if they had stopped muttering amongst themselves long enough to listen.

He watched them climb on to the crag, lifting the overhanging heather with their bayonets and peering inside. Shaking their heads, one called to his commanding officer: `Empty, sir. And very small. Not big enough for more than one or two men. Could be just the rain shelter of a hill shepherd.'

`Has it been occupied of late?'

`I wouldn't say so, sir. No sign of the makings of a fire. Just a layer of old straw.'

`Move on then.'

And they moved on, towards that part of the mountains where he had no camps and none of his men lay, for his camps had been chosen carefully, and were almost inaccessible to the stranger.

Fools, he thought idly. If they had just taken the trouble to bend down and feel the layer of straw, they would have found that the straw was warm to the touch, signifying that a body must have been lying on it only minutes before.

He waited until they were well out of sight, then rose to his feet and moved on, his mind returning to the dream, the *unbelievable* dream. Was it Sam McAllister who had warned him? Or was it simply his own instincts?

It was Sam.

He was certain of it. He had seen him as clearly as if he were alive. Heard him as clearly as if he were alive. `*Wake up, Michael, wake up. Don't die in your shoes like a trooper's horse.*'

It was Sam.

By the time he reached a small mountain stream he was in a daze. He bent to water his face, and then gazed slowly around him. Nobody would *believe* him. Nobody! But he would tell them anyway. He would tell his men, tell Mary, tell his mother and father and sisters and brothers, he would tell anyone who would listen.

And later, if God spared him, he would tell his son. He would tell his son that it *was* possible – for he had known it and still cherished it – the bond of brotherly love and comradeship that could exist between a Protestant Irishman and a Catholic Irishman; and it was only the Devil that sewed evil and hatred between them. But himself and Sam McAllister had never allowed old Lucifer such a victory.

*

By noon, the news that travelled like wildfire all over Wicklow was certain and without doubt. Michael Dwyer was alive and back to protect his people, and every soldier in Wicklow was searching for him.

The hunt was furious. A week went by, then two and three, but still the game could not be tracked.

*

Towards the end of July, Michael was making a prearranged call at Reilly's house in Coolamaddra to collect some provisions for his men. As he approached quietly along the trees he saw Reilly's youngest daughter sitting on the wall outside the house. She was singing to herself, as sweetly as a blackbird; and as arranged, she was combing her chestnut hair.

It was safe to approach.

He strolled towards the wall and smiled at her. She did not smile back, just frowned at him sullenly, then turned her face to the sky and continued singing in a low voice:

`If I was a herring, I would not wait to be caught . . .'

A herring to catch a trout – instantly his eyes flashed to the house. A second later he had vaulted over the wall down into the hollow and was running for the fields when the six yeomen waiting inside the house dashed out and fired a number of unsuccessful shots after him.

`Did you warn him?' they shouted at the girl.

`What! – warn that villain who ditched me for another girl!' She tossed her head angrily. `I never even spoke to the scoundrel. And I never will again, not as long as I live.'

The yeos were eyeing her suspiciously, uncertain.

`Who was this other girl? Was it the daughter of Doyle at Knockandarragh?'

`No! He only dallied with her at the Baltinglass Fair and on an evening or two afterwards.' She curled her lip contemptuously. `Doyle's daughter was not for him. He found her very quiet and dull in her ways when she wasn't swirling her skirts and brazenly showing her legs at the dancing. He ditched her too, quick enough, and came back to me.'

`Who was it then? The last girl he ditched you for?'

`A girl from the County Clare,' she said sulkily.

`Do you know what this girl looks like?'

`No, I do not, because I've never been to the County of Clare. But as for ye lot!' she suddenly stormed, `If ye had been quicker on your feet ye would have caught him – him who led me up the mountain path then ditched me!'

She strutted furiously into the house where she flung herself into the arms of her sister and clung quivering until, with great sighs of relief, they heard the yeos march off.

`Oh, that was a close one,' her sister breathed.

`Aye, but wasn't I a genius to come up with that melodic warning? I hope Michael tells the other lads about it and all ... especially Andrew Thomas.'

`Andrew Thomas? Is it him who's taken your fancy now?'

`Well, we have talked a bit lately, and I have always liked Andrew.'

`I thought it was Michael you would love to your grave.'

`Well there's no sense in that now, is there? Not now he's married to Mary Doyle. And anyway ...' she withdrew her looking-glass from the pocket of her dress and held it up as she pushed a few chestnut curls away from her eyes, `Michael always treated me no warmer than a friend, but Andrew Thomas looks at me something smoky.'

*

At that moment Andrew Thomas was standing alone amidst an avenue of trees that led up to the great house of Thomas

Hugo in Drummin, near the village of Annamoe. It was late evening, and the boughs of the ancient evergreens sheltered him from view. He was waiting for someone, someone who obsessed his thoughts.

The evening slipped into darkness, the glow from the lamps in the long windows cast beams into the shadows over the dark neatly cut lawn in front of the house.

Andrew smiled – Ruggedy Jack was responsible for that – the neatly cut lawn. Ruggedy Jack was very proud of his lawn. It was the only thing Ruggedy Jack ever had to be proud of. And if someone was ever to steal his tools, Ruggedy Jack would cut that lawn with his teeth rather than let its appearance shame him.

Poor old Ruggedy Jack.

Another hour drifted by, but he continued to wait, calm and patient. He passed the time recalling the lines of Irish poems his mother had taught him as a boy, beautiful poems that stilled his mind. Then his thoughts wandered over old ballads that told of Ireland's history.

Funny how the Anglo gentry had never grasped the secret behind the Irish ballad. Funny how their noses would twist and their lips curl to see the peasants gathered and hear them sing for hours into the night. Some ballads were happy, but most were sad, and all contained the core of truth.

But what the gentry had not yet understood, and probably never would, was that to an oppressed people long forbidden an official education by the words of books – ballads were their vocal literature. And through them they recorded the events of history as they happened, and passed them on in song, from generation to generation, so their descendants would know how it was, and how it had been, for their forebears.

In the distance he heard the sound of horses, the rolling of wheels. He jerked alert and peered through the trees. The carriage had turned into the avenue. For a minute he thought of what he intended to do, the ultimate sin, and he would burn for it. But then he stifled his conscience and raised the gun he was holding.

His arm was outstretched, the pistol was pointed straight in front of him, and when the carriage rolled by, and the man at the window was level with the gun, he pulled the trigger.

The startled horses took fright and reared. By the time they reached the great doors the driver had managed to calm them. The driver shouted wildly, ran and banged on the doors. Servants rushed out, gasped in horror and rushed to help out the man inside the carriage – Thomas Hugo of Drummin, their master. The bullet had missed him, passed an inch from his nose and straight through the other window.

Another bullet cracked and flew. It would have hit Thomas Hugo straight between the shoulder blades if Ruggedy Jack had not heard the crack and pulled his master forward, a second before the bullet chipped Hugo's arm, removing the cloth of his coat and lodging in the wall beside the great doors. Blood began to ooze down his sleeve.

`Your arm this time, Hugo,' a voice cried. `I'll have the rest of you yet!'

The servants ushered their terrified master inside.

Thomas Hugo of Drummin was a thickly built member of the landed gentry who, every season, was Master of the Hunt. When his wound had been dressed, he entered the drawing room to find his daughter standing by one of the long windows, staring into the night.

`Was it him?' she asked.

`Yes, it was him,' he answered, white as a sheet.

`You'll have to go very carefully, Papa. He truly does mean to kill you.'

`I'll see the bastard hang first.'

Mary Hugo, a pale-faced girl with loops of dark hair coiled around each ear, turned searching eyes back to the window. Was he still out there? Was Andrew Thomas still lurking somewhere behind those trees?

`He will never forgive you,' she murmured.

The brandy decanter clinked behind her. `Let the bastard go to hell.'

She stood silent, thinking of the young man she had

58

known since childhood. Her first memories of him were of a small, skinny lad with thick brown hair and cheeky brown eyes. Now he was twenty-two, straight and well made, and the last time she had seen him, his eyes had been flaming with disbelief and anger.

He had lived here, a servant below stairs, serving his master devotedly and in every way possible. His master had never thanked him, but Andrew had never seemed to notice that. She has been greatly drawn to the young servant-lad, liked being in his quiet company, often sat in the stables talking to him for hours. And one day when she had sneaked off after him and persuaded him to teach her how to tickle a trout, he had whispered something in her ear, something that had made her very happy and very unhappy all at the same time. She had been thirteen then, and he fifteen, and to this day she had never told another soul what Andrew Thomas had whispered to her.

Then one evening last year, before the rebellion broke, her father had hosted a supper for some of the yeomanry officers of the neighbourhood. She had been present, and was quite pleased to hear one mention that he had seen young Andrew Thomas shoot a sparrowhawk that very day. He showed great skill with a gun.

His fellow yeomen were not pleased; talk of a rebellion was rife then, in the previous spring of 1798. And as the night moved on they had mentioned Andrew again, saying it might not be wise to leave a young man so skilled with a gun at large, in the home of a gentleman of property. They suggested that Andrew be arrested that night and despatched into His Majesty's Fleet. In Ireland a man only had to be *suspected* of being disaffected to be sent to the Fleet. A trial was unnecessary.

She had waited with breath trapped to hear her father refuse, refuse angrily, for Andrew Thomas had been his faithful servant from the day he had learned to walk.

`Perhaps you are right,' her father had said. `Yes, you may as well take young Thomas with you when you leave.'

She had been the only person to see the serving-maid slip swiftly out of the room. She excused herself and hastily followed, down to the kitchen, just in time to see the maid bend and whisper in Andrew's ear. He had left immediately, pausing to take his master's favourite gun with him. At the door he had turned and looked directly at her – at his master's daughter. `I will be back,' he had promised. `And I will kill him.'

Mary Hugo emitted a trembling sigh as she stared into the night with tear-filled eyes. The land outside was black. And Andrew Thomas had returned to fulfil his promise.

*

When Michael Dwyer heard about the assassination attempt, he was furious. He called Andrew Thomas to account.

When Andrew gave his explanation, Michael told him it was unacceptable.

`Why?' Andrew cried, hardly able to believe his ears.

`It was a cold-blooded murder attempt, the same as that on William Hume Senior,' Michael said. `I will not accept such behaviour from one of my men.'

`You have killed enough men in your day, Captain!'

`Aye – on the battlefield, soldier to soldier. When they come towards me, or after me, wearing the accoutrements of battle and try for my life or the lives of my men, then I fight them. But I am no hidden sniper! And I will not allow any cowardly sniper to remain in my division.'

Hugo backs the shooting-and-burning militia! What's the difference?'

`The difference is premeditated and cold-blooded murder of a civilian. And you swore the oath of the United Irishmen, Thomas, you swore that you would not shed innocent or civilian blood!'

Andrew Thomas sought to argue, but his captain would not be swayed.

`I'm sorry,' Michael said quietly, `but if you again attempt the murder of Thomas Hugo, you will afterwards go your own road, for I will not allow you to stay in this company.'

Andrew Thomas looked around at the small army of

silent men. Their faces more than anything else told him that the captain meant it.

He shrugged angrily and walked away, walked for hours until it was dark, then returned to camp. Most of the men were deep inside the huge cavern, candles were burning brightly and a fire flaming, the glow from the cavern's entrance unseen from the land below, for across and beyond this side of the Lugnaquilla was nothing but miles and miles of wilderness.

Outside the cavern a group of men were playing cards around a fire. They were Dubliners, half Protestants and half Catholics. There had been a series of raids in the capital, searching for United Irishmen who had taken part in the rebellion, and these twenty had managed to flee Dublin to join Dwyer in the mountains. They were a merry bunch, always singing and joking.

`How goes it, Andrew?' one called cheerily.

Andrew nodded silently to them as he passed into the cavern. He looked around, and saw the captain sitting away from the main body of men. As usual he was in the midst of his three staunch companions, Hugh Vesty, John Mernagh, and Martin Burke; an unbreakable foursome; each would risk their lives for the others.

The captain looked up at him, smiled and beckoned him over as if their angry exchange earlier had never happened. Hesitantly, he sauntered across, and the unbreakable foursome broke apart to let him sit amongst them.

Later, when they had all lain down to sleep, Andrew Thomas lay awake, his choice stark and hard before him; the choice between killing Thomas Hugo or staying with the captain and his men. He didn't know which he wanted most. All he knew was that he wanted both.

*

Two weeks after the assassination attempt, Thomas Hugo's arm was almost healed. Then luck decided to strike him a nice turn. He was breathlessly informed, by a very reliable and well-paid source, that Michael Dwyer and only two of his men were near Stranahely, on a low hip-edge of Table

Mountain.

`Are you sure it's him?' Hugo demanded.

`Aye, tall, lithe, black curly hair; and one of the other two rebels was just as tall with fair hair – now *he* was definitely Hugh Vesty Byrne – the reb-chief's cousin and second-in-command.'

`You're sure?'

`I'm sure.'

So Thomas Hugo, Master of the Hunt, collected together a hunting party.

`Right, men!' Hugo cried. `Let's bring that reb-chief to the whip!'

They rode from Annamoe up Glenmalure and over the Black Banks where they rode quietly and in single file through a small forest, their horses hooves covered in leather to quieten their steps, making barely a sound on the thick ancient layer of leaves. Before they reached the edge of the clearing, they stopped in the density of the forest and sat in silence for some long minutes, waiting and smiling at each other.

Then Hugo gave the signal, and they came out at a gallop and succeeded in forming a circle around the ledge. Even to Hugo, the rebels appeared to be taken by surprise. The three sprang to their feet and sent down a volley as they ran for cover.

The huntsmen plunged their horses into the dykes and took shelter along the ditches. Only Hugo's large brown hat could be seen above the high hedge.

`You may as well surrender, Dwyer!' Hugo shouted. `Any way down and we have you.'

In the silence that fell, the huntsmen horses could be heard snorting.

`Do you hear me, Dwyer? I give you my word that nothing ill short of the law will befall you, if you throw down your arms and come in peacefully.'

In the continuing silence, Hugo's hat bobbed above the hedge in his impatience. `Are you there, Dwyer?'

`I am, Hugo.'

`Then you must see that we have you surrounded and

there is no way down. Now, will you surrender peacefully, or do we have to come and get you? Give me your answer!'

`Here it is, avic.'

The bullet whistled into Hugo's hat and carried it flying across the air. Hugo was so startled he fell off his horse into the ditch with a splatter of curses.

The huntsmen began firing.

The exchange of volleys went on for some short minutes with the rebels' fire becoming more and more intermittent, then ceased completely. At first the hunstmen were jubilant, sure the rebels had used up their ammunition, or were dead. But on dismounting from their horses and clambering up the slopes, it slowly dawned on them that Dwyer and his men had been quietly moving up and up, toward the shoulders of Table Mountain, and now were gone.

Hugo had to be helped back onto his horse, emitting a furious string of oaths at being foiled in his quest to bring in the rebel captain.

`Damn him for a dog-fox!' he bawled. `Not only has he lost me a bounty of five hundred guineas, he has lost me a hat that cost a small fortune in Dublin's Sackville Street!'

The three rebels were far away, moving across the high grassy slopes of Table Mountain. Michael shook his head in bewilderment.

`What an eejit that man is,' he said. `Sitting there talking through his hat.'

`He's got no hat now,' Hugh Vesty reminded him. `I think it flew all the way to Arklow.'

`Good enough for him,' Michael muttered. `He's lucky I didn't decide to shoot his block off. Without his hat his brain will get an airing now anyway. Did you hear the stupid tongue of him – "Any way down and we have you!" Sure any fool knows that what can't go down, must go up.'

He gave a bemused sigh. `And they say we're the ignoramuses.'

*

This time it was Andrew Thomas's turn to be furious when he heard. He rushed across the camp and pulled roughly on

Michael's arm.

`You let Hugo get away! He came after you, gun in hand, and you played with him instead of shooting him!'

`That's right.'

Andrew sucked in a breath and clenched his teeth. `I played fair with you, Captain. You offered me a choice of killing Hugo or staying with you, and I elected to stay with you. Now you insult me by playing games with Hugo and allowing him to bob away on his merry way home.'

`It was nothing to do with you, Andrew. You never entered my thoughts at the time.'

`Why did you not kill him?' Andrew demanded. `Mernagh tells me that you could have done it if you had wished.'

`There was no need to kill him. He was no real threat to us, just a nuisance.'

Andrew was trembling, his eyes glistening with tears of rage.

`Forget Hugo,' Michael commanded softly.

`No!'

`Then he'll kill you long before you kill him. He'll mangle you up into a sick knot of hate without lifting a finger. Don't give any man that power.'

Andrew sagged at the truth of it, but he managed to rasp an angry parting shot at Michael for letting him down.

`I'm beginning to think that what James Horan often says about you is right, Captain.'

`And what does James Horan often say about me?' Michael asked softly.

`That you have a particular partiality for the Protestants,' Andrew snapped, then turned quickly and marched off.

Hugh Vesty moved to Michael's shoulder. `That boy is in bad pain,' he said. `There's something more in it than he says. I think you should go after him and find out what it is.'

Michael looked at his cousin. `At this minute he hates me more than he hates Hugo.'

`Ach, he doesn't. Andrew is one of our best. He needs help to get that large weight off his shoulders. And it should be you that goes after him – being his captain and all – I'm

64

only a mere second-in-command.'

Michael finally found his man half a mile away, leaning back against a boulder and staring into space. He stuffed his hands into his pockets and took up position beside Andrew Thomas.

`So ... ' Michael said quietly, `you spent your life serving at the heels of your master and he never gave you the time of the day. Most masters are like that with their servants. Didn't you know that?'

`He agreed to my disposal,' Andrew snapped his fingers – `just like that! Without even a moment's hesitation he agreed they could send me off into a life of hell below deck.' Andrew snapped his fingers again. `Just like that!'

`Then he's not worth a thought. Do as I advise, Andrew, and forget Hugo.'

`I can't.'

`For God's sake, Andrew – why not?'

`Thomas Hugo is my father,' Andrew Thomas said. `He took my mother when she was a young kitchen maid. She still works in his kitchens. He refused to let me have his surname, so she gave me his first – Thomas.'

`Ah, man!' Michael didn't know what else to say, so he put an arm around the shoulders of the younger man and pulled him close.

*

A very long time later, when they finally arrived back together at the camp, Hugh Vesty and Mernagh and Burke were waiting. They took one look at the face of Andrew Thomas and smiled in relief.

`Here, Andrew, drink this, it will settle you down nicely.' Hugh Vesty held out a small wooden cup almost full with pure white poteen.

`Mountain dew, drink it down,' Hugh urged briskly as Andrew held the cup and stared at its contents. `Although you may find it a bit smoky. Mernagh only got it yesterday.'

Andrew tasted the brew, then eyes wide, he made a deep rasping sound in his throat as he blew out the invisible flames.

`And a drop for you, Captain,' Mernagh offered, holding up a cup.

Michael shook his head. `I have something to do first. I'll be back in a while.'

James Horan was a big lad, and very malicious and quarrelsome of late. He was having a heated conversation with a few of the Dublin lads. He turned as Michael approached.

`Ah, here's the man himself! He'll lay the bones of this argument once and for all because he was there. Listen, Captain, do you remember – '

`You're out of this company, Horan. You have two minutes to pick up your things and get out.'

Horan's face straightened muscle by muscle. `Why?' he rasped.

`You're a pissed up bloody trouble-maker, that's why.' Michael motioned with his head. `Look over there.'

Horan turned his head towards a group of men sitting away from the main body of small groups. They were Protestant deserters from the Antrim militia regiment once stationed in Arklow. Men from Sam McAllister's regiment. Men who found they could not fight their own countrymen during the rebellion and deserted to the rebels.

`They used to sit amongst us before I took my leave,' Michael said. `But when I came back I noticed how they sat apart. Now I know why. They're no longer comrades-in-arms, are they, Horan. Not on your tongue. They're just Protestants. Well let me tell you, boy, this camp is still United Irish, and those boys have risked their lives with us, just as Sam McAllister and the Little Dragoon and many others did before they died.'

`I don't want out,' Horan cried. `It was just idle talk. I'll not bother with it again.'

`You're out whether you want it or not. This camp is no longer the place for you. You're turning bad inside and looking for a reason. Next you'll be looking for blood.'

James Horan looked at the ground for a few moments. When he looked up again the message had sunk in. His face was full of furious contempt.

`My, but you do love the Prods, don't you, Captain? First you start dreaming about one, then you let another ride off. Next I'll be hearing how proudly you wear your orange sash and sing the Lillibulero.'

Michael's face turned ashen. `Run now and you'll be lucky to get out undamaged. Anyone else who feels the same and wants to go with him – move now!'

No one moved but Horan. He lifted his musket and hefted it onto his shoulder.

`And you know the rules, Horan,' Michael warned. `A whisper about anything you know and every rebel in Wicklow and the surrounding counties will be looking for an informer. Remember what happened to Patrick Lynch after Derrynamuck. He's now in solitary confinement in Kilmainham Gaol – for his own protection from the people of Wicklow. He was lucky to make it to Dublin alive. Hear me, Horan, don't use your mouth to dig your grave.'

Horan shrugged and strolled off. He hadn't a clue where he would go, but he couldn't stay, not now he'd been given his marching orders. But he would go out defiant!

`Now why would I do that, Captain, when I can use my mouth to sing a true old song or two instead.'

Then as he passed the group of Protestant deserters he smiled maliciously and began to sing.

> `Ara! what makes the noose creak and swing?
> Lillibulero, bullen-a-la.
> Ho! by my soul tis a Protestant wind
> Lillibulero, bullen-a-la.

Every Protestant and Catholic stared in edgy silence. James Horan looked around the camp and grinned brazenly, then stumbled into a half-run before falling flat on his face from the force of the kick to his backside.

`Get up and get out!' Michael snapped.

Horan scrambled to his feet and turned around, humiliation and rage dripping from every pore. `Oh, do me a favour, Captain. Go back to your bed and curl up with a dream of your darling Prod McAllister –'

`Don't you even mention his name,' Michael warned,

eyes flaming. `His name is too good for your filthy tongue! And as big as you are, Horan, you could never in a lifetime be the man that McAllister was.'

`Oh no? Well there's something you should know, Dwyer. What McAllister did at Derrynamuck was not for you. No, sir! The bastard knew he was finished and just wanted to go out in a blaze of glory.'

It was all over in two swift moves. The blow to Horan's stomach sent him gasping to his knees, but it was the force of the boot slamming up to his jaw that broke it and laid him back unconscious.

*

`He'll have to stay with us now,' Hugh Vesty said to Michael after Horan had been carried far into the cavern.

`But as soon as he's fit again he goes.' Michael was still white-faced with anger.

`He might not be fit for months,' Hugh said, but Michael did not hear him, because, as he usually did when he was angry, he had wandered off alone.

`I shouldn't have said anything to him about Horan,' said Andrew Thomas quietly to Hugh Vesty. `But at the time I was that mad myself over the business with Hugo, and Horan got me all fired up about the captain, telling me how he made the men let Joseph Holt go just because he was a Protestant and even though he was a traitor.'

`Joseph Holt was a great United commander in his day,' Hugh Vesty said sternly. `Never forget that, boy. And the business with Horan would have flared soon enough. I've had to speak to him myself about that tongue of his. Michael is right, Horan has turned bad inside. And it takes only one bad apple to rot an entire barrel. We have enough to do fighting the armies of the oppressor without faction fighting amongst ourselves. We're supposed to have put all that behind us when we became United men.'

Hugh lifted his drink, and then looked squarely at the young man sitting beside him. `So, what now about Hugo?'

Andrew Thomas gave no answer for a long time. Then he shrugged. `What's done is done,' he said. `I reckon if I don't forget Hugo, I'll end up turning as bad inside as Horan. I've decided to let Hugo go to Hades in his own way.'

Hugh Vesty grinned. `Smart thinking. Save your passion for Reilly's daughter at Coolamaddra, and leave the devil to deal with Hugo.'

*

Less than thirty-six hours later, Andrew Thomas was dead. In the company of only two others, for they never travelled in large groups for fear of drawing attention to themselves, he travelled over to the house of Edward Byrne on the northern slope of Derrybawn Mountain to collect provisions for the camp. The rain had been falling since morning, the ground heavy.

They headed on to Matthew McDaniel's house at Castle Kevin. McDaniel was one of those given the job of procuring ammunition for the rebels with the money supplied through levy by the people of County Wicklow. It was still raining and very dark when they had packed their sacks, so they decided to rest up at McDaniel's for the night.

The following morning, breakfast over, they lifted their sacks in readiness to leave, grinning and making faces at Matthew McDaniel who was standing outside and appeared to be peering in through the living room window at them, but was actually peering into a small mirror perched on the window while shaving his face by the full light outside.

Then, suddenly, Matt McDaniel gave a shout and disappeared. They came out the door to see what he was up to, and saw him running for his life and a troop of the Rathrum Cavalry spurring towards the house.

The three rebels dropped their sacks and scattered in different directions. Andrew took the left-hand, downward path, slipping as he crossed a stream. He scrambled to his feet and fired a shot at his pursuers but his gun did not go off. He fired again, a dull click and no more; the powder had got wet in the stream. For a second he just stared in disbelief at his master's favourite gun, the gun he himself had nicknamed `Roaring Bess.'

`You never failed me before!' the approaching yeomen

69

heard him cry, a moment before he disappeared like an experienced fox, hard pressed, through the trees; and eventually lost them.

He might have made it, had he not been seen by a yeoman named Lieutenant Weekes, an immensely lanky man whom the rebels had nicknamed `Long Weekes' as he pushed through a sloe hedge onto rushy ground which led to a pond where Weekes was crouched duck shooting.

Weekes turned, saw a young man with a gun, an obvious rebel, saw him about to make a run for it, and quickly brought him down with a shot in the leg. The pursuers from the Rathdrum Cavalry came along a few minutes later and dismounted. For a moment they looked down at Andrew Thomas, then lunged into kicking him unconscious, before emptying their firelocks into him.

`I say!' declared Long Weekes, the son of a Reverend. `There was no need to finish the business with such barbarous brutality!'

*

Thomas King of Kingston, a magistrate who lived two miles from Rathdrum, spent most of his leisure hours busily writing reports to his friends at Dublin Castle. He employed a number of spies, paid them poorly, and occasionally they gave him as much information as he had paid for.

He rushed in to his study and almost knocked over the inkstand in his haste to report:

> `A rebel of note has been killed. Who he was, I have not yet been able to find out, but the rumour is that Dwyer's party are grieving much at his death and all the Females on the mountains who favour the rebels are wearing black ribbons by way of mourning.'

*

Two days later, the magistrate held another report in his hand, although he could not truly believe its contents. He stood by the window gawping after the young woman who was walking slowly back down the lane ... Mary Hugo.

His wife poked a sharply chiselled face round the door. `What did she want with you, Mr King? She was very curt with me!'

The magistrate was still in shock. `She has signed a sworn statement for the authorities at Dublin Castle. But I don't believe it. I *refuse* to believe it. Here, here, read it for yourself.'

His wife stepped in brusquely and did read it, but far too short-sightedly for the bursting magistrate to await her reaction.

`See,' he cried, his finger prodding the paper. `She has sworn that the body now lying dead in the Flannel Hall at Rathdrum is the body of the late Andrew Thomas of Drummin and for the taking of whom a reward was offered by Government and sayeth that he was born and reared in the same house as herself and that ... and that ... she is his half sister!'

`Well!' Mrs King curled back and stared at her husband. `Oh, how wicked. How very, very wicked! What are you going to do with the statement?'

`I will have to send it to Dublin Castle! They rely on my reports and would not like it if I kept anything from them.'

`Then let this be a lesson to you, Mr King,' she said sternly, flouncing towards the door. `And take heed when I speak to you in future. I *told* you I did not like that young woman, and now events have proved that I was right about her. She is a wicked, *wicked* person to write and sign such a false and scurrilous statement like that one.'

Chapter Five

Mary's stay with the old couple was much happier the second time around. The white-haired woman was very kind to her; spending much time in teaching her the `old' remedies and cures. She had even taken Mary to a secret Holy Well where she had been urged to drink the water and make a wish for a safe birth for herself and the child.

And she had started to bloom; within days of going to the old couple, she suddenly bloomed and bloomed until she was as a big as a late summer rose. She wondered if it was all the raspberry-leaf tea the old woman kept making her drink. She felt so relaxed in mind and body she often dozed off in the day, but barely slept at night with the baby's movements.

At the beginning of August, as promised, Michael came just before dawn to take her home to Knockandarragh, and found the old couple in a frantic state and Mary in the pains of labour. She was standing in her nightgown by the table, bent almost double, one hand gripping the edge of the table and the other pressed into her back.

`But it's not due for weeks,' he said in confusion. `Are you sure it's not just backache?'

`It's not any kind of ache,' Mary cried. `It's pain!'

`She'll not be able to travel,' the old woman said to Michael. `But she must keep on her feet a while longer. Now you go running for the doctoring woman quick as you can.'

Suddenly he was terrified to leave her. He put an arm round her. `Will I, Mary?'

She looked at him and nodded urgently. `It started before I went to bed last evening, but I thought it was just very bad backache, before the stabs of pain woke me.'

`I'll be back in no time,' he assured her, then shot out of the door and started to run, across the yard and through the small wood nearby, speeding through the trees until he came to the edge of the clearing where he suddenly stopped dead – and stared at the unexpected figure of a woman stalking towards him; a great dark vulture of a woman with black hair tied up in a knot who was as strong as a bull and knocking on six foot two.

For a moment he almost sidestepped behind a tree in fright, but she had seen him – Midge Mahoney! A terrible woman, and mad about men, especially young men. He would never forget the time she had got him into her bedroom, on the pretence of lighting the fire for her, and then had grabbed him in a clinch that had nearly broken all his bones in his struggle to escape.

`Oho!' she cried in glee.`They say the early bird catches the worm – and now I have you!'

He wondered what she was doing so far from her own home, then remembered she was a niece of sorts to the old couple.

She let out a teasing laugh and bellowed towards him. `Ach, surely I don't frighten ye now – a big lad like you!'

`I've no time for wrestling with you, Mrs Mahoney,' he said impatiently. `I have to get to the doctoring woman?'

`What for?' Then her face sharpened, she looked at him hawk-like. `Has Mary started?'

`Aye, early. And she's in bad pain.'

`Oh, the poor lamb!' Suddenly her whole demeanour changed at the news that one of her female sisters was suffering. As lusty and brutal as she could be with men, Midge was terribly tenderhearted towards her own sex.

`Then you don't need no doctoring woman – not when Midge Mahoney is at hand.' She shook herself like a fierce mother-hen and began striding in the direction of the old couple's house.

`Well don't just stand there!' she cried over her shoulder. `'Tis you that put her in that condition, so you may come back and help me.'

She began to stride again. He caught up and looked at her warily. `Do you know anything about birthing babies?'

`Nothing at all.' She fired a derisive glance at him. `I only birthed four of my own. Four lads that are turning into great lovely brutes of men like their father.'

He thought of Midge's timid little husband only half her size, and said nothing, recalling to mind Midge's four boys –

all hawks in her own image.

When they returned to the house Mary was still on her feet, doubled up in pain and tears spilling down her cheeks.

`Ach, my lovely lamb!' Midge cried, gathering Mary inside her arms. `Into the bedroom now and I'll have the sharp edge off your pain in no time.'

Midge turned and fired a command at Michael. `You – make yourself useful! Go and collect some marigolds.'

He stared at her. `Marigolds?'

`No other will do,' Midge said, leading Mary away. `And when you have a handful collected, bring them back to me, then start hefting in the water.'

Michael looked in sceptical wonderment at the white haired old woman, who nodded her head solemnly. `Marigolds, she confirmed. `Midge has the ancient knowledge.'

Michael turned to the old man. `Will you do something for me, Paudeen? Will you go to Eadstown and tell my mother to come here – as swiftly and as secretly as she can.' He looked at the bedroom door. `I don't trust that witch with my wife.'

`She'll not fare better with anyone else,' the old man said. `Midge can work wonders with her flowers and plants. She knows more than the doctoring woman – she has the gift.'

`Do as I ask!' Michael pleaded. `Fetch my mother.'

The old man nodded genially and reached for his hat. `I'll go on the donkey. He's a swift old thing.'

When Michael returned with the marigolds, Midge came out of the bedroom with an anxious expression on her face. `It's not going to take as long as I thought,' she said to the old woman; then Michael watched as Midge pulled the green leaves off the marigolds and deftly began to chop them in shreds.

The old woman creaked over to the table with three or four small glass jars of chopped-up plants, then an iron milk-pot, then a jug of steaming water. Midge lifted a spoonful from each bottle and dropped the contents into the pot, then sprinkled in a handful of the chopped marigold leaves.

`Now give it just a second or two of brewing on the fire,' Midge ordered the old woman. `Then we'll temper it down with a little cold water.'

Mary groaned out in pain as another contraction knifed her body.

Midge looked at Michael and snapped a command. `You! Go in and hold her hand till I'm ready.'

He winced as he stepped into the bedroom and saw her, her eyes glazed with pain. She gripped his hand so tightly, digging her nails into his palms, he winced again.

`Don't leave me,' she pleaded.

`Never,' he promised, and kissed her hand passionately.

`You – out!' Midge ordered, carrying in a cup of her brew. `Now my darling girl, drink this and the nightmare will vanish.'

The old woman creaked in behind her and moved to hold Mary's head up while Midge held the cup to her lips and made her drink.

He hovered at the door watching. Within minutes the glazed look of pain disappeared from Mary's eyes and she relaxed down on the bed with a dreamy sigh of relief.

`There now,' Midge declared with satisfaction. `I think we mixed the ingredients just right. Too much of one or the other can cause problems, you know.'

`Aye, to be sure.' The old woman nodded her head in solemn agreement.

Midge sat down on the edge of the bed and gently held Mary's slender hand inside her own large-knuckled two. Mary smiled dreamily at the big woman in drugged adoration.

Midge smiled back tenderly, and then turned a wry face to her old aunt. `Did you hear about that gentry woman who picked up a whisper about our knowledge of the marigolds? Aye, thought she was clever she did, knowing one of our secrets. And when she got badly sick, she ate a handful of marigold leaves and swelled up the size of a house. Aye, writhing in agony for days she was and the Quality doctor unable to do anything for her.'

Midge sniffed. `I could have made up a mixture and

75

relieved her in no time, but when I learned who she was, I remembered once hearing that particular madam declaring that us Irishwomen were good for nothing but making babies. So I decided not to disappoint her by offering to make anything else.'

The morning was well on when Michael's mother appeared like a silent vision from nowhere. She spoke to him distantly as she threw off her cloak then turned and entered the bedroom leaving him in mid-sentence.

She stared down at Mary for a silent moment, and then looked sternly at Midge.

`What have you given her?' she demanded.

Midge was reluctant to discuss the exact details of her potions. She was also instantly subdued by the presence of this cool, efficient-mannered woman whom she had known for many a long year.

`Well?'

Midge shrugged. `Sure it's her first and hardest and longest. A little easing of her pain for a while is no harm. Is it now?'

`The old and pagan practices are gone,' Mrs Dwyer said coldly.

`Well begor and who says so?' Midge cried, flaring into a pet passion. `There's no virtue in pain. And if I can give a little help to one of my poor sisters suffering the punishment of Eve – then I will and bedamned!'

Across the bed the two women stared at each other in a dark look that held centuries of female anger and female sympathy in its depth. Then a ghost of a secret smiled moved reluctantly on Mrs Dwyer's lips and Midge smiled too.

Michael watched in puzzlement. He had seen that look pass between women before. A secret way of communicating that seemed to speak volumes without words.

`But not a drop more,' his mother said softly to Midge. `She will need all her wits and strength to deliver the child. It will not be able to come without her help.'

Midge nodded in agreement, then turning her head and

76

seeing him standing there, perked up in female superiority. `You – out! And make sure there is plenty of water hissing and steaming when we need it.'

Before he could reply she had marched over and slammed the door in his face.

Evening was falling. The old man had long returned and was now kneeling humbly beside his white-haired old wife on the hearth-mat, quietly murmuring prayers together for a safe and successful birth.

He stood by the closed bedroom door silently watching them, inwardly distraught. The water was hissing and steaming. The awful screams from inside the bedroom made him want to cry. What had Midge called it – the punishment of Eve.

He looked at the old couple who never halted in their litany of prayers. The screams became worse. He could stand no more. He wandered outside and stood against a tree not far from the house. The screams reached out to him. He bent and lifted a stone, then withdrew the knife sheathed inside the top of his boot and began to sharpen it, slowly and methodically. His frustration and impotence was boiling to danger point when the screams abruptly ceased.

He stood waiting, like a stone statue, terrified to go near the house which had fallen into a sudden silence. He had known since his childhood that some women, and some babies, did not always survive the pain and travail of birth.

He waited for what seemed like hours.

Then Midge Mahoney came out carrying a bowl of water that she threw violently towards the field, and then turned back indoors.

She came out again carrying a bucket this time, and sent the water flying in the same violent motion towards the field.

The third time she came out she was carrying a kettle. She stalked towards the rain-barrel, and then saw him standing there in the dusky shadows of evening.

`Lord save us!' she cried. `In all the excitement we forgot about you!'

He had never hit a female in his life, but he wanted to hit

her. Only hours before he had felt a new respect and liking for her. Now he glared at her in sheer hatred, but she didn't seem to notice.

`A girl child!' she crooned, smiling rapturously. `And so beautiful after she was washed that your mother and me cried all over her.'

There was a great deal of bustle and smiles between the old couple when he entered, like two excited children who had suddenly experienced a great event in their humble and humdrum lives.

His mother came out of the bedroom and stood for a moment pinning her fair hair back into a neat knot. She looked as careless as he had never seen her. The sleeves of her dress were rolled up high, the buttons of her bodice thrown open at the neck.

`Mary?' he asked.

His mother turned and smiled at him. `Go in and see for yourself.'

She had been washed and tidied up. She looked as fresh and peaceful as if her pain had never been. She lifted adoring eyes from the swaddled bundle in her arms, then seeing who it was, a nervous smile twitched onto her face.

`A girl,' she said.

`I'm glad,' he lied.

`A lovely girl,' she repeated.

A half-smile of pretended delight hovered about his mouth.

`Come and see.'

He moved over to the bed, then bent and gently pulled back the swaddling and looked into the tiny face of the child.

And the world stood still.

Sheer wonder came into his eyes. Six months of knowing a child was expected, three months of hoping for a boy, had not been long enough to prepare him for this first sight of his daughter.

Her blue eyes stared back into his unseeing; blue eyes that would shortly turn to brown or hazel. Her skin was smooth and tawny pink, her hair soft and thick and silky black like Mary's; her little rosebud mouth shaped as if she was saying a silent ooo.

`Your mother and Midge say she's a full nine months,' Mary whispered. `So the doctoring woman must have got it wrong. She must have been conceived not long after we were married.'

It was an effort to tear his eyes away, but he managed to look at Mary, smiling joyously and swallowing his breath. `She's tiny?' he quivered.

`She is, but then she's a colleen and not a buachaleen.' Mary sniffed her offspring with loving pride and covered the tiny face with gentle kisses.

`You can hold her if you like,' she said suddenly.

`Can I?'

`Aye.'

She placed the child in his arms. He held her nervously, unable to speak as he stared down at the little scrap of magic that he and Mary had concocted between them. The baby turned her face into his chest in blind curiosity, her little mouth working in a searching movement; then her lips began to quiver and her face screwed up and she let out a small cry of disappointment.

`Maybe she's hungry,' Mary said anxiously. He quickly handed the bawling child back to her, then sat down on the edge of the bed and propped his head against the bedpost and watched as she uncovered and attempted to feed the child at her breast.

Strangely, there was no embarrassment between them, these two country people, for although unwedded men may blush at the glimpse of a bare leg or ankle, a husband watching his wife feeding her child was as natural as watching a ewe suckling her lamb.

But the sharing of it, the newness of it, filled them both with a silent awe as they looked at the child that belonged to them both. They looked at each other, and both knew what the other was thinking, and their new happiness was tinged with sadness as they realised the struggle that lay ahead.

Then he realised the child was getting fretful, Mary too, moving about on the pillows and wincing as if in pain.

`What is it?'

`I don't know how to do it!' she cried, her face hot with shame at such an admission. `And it hurts so.'

The baby cried fretfully, and kept on crying.

`I'll get my mother,' he said quickly, then fled out the door. His mother came at once, told him to leave them alone for a while.

`Huerta, my lovely girl!' Mrs Dwyer murmured to the baby as she positioned her correctly against Mary's breast. `You have to learn to do it right, otherwise your poor mammy will end up as sore as can be ... there now!'

Soon both mother and child were feeding more easily, the rosebud mouth sucking contentedly, a tiny palm pressed into the soft milky flesh.

Mrs Dwyer smiled.

`I feel so foolish,' Mary whispered. `Not knowing how.'

`And why should you know? The ways of motherhood don't always come so easily or naturally as men may think.'

Mary lifted sooty eyelashes and looked at her mother-in-law. She had always been slightly afraid of her, until this day. She could be so cold, so unemotional at times, you never knew how she was truly feeling. It was only during the birth, when they had struggled and suffered together, that she had discovered just how soothing and tender this woman could be.

Mrs Dwyer suddenly smiled again, a soft smile of amusement. `I remember a young black cow we had once, lovely she was, and very young going through her first birth. And so natural, they tell us, is motherhood to animals, that when her new-born calf smelled the milk and tried to suckle her, she darted away in fright.'

Mary started to laugh, and then laughed and laughed with such relief the baby whined indignantly.

`So it is with women,' Mrs Dwyer said gently. `The ways of motherhood do not flow into us as naturally as the milk. We must learn from each other.'

The two women looked at each other and a flicker of a new intimacy showed in each face. They smiled in silent understanding. Then the older woman lifted the baby to the other side, and again nodded in satisfaction.

`Will you send Michael back in?' Mary whispered.

`I will, for I think he's had a hard day of it. Midge has treated him something contemptuous. She always hates men badly before a child is born, then loves them madly again as soon as the pain is over and the joy begins.'

`I do like her,' Mary said.

`So do I,' Mrs Dwyer agreed. `But she's still a terrible woman!'

Midge was on her third glass of poteen. She herself had brought the bottle to the old couple last Christmas but they had never touched it, believing drink to be sinful. Midge was talking and laughing so heartily that, as always, every bulging proportion of her great body shook. The old couple paid no attention to her, just smiled foolishly at each other, for the glass of poteen she had forced them to drink had gone to their heads. The old man stood up and sat down again, then wondered why he had done so.

Midge turned her attention to Michael, sitting beside her on the settle. She ogled him silently for a minute then edged her massive body closer until he was jammed up against the high wooden arm.

`As I recall, Michael asthore, the rule of abstinence is six weeks before the birth and six weeks after – three months. Isn't that a long old time for a lusty young stallion to go without his oats?' She fumbled slyly at his thigh and blinked her eyes wickedly. `Doesn't it make you glad you're a rebel and not a priest?'

Michael scrambled to his feet and out of her clutches as his mother walked back into the room. She glared coldly at Midge, and then motioned to him with her head to go back inside.

`Now Mrs Mahoney...' He didn't wait to hear his mother's words, but as he closed the bedroom door behind him, Midge boomed out a laugh that made the rafters shake.

`A terrible woman,' he murmured as he moved back to the bed and sat down on the edge, then smiled as he again feasted his eyes on his daughter. She had collapsed in sleep, a bubble of milk still on her upper pink lip.

`I'll teach her all the good things,' he whispered passionately. `I'll teach her how to tickle a fish and make a wish when she holds her first ladybird. I'll teach her to hear the heartbeat of the land and see the sun flaming through the wings of a butterfly '

Mary whispered: `I thought you would be disappointed with a girl child, but I can see that if I'm not careful, she may end up weaning your affection away from me.'

Still smiling, he looked at her, and the smile wiped from his face as he saw she was not jesting in any way. Her eyes were dark and sullen, and for the first time he knew the frightening extent of what Sam McAllister had once called, `Mary's obsession.'

And it did frighten him. For the weight of responsibility it put on his shoulders was heavier than any five hundred guineas. Her emotional dependence on him was total. It had been so since the day they married, and seemingly not even the birth of the child had changed that.

`Don't be silly,' he said. `Love of a daughter is different to love of a wife.'

The expression on her face changed, became odd and little strained.

`I was only jesting ' She began to mumble in agonised shame, and suddenly the hardness of her unsettled life, hiding and running, always having to be one step smarter than the soldiers, the constant terror of it all, and the exhaustion wreaked on her body by the birth crashed down on her.

`It's so unfair!' she cried. `All you did was fight for the freedom of your country and the protection of your people. It's so unfair...'

He looked away, acutely aware that he was the cause of all her worry and pain. If he had not joined the United Irishmen, if he had kept his nose deep in the mud and licked the horse-dung off their boots whenever they asked, he might now be living in peaceful humiliation with his wife and child on a few rented acres that could never be his, no matter how hard he worked.

All men are born and continue free and equal

in respect of their rights. The aim of all political associations is the preservation of the natural and imprescriptible rights of man. And these rights are liberty, equality, property, security, and the right to resist oppression.

That had been the dream. That had been the failure.

He turned and slipped an arm under her shoulder. She turned her face into his chest and allowed him to rock her gently.

`A baby needs a father and a future,' she said drowsily.

`Yes.'

`I need you.'

`Yes.'

Never had he understood her so well. She had given him everything, everything she had to give, and now she asked for just one small thing in return – his continued survival. She depended totally on it.

`It will be all right, Mary, I promise.'

She twisted in his arms, eyes closed. `Do you. Michael. Do you promise?'

`I do.'

`You're not lying again?'

`No.'

Finally she drifted into sleep. He looked towards the window now black with night. Survival – such a hard thing to ask of a man to whom survival was a day-to-day business, and a night-to-night achievement.

*

Hugh Vesty, John Mernagh and Martin Burke came anxiously looking for him a short time later. He left with them, promising to return as soon as he could. Midge assured him she would come every day to keep an eye on Mary and help out.

When he reached the camp the men all congratulated him and started a celebration. Some were dismayed at his subdued manner, but then they whispered it must be because the child was not a son.

83

The moon glided slowly on its course through the night sky. In the rebel camp the mood was merry, the jokes witty. But deep in the wild fastness of the Glen of Imaal, the black-haired girl stood by her window, her sleeping baby in her arms, her dark eyes fixed in a melancholy stare on the dark outline of the hills, as if in a trance. Her body was rocking gently, her voice crooning softly.

> `I know my love by his way of walking,
> I know my love by his way of talking
> I know my love by his coat of blue;
> But if my love dies what shall I do?'

Chapter Six

`Jacks are high,' said John Mernagh, shuffling the cards to deal again.

Six of the rebels were staying at the house of a harbourer, John Martin of Kilranelagh, a land-steward of Mr Greene of Greenville House.

John Martin was at the table with them, playing cards and engrossed in the men's conversation. He felt contented, for there was nothing he enjoyed more than sitting with men in a card-game and listening to man-talk; politics, wars, cards, kings and jacks. He loved it.

Around the fire his wife and three daughters sat gossiping as they sewed.

Hugh Vesty consulted a paper at his elbow, and then looked at the proprietor of the house. `And according to my notes, Martin old boy, that's three chickens and a hog our Rory has won from you.'

`Three chickens and a hog? I'm down that much?' John Martin stared at Rory Derneen who he had always thought of as being something of a young gentleman – a rather pretty young gentleman – turned into a rebel. `Where did you learn to play such sharp cards?' he demanded dourly.

Derneen smiled. `In my cradle.'

Hugh Vesty grinned. `That's right, Rory. I reckon you could win the crown off the King of England if he would just agree to a game.'

John Martin turned his gaze away from Derneen, and for the umpteenth time that night, stared longingly at the bottle of red-sealed parliamentarian whiskey which he had been trying to win from the rebels for over an hour. A great prize – not homemade poteen, oh no, but a bottle of pure and golden red-sealed whiskey that tax had been paid on.

`Tis not a leprechaun's shilling,' he said to Derneen. `It can be taken, even off a knave like you.' He rubbed his hands at the challenge. `I'll win it if I have to stay up all night.'

`Good for you, if you can manage it,' Hugh Vesty smiled.

`We've had that bottle for months and not lost it yet.'

`Well tonight's the night,' Martin returned. `I'll win it even if I have to lose my wife and daughters in the process.'

The men all glanced towards the four muslin-frilled females at the hearth.

`You may keep your wife,' Rory Derneen said. `But if you lose your daughters, I put all three in my pocket and take them away with me. Is that agreed?'

John Martin nodded happily. `Agreed!'

The three daughters, who had paused in their chatter to listen with heads bent, exchanged a silent and significant look with each other, and then with their mother.

Mrs Martin snorted, then called out brightly, `Isn't that grand now? The head of our house thinks so highly of his womenfolk who wait on him hand and foot, that he's ready to lose them in a card game for a bottle of parliamentarian whiskey!'

`Oh, stop your yammering, woman,' her husband snarled irritably. `Tis not a serious consideration or risk, for I intend to win. And as head of the house, let me remind ye that it is not your place to interrupt or comment on my conversation when I am in the company of men.' He glared at her coldly. `Ye'll not do it again, woman. I forbid it!'

`Indeed now.' Mrs Martin laughed jocularly and looked at the younger men around the table. `Boys-oh-boys but that's a real man you have in your midst now,' she advised them. `Listen well to him, and he will teach you how to give your women fair stimulation on ways to be loyal and loving to ye.'

Martin knew that she was taunting him, in front of the men too. In front of the *men* too!' The shame of it almost choked him. He showed his teeth to her and was about to reply cuttingly, when a breathless youth hurried into the room from the hallway, and stood panting at the table beside Michael Dwyer. Underneath his cloak the youth was dressed in the elegant livery of a footman.

`What is it?' Michael asked.

`Military operation in search of you, planned for tonight, the 38th regiment and a corps of yeos.'

`Are you sure?'

The youth nodded. `I heard them talking to Mr Greenville.'

`What time do they plan to move?'

`Nine o'clock.'

Michael glanced at the clock on the dressers. `It's that now.'

`I couldn't get away any earlier,' the youth explained. `I had to pretend a gippy stomach and pretend I was about to get sick all over Mr Greenville's Indian hall carpet before I was ordered below stairs.'

`Did you hear their planned route of march?'

`No. But they feel sure you are hereabouts. You were spotted earlier by a yeo out riding.'

`Thanks, avic. We'll not forget this. Now high-tail it back before you are missed.'

The youth was gone in a flash of heels. Michael sat mentally working out all routes to the area.

`There is only one,' he said. `One certain route. But a few good men properly placed should cut the whole of them off.'

`And what shall *I* do?' John Martin asked.

`Get one of your daughters to tie you in a chair,' Michael replied. `If things turn out badly, we forced ourselves on you against your will.'

Then the men stepped outside to the silence of the hills, a natural silence that had become their greatest ally, for it carried the sound of their whistling birdcalls for miles. To the stranger the whistling would have genuinely sounded as those of birds, but to the rebels each wavering note carried a message.

Less than half an hour later, after a series of calls from restless nightingales and irritable owls, twenty more rebels had mustered to Michael's assistance in a field near Martin's house where he instructed them in his plan, then divided them into four sections.

Three small parties hurried away, under the separate command of Hugh Vesty, John Mernagh, and Martin Burke.

Those men left behind followed Michael to an unfrequented avenue not far distant, where he placed them in alternate positions behind the hedges, ensuring their crossfire could not injure each other in the darkness which would soon fall.

He walked backwards down the avenue, his eyes roving the hedges to make sure all men were well enveloped in the cover of bushes and trees, stopping at the top of the avenue where Rory Derneen stood behind a hedge in the foremost sentry position.

Michael put a hand on his shoulder and moved him back a few paces. `You stand well behind me,' he whispered. `You are one man I don't want to lose.'

Surprise was evident on Derneen's face at this unexpected sentiment from the captain, who was now training his rifle over the hedge and positioning himself for firing.

`And why would you not want to lose me in particular?' Derneen asked. `As a matter of interest only.'

`Because if we lose you, avic, we lose a very good provider.' Michael smiled. `Three chickens and a hog ... and nearly three daughters!'

`Ach, I was only jesting about the daughters, I have my own darling girl to be true to,' Derneen said with a smile; then added seriously, `But I'm surely going back to collect the chickens and the hog, fair play and fair game. They'll make us a nice supper one of these nights.' Then he also took up firing position and stood in readiness.

*

The night was cold, unseasonably cold, and darkness came. The two lines of men down the avenue waited in silence.

They had been waiting for over half an hour when Rory Derneen suddenly broke the silence.

`Isn't it a terrible thing they do to hogs, though?' he whispered. `Gelding them and depriving them of a love life with some little piglet, and rearing them just for meat.'

Michael slowly turned his head and stared at Rory Derneen.

`Still,' Derneen sighed. `I suppose that's how all animals finalise in the end. As meat. But the poor hog never gets a bit of happiness beforehand.'

`Shove the hog!' Michael rasped. `Now whisht, and be ready as soon as you hear even the faintest footfall.'

Time passed slowly as they waited, and although it was extremely cold, not a whisper could be heard save the fluttering of the beech leaves along the hedgerows. They had taken their positions at half past nine – it was now one o'clock.

`Listen, Captain,' Derneen finally whispered. `I don't think they're coming. Not a hint of a footfall of any mortal, never mind the enemy.'

Michael made no answer, just continued waiting for his enemy.

`Captain – '

`We wait!'

At two o'clock, soft whistling was heard over the hills.

`Hear that,' Derneen whispered, `even Hugh Vesty thinks we should quit. And truth to tell, Captain, even if the enemy were to come along this freezing minute, my fingers are too cold to crook the freezing trigger. Same for all the other men, I expect.'

`Aye ... perhaps you're right.'

Michael passed down the lines and across the fields and consulted with his principal men. When he returned, the men were all greatly relieved to hear the command to fall out. Shivering with cold from standing without motion for so long, they all headed for the fire at John Martin's house. Once inside, Michael withdrew from his rucksack two bottles of poteen. A round of it quickly revived their flagged spirits and warmed their blood again, making them drowsy with tiredness.

John Martin was not a bit tired; he had fallen into a few hours warm sleep while tied up in a comfortable chair near the fire. The females of the house were all tucked up in bed. Martin yawned, then smiled as he rubbed his arms and hands when Rory Derneen untied him.

`Shall we play the game now?' John Martin asked eagerly. `For the bottle of parliamentarian?'

`Do I look fit and snappy for a card game?' Derneen said

irritably. `Or do I look frozen stiff after standing like a stone statue in the cold night for over five hours?'

`You don't want to play cards then?' Martin queried.

`No!'

`Ah, come on, avico, just one game?'

`Go piss at a star!' Derneen snapped, and then threw himself down on a fairly good chaise-longue on the far side of the room. `I'm jacked,' he moaned. `I was up most of last night too. Oh God, I'm jacked.'

`Jacks were high, last we played,' Martin said dolefully, looking towards Michael and the others.

`It's a big enough house you have,' Michael said to John Martin. `Can these men squeeze in here for tonight. They're tired and cold.'

`Sure they can, avic,' Martin replied. `Let them spread themselves around any place they can find. Wait now, there's a few straw mats in one of the bedrooms. I'll bring them out.'

The men fell down on the mats and floor and were soon asleep. The candles were snuffed, the house fell into darkness and the four leaders sat tiredly around the glow of the fire, quietly discussing the false information.

`Not false,' Michael said. `Not from him. He either got the night or the neighbourhood wrong.'

`Every minute out there was like an hour,' Hugh Vesty said. `But my lads never made a word of complaint.'

The proprietor of the house stood looking at the four men talking quietly around the fire, and knew all chance of the card game was gone. `Well now,' said John Martin, `I think I'll just nip out and look at a star before I retire to bed. I'll be back in a – '

He was pushed back into the room by one of the two lads on outpost duty who rushed in from the hallway. `They're coming, Captain, on yonder hills!'

The four leaders sprang to their feet, and then had a little difficulty rousing some of the sleeping men who groaned at the thought of going out into the cold night again. Rory Derneen was sleeping so soundly, Michael had to shake him violently before getting a response.

`Ach, I'm near dead, Captain.'

`You will be if the yeos get you.'

Michael pushed John Martin back into his chair and swung the rope around him, tying him securely and yanking the knots tight. Then he went to the door and, standing by it, ordered every man out.

As the men quickly and quietly filed past him, Michael looked back into the room and saw Rory Derneen still sleeping soundly. He went over and jabbed him with the butt of his rifle.

`Get up for your life, man.'

`Ah, Captain – ' Doreen forced open a bleary blue eye. `Leave me be. The sleep has such a lovely hold of me I can't seem to banish it.'

Michael pulled him to a sitting position and slapped him a stinging back-hander across the face. `There now, has that banished it?'

`Aye, it has, Captain, and nearly my poor head along with it.' A few seconds later Derneen was running after the others, who only had time to take cover in the fields as a number of the Yeomanry Corps rode in their direction.

As soon as they were close enough, a rebel fired. A shout rose up from the Yeos and, realizing they had a welcoming committee, the whole party immediately turned and rode off at a gallop.

`Some military operation,' Rory Derneen yawned. `One man was all it took to send them off. The rest of us could have stayed in slumber.'

`Back to your original defence positions!' Michael commanded.

Derneen moaned as the three other sections took off. `Holy St. Patrick,' he muttered, `here we go again.'

`Derneen and I will try to skirmish,' Michael said to his men as they lined the avenue, `but if they come galloping, you know what to do.'

Michael turned to Derneen. `Come on – I'm changing our position to a forward one.' He then set off on a swift run beyond the avenue into a field where a very large rock stood perpendicular in the centre, between six and seven feet high, placed there for the cows to rub against. They took up positions either side of the rock and waited, raising their guns at the sound of a troop of horses, then took aim as the 38th came into view.

Derneen in his enthusiasm moved forward a few steps and slammed the trigger so hard the butt kicked against his shoulder.

`Rejoin,' Michael quietly called to him, as superbly calm at the onset of battle as ever, even though the redcoats were now closing in, hammering forward in a gallop.

Michael let out a high vibrant whistling sound, then the three other sections under the command of Hugh Vesty, John Mernagh, and Martin Burke, appeared on different parts of the hills.

`Fire!' The four leaders yelled in unison. `Fire, fire, fire, fire!'

Preconcerted, the rebels fire came from four directions and the only line the military commander could form was a disorderly retreat, thinking they were completely surrounded by great numbers. `There's hundreds of the bastards!' he roared, turning his horse around. `Go! Go! Go!'

The drumming of hooves died in the distance, complete silence fell over the land.

`Now run!' the leaders commanded. And the entire body of rebels took off in different directions, disappearing into the darkness of the night like fleeting ghosts.

Michael sprinted back towards John Martin's house with Rory Derneen ten paces behind. When they entered the house John Martin was still in his chair, tied up securely, his face questioning in the firelight.

Michael smiled, and then flicked into his lap the bottle of sealed parliamentarian whiskey.

`For you, avic,' he said.

`Me?' Martin tried to struggle out of his binds. `For me?'

`But mind,' Rory Derneen warned. `I'll be back for the chickens and the hog. Fair play and fair game.'

And so they swiftly disappeared again, and when the military returned with reinforcements a short time later, all they found was a dark house surrounded by dark deserted fields and not a hint of a rebel in sight or earshot.

Captain Woollard crashed into the house, marched into the living room and stood staring at the man tied in the chair, a bottle of whiskey in his lap.

`Was Dwyer here?'

`Rebels were here,' Martin confessed. `Rebels for sure, but who they were I couldn't say, for isn't it just out of a coma I've come.' He nodded down to the bottle in his lap. `They must have hit my head with that, knocked me clean out.'

He aimed an angry spit at the fire. `Vicious bastards. They hate me just for being a loyal land-steward to Mr Greene of Greenville House.'

Woollard halted at that. He could not manhandle an employee of Mr Greene without possible consequences. And the dozy bloody clod truly looked as if he might have been clobbered.

`Would you be so kind as to untie me, sir?' John Martin asked politely.

`Go piss at the moon!' Captain Woollard shouted in furious frustration, and then marched outside.

`I'd try for a star anyway,' Martin grumbled sulkily. `If someone would just untie me.'

Minutes later his wife and three mob-capped daughters appeared in the doorway. `Well, don't just stand there like gawping hens,' Martin shouted. `Cut my bonds and let me loose!'

`Of course we will, our manly hero!' Mrs Martin bustled gaily into the room. `But not until we decide which one of us lowly females shall perform such a noble task.'

Martin pitched his brows in puzzlement as his daughters breezed in carrying a plate of scones, a jug of lemon water, and four glasses.

`What the blazes are you doing?' he cried.

The three daughters chuckled and sat around the table while Mrs Martin lit the candles, then sat herself and shuffled the cards.

`What are you doing?' Martin shouted again. `Put down

those cards and come and untie me.'

Mrs Martin ignored him and smiled at each of her daughters. `Now then, darlings,' she said in a jocular tone, `whoever has the highest score at breakfast time, wins the honour of deciding if and when we should untie him. Is that agreed?'

The daughters nodded happily. `Agreed!'

`Good!' Mrs Martin levelled a long and wicked smile at her gaping husband as she dealt out the cards with an experienced hand.

`Queens are high,' she said.

*

Michael and Derneen were far away, running through the darkness together, then with a salute of farewell, split in opposite directions.

Michael headed towards the old couple's house where Mary was still living, quite content and blissfully drooling over Mary-Anne who was now almost ten weeks old.

Mary's yearnings for him to spend more time with her and the child had conflicted with the need to keep his survival unendangered, until a week ago, when he and Hugh Vesty had erected a false timber ceiling in the bedroom which would facilitate a quick hoist up to concealment in case of a random search.

The old couple made no objections, so pleased and rejuvenated were they by the girl and her child. They cared little about the risk and possible penalties of being discovered as harbourers. `Sure we were as dull as dead anyway,' the old woman said calmly to Michael, `before Mary came and brought new life into our existence.'

And so when he tapped on the window, old Paudeen happily got out of his bed and let him in, then chained and re-barred the door and shuffled back to bed and sleep again.

The house was warm after the cold outside; the fires in the living room and bedroom were banked down for the night in a slow smoulder of little piles of glowing turf under a weight of smoored ashes.

In the bedroom the baby was sleeping soundly. He sat on

the edge of the bed and began to undress. Mary stirred and stretched over to peer into the wooden cradle beside the bed, then moved back to make room for him.

`Have you met any trouble since I saw you last?' she whispered as always.

`Not a bit,' he said, and she questioned him no further. She had come to know that in his short times with her he sought only peace and a space of forgetfulness. She also knew that her gentleness and natural lack of aggression always lulled and restored him.

`Stay with me,' she whispered when they woke in the morning. `Stay with me and Mary-Anne for a few unbroken days.'

She felt the sudden tension in his body, and sensing his refusal stopped his mouth with her own. As always, the efforts of his cold reason were washed away by the warm softness of her persuasion.

And he stayed, time and time again, as often as he could, for he truly adored her. He lied to her continuously, swearing he had glimpsed neither hilt nor hide of a redcoat in weeks, often only hours after escaping death by inches or minutes.

Although the daily round of her life was secret and hidden, Mary continued to be happy living with the old couple, and he was happy for her, agreeing she could stay for as long as no one suspected she was there. And in her new contentment, the nineteen-year-old mother bloomed with a new radiance. She was beautiful, he told her so, every time he made love to her, which was often. So it was not too much of a surprise when shortly after Christmas, Mary discovered she was expecting another child.

Chapter Seven

In the spring of the new century of 1800, Martin Burke married a Wicklow girl named Rachel, leaving John Mernagh as the only single man in the unbreakable foursome.

The militia and yeomanry forces still carried out occasional atrocities in Wicklow, and would have indulged in outright carnage had it not been for the fear of reprisals from Michael Dwyer and his small force. House burnings became less frequent, as did rape; for the militia knew that the reprisal for rape was certain death. Of all crimes, the one beyond all toleration to the rebels was the brutal violation of their girls and women.

And so life began to stabilise a little. Reports on Dwyer continued to flow into the secret service files at Dublin Castle. One report even admitted that he had put a halt to religious faction fighting amongst the young men of the county, pointing out to those who indulged in it that, when real fighting was needed during the rebellion, they had been very noticeable by their absence.

The Castle officials carefully read every report on Dwyer, especially those sent in by Thomas King, the resident magistrate at Rathdrum, and the latest contained only bad news, as usual.

> `Be assured that from the day Dwyer appeared as a Rebel of note I have used every means I could devise to bring him in. But he is very cautious and 'tis almost impossible to get acquainted with his movements. Had I not a very particular Influence in another way over my spies (being a magistrate) I should often be inclined to think they were deceiving me, but as I have nothing definite to warrant that conclusion, I still have hopes.

> Captain Myers, the Inspector of Yeomanry, also sent a report on Dwyer to the Viceroy's military secretary, Colonel Littlehales, giving more or less the same information and concluding with the

fact: ` . . . *The attachment and loyalty of the country people to him is without parallel.*'

*

Michael and Hugh Vesty were strolling through the moonlight on the north side of the Keadeen Mountains. At length they stopped in the midst of the dark dense wilderness by a large rock next to an equally large bush of heath.

Michael turned his back to the rock, struck it with his heel, and called out a command. Less than a minute later, the bush of heath was lifted aside, quite detached from the surface, and a flickering gleam of a candle appeared.

The young man who held the candle let out a cry of greeting, and then proceeded to light them through a passage which led into a large mountain cavern which had its own natural airlets. The interior was afloat with candleglow and, as was usual in every cavern they used, the walls had been well lined with moss to protect them from loose clay and damp. There were twelve men inside and, as usual, their arms and accoutrements were hung up in military order.

Thomas Halpin was sitting near the rear of the cave playing cards with three men. He had stopped playing as soon as the command echoed through to the cavern and the lad had run to see who it was.

Now, as the two men walked into the interior, Halpin's eyes were riveted on the tall young man with black hair – the Reb Chief himself.

Halpin's heart began to thump wildly; a rush of perspiration came to his face. He had waited seven days for this meeting, seven long impatient days, and now the waiting was over. He took in every detail of Michael Dwyer, his lithe figure and manly appearance. Then he noticed the Rebel Captain was viewing him with a curious eye and Halpin got to his feet, feeling slightly faint in case the decision would go against him.

James Doyle of Ballynecor, the man in command of this particular group, was talking to Dwyer and waving a hand towards Halpin as he explained who he was. Then Doyle beckoned Halpin over.

Halpin braced himself, walked across and stopped directly in front of Dwyer and Hugh Vesty.

`He wants to join us,' James Doyle said to Michael. `He's been with us seven days now. I explained that the decision was yours. He has brought us two guns – a musket and a fowling piece – and a supply of powder.'

Halpin smiled, but Dwyer was still viewing him with a long, cool look.

Michael saw before him a man about thirty-eight-years old and five feet six high, brown hair and blue eyes, long face, long sharp nose, round and narrow shouldered and weakly built.

`Why do you wish to join us?' he asked.

Halpin's lips had gone dry under the measuring gaze. James Doyle nudged him with an encouraging grin. `He won't eat you or shoot you – just explain to him what you explained to us.'

Halpin nodded, then explained. He was a Munster man who had lived in Wicklow since 1798. When the rebellion had flared he had burned to join it, but not being a Wicklow man, and not being part of a `young' set of lads, the opportunity never came to him as it was all the young men who were taking off in groups to join up.

He had then gone to work at the mansion of Mr Fawcett of Ballynockan near Rathdrum. Not long after going there he became friendly with the family of Brian Devlin of Croneybeag, them that are relations of the Dwyers of Eadstown, and the daughters had often discussed their first cousin Michael Dwyer whom they were very proud of. Anne Devlin, in particular, spoke of him often.

Halpin paused, still no reaction from Dwyer but Hugh Vesty Byrne asked indignantly, `Did they not talk about me? I'm their first cousin too, you know.'

Halpin smiled, but before he could digress, Dwyer, in a neutral voice, told him to continue, and he quickly did.

He was employed as a gardener by Mr Fawcett who was extensively engaged in planting his grounds with young trees and shrubs. He had liked working there, and did a fine job of it, but then Mr Fawcett discovered that he had allowed some rebels to shelter in the garden-house, and so he had fled for his life. He didn't know where to go, what to do. Then a neighbour suggested: `The best thing you can do is to go to the boys on the mountains.'

Halpin moved his hands in a pathetic gesture. `And, well, I thought that would be great, because I always longed to be one of the boys. And, well, I hope now that you will decide to take me in ... I'm prepared to fight if need be, do whatever task you may give me' He flushed a deep embarrassed red. `I know you may think I'm a bit old to be a rebel, but I hope that won't disqualify me.'

Where did you get the guns and the powder?' Michael asked.

`I sneaked back during the night a week ago and stole them from Mr Fawcett,' Halpin confessed. `I may as well be honest about it. But I felt I ought to bring something with me ... as a contribution towards my food and that. I'm sure there are lots of ways I can help you, I can fix broken guns, I can cook, I can – '

Dwyer cut him short. `I think we have your situation now.'

Halpin looked at him. `You'll... take me in?'

`Well, I have little admiration for thieves,' Dwyer said neutrally, `but you did risk your employment by giving shelter to rebels. You may stay here with this group, for now.'

Thomas Halpin beamed, began to gush his thanks, but Dwyer was already walking away from him.

Go back and play your hand,' James Doyle said, motioning his head towards the card-playing group Halpin had been sitting with. `Looks like the men have held the game for you.'

Halpin flopped back down in delight amidst the three men who slapped him on the back and told him they knew there would be no problem.

Thomas Halpin was so overjoyed with his luck that he won the next three games, but throughout his eyes kept straying to Dwyer, Byrne, and James Doyle of Ballynecor as they stood in a group quietly talking together. Then the three sat down on one of the straw beds and started up their own card game. Dwyer propped his back against the cavern wall, leaning languidly back from the hips as he surveyed his cards, eyes half closed as his lips moved in low conversation.

`Drink?'

A rebel had taken out a hip-flask and handed it to Halpin. `Take a slug then pass it around, Tom,' he murmured.

Halpin looked at the flask, took a deep slug of the poteeen, passed it on. Then he laughed and said: `Isn't it great all the same? Isn't it great!'

`The poteen?'

`No – myself being one of the boys on the mountains.' He laughed again and thumped his knee. `If my old father in Munster could only see me now – one of the rebel boys – he'd be right proud of me!'

The three rebels looked at him as if thinking his father must have very little to be proud of. `Tis a hard life,' one murmured. `You never know the day you might be killed. Are you playing your hand or what?'

`Eh? Oh, sure...' Halpin looked down to see he had three aces and two jacks. He smiled and, studying the face of each man surveying his cards, Halpin knew the game was his. Then he saw Dwyer and Byrne suddenly move to their feet and walk out of the cave with a salute of farewell to James Doyle of Ballynecor – only minutes after they had started their own game. Halpin was puzzled ... they had been holding cards and talking low, but they had not been playing a card game ... and why had they gone out again?

`Is the captain not lying with us here tonight?' Halpin asked curiously.

`Who knows?' a lad named Browne replied. `He comes and goes and he doesn't trouble himself to confer with us. All we know is that he is the chief and he never lets us down and is never long acoming when we whistle a signal of trouble. Let's see you?'

Halpin laid down his cards and let him see – three aces and two jacks – a full house. `Can you beat that?'

'Nah!' Browne threw down his two pairs and Halpin collected the pennies. 'Well, I'm for a stretch,' he said. 'I'm done in. All that worry about whether the captain would take me in or not.'

He moved over to where the straw mats were laid out and threw himself down under a blanket. Shortly afterwards the entire group were lying down and the candles snuffed.

The lad on the straw mat next to Halpin was fussing with his blanket, the one named Browne who had given him the poteen. 'When will the captain be back?' Halpin whispered.

'Who knows?' Browne shrugged. 'He usually sleeps at headquarters, or at some harbourer's house, but sometimes he does sleep here. He may be back in an hour, or not for a few days. Who knows? But if he needs us, he knows how to fetch us.'

'Listen, brother,' Halpin whispered. 'Have you e'er a drop of poteen left in your flask?'

Browne fussed with his blanket again then handed over the flask. 'You may finish it,' he whispered.

'Thanks.' Halpin smiled, held up the flask. 'To the boys,' he whispered gleefully, then gulped and drained, wiped his mouth, and leaned closer to Browne. 'Tis from Wexford you said you come from, eh?'

'Aye, the rich corn country.'

'Have you been a rebel since the ninety-eight rebellion?'

Browne chuckled. 'Man, I was born a rebel. I come from a long line of rebels. When my mother crooned me to sleep she always did so with a rebel song.'

'Why was that?'

'Curse you for an ignoramus.' Browne peered curiously at Halpin. 'Did you never learn your history down in Munster?'

'I never learned much of anything,' Halpin confessed.

'Then I shall tell you my history for a start?' Browne whispered, rising onto his elbow and resting his head on his hand.

'Go ahead.' Halpin leaned closer until their heads were close together like whispering conspirators.

'From the days of Strongbow,' Browne said, 'my family

lived at Rathronan Castle in Wexford. We were a grand family, a rich family. But when the Devil came to Ireland carrying a Bible in his hand, we fought with the confederacy against Cromwell, and lost, and were dispossessed of our home, everything. In his victory Cromwell gave Rathronan Castle as a gift to one of his roundhead soldiers, a man called Ivory. And that man called Ivory very generously took the Brownes back onto the lands of Rathronan Castle – as labourers – as his tenants. *Le Brun* we were called then, until we were forced to anglicise to Browne.'

'That's a hell of a story,' Halpin whispered. 'But I've heard similar many times before, except few came from castles. But now, lookit – I'll call you *Le Brun* if it'll make you feel any better.'

'Just call me in the morning,' Browne said, turning over and fussing with his blanket again. 'I'm a very heavy sleeper.'

Halpin lay back with one arm under his head and wondered where the captain and his second-in-command had gone so late? From the reaction of the other men it appeared as if those two often drifted in and out of the various camps. Although Halpin only knew about this particular camp. The main camp, the one they called *Headquarters* could not be told to him, not even after he had been sworn in under oath – as a member of the United Irishmen.

One the United boys! He smiled to himself and snuggled down to sleep.

The following day James Doyle kept Thomas Halpin busy cleaning guns while others went out shooting game in the high woods of the mountain.

In the early afternoon Pat Harman came in, and after being introduced to Thomas Halpin and shaking his hand, Harman said to Doyle: 'I've just received intelligence that some of the yeos were heard swearing this morning that as soon as soon as the day is done, they will go tonight and shoot the parish priest of Imaal.'

'Bastards,' Doyle muttered. 'We'll have to send a detachment there so.'

A great idea suddenly came to Thomas Halpin. He jumped to his feet. `I say, boys, why don't we go tonight and shoot their minister Weekes?'

Pat Harman swung round and glared dangerously at Halpin. `I'll blow the head off any man that injures Reverend Weekes.'

`But ...' Halpin looked stunned, `but ... wasn't it Reverend Weekes's son that brought down Andrew Thomas with a shot in the leg?'

`No mind about what his son does,' Harman snapped. `Reverend Weekes is good and decent man. So you better keep your stupid tongue in your stupid mouth, man!'

`Sorry, sorry, didn't really mean it,' Halpin muttered weakly, and slouched back to his guns and rags. He'd only been trying to talk and act like his idea of a rebel. Halpin was relieved when Pat Harman eventually left, and delighted when Michael Dwyer and Hugh Vesty came in close on evening time. Neither seemed to notice him sitting in the corner, so busy were they organising the men in low voices and giving them orders of some kind.

Then Dwyer strode over to him. `Now you – Thomas Halpin.'

`Aye.' Halpin jumped to his feet, surprised that the captain had remembered his name.

`How well can you cook?' Dwyer asked.

`Quite well.'

`Good. Now here's what I want you to do. About two miles from here is a small crevice. I'll tell you in detail where to find it. Inside you will find, wrapped in a tablecloth, a large joint of beef and some other provisions. I'm told it is there now. Collect them, then come straight back and start cooking.'

`Aye.' Halpin nodded. `But what about the lad who normally does the cooking?

`No.' Dwyer shook his head. `Every single one of these lads is needed somewhere else tonight with Hugh Vesty. And I need this cavern cleared. There will just be myself here all night.'

`Just you here all night?' Halpin could not believe it.

`Just you – alone? And me?'

`Just me and you,' Dwyer confirmed, then smiled. `And two men coming down from Dublin to talk business. It's them I want you to cook a palatable meal for. And while they are here, will you do guard-duty outside? You can sleep when they've gone.'

`I'll do whatever you say, Captain,' Halpin snapped keenly. `Now where do I find the beef and stuff?'

Michael grinned at his keenness and patted his shoulder. `Not yet, wait till I see to these lads and then I'll come back and tell you where.'

Halpin waited around as each man collected their guns and took off with Hugh Vesty. Suddenly there was only himself and the captain left inside the cavern.

`Come on, avic,' Dwyer said urgently. `The city boys will be here in a few hours and I want to have a sleep before they come, as I shall probably be up all night discussing business. And, man, I am already very tired.'

`Then you go ahead and have a sleep,' Halpin said kindly. `But now listen ... they've taken all the guns. I'll need a gun if I'm going abroad.'

`And maybe get stopped for being armed?' Dwyer grinned. `Are you crazy? Even the yeos know that no one goes sporting at night. Now look, the reason I've picked you to go down there is because you're not known as a rebel, and therefore not likely to be followed back.'

`What about when I stand guard duty? I'll need a gun then, won't I?'

`I'll give you one of mine.'

`Oh, right, right.'

Halpin listened carefully and nodded several times as he was given instructions. Then Dwyer escorted him to the entrance of the cavern. `It will be dark when you get back,' he said, `and I'll be sleeping. But if you kick hard against the rock it will echo through and wake me, and I'll come to light you in with a candle. All right?'

`Don't you worry about a thing, Captain.' Halpin's thin lips snapped out every word like a command. `You just rest and leave it to me. But listen ... the boys said only a captain or higher could do it officially, so will you take the time to swear me in as a United man when I get back?'

Dwyer gave him a long measuring look. `I'll think about it while you're gone,' he said. `Now go.'

The bush of heath was placed firmly back in position and Halpin ran off like a bandy rabbit scurrying after a field mouse.

Darkness had fallen when Halpin returned to the cavern, protesting frantically as he stepped into the interior lit by a single candle.

`I tell you he was here! I swear it! He was planning to settle down for a sleep!'

Captain Woollard peered around the cave which had been stripped bare – no straw mats, no moss on the walls, no remains of a fire, nothing to indicate it had ever been used by anybody as a shelter.

The cavern was filled with redcoats. Halpin staggered amongst them with his hands to his dazed head. `The fire was there ... the straw mats were along here ... that's where Dwyer sat holding some cards ... the moss, where in damnation is the moss?'

`And where's the bush of heath that was supposed to be at the entrance?' Woollard demanded. `That's also gone – if it was ever there!'

`But why would I lie?' Halpin cried. `It took me weeks to wangle my way through the people and get to this small group. Then seven days I lay here waiting for my prize. Seven days when I was kept a prisoner and not allowed outside again until Dwyer had given me the once over. The only times they let me out was to relieve myself, and even then I had a guard on me.'

`And after all that,' Woollard said sneeringly, `Dwyer comes along, a man with five hundred jinglers on his head, and tells you that he's going to be all alone and sleeping, with no bodyguards nearby – then sends you out with that valuable information. I knew you were lying!'

`But he was here, I swear it! They were all here – Hugh Vesty Byrne, Pat Harman, James Doyle, eleven other rebels.'

`No rebels were here,' Woollard snapped. `You've just wasted our time to justify your pay.'

He turned to go, taking the candle with him, and in the swift beam Halpin's eyes noticed something on the floor in the far corner.

`Wait! Wait!' He darted over to the corner and felt blindly, then clutched. `Wait! I've found something that'll prove they were here!'

Captain Woollard was standing at the entrance with the candle still in his hand when Thomas Halpin scrambled towards him and held out a book.

Looking greatly surprised, Woollard passed the candle to Halpin who held it up while the Captain read the title, opened the front cover and jerked his head down to peer at a name written in ink on the flyleaf – *Hugh Vesty Byrne.*

`What's it say?' Halpin whispered, peering also, but totally illiterate.

Captain Woollard suddenly bashed Halpin's head with the book. `You fool! The bastards were here right under your nose, but it was *you* they smelled!'

Halpin dropped the candle as the book whacked him left and right. He let out a cry and protected his head with his hands until Woollard began kicking him, then Halpin started to run.

*

When the redcoats had scrambled back down the craggy slopes and out of sight, the fourteen rebels standing motionless behind the trees and watching, stepped out and began their rugged journey through the darkness over to headquarters on Lugnaquilla.

`God, I'm sorry about the book,' Hugh Vesty said to Michael. `I took it out last night to read before I slept, then forgot it when you suggested checking Halpin out. I picked it up again today, but left it down while I was stripping the moss.'

Michael shrugged. `No matter. At least we found him out for sure. Pity about the cavern though. It was a good and comfortable hideout. We'll not be able to go anywhere near

106

it again.'

`What made you suspect him?' Browne asked.

`His name,' Michael answered. `Yesterday the new list of "Rebels Still in Arms on the Wicklow Mountains" was published. Fifty-four names were on it. And the last name was Thomas Halpin.'

He looked in astonishment at the group of men walking each side of him. `Now isn't that a funny thing? The government knew Halpin had joined us even before we did!'

`We reckon he must have expected to hang around for a while,' Hugh Vesty said to Browne. `Sifting out whatever information he could – and being a listed rebel, harbourers and picquets would trust him. But when he got his chance at the captain so soon, he couldn't resist it.'

`The blatherumskite,' Browne said. `Is that where you went last night? To check him out?'

`Aye,' Michael said. `We went across Wicklow to my cousin Anne Devlin at Croneybeag, one mile from Rathdrum. She warned us off Halpin straight away. She's convinced he is a spy and informer, employed by Thomas King. Her younger brother, Little Arthur, has spotted Halpin slinking into the magistrate's house a number of times.'

*

`Two shillings a day, Mr Halpin!' Thomas King declared. `That is the price we agreed. A very generous amount if I may say so. And that is the price Dublin Castle allows me for you.'

`Bedamned to the Castle then!' Halpin cried angrily. `I'm now a marked man, a known informer. The risk I took is worth more than two shillings a day!'

`And that two shillings a day will continue to be paid only as long as you remain useful,' King informed him coldly. `And how, I wonder, may you continue to be useful to me now? Now that you have become a known informer?'

The implication of the magistrate's word knocked Halpin's aggression clean out of him. He fidgeted about and scowled, then looked at King sharply. `What are you saying?'

'Simply that you will have to change your occupation. From a spy – to a prosecution witness.'

'Eh?' Halpin stared at him as if he was mad. 'A witness in open court!'

'It is your choice, Mr Halpin. You may remove to the barracks and live there as a protected witness on a very generous allowance of two shillings a day. Or you may go your own road and take your chances with a population that favours the rebels ... a population that will shortly know how you tried for Dwyer's capture.'

There was a silence. Halpin slouched over to the window, gnawing his nails as he looked out.

'I can assure you, Mr Halpin,' said King in a gentle tone, 'that you will not be harmed while under my protection.'

Halpin slowly turned to him; all the blood seemed to have drained out of his face.

Thomas King threw a glance at the clock on the mantel. 'Come along,' he said brusquely, 'it's almost my breakfast time. If you are to serve as a prosecution witness we will need accused men in the dock.'

He adjusted his wig and sat down in the chair at his desk. 'Dwyer,' he snapped, lifting his quill. 'What did you manage to learn about him?

'Nothing,' Halpin muttered, 'I could learn nothing about him at all.'

King looked up, disbelieving.

'It's the truth!' Halpin insisted. 'Even his men seem to know only what they see of him, when they see him. Dwyer confides in nobody save a small group of his principal men.'

'Does he look like the two pictures drawn of him by the artists?'

'Well neither picture looks anything like the other,' Halpin grunted, 'and neither picture looks anything like Michael Dwyer. Not as I saw.'

Thomas King laid down his quill and folded his arms on the desk. 'You are beginning to spoil my appetite for breakfast, Mr Halpin. You really will have to do better than this if you wish to secure my protection.'

`I'm only telling you what I saw and heard,' Halpin said defensively.

`And so far you heard nothing worth a spit!' King cried. `And there's still the matter of your theft of Mr Fawcett's property, don't forget that! Even the mildest court in England would give you the rope or life in Botany Bay for such a crime – but we in our benevolence are giving you two shillings a day!'

`Yes, sir,' Halpin stammered nervously, `and very kind it is too, but –'

`It's Dwyer's woman that interests me now,' King snapped. `I'm intrigued to know if you heard her name mentioned?'

`I did!' Halpin brightened. `I heard her name was Mary.'

`Mary what?'

`Just Mary, I heard no other.'

`Good God, man!' King's fist banged down on the desk with impatience. `Every second Catholic girl in Ireland is called Mary. What else did you hear about her?'

`Only that she's a sweet-looking wench and Dwyer would kill any man that looked crooked at her. So she's obviously more to him than just a whore to lay with. I did ask her surname but they froze up as if they had said too much already.'

`They consider her a dangerous subject for idle discussion?'

`You've hit on it exactly!' Halpin nodded his head vigorously.

`Is she from the County Clare, did they say?'

`They didn't say,' Halpin admitted lamely.

The magistrate pulled a cambric handkerchief from the pocket of his morning robe and dabbed at the exasperation on his forehead. `Let us forget Dwyer's whore for now,' he said tiredly, `and move on to any other snippet of information you might have overheard.'

`I did hear one interesting thing,' Halpin said suddenly. `It seems a letter was sent down to Dwyer from Dublin signed by many names and assuring him of continued support as long as he stays out and free. And with the letter was a sum of money.'

`You pox-faced wretch!' King cried angrily. `Why did you not tell me this in the first place? Did you hear any of the names on the letter?'

`No particular name was mentioned as I heard. Only that the letter came from the Dublin Executive Committee of United Irishmen.'

`Good God!' King sat back and stared at the ceiling. `Good God!' he said again, then lowered his eyes to Halpin. `The twelve men in the cave? Do you know their names? Could you identify them if they were brought in?'

`I most surely could,' Halpin drawled, complacent now he realised he had given some valuable information that would ensure his maintenance and protection. `I could name and identify every one of the bastards.'

`Then, Mr Halpin, I think we should get you to a safe place of concealment until you are needed as a crown witness.' King moved to his feet and the window. Halpin watched him as he scanned the garden.

`Dublin, I think,' King said at last. `As soon as we have breakfasted I will arrange a carriage and military escort to take you to Dublin Castle, where you will be placed under the protection of Major Sirr, the Chief of Police, until you are needed back in Wicklow.'

PART TWO

Twenty men from Dublin town,
At night gathered round the fire
Brimming poteen we toss down
To our Captain, Michael Dwyer.

Slainte, Michael, brave and true,
Then there rings a wild "Hurrah"
Also we drink, dear land, to you,
Eire, sláinte, geal go bráth.

`Twenty Men From Dublin Town' – Arthur Griffith.

Chapter Eight

In the old couple's house, on a warm night in the month of July, the gentle white-haired old woman said her last prayer and drifted away in sleep to the land of the Ever-Young. Her husband Paudeen was heartbroken, as was Mary.

Midge Mahoney came and took her grieving old uncle back to her own house for a while, but all knew he would not last long without his soul mate.

Michael took Mary home to her parents at Knockandarragh, and at the height of summer in late August; John Doyle breathlessly climbed the steep ravines and gave him the news that Mary had gone into labour.

Six men were collected to act as picquets outside the house at Knockandarragh. When Michael entered the house he found Mary's parents babbling and flapping excitedly and his mother being the only sensible person present. She came towards him with a smile.

'You have a son,' she said.

Before Michael could reply, a strong hand thumped him hard on the back and almost sent him toppling off his feet. `I have a grandson!' William Doyle roared. `Are you not going to congratulate me?'

Michael shrugged his shoulders back into place and turned towards the man who was grinning at him like a horse yawning.

`Congratulations,' he said, then whisked over to the hallway, which led to the bedrooms. At Mary's door he hesitated, then slowly creaked it open.

She was bright-eyed and flushed and he saw straight away that she was as giddy as a girl in her first romance. `A boy!' she cried. `A darling little boy. Come and see!'

Once again she held out the child to him and he took the small bundle in his hands. His eyes moved over the sleeping face, the tiny clenched fists

`I think he knows he is born in Ireland,' Michael finally whispered. `Look at his little hands, all clenched and set up for battle.'

`Isn't he bonnie though? `What would you like to name him?'

`John,' he said. `After my own daddy.'

The door opened and William Doyle poked his head inside, searching out another look at his grandson and grinning stupidly – someone yanked him away.

`John William,' Mary whispered. `And say the two names or Daddy will be hurt.'

When darkness came the house in Knockandarragh was full with people. Michael's father was quietly delighted as he looked on his first grandson, but William Doyle was still loudly exclaiming his ecstasy to all who would listen.

The two grandmothers were busily handing round plates of food. Michael dispatched his brother-in-law to fetch John Cullen. When the old man arrived clutching his fiddle, and saw the child, he nodded his head up and down.

`A lad, as I prayed it would be. Amen I say for a prayer answered, Amen.' His eyes misted. `John, is it? Troth, but I never dreamed youse would name him for me.'

Neither Michael nor Mary had the heart to correct him.

In the parlour, Michael passed money to Mary's brother and sent him up to the tavern at Donard for some bottles of refreshment. When John Doyle returned, he was followed into the house only seconds later by Pat O'Riordan, who got very excited when he saw the whiskey.

`Is he still as mean as ever?' Michael whispered to William Doyle.

`Mean? That man wouldn't spend Christmas! But we must take our friends as we find them. And Pat is the best friend I ever had.'

`You could do worse than O'Riordan,' Michael supposed.

`Not much,' Doyle said gloomily. `But still, no matter. My grandson is born and I want you all to celebrate with me!'

`O'Casey the blacksmith sends his felicitations,' John Doyle said, `but he said he couldn't do the walk down here on account of the weakness in his legs.'

`I know that weakness,' William Doyle grunted. `Tis called poteen.'

`He gave me a present for Mary.' John pulled out a twist of paper from his pocket and laid it on the table. Mrs Doyle opened the paper and stared at the contents in puzzlement. `What is it – tobacco?'

`Tis two ounces of leaves from China that makes a drink called chah,' John told her. `O'Casey got it from a smuggling man who said it makes a drink like the tea from India the gentry drink, but is not at all like our own and much better.'

`Oh, musha, I'll make some for Mary so.'

`Huh!' William Doyle cried. `I'd be whipped before I'd drink any chah from China.' He lifted a bottle of whiskey. `Now then, who's for a drop of the right stuff?'

Hugh Vesty, Mernagh, and Burke, took it in turns with the three others to do outpost duty while the occupants of the house toasted the health of the new baby. Michael sat holding his one year-old daughter, Mary-Anne, who was yawning tiredly after the excitement of cooing at all these strange people.

`Faith and troth,' Cullen declared, `they say when a man and a maid get wed they become one, but from what I've observed they usually become three or four or more.' He stuck his fiddle under his chin and before long a party was in full swing.

Mary did not even hear the music, so enchanted was she with her son. She scarcely heard her mother enter the room. `Drink this,' Mrs. Doyle said. `It's been sent to you from China all the way and is supposed to make you feel as fit as a young war horse.'

Mary almost choked on her first taste; became distressed almost to tears when her mother kept insisting she drink more. `Twill poison me!' she cried.

`Hush now, pet,' her mother soothed. `If you upset yourself you're liable to sour the sweet milk in your breasts. I'll bring you a nice cup of our own tae mór.'

Outside the door Mrs Doyle took a taste of the China chah and thought it tasted damned nice. She decided to make some more up for the neighbour-women who had come acalling, and bring Mary a cup of the usual herbal beverage made from the leaves of Ireland's own tae mór plant and

115

chamomile.

When she returned to the parlour Mrs Doyle found her husband and Pat O'Riordan dancing together, clapping their hands and hopping and jigging, moving far apart then towards each other with heads down like two charging bulls. Mrs Doyle laughed at their antics, and sent up a `Whoosh!' when it seemed the two might crash.

At the end of the dance William Doyle mopped his forehead and was moving towards the bottles when he noticed Michael's gun leaning against the wall. He frowned and turned to his son-in-law.

'You haven't been shooting any ducks with that, have you?'

`Ducks?'

`Aye, male ducks – drakes.'

`No, why?'

`Have you not heard about the curse?' Doyle shook his head gravely. `Oh 'tis all around the country about some woman named Nell Flaherty who's put a terrible curse on whoever it was killed her pet drake. Wait now and Pat'll tell you. He knows it by heart.'

Doyle turned and put a hand over the glass journeying up to O'Riordan's mouth. `Pat, the curse that woman Nell Flaherty made, how did it go?'

O'Riordan paled and shuddered. `Oh wisha, tis a terrible curse for any woman to send forth of a day. And God help the man it falls upon. The travelling man who brought it to us in the tavern, a man from Limerick way, said this woman Nell marched right into the centre of the village and stood for all to see and hear as she threw the curse to the wind.'

`Tell him how it goes, Pat.' Doyle was getting impatient, he reached for a drink. `Tell this son-in-law of mine.'

O'Riordan, shivering nervously, cleared his throat and recited the woman's curse as she had shouted it and he had been told it.

`May his pigs never grunt! May his cat never hunt!
May a ghost ever haunt him at dead of night!
May his hens never lay! May his horse never neigh!
May his goat fly away like an old paper kite!

116

May he swell with the gout! May his teeth all fall out!
May he roar, yell and shout with the pain of
headache.
May his hair stand like horns and his toes with many
corns,
The monster that murdered Nell Flaherty's drake!'

`Listen to that now.' Doyle looked warningly at his son-in-law. `See what could befall you if you don't mind whose duck you're shooting.'

`A terrible curse like Nell's could befall you,' O'Riordan whispered gravely.

`Sure now,' said Michael calmly. `I have always heard that a curse comes home to roost on the person that made it.'

Doyle and O'Riordan stared at him, then stared at each other with mouths open. As big as they were, they looked liked two children who had just had their favourite party game spoiled.

Michael looked with innocent eyes from one to the other. `Isn't that what they say? A curse always comes home to roost.'

`Well now ...' said Doyle, and then frowned at O'Riordan.

`Oh, well now...' said O'Riordan, and then frowned at the floor.

Michael spied his mother coming into the room carrying a bundle of swaddling flannel. He moved away from the two confounded men and asked her:

`Is Mary left on her own?'

`Aye, but don't think of going in to her. The baby is changed and fed, Mary-Anne is asleep, and Mary also needs to sleep now. Leave them be.'

He did not argue with her, just nodded, but continued loitering by the door as she moved into the crowded parlour. He looked towards Doyle and O'Riordan who were still frowning, as if trying to decide whether the curse would go where intended, or come home to roost. Then, panting with the effort of thought, both reached for a drink.

Michael saw his mother in deep conversation with Mrs Doyle, and moved to open the door and was about to slip out to the hallway leading to the bedrooms when O'Riordan suddenly cried: `I have it – I have the answer! Where are you, Dwyer?'

Michael turned and glared venomously at O'Riordan.

From his seat on the settle O'Riordan smiled back at him triumphantly. `Tis said that only the curse of the *innocent* brings no evil on those that utter it.'

William Doyle was astounded. He took O'Riordan by the hand and began shake it as he praised him. `Oh begor, you clever varmint, but aren't you right! And Nell Flaherty and her drake were innocent. So the curse stands.'

O'Riordan nodded. `It does! Horns and corns and swelling with gout and teeth dropping out – the lot!'

William Doyle looked over his shoulder and, with a smirk of satisfaction, regarded Michael. `Well that settles it then. There's no more to be said.'

`No more to be said,' O'Riordan repeated.

Then the two of them, almost in a state of delirium, laughed and knocked back their drinks.

`Now then, Michael ...' Doyle cried, smirking smugly at his empty glass. `You thought you were right but you were wrong and no hard feelings, boy. And to prove I hold nothing against you, one way or another, I'm inviting you to join me in a long and hearty drink, to celebrate the birth of my grandson.'

O'Riordan nudged Doyle, who looked around, and saw Michael was gone.

`My soul!' Doyle cried. `He was nippy enough with his mouth when trying to confuse me about the curse, but where is his mouth now that I want to drink with him?' He stared at O'Riordan. `Isn't he the strangest son-in-law for a man to have, Pat?'

`He is,' O'Riordan agreed good-naturedly. `He is indeed.'

*

A candle was flickering inside a table-lantern when Michael entered the silent bedroom. He saw that she was fast asleep, the baby in the rocker beside her. A drawer had been made into a bed for Mary-Anne, his best- beloved child.

He pulled the chair nearer to the bed and sat for a time watching the girl in the bed. The music and gaiety in the parlour went on. There was joy in the house, the joy that always comes with the birth of a child. Only this bedroom was dim and silent.

From the parlour he could hear William Doyle singing loudly and passionately. The words were blurred at the edges from drink, but he recognised the song as Doyles's favourite, `*My love from Aughavannagh.*' It had forty-two verses, even more when you counted the verses Doyle made up and added on. He loved the song and his singing of it so much that he couldn't bear it to end.

Michael sat back in the chair, deciding to remain where he was. The candle was guttering low. In a kind of languorous ecstasy he sat watching them sleep, his wife, his daughter and his son.

He looked at the little chubby form of Mary-Anne in the bed-drawer beside the cradle – she was his firstborn, his delight, his pride – but his son was his hope. Maybe by the time he had grown to a young man, things would have changed for the better in Ireland.

At the first threads of dawn, his son whimpered, then cried hungrily. Mary stirred and opened her eyes, and seeing her husband sitting there, smiled and assured him, `I feel fine.'

When he finally returned to the parlour it was still full with people. Cullen was slumped in sleep on a chair in the corner, his fiddle still under his chin. Mrs Doyle was still surrounded by neighbour-women at the table, holding court around a pot of the China tea and all praising it to glory while bidding to best each other with horrific tales of their own childbearing days.

William Doyle had dissipated all his earlier horse-like energy. He sat scowling at his son-in-law like a peevish bulldog.

`Tis unmanly and unnatural and uncalled for,' he growled. `Tis the most unmanly thing I ever knew of. Tis shame you have brought on the surname of my grandson!'

`What grieves you now?' Michael asked, moving over to

the hearth where a neighbour-woman was lifting hot griddle breads off the gridiron. As he helped himself to one, William Doyle stretched his legs and folded his arms and enlarged upon his grievance against his son-in-law.

`Tis shame you have brought on me too. Shame that'll be known all over Wicklow by nightfall. These neighbours of mine will see to it. Troth, scandal travels faster than the horses on a mail coach! And the scandal will be that Michael Dwyer, the sire of my grandson, chose to spend the entire night in a room with a woman and two bairns instead of acting like a man and staying with the men and celebrating with a toss of the right stuff.'

He bowed his head and gloomed. `Faith, but I'll never live it down. A son-in-law as unsociable as an Englishman. And what have you been doing all this time, may I ask?'

`Sitting in the dark,' Michael answered truthfully.

Doyle winced at the shame of it. He sat looking at the ground for several moments, shrugged and muttered dolefully, `I used to know another man who preferred sitting in the dark instead of jollying with the men, but he was a lame monk.'

Pat O'Riordan tittered.

Doyle jerked round. `What are you tittering about, you great spawn of a beggar-woman.'

`O'Riordan tittered again, swayed backwards and forwards, then slumped back unconscious in a blissful stupor.

`Now there's a man who knows how to celebrate!' Doyle cried admiringly. `Tis him should have been my son-in-law!'

`Let's go,' Michael whispered to John Mernagh, `while Doyle is searching for another drink. I think he intends to join O'Riordan and drink his grievance into a coma.'

As they slipped out, Mernagh looked back at O'Riordan. `That man shouldn't drink,' he said. `There's two essential rules to drinking and O'Riordan follows neither of them – pay your share for it and know how to carry it.'

Michael shrugged. `God help him though, alone and lonely as he is. The drink is killing him but he'd be dead without it.'

Outside in the field he saw his mother perched on a stool milking a red cow. As he approached her, he got the scent of the pure sweet milk as it fell like a shooting waterfall into a whirlpool of white froth. The cow stood in docile contentment, almost asleep with the pleasure of being milked by a gentle-fingered, crooning woman.

`This poor girl was crying piteously to be milked,' his mother said, looking up. `I've decided to make myself useful and stay around here for a day or two. That lot in there are too busy enjoying themselves to remember that work on a farm never stops. How is Mary now?

`She says she feels fine.'

`Well, I reckon she'll need some help too. I'll go in to her shortly.'

He rubbed the cow's forehead. `Has Daddy gone home?'

`Aye, he said he'll speak to you about the boy in his own time.'

Michael was disappointed. `Has he been gone long?'

`Since the fifty-fourth verse of *"My Love from Aughavannagh"*. He couldn't cope with another line of it. Doyle didn't even see him go, so tight were his eyes shut with the ecstasy of his own voice. I couldn't make out a word he was singing.'

They smiled together, then she bowed her head, crooning again, her fingers had never stopped working as she talked, the milk kept falling as sweetly as a lullaby.

`I'll be off so.' He patted the cow's side, and then slyly brushed a tender finger against his mother's cheek before striding on towards the trees where his men stood silently waiting for him.

When they returned in a quiet fashion to the camp, the rest of the men were awake and waiting. Many came forward to greet him, but seeing his expressionless face, none dared to ask the result.

Michael gazed around at the men, then his face split into a wide smile and his fist shot victoriously into the air.

`*I have a son!*'

The men roared their cheers, and the real celebration

began.

*

The afternoon came on mild and beautiful; but all decided it was time to send for the moonshine.

The detachment of men sent out for the purpose came back carrying a keg and were accompanied by the man who had distilled it. He was a fine big tall man and strode along as if he was the king of his trade. Not only did he make the most exquisite brew ever tasted, he knew every historical detail about the making of it since way back when:

`Our Viking invaders who came around eight hundred and six and stayed awhile. They were the men who taught us the secret of brewing the magical nectar,' he told the men sitting around him and sipping.

`I know all about them,' Hugh Vesty the history expert said. `It was them who named our own Wicklow for us – Wyking alo – which means Viking meadow. Though how you can call these uplands a meadow is beyond me!'

`And it was the Danes who taught us how to put the white froth on a drink,' the distiller king said, returning to the subject of his own expertise. `But there was one drink the Danes made, the secret ingredient of which no one could get out of them – a drink as pure and clear as a golden pond, with the pure white head on it – heather beer.'

The men all looked at each other; none had heard of it.

`And so the time came when there was only one Danish chieftain left on these shores,' the distiller king continued, `the others all having been routed by the Celts. And it was put to this last remaining chieftain, very nicely, that his life would be spared if he told the secret ingredient of the *beer* drink. But, begor, he died rather than tell it!'

He sat back and blithely regarded the mesmerised men. `Indeed! Many suspected the secret ingredient was heather, so it was called heather beer, but none learned how to make it, not like the Danes, so the people decided, ah well, they may as well forget it and concentrate on malting the barley.'

The flute, which had been crooning softly, was now joined by a happy fiddle and the clinking of spoons; a

122

bodhran began to thump thump thump and the music turned from easy to itchy.

The distiller-king didn't even hear the music, his mind intent on the perfection of his brew. `Now then,' he said, finishing his drink and moving to open a second cask. `I want you lads to taste and give your opinion on this particular keg. It has a quality and texture so fine and excellent, I am prepared to stake my reputation on it.'

Michael was smiling and looking across the camp. `If it's all the same to you, avic, I think we'll get the Dublin boys' opinion on it first. As you can see from the way they're dressed, their velvet coats and breeches and all, many were fine bucks of the gentry before they joined us here.'

The Dublin men were clapping in time to the music; they stopped when Michael approached with a grin and the keg.

`Moonshine, boys. Its maker would be greatly obliged for your verdict on its quality.'

`Sure we'll give it try anyway,' the Dubs agreed pleasantly. When it was poured they sat studying the colour of it in their wooden cups. `This moon looks mighty pale in the face to me,' one said. `As pale and clear as a silver lake.'

`Well then,' said another. `Are we all ready – down the hatch!'

Michael laughed at their wide-eyed reaction and gave them a toast as he joined them in another cup of the exquisite substance.

`Good health boys, one and all, and may God keep up our luck.'

`*Sláinte!'* the Dublin men chorused merrily. `Down the hatch!'

Another round was poured. Michael raised his cup and toasted again.

`And here's that we may never see hell or the hangman.'

`*Sláinte,*' the Dubs all sang. `Down the hatch!'

`And here's to you all, as fine as you are.'

`*Sláinte* – down the hatch!'

`And here's to me, as bad as I am.'

By the time Michael had proposed his umpteenth toast, the Dubliners were all cock-eyed. Then one blinked his eyes, focused on the captain, and suddenly remembered with a yelp of delight just why they were celebrating. He stumbled to his feet and proposed another toast.

`Here's to the man that has a bonnie son!'

Another Dubliner scrambled to his feet and merrily held up his cup. `And the blazes to any man that has a bonnie daughter – and won't give her to me!'

Chapter Nine

A meeting of the most determined rebel-hunters took place at a lodge in Rathdrum. Dwyer had to be caught! And so far only one band of men had proved equal to the task – the Highlanders. The plan was agreed. Set a Celt to catch a Celt.

Michael was shooting game on Knockamunnion with only five of his men when he heard the frantic birdcalls and whistles of warning echoing over the mountains. He ran to a crag and, in the grey of the morning, saw a detachment of Highland infantry only a few yards below, ascending at a furious pace. `Too many to stand and fight,' he said as he ran back to the men. `Separate and confuse!'

`Who are they?' asked Hugh Vesty. `Yeos or English?'

`Neither.' Michael smiled. `'Tis the gallant Scotsmen!' Despite Derrynamuck, he still considered the Highlanders to be the best soldiers in Ireland. Moments later the Highlanders appeared on the ridge. Their colonel let out a shout, `There's t'canny laddie!'

And the chase was on, fanning in six differing directions.

Each of the five other rebels soon confounded their followers as they disappeared, seemingly into thin air, down the ravines into the many secret caverns in these their own mountains, but the group of staunch highland lads chasing Michael Dwyer never let him out of their sight. Glensmen themselves – they could run as fast, jump as far, and were every bit as expert and natural climbers as he was.

The chase continued through morning to afternoon, the whole day, across the mountains; in and out through wood and glen, over the Glenealo river and across to the lovely valley of Glendalough with its two small lakes lying in the hollow of its pine-covered hills.

Michael was running towards a stone tower that had been built almost a thousand years earlier as a fortress against the Danes. The door was high, ten feet up in the wall, with a scaling rope still hanging from it, put there no doubt by the children who played in the tower. He glanced over his shoulder and frowned to see the Highlanders still close on his tail. No time to scale up and pull the rope inside with him without the Highlanders seeing. No sense in being trapped.

He sprinted on through the trees, up towards the ruins of a monastery where Mass had been said by St Kevin's monks centuries earlier. In and out through the ruins they chased him, and on and on until he reached the trees of the Upper Lake where he suddenly gave the Highlanders the slip.

They looked around them in bewilderment, and then searched high and low, refusing to accept defeat after tracking their game so long and so far. Eventually they grounded their arms in fury and exhaustion.

`He's a Hieland born laddie, nae doot,' said one. `Knew every larch and hole of the mountains back awa'.'

The seven men sat down for a breather, and held a council of war.

`Och!' exclaimed the youngest highlander, a sandy-haired lad named Sandy. `I cannae help but think o' the days when my own clansmen were chased o'er the Hielands by English soldiers. We gave yon tiger a good run o' it. Let's push awa' back to barracks.'

`Hold yer wheesht, mon. Five hundred English guineas. Think o' that!'

While they sat and thought of it, a strange noise reached them. A bump-bump-clop-clop sound which they could not discern.

`Tis over yonder!' cried one.

They jumped to their feet and held their weapons in readiness as the sound drew nearer, then they stared in awe as a grotesque sight emerged from a young grove of larches. Sitting in a wooden box came a legless cripple pulling himself along at amazing speed with the aid of two hand-stools which he used to push the ground behind him.

`Aha, my gallant Sawnies!' the cripple cried as he bumped towards them. `And is it a copper or a shilling ye have for a poor deformed one like meself?'

The Scotsmen stared at the miserable piece of humanity. Pity was their first emotion as they stared down at the two stumps of legs which had been snapped off at the thighs by the steel jaws of a poacher's mantrap when the cripple was eighteen years old.

Pity was their first emotion, but on closer inspection they saw the long bony face had a cruel look to it and the eyes held a malicious gleam.

The cripple dribbled a cackling laugh. `No mind about coppers or shillings. Would ye be interested in guineas? Five hundred of the darlings. And me for a rightful share.'

`Five hundred guineas? D'ye ken where he be?'

The cripple nodded. `Aye, but before I tell ye, do I have yer word on my share of the reward?'

`Wha' kind of mon are ye?' said the youngest Highlander tiredly. `Selling oot yer own clansman?'

`Hold yer wheesht, Sandy. Let the mon speak.'

`Dwyer's no clansman of mine!' the cripple shouted furiously. `I hate the varmint! Detest and despise him something aggravating. Do I get me share of the money if I tell ye where he is?'

Aye. One tenth part.'

`Tenth? But there be only seven of ye?'

`Aye, but wha' about our colonel and captain?'

The cripple set down his hand-stools and rubbed his long bony hands together as if wringing soapsuds from them, then he said: `He's up there, in St Kevin's Bed. I seed him go up there a few times before, when he was a youth, with some of his pals. I seed him go up there only a few months ago, with that other varmint, Hugh Vesty Byrne. But this time – I seed him go up alone.'

`Dwyer? Definitely Dwyer?'

`Aye, the Reb-Chief himself. I seed him get away from ye by slipping into the lake and swimming underwater like a mermaid. Then while ye were sitting and gossiping, I seed him climb up to the Bed as swift as a cat.'

The Highlanders rushed down to the borders of the lake with the cripple bumping after them. They stared across the water to the historic hiding place – St Kevin's Bed – a cave high up the face of the cliff where the young monk had hidden in the sixth century – a perilous climb.

`Wha' can a mon do up there?' asked the youngest

Highlander.

`He can sit and wonder how he's going to get back down again?' cackled the cripple.

`Have ye been up there?'

`Feck yer gab, ye Scotch beggar!' screamed the cripple, banging his hand-stools on the ground in fury. `How in hell's flames could I get up there?'

`I'll gi' ye a blow in the weisin if ye call me a Scotch beggar, ye Irish Iscariot!' cried Sandy. `Why d'ye hate your own countrymon so anywa'?'

`I don't hate all of him!' the cripple cried peevishly. `Leastaways, not the top half of him.'

He began to grumble angrily. `I used to seed them at the Hurley matches and ball-kicking games. All them young men running over the green grass on their long strong legs. Dwyer's legs annoyed me something vexatious. I used to seed him like I seed him this evening, running like the wind through the trees, swinging the Hurley bat and laughing his head off when they won the contest. I knowed he was laughing at me. I knowed it as sure as my name is Danny of the Lake.'

He wrung and pulled at his hands as if he was strangling some invisible person.

`But after Dwyer's, the legs I hate the most are on Hugh Vesty Byrne. I seed him once pole-vault over a wall nine feet high with no problem. Then I seed him and Dwyer trying to ride the horses standing up – not sitting like gentlemen, but feet balanced on the horses' haunches and arms spread as the horses cantered along. And they was laughing, even when they fell off they was laughing.'

`Curse them!' he screamed in sudden savagery. `Curse them to hell and beyond! And ye Jocks can give me a shilling now on account of my imparting the intelligence to ye! Youse shameless hoors – going around in yer skirts! Showing off your legs like any Jezebel hoor!'

The Highlanders quickly gathered a shilling together and threw it into the box. Anything to get rid of the horrible deformed man who screamed like a woman.

`The mon's demented,' said one, when the box had

bumped away into the shadows. Darkness was falling and they realised no more time could be wasted if they were to bring Dwyer in.

They looked again up towards the high cave inside a projecting rock that hung over the water.

`We cannae even be sure he's up there. Mebbe the cripp just said tha' – on account of our kilts?'

`Och, nae. He hates the rebel's knee-breeches mair. He be looking a' 'em longer.'

They quickly formed their plan. Although it was a hazardous and dangerous climb, they were all cragsmen and thought they could do it if Dwyer had, although – not if they carried their muskets – the powder would get wet in the water.

The stripped off their coats, then armed with only bayonets, they left their guns behind and slipped into the still waters of the lake and swam across to the crag's feet at the opposite side. There they separated into two groups, three started the climb to the right of the Bed, four to the left, their plan being to converge on Dwyer from each side of the ledge.

From where he stood just inside the cave, Michael could not see the Highlanders moving upwards, but he knew they were coming, having watched them swim across the lake.

He smiled to himself. It took a Celt to understand a Celt, and the Jocks could be every bit as superstitious as the Irish. Such a pity he had lost his sea-whistle at Derrynamuck.

He glanced up at the darkening sky; a purple hue hung over the land like a lamenting shadow; the moon was rising slowly from behind a few whisps of cloud, like a ghost rising out of smoke.

He waited a few long minutes, and then cupping his hands around his mouth he sent out a high shrill scream like the cry of a soul burning in hell. The noise echoed and reverberated across the dark waters of the lake.

`Hoot!' cried one of the highlanders almost losing his balance. `Wha' was tha'?'

Again the high-pitched quivering wail echoed over the

dark lake, freezing six of the seven Scotsmen to the face of the cliff in numbed terror.

`Isnae a mon made a sound like tha" one cried. `Isnae a mortal!'

`Och, ye bluidy bairns,' snapped the seventh. `Tis Dwyer actin' the fool an' hopin' t'frighten us wi' the shreikin' cry o' ghostly bogles. Stave on!'

Only duty to the regiment, and nothing short of duty, forced the other six to continue upwards. They had almost reached the ledge of the saint's bed when Dwyer suddenly appeared on the ledge and stood calmly smiling down at them for a moment – then disappeared – then came back to the ledge on a run and jumped past them down into the water.

Over their shoulders they gaped down at him as he swam across to the opposite shore. `Bluidy hellfire!'

Too late the Highlanders realised their mistake. They had left their guns behind and no guard!

`Och, nae, Dwyer!' one shouted as Michael lifted the stacked muskets and moved to throw them into the dark waters. `Dinnae droon our weapons, mon! Just b'thankful ye got awa' an' free!'

`Aye!' Michael shouted cheerily, `Scot-free!'

`Nae need t'make it personal, mon.'

`Did the Glengarry's tell you what happened at Derrynamuck?' Michael shouted.

`Aye.'

`Then you'll understand why I can't oblige you, avics.' Michael consigned the muskets to the depths of the lake, then turning away, almost stumbled over the legless man in the box.

`Hello there, Michael me hearty,' the cripple cooed in a whisper. `I was just coming to see if it was ye or yourself the Jocks were seeking. I was just on me way to warn ye anyhow.'

Michael moved into the trees and retrieved the gun he had hidden there before going underwater along the edge of the lake. He came out again into the early moonlight and examined the gun with an experienced eye, while Danny looked on, beads of sweat beginning to form on his frightened face.

`You saw me, didn't you, Danny. You saw me take to the lake. You saw me go up to Kevin's Bed. You told the kilties where I could be found.'

`No, no!'

`Lucky for me you didn't see where I hid the gun.'

He looked at Danny, his eyes as cold as ice. He placed the muzzle of the gun against Danny's heart, `Cripple or no, you're an informer, Danny, and you know the fate of informers.'

`No! No!' Danny screamed. `In the name of St Kevin I'd never inform on one of me own race. What? – inform on the Reb-Chief of Wicklow? On the Glen-King of Imaal? Nay, never! And not to those shameless hoors in skirts! Did ye see them climbing up to the Bed and showing off their big wet legs?'

Inwardly Michael recoiled at Danny's sickness. He glanced over his shoulder at the sound of the Highlanders splashing back into the water, then looked again at the man in the box, at the long bony face that could have been sixty but was only thirty-five. He drew away the gun.

`I reckon I'd be doing you a kindness to kill you, Danny, but I wouldn't have you on my conscience. Go to the devil your own way.'

Danny stabbed him an evil glance between the eyes, but said nothing.

`At least I know where we stand now, Danny, you and me.'

`Stand?' As abruptly as Danny's fear had vanished, his anger came back. `*Stand? Stand?*' He screamed like a fox and grabbed at one the legs standing before him. Michael tried to jump back but gasped in shock as Danny's teeth bit savagely into his knee. He raised his hand and whapped the cripple hard across the neck which brought a howl and instant release.

Michael shuddered, and moved away from the man who screamed as if insane. He turned and ran on; had only gone a short distance when he heard Danny's voice ringing out in renewed rage, and knew the Highlanders had reached the banks.

`Ye hoors! Ye let him get away! Ye shameless Scotch hoors in yer stupid skirts! Give me the yeos in red coats any day to ye lot – at least they managed to run down their game at Castle Kevin when I gave them the word. Only one they bagged, Andrew Thomas, but at least they didn't lose their guns like ye shites! Scotchmen me eye! Botchmen!'

`Oh, mon, ye've asked fer it!' young Sandy hissed in rage. He lifted his foot to boot the cripple in the face but Danny was quicker. He whipped up the club he always carried in his box and swung it, sending the highlander sprawling.

`Kill me would ye?' Danny screamed at the others, holding the club up threateningly. `Six more of ye against a poor cripple! Even Dywer, bad as he is, couldn't hurt a poor legless cripple. But then Dywer is a man – not like ye hoors in skirts!'

Still waving the club, Danny let out an angry peel of laughter. `Hoors! Hoors! Hoors!'

`God almighty!' a Highlander whispered, backing away from the grotesque man in the box. `I'm no' even dead – but already I know what the Devil looks like. In God's name, come awa' lads. The mon's a demon from hell.'

Danny watched them narrowly as they helped Sandy to his feet and dragged him away. He listened to their movements and voices and knew they were heading in the direction of Lugduff Mountain.

The darkness was now like a blanket over the mountains of Glendalough. The moon sent silver beams over the dark waters of the upper lake around St Kevin's Bed.

Danny grinned and turned his box down towards the water, then cackled to himself as he wondered what the Highland hoors would do – if on their journey back they happened to hear the haunting tune of bagpipes and meet the gliding ghost of Lugduff?

He lifted a bottle out of his box, threw back his head and took a long gulping slug, then re-corked it and wiped his mouth and chin. He put the bottle away and sat motionless, staring with evil eyes at the dark rippling waters of the lake.

He often sat at night staring at the lake, for deep in its depths was the bones of the gamekeeper who had set the mantrap that had taken his legs.

He heard a quiet movement in the dense undergrowth beside him and shifted his narrow eyes sideways in fear ... it was a badger, nosing its way along the ground. Suddenly there was no fear in Danny's eyes; they became bright and glowing with yearning.

He sat motionless, quietly smiling as the badger nosed closer, and when it was near enough, Danny swung up his arms and brought the club down, blow after savage blow, until the badger lay battered and bloody and dead.

Then he sat again, his anger spent, looking over the lake surrounded by pine trees and wilderness. He stared at the rippling water as if hypnotised. There was no other motion, no other sound.

Then he heard the footsteps coming through the trees, strong footsteps that did not try to disguise themselves. He quickly pushed his box around and raised his club, grinning slyly when the tall young man strode into the moonlight.

`Ho, ye rascal! Ye gave the botchmen the slip, did ye? Well, fair play to ye, Michael me hearty!'

Michael stood a few paces off, staring down at him with eyes that seemed aflame.

`So it was *you* that sent them to get Andrew Thomas. You traitorous bag of scum! I'd take my chances with you any day, Danny – but Andrew Thomas, I'll not forgive you for him.'

`What are you talking about?' Danny cried in amazement. `I know no Andrew Thomas.'

`But you knew Matt McDaniel's house at Castle Kevin. And you knew three rebels were lying there. And it was you who told the boys in red coats where to find them. And you knew it was Andrew Thomas they caught.'

`Me?'

`I heard you with my own ears,' Michael said. `I heard you boasting it to the kilties.'

`Did I?' Danny shrugged indifferently. `I have a poor memory these days.' He unplugged the bottle in his box and held it to lips. `So, ye've come back to kill me, eh? Come back to kill an informer. Then get on with it!'

He took a deep draught from the bottle, and then looked savagely at Michael through almost closed eyes. `Well, what ails ye? What are ye waiting for?'

Danny was not a clever man, but he possessed that genius of cunning quite common in those bordering on madness. He knew Dwyer was capable of killing an informer, but not a cripple.

And when Michael suddenly let out an angry breath then walked a few paces down to the lake's edge, Danny knew he was right in his deduction. If Dwyer was ever going to kill him as an informer, he would have done it earlier, when it was himself who had been betrayed.

Michael was studying the waters of the lake, he spoke quietly without turning round. `I reckon I'd be doing you a kindness if I killed you, Danny,' he said again.

Danny shrugged. `I reckon you would, but go ahead, kill half a man and feel proud of it.'

Michael moved to one of the stone boulders along the edge of the lake and sat down, a few feet away and facing Danny, looking at him with a mixture of revulsion and pity. But all Danny saw was the long rifle Dwyer held in both hands, the muzzle pointing at the ground and out of harm's way.

`You've turned bad inside, Danny, real bad. And if there's one thing I hate to see, it's a man turned rotten.'

`Then look in your mirror, boy. From what I hears you're as bad as they come.'

Michael glanced at the waters of the lake then slowly looked back at the cripple.

`There's bad and bad, Danny. You should know that, all the time you spend sitting in that box watching the ways of nature. Even the birds of the air defend their territory and fight to protect their own. But real badness, in man or beast, is nothing to do with situation and everything to do with heart ... and when the rot starts the signs are clear, same as they are in nature; the bird that fouls its own nest, then wrecks it. The sheep dog that begins nipping his own sheep, then ends up tearing their throats out. The man who clasps hands with his comrades, then steps out and sells them like Judas.'

`Well I couldn't do that, could I?' Danny said plaintively. `Step out.'

`You still grinding that old bone? Man, you haven't heard or heeded a word I've been saying. Sure you've got no legs, but worse, you've got no heart, it's all withered up and rotten inside you. As dead as that poor badger you just beat to death.'

`Never liked badgers,' Danny said, taking another drink. `And any heart I once had went with my legs.'

He held up the bottle as if measuring its contents against the light of the moon. `But seeing as ye know so much about the ways of nature and the ways of badness, bucko, then ye should also know that only a wicked rooster will sneak into another cock's barnyard and lie with one of his hen-wives.'

Michael frowned in puzzlement. `What the hell are you talking about?'

`Pat O'Riordan of your own Imaal,' Danny said. `Only the other day I heard he got wed and brought a mate home to his nest. A lovely black-feathered hen that already had a chicken. And now she's clucked another one. But only this afternoon, I learned that you were the rooster on that roost, not O'Riordan.'

Michael looked at the cripple with eyes half closed. Danny laughed contemptuously. `And ye talk to me about badness. That's boiling!'

`Who told you such nonsense?' Michael said softly.

`What's that?' Danny snapped angrily, as if he resented the question. Then he shrugged. `Nobody told me.'

`So where did you get the notion that the children are mine?'

`Oh, no notion in it! 'Tis the truth and no mistake.'

Danny paused with the bottle to his lips and bared his teeth in a savage grin. The conversation had lulled him into a calmness and he was enjoying it, sharpening his wits against the bright young spark who thought he was so clever.

`This afternoon it was I learned it. Only a few hours before ye and the kilties showed. I was behind those trees, keeping my eye on the lake as is my fashion, and watching two men fishing. They were talking together about the christening that O'Riordan is having for the second child this Sunday, at the chapel at Rathdangan. According to O'Riordan, everyone will be there. Then one man laughed and said, `But will the *father* of the child be there?' And as they talked on, I realised they were talking about the Reb-Chief himself.'

Michael looked calmly at the cripple, his eyes now as remote and cool as the lake.

`Way I see it,' Danny drained the bottle in a gulp, `you and her must have been mating long before she went to the priest with O'Riordan. Although I reckon now that she never went anywhere with O'Riordan, never married him either. I reckon you've had her tucked away in some little nest somewhere, and this christening on Sunday is just a trick to take the militia off her scent.'

Danny cackled. `But I'm smart, boy, smarter than most of the militia who're as stupid as flies in a whiskey bottle. A lot of them do reckon the children might be a gentleman's by-blows, and O'Riordan is happy enough to make a respectable woman of her, as long as he gets the next shot.'

Danny shrugged. `Sure half the bloody population of Ireland is gentry sired.'

Michael suddenly shivered. A chill wind blew over the lake and his clothes were still wet from his swim.

`Finished,' Danny said, throwing the bottle into the undergrowth. Then he chuckled and rolled his tongue in his cheek, all the fine cunning of his mind mulled by the warming whiskey in his belly.

`Come now, Michael me hearty, admit I have the cat by the tail. Admit those two chicks are yours. I'll not tell a soul.'

Michael looked at him, a small enigmatic twist to his lips, and Danny smiled in the certainty that he was right, a slow delighted smile. But he had to be sure.

`Tis right then, the child to be christened on Sunday is yours, eh?'

`Yes, the child is mine.'

`And the woman? Is she yours too?'

`The woman too,' Michael confirmed, then slowly raised up the muzzle of the gun and shot the informer in the place where his heart had once been.

Chapter Ten

At the little village chapel of Rathdangan, at a place where four roads meet, the Christening Mass went off without a hitch, except no christening took place, only the Mass. The seven-week old son of Michael and Mary Dwyer had been baptised secretly a week after his birth, in the presence of both parents, in the parlour of the priest's house at Green's River.

The military waiting on their mounts outside the little chapel didn't know that. And when the people began to come out, Captain Woollard's eyes sought keenly for a woman holding a newborn.

He recognised her at once, the girl in the square at Donard. She wore a large tortoise-shell comb in her dark hair, gypsy fashion, and despite having a child she was as slim as an unbroached filly. He sat more erect on his horse as he stared at her. Primitive in mind and race she might be, but she was outstanding amongst the sombre huddle of people around her. He looked amongst them for the one who might be the father, but there were no young men present, only middle-aged and old men.

He kneed his horse forward and within seconds the military had formed a cordon around the entrance to the church. Everyone fell silent and looked at the soldiers, their faces cold and sullen, like a people under siege.

Woollard surveyed them, his expression pure arrogance. A number of the women moved to form a silent second inner cordon around the girl holding the child, and Captain Woollard knew at once that he and his soldiers would likely be torn to pieces by these females if they as much as touched her.'

`Is the child illegitimate,' he said down to the girl. `Or are you married?' `No grandson of mine is ill-anything!' William Doyle cried, pushing forward. `And is it insulting a virtuous woman ye'd be on a holy Sunday?'

Woollard coolly regarded the sturdily built man who had a strong face, great rakish dark eyes, and a voice like a foghorn.

'Where is the husband then?'

'God save your honour, but isn't he looking at you.' William Doyle nudged Pat O'Riordan forward and spoke through the corner of his mouth. 'Act like a half-wit,' he whispered unnecessarily.

O'Riordan stumbled forward in genuine terror, twisted the hat in his hands a few times, then offered a red twitching smile to the officer.

'Are you this woman's husband?'

'I am, sir.' O'Riordan tugged his forelock with a trembling hand.

Captain Woollard could not believe it. His eyes moved to the tall beautiful girl, then back to the ungainly heap of an ignorant-looking man beside her; at least twice her age.

'Pat here,' cried William Doyle, putting an arm fondly around O'Riordan, 'is the son-in-law I've always wanted. And no finer husband could my daughter or indeed any woman wish to have. Always up at the crack of dawn and out on his farm working like the land slave he is. As fine as any man ever bred in Imaal.'

Woollard was staring scornfully at O'Riordan whose head was now bowed in embarrassment at such praise.

'As fine as any man ever pulled on breeches!' Doyle clasped O'Riordan tighter. 'No matter about the colour of his face. I wish I could grow apples the red of Pat's face. And so what if his hair stands up here and there like horns — twas not him that shot the woman's pet duck! I'd swear that before a judge even — '

'Michael Dwyer?' interrupted Woollard. 'Your daughter knew him, I'm told.'

'Knew him?' Doyle squared his shoulders and glared at the redcoat with a colossal air of offence. 'What do you mean she *knew* him?'

'What I say. She knew him well enough to dance with him and be considered his companion at one time.'

'Oh, is that what you mean?' Doyle's wrath instantly fell with his shoulders. 'Sure stone the crows,' he said in a bewildered tone, 'tis hard to be knowing the true meaning of words these days. His Reverence in there was just telling us about a place called Genesis where Adam knew Eve and she conceived ... But my saintly daughter never knew Michael Dwyer that well, not before she was married ... to Pat here.'

Woollard sniffed at the big nonsensical man. He decided to speak directly to the girl. `Just how well did you know Michael Dwyer?'

`Knew him only long enough to find out what a rascal he is!' William Doyle answered, and then regarded the officer with a look of sneering disdain. `Dwyer? Tch! A womanish sort of fellow in my opinion – likes sitting with women and bairns. What sort of man is that? And no respect for the traditions of our County either. In the old days a Wicklow boy always courted a Wicklow girl, but not the rebel Dwyer! No, that gypsy had to wander as far as the County Clare to find a girl good or bad enough for him. Isn't that right, people?'

The people all nodded in murmured agreement.

`Do you know any of his hideouts?'

`Faith, I don't!' Doyle declared. `And don't want to neither. Why should a sensible man like myself be foolish enough to seek out trouble? But I'll tell you this, my good man, if that – '

But Woollard had heard enough. `Thank you and good day!' he snapped.

`And the same to ye!' Doyle replied, and then turned brightly to the crowd. `Isn't he a very civil young man all the same? Wishing us a good day. Well, anyone who wants to may come along with meself and Pat now. There's going to be some acelebrating at my house!'

Captain Woollard motioned with his head to his men and they side-stepped their mounts away from the huddled crowd, then sat on their horses along the edge of the fields where the corn was all reaped and stood in stooks, watching the people as they drifted towards their homes. The people from north Imaal piled into two hay wagons that trundled down the country road.

`What do you think?' Woollard asked the young

lieutenant sitting alongside him. `Do you think she is married to that stupid-looking man?'

`I think she is, sir, if the father says so.'

`He could have been lying.'

`He could have been, but matches like that are not unusual among these natives, especially the agricultural tribes. So many of their young men die in their continual war against us that many fathers prefer to settle a land-match for the girl and ignore her plea for a love-match. But once the marriage-tie is made, it is accepted by both as forever binding.'

Captain Woollard looked at him in surprise. `You sound like an expert on the subject.'

The soldier shrugged. `I should be, sir. I spent over six months up in Connaught after the French landed.'

`And became acquainted with the natives?'

`Just one, sir.'

When the soldier said no more, only sat with a blank face watching the last few stragglers standing in chatting groups, Woollard said impatiently, `Well?'

`A girl, sir. She was lovely, and very dainty, except for the fact that she wore a broken old pair of men's boots under her skirts. She had no real shoes, you see. The Connaught people are poor almost to starving, have been since Cromwell shunted them to the barren patches where nothing grows. I was even thinking of marrying her myself, and buying her a pair of shoes, but her father quickly set off and agreed a match with a man from miles away. Neither she nor I saw him until he came over the hill for the wedding. He was that old, sir, older than her father, and very bent from working the land.'

`Awful,' Woollard muttered, then looked curiously at his lieutenant. `Were you really that willing to surrender to the foe?'

`I was hoping she would surrender to me, sir.'

`Then why didn't you just whip her back to barracks and break her in before her father could do anything about it?'

`She wouldn't have come, sir. She was a good girl, not a doxie.'

`Too many good girls in this rotten place,' Woollard muttered glumly. `All Mary Virgins and very few Magdalenes. Black-haired, was she?'

No, sir, golden.'

`Ah, a Viking throwback. Good God, I saw one the other day that looked like a chieftain herself. A magnificent fair trollop with yards of yellow hair and a skirt so thin you could see she had thighs as strong as any Viking or Highlander. But when I spoke to her she ran away like a frightened kitten, God damn her! God damn them all! Did your Connaught girl have thighs like a Viking?'

`I doubt it, sir, she was petite as a fairy.'

Woollard glanced at the handsome young face still staring blankly at the deserted chapel. A face as blank as the voice.

`Oh come now, Lieutenant Lowe,' he said in a teasing tone, `don't tell me she turned her back on a fine young soldier like you and went with the bent old codger?'

`She had no choice, sir. Her family lived solely from the profits of a potato garden the size of handkerchief, but the man she was matched with had fertile land, four whole fields of it, if only rented. Besides, her father would have killed her for even associating with an English soldier. The only time he ever saw me, he stared at me as if I was the ghost of Cromwell himself. Accused me of stealing his land. Accused me of shunting his people to starve in the barren hell of Connaught. Then he ordered the girl inside and slammed the door in my face. Yes, sir, he would have killed her first.'

`Awful moody people these Irish. Won't accept that bygones should be bygones.'

`Last I saw of her, she was walking back over the hill with the bent old man, as his wife, still wearing her broken old boots.'

`Well,' Woollard said in a cheering tone, `now you will think twice before getting involved with any other native girl while you're here.'

`I'll not even think once about it, sir.'

`Jolly good!' Woollard turned his horse around. `But

don't sound so forlorn, boy. Think of England! And besides, where could your little romance have led? She would never have fitted into English society, not even in shoes. Remember that.'

`Yes, sir.'

Woollard raised his hand and signalled the column to move.

`I'll remember it every time I see a fine lady wearing fine shoes and hear her complaining about having to make another tedious journey with her husband to his Irish estates on the rich fertile lands of Longford or Drogheda ... sir.'

Woollard responded with a tolerant sneer. `Wonderful victory Cromwell had at Drogheda.' Then he breathed deep in his lungs and fixed his eyes on the mountains as they rode in slow double file past the reaped cornfields. `Well, there are still plenty of young men left in Wicklow,' he said, `athletic-looking bastards every one of them, and most are up those mountains with Dwyer – a ruddy hard bugger to catch.'

`Yes, sir.'

`Damn it all!' Woollard cried irritably. `At times I think I'd give my commission just to get a glimpse of the insurgent chief.'

When the military party had ridden well out of sight, the detachment of armed men concealed amongst the corn stooks who had observed the whole proceedings with guns primed and aimed, broke cover and shook themselves down.

`Did you hear that now,' Hugh Vesty said to Michael. `That there redcoat would give his commission just to see you.'

`And who the blazes would want his commission?' Michael asked.

Hugh Vesty thought about it, and then smiled. `You're right, who the blazes would? Now come on – let's go and see our wives and children.' He strode off eagerly and Michael could not help smiling as he followed his cousin. Hugh Vesty's wife Sarah had now also given birth to a boy, and

Hugh was delighted as could be, and already planning his history lessons.

*

The Mass-attenders had long gone. The rebels broke away in pairs and disappeared into the hills towards Lugnaquilla. At Camara, Michael and Hugh Vesty, with Mernagh and Burke following close behind, turned off towards the isolated land of Knockandarragh where, all going well, their wives had arranged to meet them.

The house at Knockandarragh was once again filled with people. In the centre of the room the table was furnished with numerous uncut loaves and plates of butter, cheese, ham, and cold pork, and tumblers for cold ale or seasonal blackcurrant juice, the cost of which Michael's father had agreed to pay half, even though he did not attend, seeing as it was all a charade – and just another excuse for Doyle to revel.

William Doyle was standing in a pool of importance by the fireplace, master of all the news, which he imparted with great aplomb to those neighbours who had come just to hear the gossip.

`The husband?' Doyle cried. `God save your honour, says I, but isn't he looking at you – and me knowing himself was beyond in the cornfields doing just that.'

The laughter was lively when the four rebels walked in. Michael smiled warmly at O'Riordan and patted his shoulder. `You did a grand job, Pat.'

`And what about me?' Doyle demanded. `In all modesty but truth you have to admit that it was me carried the whole thing off.' He smiled rakishly at all the neighbour-women.

Michael looked at the laden table and ale casks. `What are you celebrating?' he said curiously to Doyle.

`What do you think – a christening.'

`A christening?' Michael looked perplexed. `And who was christened?'

`Nobody.' Doyle was all puzzlement. `You know that right well.'

Michael looked at Hugh Vesty with a sly gleam in his eye.

`It seems foolish, doesn't it, to celebrate a christening without someone getting watered.'

Doyle let out a roar when he was suddenly scooped off his feet as lightly as if he was a sack of oats then carried struggling and shouting through the room of gaping neighbours.

Put me down! Ah here! Fair play now!' But Michael and Hugh Vesty continued out to the yard and across to the long cattle-trough where Doyle was dumped in the water without ceremony.

God Almighty!' Doyle roared, trying to get up, then slipping back again until his head and every screed of his clothing was soaked. `God Almighty!'

The sight of him was so ludicrous the neighbours were all carried away into an ecstasy of hilarious laughter. Even Mrs Doyle, holding her grandson, was laughing; but the one laughing the most was Mary. Her laughter floated merrily over the rooftop, while her father struggled and slipped and spluttered.

'*God Almighty!* Doyle roared up at Michael. `Why the blazes did you do that?'

`You only got what you asked for,' Michael told him. `Slandering the father of your grandchildren – a womanish-sort of fellow indeed!'

`Devil roast you, I was only playing the game!' Doyle cried as Mernagh, Burke, and O'Riordan helped him out. `Oh, would ye look at me clothes!'

Doyle stood staring down in horror at his soaked Sunday best, while Michael and Hugh Vesty doubled up in laughter.

`He wanted a christening and he got it!' Hugh Vesty cried, thumping Michael in the chest.

Still laughing, Michael turned towards the house, and saw Mary looking at him with approval. Her cheeks were flushed from her merriment. He approached her slowly and smiling, the sly gleam back in his eye.

`No, no,' she said with laughing lips, backing away. `No, don't...'

`To the devil with this for a story,' William Doyle muttered. `I'll not live this down in a hurry.'

`William, oh, William,' O'Riordan said plaintively. `Don't get upset now. He's just in good humour because the whole thing went off as planned.'

`Holy Moses,' said Doyle, slumping wearily down on the edge of the trough and wiping the water from his face. `Holy Moses, if he does things like this in a good humour, what would he do in a bad mood?'

They heard a scream of excited laughter and looked round to see Michael chasing Mary through the field. A loud cheer rose up from the neighbours when he caught her and kissed her passionately in full view of them.

`Look at him,' Doyle grunted. `As playful as a buck hare with a doe rabbit, and not an ounce of remorse in him. He's turned my fine celebration into a rowdy debauch.'

Still dripping from head to foot, he turned and stared dolefully at O'Riordan, his hair a matted mass about his face. `Isn't he the *wurrst* son-in-law a man could have, Pat?'

`He is,' O'Riordan agreed good-naturedly. `He is, by jiminy, he is indeed.'

*

Over in Eadstown, the priest from Green's River was at the Dwyers' house that night. When Michael slipped in, no one noticed him, all their backs to the door as they gathered round the priest seated at the table reading a newspaper that Michael's father had pushed into his hands.

`Tell me is it true, Father?' John Dwyer said anxiously. `Tell me it is *not* true. There are many words there that I don't understand.'

Father Richard's eyes, deep and far-seeing, opened slightly as he looked up. `Ah, here is your wayward son,' he said, handing the paper back to John Dwyer. `I would like to hear him tell you what it means – him that had the benefit of an elementary education from a barn-master, but more from a scholastic priest.'

`Michael ...' John Dwyer held out the paper to his son.

Michael took the paper and read it, then contemptuously flicked the paper back onto the table.

`What difference will it make to us?' he said to the priest coldly. `On a practical level it will make no difference at all. We will still be denied every right of the citizen, no right to own land, no right to vote, no right to public assembly, no right to any of the natural and unalienable rights of man!'

`The natural and unalienable rights of man ...' the priest recognised the words and sighed sadly. `So, you have found a new doctrine?'

The family looked at each other in blank bewilderment. The priest turned to the fire and held his hands out to the blaze. `So tell us, Michael, in the true parrot-fashion of the inflamed disciple, the philosophy of Thomas Paine that led thousands of young Irishmen to their futile deaths in 1798.'

`It also inspired America to freedom and France to overthrow the tyrants.'

`Good God!' the priest cried. `Thomas Paine is not only an Englishman, he is an atheist! If you begin by believing part of what he says, you will end up believing *all* of what he says!'

`I believe,' Michael said steadily, `that men are born free and equal in respect of their rights. And those rights are liberty, property, safety, and the right to resist oppression.'

`Very good,' the priest commended in a sarcastic tone.

`Don't you sneer at me,' Michael said irreverently. `I have been fighting for those rights since the spring of ninety-eight! Now you sin in your heart, and lie with your tongue, and tell me that you do not agree with those words also!'

`I do,' the priest admitted, `but it does not have to be achieved with the gun and the sword. There is another way, and it is coming. You say it will make no difference, but it will. To us as people, it will. If not as patriots.'

`Father, please ...' John Dwyer was losing his patience. `What it says in the newspaper, explain it in its truth not its words.'

`The Irish Parliament is to be dissolved, and we are to join with England in an Act of Union that will elevate us from slaves to citizens.'

`But ... but it says ...' John Dwyer had read it differently.

`It says Ireland will now be ruled solely by English politicians – direct from the Parliament at Westminster.'

`English Crown servants still ruling us from Dublin Castle,' Michael said. `What difference will it make? We will still be the most cruelly oppressed nation in the world.'

`Wrong,' the priest corrected. `It is all going to change. You see, the Bishops of the Catholic Church in Ireland have agreed to the Act of Union ... in exchange for Catholic emancipation.'

The priest looked around at the family, smiling joyously. `Yes, yes ... in exchange for the emancipation of our people.' He looked at Michael. `What say you now, revolutionary? Is this not a better way to achieve the natural and unalienable rights of man?'

Michael met the eyes of the priest, look for look; then turned and strolled through the kitchen towards the scullery at the back, loudly whistling a tune the United Irishmen had whistled many times while marching to battle in 1798, the tune of the French Revolution, `The *Marseillaise'*.

`He may whistle `The *Marseillaise'* now,' the priest said, unperturbed, `but come the Union ...' He smiled.

`Is it true, Father?' Mrs Dwyer asked. `Emancipation is truly coming for the Catholics at last?'

The priest stood up and laughed. It is true! Not our liberty as patriots, but the liberty of being treated as citizens in our own land.'

`Oh my,' said Mrs. Dwyer in the daze of a miracle. `Oh my, my, my!'

*

The vote was passed through both Houses of Parliament, and on 1st January 1801, the Act of Union between Ireland and England was established.

The three hundred members of the dissolved Irish Home Parliament were now reduced to a small delegation at Westminster, and amongst the great numbers of that political House, they were hard to find in the crowd.

Catholic emancipation did not follow. William Pitt had genuinely tried to bring it about, some believed, but King

George would not even consider Pitt's Irish relief measures, flaring into a bout of insanity whenever they were mentioned. The King's refusal to consider emancipation of the Irish Catholics was given colossal approval by the ruling Tory Party of the British Parliament, and Pitt resigned as Prime Minister.

Lord Cornwallis was heartbroken. He had convinced both sides of the divide that they would benefit from the Union. Under Pitt's instructions, he had wheeled and dealed, promising peerages and government pensions to the land barons who insisted on recompense for abandoning their political privileges. He had secured government posts for defunct members of the Irish Parliament, secured bishoprics for others, and bargained huge financial bribes to secure the vote. He had grumbled privately about `trafficking with the most *corrupt* people on earth,' blind to his own part in the corruption. But he had also truly believed that the Union was the answer to the Irish problem.

`But what we have now,' Cornwallis wrote, `is not a Union with Ireland, but a Union with the Protestant Party of Ireland.'

To the seven-eighths majority in Ireland, the only difference the Union brought was a new Viceroy and a new administration at Dublin Castle – and a new flag! The English cross of St George and the Scottish cross of St Andrew, were now joined by the Irish cross of St Patrick – in a single flag known as the Union Jack.

*

`Jacks are high,' said Hugh Vesty Byrne.

`Not me,' said John Mernagh, viewing the cards in his hand.

`Nor me,' said Martin Burke.

`What about you, Michael?' Hugh Vesty asked. `Can you open with a pair of jacks or higher?'

Michael looked up vaguely. `I'm thinking about the priest,' he said. `He truly believed them. He truly believed they were going to grant us emancipation and treat us as

149

citizens. He was not expecting King George to piss in his eye.'

He looked at the men anxiously. `I'm worried about him. I think I'll go over there and see if he's all right. He's done me many favours, even though we disagree on many things.'

*

The priest was stumbling unsteadily along the banks of Green's River. His eyes bloodshot from lack of sleep, his grey hair straggling down his back. His bones hurt violently. He was stiff from walking – walking here and there and everywhere – seeking respite from his rage and finding none.

`Oh what fools we were,' he muttered to the ground. `They spit on their own people, so why should they not spit on us too.'

He raised his eyes from the ground and let out an ironic laugh. `By God, you are right, Mr. Paine! They govern not in service of the people, but in *contempt* of the people.'

He stumbled on. `And yes, Mr. Paine, after all, what is this thing called a crown? And if the crown makes a king, what does that make the goldsmith who made the crown? And when they, the politicians and placemen and pension-men and lords of the chamber bow down and worship that crown, why do they not see the daily labour of the *people* who pay for it in taxes. Why do they spit on them?'

He let out another small laugh. `You see, my young revolutionary. I too have read Thomas Paine, and see him for the dangerous man that he is.'

And then as he walked, looking around at the wild hills, he saw the haze of people marching to the mountain top. As they always did in his dream. But now they were no longer singing joyous hymns, they were singing a war cry. He stared at them and trembled to his bones. Then he sprang to life and rushed to join them, stumbling in his movements. A young man came out of the crowd, walking towards him, a dark-haired young man holding a long gun at his side.

`Yes!' the priest cried, reaching to take the gun. `It is the only way now. They have sown the wind so must reap the whirlwind!'

`What ails you?' the young man said. `Are you sick in your head or what? Stumbling and raving like a madman.'

Then the haze cleared, the face came into focus, and his sleep-starved mind stabled on a shaky balance. `So it is you,' he whispered. `You have come to taunt me with `The *Marseillaise*'. You have come to gloat over my stupidity and shame.'

`Ach, stop talking like a fool and come along now. Your house is just beyond.' Michael took his arm. `We should get you to bed, I'm thinking.'

The priest awoke three days later, with no memory for what had passed. He opened his eyes and looked up at the dark-haired girl bending over him. She smiled, then with a litany of gentle phrases, forced him to sit up and spoon-fed him a bowl of broth.

`It tastes good,' he said. `Was I sick, Mary?'

`Just bone tired and mind-weary, Father,' Mary said softly.

Then it all came back to him. The betrayal. The lies he had believed, and encouraged so many others to believe. He wondered if he had said anything in the turmoil of his dreams.

`Did I ... say anything ... in my sleep?'

Mary threw a glance at Michael standing over by the wall. `No, nothing at all, Father,' she replied quickly. `You slept like a corpse.'

`And now it seems, I am restored to life again.'

He looked bleakly at the young couple who had helped him, and whose future was as dangerously uncertain as his own. How could he, as their pastor, help them in return? And then he realised there was only one way.

`Listen to me now,' he said softly, `listen while I tell you what our beloved Redeemer said in the Gospel of St. Matthew ... Love your enemies, bless them that curse you, do good to them that hate you, and pray for them that use you and persecute you.'

Both stared at him silently.

Then the sorrow of it all rose in him, and his eyes misted.

`Oh, Father,' Mary whispered, `why are you crying?'

`Not for myself, child, not for myself.' He looked up and smiled. `There, you see, a tear and a smile. One usually follows the other in the up and down of life. Is that not so?'

`That is so,' Mary agreed.

The priest was silent for a long moment, then he sighed deeply and pulled the bed covers high up over his misery. He lay back and closed his eyes.

`Thank you both,' he said. `But now you may leave me. I will be fine. I will rise soon and pay a visit to some of the hearty men of the parish who enjoy arguing with me. Just like himself there.'

Mary reached out and touched his hand. `Father..'

`God bless the two of you,' he whispered. `May you live to see your children's children.'

Michael motioned with his head to Mary. Outside the house he looked into her anxious face.

`No,' he said quietly, `leave him alone to get back his self-respect and dignity. It was just a brainstorm, but it's cleared now. The stubborn old martyr has a good few sermons left in him yet.'

Then in the bright winter sunlight they walked back along the riverbank, hand in hand, with the three companions who followed their captain with avid loyalty close behind.

At the hedge of a field, the five of them paused to watch a lone young bull having a fierce fight with his shadow in the sunshine, running in circles and charging and snorting in fury.

`Which one do you think will win?' Hugh Vesty murmured.

The five laughed, and walked on.

Chapter Eleven

To the fury of the ruling class, the new Viceroy of Ireland, Lord Hardwicke, soon made it very clear that, in the same way Lord Cornwallis had refused to be dictated to by generals of the army or officers of the militia, he in turn would not be dictated to by the land barons. He was an Englishman, and intended to rule as an Englishman, and as an Englishman he would not bow to the whims and wishes of the Irish gentry.

With all the hullabaloo of the Union, and the recall of many English regiments, Michael Dwyer began to entertain a small hope that maybe the Castle authorities would forget all about him.

They did not forget him, but they were no longer very troubled about him. The rebellion was long over and all radical movements crushed. So as long as Dwyer continued to confine his military strategy to one of defence and not attack, and as long as he continued to confine himself to his own mountains of Wicklow, he posed no real threat to country or government.

Nevertheless, the militia and yeomanry forces were kept on full pay and incentive to capture Michael Dwyer and bring him in. But the English regiments had been taken off the offensive and were now employed mainly in policing the country.

*

He had just stepped into the house of Laurence Mangan at Talbotstown when Mangan's daughter, Grania, cried a warning that an English regiment were riding down the road!

Mangan and Michael looked at each other; there was no way out, the house backed into the high ground of the hill-face and there was nothing but solid rock beyond the fireplace. If he attempted to run he would be seen the length of the road.

Grania rushed over to Michael and clutched on his arm.

There were only the three of them in the house. Minutes later a hammering came on the door. Mangan opened it.

`Routine search,' Captain Woollard said with a bored air.

Mangan opened the door wider. `This house belongs to Mr Hume of Humewood,' he said, thereby warning the officer that it could not be burned down at whim. `My tenancy is with Mr. Hume.'

Captain Woollard ignored him as a number of redcoats moved through the house, opening the settle-bed, moving the pine table and black-oak furniture, searching in and under the beds in the rooms off the kitchen.

Throughout, Captain Woollard stood officiously beside the silent Mangan whose very countenance fumed at such indignity. His daughter, on the other hand, was looking at the military officer with mild curiosity. She was a handsome girl with golden hair. Her eyes were blue, her lips naturally red, and her figure well shaped, as clearly emphasised by the tight black bodice laced under the white cotton cups of her breasts.

Involuntarily, Woollard smiled at her, and she smiled back. He looked down the room at the searching soldiers and wondered about her. Most of these females were rebel-lovers; but there were those few who – when confronted with a handsome officer in his scarlet uniform – instantly contracted a dose of scarlet fever.

Woollard stood taller in his uniform and found himself sympathising with such females: how could a rebel dressed in the country style, ever compare with the splendid scarlet gallants of His Majesty's army?

He looked at her and smiled again. She turned her eyes to the fire but a flush stained her oval cheeks, Woollard noticed, a *scarlet* flush!

His posture relaxed into one of arrogant charm. He moved a step or two towards the hearth and addressed a question to her: `What is your name, Miss?'

`Her name is Grania,' Mangan snapped.

`Gran-ya,' Woollard repeated the name as if it belonged to an angel, but before he unleashed all the seductive power of his charm, he decided to clarify one point: `Are you one of those females afflicted with a favouring disposition towards the rebels?'

Her eyes widened a fraction and sought those of her father.

'Well, are you?' Woollard murmured softly, placing his scarlet-coated body in front of her father and shielding her face from his view.

'*Tá a lá go dona. An bhfuil tú fuar*?' she answered, her voice a soft, musical soprano.

Woollard stared at her in enchanted puzzlement.

'She doesn't speak English,' Mangan said. 'The wife was ill when she was born so I sent her down to be reared by my sister in Cork. She came back only a year or so ago speaking only the Gaelic. Not as much as ten words of English can she speak.'

'What did she say to me in Gaelic?' Woollard queried.

'She says it's a very bad day. Are you cold?'

'A bad day? Am I cold?' Woollard looked out at the sultry late September day, and then stared curiously at the girl who smiled sweetly at him.

'She's also simple-minded,' Mangan said sadly. 'Spends most of her time talking in Gaelic to the hens and pigs.'

The girl looked from the officer to her father with the awkwardness of one in the presence of those whose language they cannot understand, then uttered a silly giggle like a child of five.

'O my sainted arse!' Woollard exclaimed wearily. 'The wenching situation in this country gets worse by the day.' He turned away from the girl, having instantly fallen out of love with her.

He realised his men were all staring at him, waiting for his command. The place had been searched without success.

'Search the outhouses and surrounding land!' Woollard snapped, then glared scornfully at Mangan and the girl before marching out also.

'A right piss-off this is,' Captain Woollard muttered in disgust to his lieutenant as he relieved himself against a hedge adjoining the property. 'How can an officer ever hope to rise to glory in this bogland – searching houses and chasing bloody rebels and no other action.'

`And the rebels always seem to have the advantage in a chase, sir, knowing every inch of the land as they do – especially Dwyer.'

`I'll have that clever bastard on a triangle one of these days,' Woollard said, buttoning his breeches. `I'll flog him myself until there's not an inch of skin left on his spine. Bloodybacks they call us – well I'll make his back so bloody he'll be screaming for me to kill him. Then I'll hand him over to the Rathdrum militia and let them stick him like a pig and slice him up between them.'

`If we ever catch him, sir.'

Woollard turned and stared at his aide. `I do believe, Lieutenant Lowe, that you take great joy in irritating me. Of course we'll catch the bastard eventually. How many times have I told you that in any game of war, when it comes to deciding a victory, God always wears a red coat.'

`He didn't in America, sir.'

Woollard looked pained. `I despair of you, Lowe, I really do! Why on earth did you ever join the army?'

`My father bought me a commission, sir. It was either the army or my inheritance.'

`Then you must be daft in the head if you think a wise old father like that would ever have accepted an Irish trollop in a pair of old broken boots!'

The other soldiers returned. `No rebels here, sir.'

`Then let's go!' Woollard snapped, then as he mounted his charger, `And I warn you, Lieutenant Lowe, if you persist in irritating me I'll have you cashiered for cowardice.'

`Yes, sir, very good, sir,' the lieutenant answered drolly.

`Oy there!' Woollard checked his mount as Mrs Mangan turned in from the road and began to walk across the yard towards the house.

`You, woman – halt!'

`Me, sir?' she asked, turning to face him.

`Do you have any knowledge of Dwyer's whereabouts?' Woollard demanded without preamble. `Answer me truthfully now, and don't even think of antagonising me,' he warned, `or I'll shoot you.'

`Shoot me, sir? Oh God save us – what was the question again?'

`Do you have you any knowledge of Dwyer's whereabouts?'

`I do,' she replied with a nod. `I was told only ten minutes ago.'

`Well?'

`Well, sir, tis said that Moiley the Bogeyman ate him a few days ago.'

She regarded Woollard with a woebegone look that said wasn't that a terrible way to go?

`*For'ard!*' Woollard screamed at his troop, then rode off at a gallop as if fearing the very real possibility of shooting her.

*

Grania stood by the window watching them with wide blue eyes until they had disappeared from view, then she turned and looked up towards the roof-tree and wide oak ceiling beams where Michael had been lying flat on his back directly over their heads, squeezed under the roof.

`All clear,' she said, and he swung down to the ground with a jump and smiled a smile of gratitude especially for her.

He was dressed in country style of brown whipcord breeches into which a black linen shirt was tucked and fastened with a wide leather belt accoutred with military pouches and cartridge-box. On his shoulders he wore a cross-belt that held a brace of pistols each side of his chest which were hidden by a brown jacket.

The girl laughed again, for she had guessed Woollard's thoughts when he had preened to a taller and firmer stance in his scarlet uniform.

`God help any maid that's foolish enough to fall into bed with him,' she said, `for the poor lass is likely to end up kneeling at his feet in praise and ordered to tell him exactly just how wonderful he was, and just how very grateful she is for the honour.'

Michael looked at Grania in mild surprise, for she was an unmarried maid and not supposed to know about such things, but then he remembered she was on the verge of marriage with one of his comrades; a good-looking lad who lately returned to camp looking unusually tousled and followed orders as if in a dream.

Mrs Mangan came in carrying a red hen which she had picked up in the yard.

`Oh, is it ye, Michael,' she said indifferently, her near-miss with a bullet completely forgotten as she held up the ruffled red hen who was trembling violently and appeared to have had some of her feathers torn out.

`Would ye look at the poor darling,' Mrs Mangan cried. `A beautiful hen she was when I brought her here last week, and the rooster fell head-over-heels in love with her, but his other wives are mad with jealousy and keep pecking and clawing at her something vicious. Will you have a glass of buttermilk or ale, Michael?'

`If you'll not be offended, I won't,' he said, and then quickly thanked her husband who assured him that every villager in Wicklow was behind him, and he could trust his life with every single one of them.

`And as for me,' Mangan added, `I have to be saying that I'm fiercely proud to have had you under my roof.'

They both laughed at that, then Michael moved to the door where Grania stood guard by the gate to make sure all was clear.

She gave him the nod, and he went out to her. He thanked her again by hugging her tightly and then swiftly disappeared.

Chapter Twelve

For almost a year Michael Dwyer's name had not appeared in a newspaper. Then the *Hibernian* brought him to public notice again in an article that endeavoured to be informative and impartial, yet trembled with exasperation:

> *At the breaking out of the late Rebellion, Michael Dwyer, being about six or seven and twenty years of age, ranged himself under the banners of rebellion; and though always foremost in danger, had the good fortune to retire unhurt through all the battles of that deplorable contest. When the rebellion was put down, Dwyer withdrew, accompanied by a chosen band, into the fastnesses of his native mountains, where he has since kept his ground, bidding defiance to all the parties sent out from time to time against him.*
>
> *It must be a matter of astonishment that an active, powerful and vigilant Government could never succeed in exterminating this banditti from the mountains, however difficult, and inaccessible they may at first appear.*
>
> *The rebel, who is intimately acquainted with the topography of the place has his regular videts and scouts in all the most advantageous points, who, on the appearance of alarm, or the approach of strangers, blow their whistles, which resound through the innumerable caverns, and are the signal for a muster. They are generally superintended by the chief himself, or his cousin of the name of Byrne, a determined fellow in whom alone he places confidence. Both are adepts at disguising their faces and persons and are thought to pay frequent visits to the metropolis. Dwyer is an active and vigorous fellow, and said to be wonderfully patient of fatigue, and fearless of every kind of danger.*

By the time 1801 had passed into 1802, the Protestants of Wicklow were as unhappy about the Union as the Catholics. Unlike the previous Irish parliament, England forbade them any say in government, except through the vote of their representative who was invariably ignored at Westminster.

By the early spring of 1802, the Protestant and Catholic farmers of Wicklow were as good friends again as ever. They discussed their differences and the space of their hostile separation since the rebellion ... In 1798 the Catholics were told that the Protestants intended to murder them, and they would not take that lying down ... In 1798 the Protestants were told the Catholics intended to murder them, so what could they do but join the yeomanry forces and assist the English troops.

No one could quite remember who had told who, but when a rumour is whispered on the wind, it breezes into every household.

Then all concluded that the English Executive at Dublin Castle was to blame – using the old system of Divide and Conquer to secure its imperial rule.

And so life stabilised as all abandoned their past prejudices and prepared excitedly for the spring planting, during which, long idle discussions were held on the prospect of the autumn harvests.

In that same spring of 1802, the war between England and France ended with a Peace Treaty signed at Amiens. The Protestant and Catholic farmers greeted this news with an indifferent shrug and returned to talk of husbandry of the land, their eyes fixed keenly on the fertility of the soil as summer progressed.

But even as the men reaped the harvest of barley and corn in the fields, and their women and children helped to collect the cut stalks of the grain which would be used as dry straw for fresh bedding, roof thatching and animal fodder, the search for Michael Dwyer continued.

*

Mr William Hume Junior of Humewood sent for his tenant, Sergeant Hawkins of the Upper Talbotstown

Yeomanry Corps.

When Sergeant Hawkins arrived, Mr Hume received him in his study.

`A friend from London is over on a visit,' Hume said. `He wishes to have a crack at the excellent game we have here. You are cognizant of the best shooting ground, Hawkins, are you not?'

`Indeed I am, sir.'

`Excellent! Just as I thought. Now report here before first light in the morning to accompany us.'

Hawkins looked pleased, he loved a good sport; and then an idea came to him. `May I bring the young son of Ned Byrne of Fearbreaga, sir? He can hear and smell the game a mile off.'

Hume hesitated. `Is he trustworthy?'

`He was too young to be an insurgent in 1798, if that is what you mean.'

`Is he a supporter of Dwyer?'

Hawkins shrugged. `They all are, sir, but it doesn't mean he bodes any ill against you. Young Byrne is a very decent and likeable young lad.'

`You trust him?'

`I do.'

William Hume sighed. `Well, if a yeoman trusts him, then I suppose I can. But he must not be allowed to carry a gun. Now, Hawkins, be here dark and early. I want my English friend to have an excellent time while he is in Ireland, an excellent time. Three days shall we allow? Three days sporting?'

`Three days should bring in a nice bag,' Hawkins agreed. `Although we will have to make some recompense to Ned Byrne for losing his son's labour on the farm for three days.'

`Naturally, naturally,' Hume replied brightly.

The following morning was fine and frosty, perfect for a shoot. Ned Byrne's fifteen-year-old son, aware of Hume's rewarding nature, was happy enough to go along, and the party of four set off sharp and early and were on the shooting ground at Aughavannagh not long after the darkness had lifted.

161

The Englishman was a fine young fellow, full of good humour and eager for the sport. They had been on the ground only a few minutes when, turning a hill, they saw six other sporting men in the distance, carrying guns.

`It seems we are not the only hunters out this early,' Hume remarked, then as his red setter bounded away to leap madly at the tall young man leading the hunting party, he stared – and recognition dawned.

`I say, that's the fellow who calmed my poor injured setter for me. What did he tell me his name was now ... Do you know him, Hawkins?'

`Yes, sir.' Hawkins pulled Hume aside and whispered in his ear. `It's Michael Dwyer, sir.'

`Dwyer ...' Hume went rigid with fright, his face blanched into a sickly paleness and his breathing quickened. It was on a morning such as this, in 1798, that his father had been killed while out sporting.

`Calm yourself, Mr Hume,' Hawkins said quietly. `We are in no danger.'

Hawkins motioned with his head to young Byrne of Fearbreaga, who ran up to the party of men who had turned to look into the far undergrowth, a shot rang out, then a rebel sprang into a race with Hume's setter to collect the dead game while young Byrne spoke to Dwyer.

`Well?' Hawkins asked when he came back.

`Yes, w-well?' Hume stammered, ushering the lad aside so the Englishman could not hear.

`He says to crack away, sir. They apprehend no fear of us and we should apprehend no fear of them. He says we should crack away while the game is wild and running.'

Another shot rang out. Hume trembled to his boots. The Englishman looked totally bewildered, not having been told there were Irish rebels in these parts.

A few moments later Dwyer himself strolled casually down to them, leading back the setter and leaving his party behind. This time he removed his hat.

`Good morning, Mr Hume.'

`Oh, eh, yes indeed.' Hume pretended no recognition or knowledge of the man's identity.

The Englishman looked him over, from the gaming-gun in his hand down to the buckskin breeches and boots and assumed he was some sort of land-steward. `Is it pheasant they are shooting up there?' he asked.

`Well it's surely not butterflies,' Dwyer answered in an amused drawl. `You are an Englishman?'

`I have that honour,' came the bright reply. `Here on a short holiday.'

`May I ask what you think of our country?'

Hume was astounded at the impertinence of the rebel, but the Englishman seemed quite unperturbed. `A beautiful country! Quite beautiful. Yes, I must confess I am enjoying my stay here very well so far. The air and relaxation have been a damned tonic after the hub-bub of old London.'

He smiled fondly at Hume and slapped him on the back. `No offence, Willie, old chap, but Sutton and Thetford still insist you are pigging it here in some wilderness. I'll soon put them to rights!'

Hume flushed. `Thank you, Kit, but I think that would be pointless,' he said in a resentful quiet tone.

`Devil take all those beggars in Dublin, though! Quite gave me the wrong impression when I landed. Reminded me of the London wit who said he never knew what the English beggars did with their old discarded rags, until he came to Ireland.'

`Oh we heard that jest too,' Dwyer said brightly. `But did you ever hear the response of one our Dublin wits on the matter?'

`No.' The young Englishman smiled, eager for the souvenir of gossip. `Do tell.'

`Ireland may have beggars in rags – but England has a king insane.'

`Oh I say! That's a bit below the belt.' The Englishman smiled in a very superior manner, and then suddenly relented. `Of course King George *is* completely batty – and worse – he's becoming less like a King and more like a national debt!'

He turned to Hume. `Did you know, Willie, that he's presently allowed to take one million pounds a year out of the seventeen millions that Parliament collect in taxes? *One million!* Now, as a liberal-minded man and a devout Whig –'

`Yes, eh, well,' the Member of Parliament for Wicklow looked whitely apprehensive as he looked at the rebel.

But Dwyer seemed to be enjoying the young Englishman, for strangely enough, although he hated redcoats, and hated the British Parliament, he was totally uncontaminated by any fanatical feelings of hatred towards ordinary Englishmen, rich or poor. And this detached sentiment was also felt by most of his comrades.

But William Hume didn't know that. He was sure himself and his English friend were about to be despatched at some unsuspecting moment by this rebel who only had to give the signal to his party of sharpshooters.

`Have you done much sporting?' Michael asked the genial young Englishman.

`Did a bit of grouse shooting up in Scotland. Lovely country, except for the people, of course. Very dour and grim in the best of their humours. The Scotsman who took us out as a guide had the set face of a Puritan elder and never uttered one word for the entire two days he was with us. Quite took the enjoyment out of it all.'

'Ach, you were just unlucky,' Michael told him. `Some are as bright and merry as Christmas.'

`Yes, um, well,' Hume said nervously. `Shall we seek out the pheasant?'

`A nice stag's head is what I'm after,' the Englishman exclaimed. `A red one, to stuff and put up on my wall back in England – will always remind me of you, Willie!'

`Ha ha ha ha!' Hume laughed miserably, knowing his friend had made an unfortunate gaffe.

`The red deer are never killed in this land,' Michael said quietly, `except by ignorant foreign visitors and plundering invaders.'

`What? Not kill the deer, not even one?' The Englishman made an exaggerated face of gross disbelief.

`It is an unwritten law of old,' Sergeant Hawkins explained quietly. `Ordered by Finn.'

'And who is he – some upstart of country bumpkin magistrate?'

'We are allowed to course the red deer in a chase,' young Byrne piped up solemnly, 'but it must reach no *kill* – not while poetry is our heritage and Ireland is our land,'

'Take my advice,' Michael said to the Englishman, 'and content yourself with the pheasant,'

'Oh well!' the Englishman declared good-naturedly. 'A pheasant or a peasant – I'll have to shoot and stuff something in Ireland to bring back and show what a fine shot I am.'

'Hume burst into a peal of tense laughter, bordering on hysteria. A country silence filled the pause, the lads on the hill now stood waiting to know if they should retreat away from the gaming grounds.

Michael nodded at Hawkins, tousled young Byrne's hair, then saluted Hume and his friend in farewell with a touch of his hat.

'Good sporting to you, gentlemen.'

'Oh maybe so, maybe so now,' Hume replied with a huge smile of relief as the rebel strolled away.

'A pleasant enough fellow,' declared the Englishman, still in the bliss of his ignorance. 'But a little strange, perhaps?'

Hume stiffened. 'Strange?'

'Rather lofty in his manner, I thought. Telling us not to shoot the deer and then striding off as if he was some lord of the acres.'

'Oh, they're all like that in these hill parts,' Hume assured him quickly. 'All think they are descendants of Irish kings or Gaelic lords. One has to humour them, you know, for the sake of peaceful relations.'

'Whisht, sir!' young Byrne whispered, holding up his hand. He stalked forward a few paces into the trees, and then beckoned the others to follow him. 'Stand well covered and ready,' he hissed.

The three men quietly prepared their guns, excitement boiling in their blood, then Hawkins stood well back, firmly holding the setter as all waited for what seemed a very long time while young Byrne stood with head cocked and eyes half closed. Suddenly he made a sound with his mouth like that of a pheasant cock yearning amorously for a mate.

Nothing happened, but he smiled and made the sound again, clucking loudly and seductively ...

... and out he came, along the beaten path, a great big pheasant-cock making angry noises and strutting like a furious army major ready to savage the rival making wooing calls to his wives.

Suddenly he stopped strutting and looked about him, his head stretching high out of his neck, jerking from left to right. He made an irritable noise in his throat and shook his feathers; then clucking angrily he scraped the ground furiously with one leg, preparing for battle.

From where he was concealed, young Byrne raised his catapult and let fly with an iron pellet at the same time as the Englishman fired.

`I say!' Hume cried. Good shot, Kit, old chap, good shot!' The Englishman scrambled forward and picked up the prize pheasant by the neck.

`Oh look at the size of him,' he cried, `and the plumage!' His face was beaming with radiant astonishment. `Wait till they hear it was my very first shot of the trip, what? And he'll make a wonderful stuff!'

Hawkins and young Byrne peered at the pheasant, then looked slyly at each other. Hawkins shook his head, the lad nodded agreeably. It would be very unsporting to point out that the pheasant-cock bore no bullet wound, just a small black bruise in the centre of its forehead where he had received his deathblow.

`Good work, boy,' William Hume exclaimed in delight. `Where did you learn to make a sound like that?'

`Tis an old trick,' the lad said, then smiled mischievously. `The dames will be out soon, sir, if I woo them a bit more. They'll be out looking for their lord or his rival. They'll not care which, as long as he's amorous.'

`A pair!' The Englishman cried excitedly. `Perhaps I could stuff a pair – a lord and his dame – put them in matching glass cases in the dining-room.'

`Good God man! Do you have to be in such good humour

166

all the livelong day!' Hume's control had suddenly deserted him without warning.

The Englishman stared at him, and then smiled slowly in understanding. `Willie, you old devil, don't tell me that you're jealous because I got the first kill?'

`I'm delighted you got the first kill,' Hume cried, taking out a handkerchief and mopping his brow. `But devil take it, Kit, here in Ireland any game that we kill is usually sent straight to the kitchen, not the taxidermist!'

The Englishman looked totally taken aback. `No need to get so temperamental, dear chap.' He looked about him, crestfallen. `Oh, damn it,' he said quietly, `I do hate arguing and you Irish are so good at it. Oh, I have a suggestion – let's split the difference, stuff only one, and shake hands and be friends again, what?'

Hume nodded and smiled a shade guiltily as his hand was warmly grasped.

`Good old Kit, so patient.' Hume grasped the hand tighter. `I *am* glad you came.'

Kit smiled self-consciously. `I cannot endure ill feelings between old school chums, or indeed anyone. I hope I have not offended.'

`Not intentionally, Kit, never intentionally.'

`So now, back to the game, eh?' Kit turned and flung an imperious finger towards young Byrne. `You, boy! Do that seductive noise again and make those feathered whores come strutting.'

He turned back to Hume. 'Then tonight, Willie, old chum, you and I should get gloriously drunk and find ourselves a couple of damsels who might oblige us with the pleasure of a jolly good rogering!'

Hawkins, who had just taken a gulp of whiskey from his hip-flask, choked and sprayed the contents of his mouth all over William Hume.

But William Hume didn't seem even to notice. He collapsed back against a tree and began to laugh until tears ran from his eyes.

*

As soon as his friend had returned to England, William Hume, Member of Parliament for Wicklow and Captain of the Humewood Cavalry, informed all his associates that he was planning a campaign to bring in Michael Dwyer. He made a number of half-hearted midnight raids on houses but all to no avail. Hume wrote to the Castle explaining the result.

In one house, he explained, while searching the room off the kitchen he found the bed still warm, and the family could not account satisfactorily for the person or persons who had been sleeping in it. He was convinced it was a rebel, maybe even Dwyer; but now that the country was no longer under martial law, and without definite evidence, he could do nothing to the family on mere suspicion.

He also had to live in Wicklow, Hume explained, depending on the peaceful goodwill and labour of his many tenants. He was fully persuaded that as the entire population was determined to protect Dwyer, it was impossible to arrest him.

*

Inside Dublin Castle, the new Under-Secretary of State, Alexander Marsden, found he had inherited a wide range of spies and informers from the former administration.Thomas King, the resident magistrate at Rathdrum, continued to send in his indignant reports:

> `If gentlemen like Mr. Hume, our Knight of the Shire, will temporise with rebels, what can be expected but they live publicly in that country without fear of apprehension. Dwyer walks about in open day, but seldom comes on this side of the great body of mountains.
>
> Above all the cause of Loyalty was much injured by granting a pardon to John Jackson a Yeoman who was clearly convicted of harbouring Dwyer, the consequence has been that Dwyer is as free in every Yeoman's house there (if I am rightly informed) as he can wish – his greatest place of resort is with one Morris who lives at

Boleycarrigeen. He is often at Wilson's at Knockanarigan, Jackson's, and William Murray not far from Ballinaclay, all Yeomen – I find these names upon report so often repeated that I have no doubt on the subject.'

Alexander Marsden threw down the report. He was now convinced more than ever that Michael Dwyer posed no threat to the safety of the country or government. He was simply an embarrassment. His defiance and evasion of capture had caused many red faces in military circles.

Marsden swept the reports on the Wicklow rebels aside. He was far more interested in the other reports sent to him from his network of spies on the Continent, who kept him well informed of the Irish émigré 1798 leaders now living in Napoleon's France. These were the truly dangerous men that Marsden feared and hated – Irish Protestants of the Class – politically inflamed intellectuals bent on achieving an Irish Republic modelled on the French and American system.

These were the men Marsden hated beyond measure. Their betrayal of their own superior class alone suffused him with an anger he could barely control. Their nonsensical theory that Irishmen of every religious persuasion could stand shoulder to shoulder as equals and united was more than ludicrous, it was insulting – insulting to every respectable member of the ruling class.

Rebels of the peasant farming class, like Dwyer, did have a few understandable grievances to justify their rebellious nature, but rebels of the superior class born with a silver spoon to feed their mouths had no justification for their views at all – and if any of these United émigré' leaders dared to return to Ireland, Marsden intended to see every one of them hanged for treason.

A fine lesson that would be. A perfect discouragement to any other members of the Class who might have similar notions about an American styled democracy where Johnny was considered to be as good as his Master.

Johnny as good as his Master?

Never.

Chapter Thirteen

The pretty Sarah, wife of Hugh Vesty Byrne, had grown up some fifteen miles away from Imaal in the vicinity of Rathdrum. The first time she had ever set eyes on Mary Doyle was on the night of her wedding to Michael Dwyer. The two girls had spoken very little to each other that night, for Mary had no eyes or words for anyone but her husband.

Sarah had not particularly liked the new bride that night. Sarah had looked at Mary with her shy smile and soft brown eyes and thought Michael had made the biggest mistake of his life. In truth, Mary Doyle was the loveliest girl Sarah had ever seen, but she looked fearful and doltishly dependent – qualities that filled Sarah with contempt, for although she herself was a frailly built girl, she had been as ready as any man to risk her life for liberty in 1798.

In view of all that had happened since then, Sarah smiled now at her thoughts on that night in October 1798. Mary lived a harder life than any other female in Wicklow, and over the years had proved herself in all ways admirable, bearing all her difficulties and discomforts without complaint. And she was now Sarah's dearest friend.

`Thank God they're all asleep now,' Mary murmured tiredly. `Are you coming to bed soon, Sarah?'

From where she was sitting on an old settle, Sarah looked up from her contemplation of the fire and silently nodded at the girl sitting on the edge of the bed in the dark shadows of the room, pulling a comb through the tangle of dark hair around her shoulders. Her dress was folded neatly on the back of a chair, her arms and shoulders were bare, she sat in a white petticoat which revealed the swell of full milky breasts that had recently given sleepy comfort to a suckling infant.

They were in a harbourer's house deep in Glenmalure, at a relative of Hugh Vesty's. The larger of two bedrooms had been given over to the two young women and their children, while the parents of the family willingly insisted on sleeping on a straw pallet in the small open loft above the living room.

Sarah and Mary shared the bed, while their children slept on a straw mat on the floor, and the two babies snuggled side by side under warm blankets in a big wicker laundry basket beside the bed. Like Mary, Sarah had also born three children now: Philip, Michael, and baby Rose. And like Mary, Sarah adored her husband.

Sometimes Sarah raged at Hugh Vesty against the hardness of their lives, the long separations, the pregnancies that resulted from a few nights of love that were more ecstatic because they were brief and stolen. And he would apologise sadly, and she would be filled with guilt at her outburst, for the women at least had the joy of the children, but all the time the hunt for the men went on, English regiments, militia regiments, Rathdrum and Baltinglass yeomanry; and occasionally, rebels were killed.

And therein lay the anger and the heartache. To the world at large they had only the name of rebels, but to Hugh Vesty and Michael and the people of Wicklow, they were friends with individual names, friends with mothers and fathers and sisters and brothers, some with baby children to care for.

`Sarah,' Mary whispered, `what is wrong, darling?'

Mary moved from the bed to sit on the settle and put an arm around her friend. It was not the first time they had comforted each other. Over the years the similarity of their situations had drawn them towards each other. More and more they sought out each other's company, for both knew the loneliness and desperation of being wife to a hunted rebel. Both knew the feeling of being cut off and living in a world apart from everything that was normal and secure in the general run of life. And when one or the other allowed their fears to overwhelm them, they would put their arms around each other in the way of all women seeking and giving comfort, and whatever the problem the other would whisper: `I know, I know, I have felt the same also.'

Sarah pushed back her tears and clutched Mary's warm hand. They were so different in many ways. Mary would never rage at Michael about the hardness of her life. His

171

love was all she considered, his love fulfilled her, the memory of their last time together sustained her until the next, and knowing his pride and delight in his children, she would go on bearing them happily and placidly, and in return he worshipped her like a queen.

But it seemed to Sarah that as different as she and Mary were, only with each other could they honestly speak their minds and share the burden of the struggle. Say the things a woman says only to another woman. Their friendship had grown slowly but surely, a friendship almost as deep and as solid as that shared by their two husbands; and now, beneath that friendship, both knew there was love.

`It's all a dream ...' Sarah whispered. `A dream that one day it will be all right ... and we can return with our men and babies to our farms and live in peace... but it's all a dream isn't it?'

`I don't know,' Mary confessed. `I used to dream, of a house and hearth of my own, but now I just live from day to day.'

She shrugged, then moved off the settle and knelt down to rake the ashes over the red embers of the fire. In the firelight her beauty had a wild quality, but when she turned and looked at Sarah, Sarah noticed the dark shadows of fatigue under her eyes.

`You look tired,' Sarah murmured.

Mary nodded, and gazed back at the fire. She was tired, so very tired of her nomadic life. Sometimes she wondered just how long she could carry on. She was no great heroine full of bravery and courage; she was just an ordinary girl with ordinary needs and three small children to take care of.

She had relinquished all her dreams in the days after Derrynamuck, especially her great dream of escaping with him to America. She knew he would never go, never leave Wicklow, and after Derrynamuck she had vowed that she would never again ask him to. He had his own dream which he carried before him like some eternal flame, and everything else had to be sacrificed to it. And the tragedy of it, she knew, was that his dream would never come true, no matter how many men tried to make it so. Thousands of young men had the same dream in 1798, thousands of young men who had not lived to see the closing days of that summer of rebellion, all in vain, all in vain ...

So how would it all end? She dared not think about it. She could only live from day to day, always wondering if this would be the day they brought her the news of his death, always wondering if she would ever see him alive again, and every day that she did not see him she counted as lost. He lived a constant battle, his days ending in neither victory nor defeat, and often happily with her. She no longer minded those times when he gave most of his attention to the children, for she loved the children almost as much as she loved him, and they were three more strong links in the emotional chain that bound him to her.

She shrugged, as she often did of late, an unconscious gesture of the acceptance of her life. This was it, this was how it would go on, and this was how she had chosen it .... and there was a sense of victory in that. Other women were bargained off in an arranged match and lived secure lives of loveless misery, but she had made her own choice, and despite everything, she had no regrets.

Then Mary tuned her head; her voice soft and puzzled. `Isn't it a funny thing, Sarah, how the yeomanry in Imaal and the surrounding neighbourhoods have become more friendly towards Michael? Almost every man jack of them seems to be on his side now. Do you know why?'

Sarah made a vague gesture. She was at a loss to understand it herself. Mary was right, though. Of late the Imaal yeomanry seemed as determined that Michael should remain free and uncaptured as the people were.

*

The relaxed attitude of the Imaal yeomanry was indeed a funny thing, an unexpected development, and in early spring of that year of 1803, Michael decided to ask Billy the Rock the reason why?

William Jackson had been given the name of `Billy the Rock' simply because of a conspicuously large rock that stood in the field across from his house. His son, John

Jackson and his friend Thomas Morris were the same age as Michael and the three had grown up as neighbours and friends since childhood. All three had been of a sporting turn and had spent much time in shooting and coursing over the mountains together. Such a strong attachment had sprung up between the three lads that the houses of Morris and Jackson, although Protestant, had been as open to Michael as his own home. Then the rebellion broke, sides had been chosen, and Morris and Jackson took the King's shilling in exchange for a red coat.

As he approached the house, Michael returned to his long-ago memories of John Jackson's father, Billy the Rock.

Billy the Rock – who had made him drink his first cup of whiskey, then roared with laughter to see the eyes rolling in his eleven year old head. But that was long past and best forgotten. Billy the Rock was now also a yeoman in a red coat.

Billy was a thickset man with a face that could be coarse or genial, depending on his mood. He threw back his head and laughed when Michael asked him the question about the change in attitude of many of the yeomanry.

There were three other men in William Jackson's farmhouse parlour besides Michael; his son John Jackson, Thomas Morris, and Sergeant Hawkins of the Upper Talbotstown Corps. And the fact that Michael Dwyer was here alone amongst them proved his faith and trust in them.

`Sure we're friends and neighbours,' said Billy the Rock. `Have been since you three lads were weans. Is that a good enough reason?'

Not for the realistic Michael Dwyer. `No, sir, it is not. I smell a conspiracy of some kind.' He sat back and looked at Morris and Jackson who were also sitting round the table drinking.

John Jackson and Thomas Morris had harboured Michael many times in the past eighteen months, and had been found out by spies of Thomas King. Both had been charged under court-martial with harbouring Michael Dwyer in their homes. Thomas King sat as magistrate, and evidence was produced maintaining that Thomas Morris had not only harboured Dwyer and entertained him handsomely, but had actually shared the same bed with him.

Jackson and Morris were found guilty and sentenced to five hundred lashes each, to be inflicted in stages of one hundred. Before the first hundred could be thrashed, Reverend Ryan of Donoughmore intervened. He petitioned the Castle on behalf of his two parishioners, insisting in all sincere belief that it was a trumped-up charge – as they were loyal yeomen who had fought at Hacketstown and lived in daily fear of the rebel chief, so it was ridiculous to believe they would harbour him, let alone settle down to sleep in the same bed as him!

The sentence was overruled and both were pardoned. And rumour had it that for weeks afterwards, Thomas King stumped around in purple fury muttering all kinds of abuse against the interfering ecclesiastic divine from Donoughmore.

`I can accept old friendship as a reason for you two,' Michael said to John Jackson and Thomas Morris, and even you, Billy, and even you, Sergeant Hawkins, but not the whole damned Imaal Yeomanry Corps!' He shook his head and smiled cannily. `Yes, sir, I smell a conspiracy.'

Morris and Jackson grinned. Sergeant Hawkins smiled subtly as he paired his fingernails on a seat by the window. Billy the Rock stared at Michael with a blank poker face.

`Conspiracy? You're talking crazy, boy. Every yeoman outside this house would shoot you down if they saw you.'

`Is that right?' Michael said. `Then how come two yeos from the Upper Talbotstown walked right past myself and Hugh Vesty this morning? Two of them came along the road towards the two of us, and as we closed they carried on past us with their eyes to the sky and without speaking.'

`Those men,' Billy explained in a fatherly tone, `are like us, Michael. Before the rebellion they were what you might call – neutral Protestants.'

`They're still bloody yeomen,' Michael declared. `But all seem more intent on farming their land than finding rebels lately.'

175

Thomas Morris, reaching for the bottle on the table, said: `Tell him the truth, Billy. He'll work it out for himself soon enough, seeing as he smells something already.'

Michael looked at Billy the Rock who sat back and folded his arms. There was silence for several seconds, and then Billy explained.

`You've become the prize goose that lays the golden eggs for the yeos, boy. Attempting to capture you is a lucrative business. Very few now believe that you can be taken. But if by some miracle you were to be captured, the present standard of living for most yeomen would suddenly drop, and a good source of income would come to an end. Every yeoman would be put back on occasional small expenses – but while you remain out and free – they remain on full incentive and full pay.'

Michael stared at each man in the room. `My God ...' he said slowly. `You are all entirely disreputable.'

`So are you,' Billy reminded him gently. `You're the most disreputable man in Wicklow.'

`I was born disreputable,' Michael said. 'But you lot were born part of the privileged class – and now you are officers of the bloody law!'

`We tell you why most of the heat is off you, boy,' Billy declared. `And is it complaining you are?'

Michael grinned. `Not a bit.

He sat back in his chair as he thought about it. `But it's a bit hard to take – after years of defeating the yeos, I now find that I'm helping to make them rich.'

`A fact of life they've come to realise,' Billy said logically. `If they can't make money out of Dwyer with a share of the reward for his capture, then make it another way by helping him to stay free.'

`It's disgusting!' Michael said indignantly.

Billy the Rock threw back his head and laughed. `But now, in all fairness, it's not only the money. Many fear reprisals from the people if they did manage to capture you; and apart from that, since the Union, most feel little allegiance to this new government.'

And you will still have to be extremely careful,' Morris

said in sudden seriousness. `The fanatical Rathdrum and Baltinglass Corps are still pledged to your murder. Their minds are so poisoned with sectarian hatred, they would hunt you on no pay at all. And the English regiments and Scottish Highlanders are duty bound to take you if they find you, and kill you if they have to.'

Michael gave a smile of wry amusement. `I have heard that before.'

`Then there's the bounty-hunters,' John Jackson said. `And there's never been a shortage of avaricious fiends who are happy to take bribes from the secret service funds and become spies on their own people and co-religionists. Remember Thomas Halpin?'

`Halpin!' Sergeant Hawkins snorted contemptuously and came over from the window to refill his glass. `Halpin testified against a man he claimed to have seen standing sentry for rebels and handing a gun to them. And the man was convicted and sent to the prison at New Geneva, even though the magistrate, Thomas King, had evidence that at the time Halpin was supposed to have seen the accused doing all this, the accused had been physically locked up in prison, and had only an hour earlier been released.'

`Thomas Halpin...' Michael's eyes had turned dark. `He's the proof that St Patrick never did drive all the snakes out of Ireland. But if that reptile ever slithers across my vision, I'll give him more than a trip to New Geneva.'

`One other thing,' Thomas Morris said. `It's now common knowledge, Michael, even amongst the English regiments, that Mary Doyle's children are your children.'

`Mary Dwyer,' Michael corrected softly. `Her name is Mary Dwyer. And has been since 1798.'

*

A week later intelligence was sent to Michael informing him that Thomas Halpin had returned to Wicklow and had spent the past five nights at the barracks, during which time he had identified three young men as being three of those rebels he had seen in the cave on the Keadeen Mountains.

Michael arranged for several people to watch the barracks

and let him know as soon as the informer came out. He then learned from a friendly yeoman that Halpin had also returned for the purpose of setting Dwyer for a capture, and had spent the past four nights, accompanied by two of the militia in disguise, and disguised himself as a wigged and bonneted woman, going around the taverns with a good deal of money in his pocket with which to pay the people for information about – "her long lost cousin," Michael Dwyer.

`Did the people take the money?' Michael asked.

`Sure they did, and they gave Halpin plenty of information, about everything and everyone, except Michael Dwyer.'

Then, on the sixth morning of Halpin's visit to Wicklow, a youth ran breathlessly up to Michael with the information that had passed along the road from farmer to farmer, and over the hills from shepherd to shepherd – Thomas Halpin, now back in his own clothes, had been escorted from the barracks as far as the road leading up to Dublin, and was now continuing his journey alone.

Michael set off at a sprint, running like the wind and jumping over ditches and skidding down hills until he came to the Dublin road and eventually got a view of the informer ... swinging along for all the world as if he had never perjured any young men to the hell-hole of New Geneva and slavery in a Prussian mining camp; and now had tried again to set up Dwyer for a capture.

When Halpin was only fifty perches ahead, he turned and spied his pursuer. He let out a yelp and jumped into a run and a vigorous chase commenced until Michael was easily running down his game.

Halpin withdrew a pistol, turned and fired wildly over his shoulder, then dropped the gun as he scurried on as swiftly as a rabbit.

When Halpin was well within range, Michael stopped, raised the gun, aimed at Halpin's leg and pulled the trigger – and the world blew up before his eyes in a thundering burst of red-hot pain as the gun exploded in his hand.

He reeled over to a tree in blind agony. Then through the haze of his pain he saw Halpin coming slowly back to him.

`You're dead,' Halpin cried in astonishment, looking at the blood spreading over Dwyer's shirt. `Holy Jakers, but you're dead this time, Dwyer! And listen, won't it be me that collects the reward!'

Halpin was almost jigging with joy. Michael turned away from him, his brow pressed against the tree; taking deep breaths as if summoning the strength for one last attack. With one hand he fumbled at the pistol in his cross-belt, remembered it was unloaded, opened it, and then plucked a bullet from the cartridge-pouch in his waist belt.

Peering closer, Halpin suddenly saw that it was only Dwyer's left hand, pressed against his chest, that was injured, and his right was fingering a pistol. Then Halpin saw him spit the bullet into the barrel and almost jumped out of his shoes.

Halpin had run so fast he was well out of pistol-range when Michael eventually moved away from the tree and aimed, then slowly lowered the gun and watched with half-closed eyes as the reptile disappeared from view, towards Dublin.

He turned and looked at the ground and the fallen rifle which had blown up in his hand; the barrel had burst at the moment of firing.

He shoved the pistol back in his belt and turned back towards Imaal, taking deep breaths and walking slowly until he had mastered his pain and his demeanour became normal again.

He walked for some time over the lonely hills and at length he saw Lawler the tailor coming towards him. Lawler instantly jumped to a salute, and then stared at the blood on the captain's shirt.

`Do you have your tailor's kit with you?' Michael asked.

`Never without it,' Lawler answered in puzzlement, holding up his bag.

`Scissors?'

`Aye.'

Michael held up his blood-soaked left hand, the thumb had been shattered and was joined to the hand only by a thread of skin.

`Then would you mind cutting this away,' Michael said, `because it looks like it can be no further use to me.'

Lawler inspected the hand, which was bloody and slightly burned but generally undamaged except for the thumb, which was beyond repair; he took out his scissors and removed it.

Michael took deep breaths and closed his eyes as Lawler lifted spare strips of linen from his bag and began to carefully dress the hand in a neat bandage.

`God sakes,' Lawler tutted, `but you must be in agony. And what about that blood on your shirt?'

`Just blood from the hand,' Michael assured him, and then in response to Lawler's questions told him about Halpin and the bursting gun.

*

When Thomas Halpin reached Dublin he rushed straight to the Castle and into Major Sirr's office in the lower courtyard. He explained everything that had happened to Dublin's Chief of Police who had sent him down to Wicklow on such a hazardous mission.

`I went in search of the rebel, as agreed, and after five nights without success I spied him this morning, sitting alone and dreaming in the sun and I closed in; but as I cocked my pistol, Dwyer took to his heels without even knowing who was near him.'

`A cautious man!' Major Sirr sat curling one of his moustaches around his finger. `Took to his heels without even knowing who was near him?'

`But I pursued him, Major Sirr, I did that! I fired several shots and chased him across two rivers and countless hills, and then I lost him. I would have carried on the pursuit but for the fatigue of the long hunt and the fact that Dwyer can run all day without missing a breath.'

Major Sirr sat thoughtful; he uncurled his moustache, and then curled it again.

`I did my best, sir,' Halpin said plaintively. `I did as much as any human could. But it wouldn't be safe for me to return to Wicklow ever again, not even as a witness in a trial.'

Major Sirr was deeply disappointed at the failure of the mission, but Halpin had done his best, and a man could do no more than that.

A sudden idea occurred to Major Sirr. A broad smile came on his face as he voiced it. `You did your best, Halpin. And for that you deserve a reward.'

`I do?' Halpin was all eyes in surprise.

`Indeed you do. I have a sudden notion to take you onto my staff.'

`But I am on your staff, Major Sirr,' Halpin said in a puzzled tone. `I have been for a long time now, as a spy on the Dublin sedition-mongers in the taverns.'

`And so I am offering you promotion.' Major Sirr enjoyed being benevolent to his minions. He sat laughing soundlessly like a panting bulldog. `How would you like to wear a red coat and white breeches and have all Dublin cowering at your feet?'

Halpin was astonished into speechlessness, and then finally he managed to stammer a response.

`A militiaman?'

Major Sirr nodded.

Halpin seemed overcome. He staggered to a chair and sat down, overwhelmed by his amazing good fortune. Then on an impulse of wild joy he fell to his knees and shuffled across the floor until he was kneeling before the Major and kissing his hand.

`I'll not let you down, Major Sirr, sir! I'll be the best militiaman that ever marched the streets of Dublin so I will! The first blatherumskite I hear singing a seditious song I'll lock in manacles and throw in the grid without mercy!'

The major looked at the man grovelling at his feet and resisted a sudden urge to kick him. Then he remembered all his good work at the Wicklow trials and his efforts in pursuing the notorious Dwyer, and gently patted him on the head instead.

`Very good. Very good. Lock them in manacles and throw them in the grid without mercy. That's what I like to hear from my men. That's the kind of enthusiasm that gets results. But now, before you rise off your knees, my good man, whip off your neckcloth and give my boots a spit and rub, will you?'

Halpin looked down at the Major's dull boots, and then up at his face.

`It would be an honour, Major Sirr, sir!' he said with an emotional quiver in his voice, and then he whipped off his neckcloth and within seconds he was spitting and polishing away.

Chapter Fourteen

For two weeks Michael went around with his arm in a sling, during which time Mary tended and changed the dressings on the wound every night. By the end of the third week he had discarded the sling, and at a month's end he had taught himself to handle his guns as if the left thumb had never been lost. But still, the loss annoyed him.

`The Ninety-Eight Rebellion and almost five years on the run and I never suffered an injury until now. And I did it myself! That's what annoys me so.'

`It was not your fault,' Mary said defensively, `it was the fault of the gun.'

`The gun was mine so the fault is mine,' he told her. `But do you know the worst thing about it? Halpin saw my injured hand. Halpin saw the thumb hanging off beyond repair.'

`So?'

`It makes me more easy to identify, even in disguise. Because now the soldiery will be keeping their eyes open for a man who is minus a thumb on his left hand.'

Mary made no answer and showed no sign of anxiety. Almost every yeoman on this side of the mountains seemed now to be on Michael's side, and she was nursing a secret hope that before long they would be able to start living a normal life again, in the peace of their own Imaal.

She was also beginning to think that Michael, like herself, was tired of the struggle. He had the heart of a lion and didn't know the meaning of fear, but more and more he seemed to want to be with his children, and more and more he had started longing for the land ... the eternal land that grips a man's soul with a passion that never cools.

This past spring she had noticed the change in him, noticed how keenly his eye had been watching, not for the militia, but the weather; sun, wind, and rain, and how it affected the growth of the crops, the behaviour of the animals, and she knew memories of his youth were arousing in him, memories of the days when the land was his mistress and his whole being moved in tune with the seasons of nature; and it was as if a new hope was growing in him too. How would it all end? She wondered.

*

The following morning Michael was dallying with his second favourite girl on the grass outside Cullen's house. She ran towards him on her little four-year old legs, carefully cupping the ladybird in her dimpled hands. He bent down, his eyes opening wide with awe as she let him peek at the red and black beetle sitting motionlessly on her palm.

`Make a wish, Mary-Anne,' he whispered.

`I wish ... I wish...' she let out a ripple of excited laughter that mingled with the sun on the grass. `What will I wish?'

`Wish that one day you will own acres and acres of land.'

She looked at him with dark disappointed eyes which were almost hidden by the mop of black curls falling around her face. `Don't want that wish,' she said sulkily.

`Then wish for whatever you do want.'

She peeped in at the ladybird in her cupped hands before throwing back her head and singing in a high childish voice. `*I wish I was a blue bud that flies over the twees!*'

Mary was standing at the door watching them. She saw him laughing, then waited for his answer when their daughter asked solemnly, `When will my wish come twoo, Dada, when?'

She saw him look up at the sky for his answer – then suddenly rise to his feet and stand to stare at the ridge where Hugh Vesty, John Mernagh, and Martin Burke had appeared, all moving to jump down onto the path below.

Then she saw him reach down and swing up the child and carry her towards the three men whose voices reached Mary, though not all their words.

`... Robert Emmet is back from France ... A number of the United Irish émigré leaders are back with him... another attempt for liberty is going to be made ... Miles Byrne has joined Emmet, and now Emmet wants to meet you. He sent Arthur Devlin and James Hope, they're waiting in the care of others to talk with you ... three miles back away ...'

Mary turned back into the house, clutching her arms around her waist as if the warmth of the sun had suddenly gone behind the clouds and left her feeling chilly. Her eyes were dark and moody and there was despair in them. How would it all end? It would never end!

*

She asked him no questions, not even when he returned from his meeting with the two visitors and told her that he was going to Dublin, nor when he returned from Dublin, for she knew that he would not tell her anything worth knowing anyway. He didn't even know that she had overheard his conversation with the men when they had brought him Emmet's summons.

All through that month of May and the following month of June she sought no explanation or made any complaint when he spent less time than usual with her. There seemed to be a great deal more activity amongst the young men of Imaal, but it could just have been the onset of summer. Young men always gathered to parley and frisk and jest on the hills in summertime. Even the older men sat on the walls and talked until after the midnight hour; the women too, young and old. The whole world came out of doors when summer's heat was in the air.

And her brain became hot and weary as she shut her mind to the hurricane that was slowly unfurling its cyclone in preparation to blast her life into chaos again. She knew it was coming, just as surely as the shepherd knows a storm is moving closer in the distance, even though the thunder is still too far away for him to hear, yet in his bones he knows it's coming.

Her sleep became troubled. She had terrifying dreams that woke her in the night. But in daylight she shut her mind and sought refuge within the shelter of her outer placidity, refusing to allow words of discussion to give substance to her fears. Only when a dream is manifest in words does it take on the possibility of reality.

She pretended not to hear him when he told her he was

185

going to Dublin again, and would not be back in Wicklow for a number of days. She pretended greater absorption in the corduroy breeches she was making for him from the roll of cloth her father had acquired in Wicklow Town for her. She made all her family's clothes, as good as any dressmaker or tailor in Dublin.

She lifted her head after he had gone, and thought about Dublin ... and her thoughts rarely strayed from Dublin for the next three days.

*

It was not to Dublin that Michael went, but a lonely country house on the outskirts, on Butterfield Lane in Rathfarnham.

There were ten men sitting around the table in the dining room, a number of maps and papers on the table, but only one of the men was speaking, pausing when a young woman entered the room carrying candelabra and set it on the table.

The light flared up, making Michael realise the evening had grown dark without him noticing it. In the golden glow of the candles he looked up at the face of the girl, Anne Devlin, his cousin, whose family had moved from Wicklow to County Dublin.

He watched her as she moved the candelabra nearer to the papers on the table, and then sat down again in the vacant chair beside the black-haired, brown-eyed young man who was her new master. She settled herself beside Robert Emmet as if she was his second-in-command and not his servant.

Robert Emmet was a Protestant of the ruling class, and the youngest revolutionary officer to sit on the secret executive council in 1798. His brother Thomas Emmet had been one of the founders of the United Irish movement with Theobald Wolfe Tone and Thomas Russell. He was twenty-five years old, had an extremely intelligent face, yet his face wore none of the arrogance so characteristic of many revolutionaries.

He saw Emmet glance at Anne only briefly, before returning his eyes to the paper on the table covered in his

186

own handwriting, and continued reading the words aloud in his soft, cultured voice.

> `People of Ireland, you are now called upon to show the world that you are competent to take your place among nations; that you have a right to claim the world's recognizance of you as an independent country, by the only satisfactory proof you can furnish of your capability of gaining your independence – by your wresting it from England with your own hands. We war not against property, we war against no religious sect, we war not against past opinions or prejudices, we war against English dominion.'

The men around the table murmured their comments, but Michael kept his eyes fixed on the young general of the secret army who had calmly read the proclamation of revolution as if it were a solemn prayer.

Then Emmet's dark eyes, with their serious intellectual expression, were looking straight at Michael.

`You appear very thoughtful, Captain. Is there anything in the draft proclamation which you do not agree with?'

`I agree with everything in the proclamation,' Michael replied quietly. `But... I would like to hear the last few lines again.'

Emmet looked down, then repeated: `We war not against property, we war against no religious sect, we war not against past opinions or prejudices, we war against English dominion.'

`So, this time,' Michael said, `they will not be able to say our fight is a religious one.'

`Oh, but our fight *is* a religious one,' Emmet said firmly. `We fight that all of us may have our own country; and that done, each of us shall have our own religion.'

`A new Jerusalem,' Michael said wryly.

`A new Ireland,' Emmet said with a smile.

*

By the middle of July, Mary's nerves were ready to snap.

She was sitting by the fire alone when Michael entered. The children were asleep in the bedroom; Cullen had not returned from his eight mile round trip to the tavern.

`I want you to tell me,' she snapped, quivering with tension.

`Then you should have asked me to tell you,' he said gently.

`Why didn't you tell me anyway?'

`I thought you preferred not to know. That is the impression you have given.'

`I know about Emmet. Have you agreed to join him in his rebellion?'

`A mutual reliance has been agreed between us,' he admitted.

`You will go to Dublin for it?'

`No, we are not to stir until Dublin has made its move.'

She stood up and stoked the fire, then remained staring at it.`It is true, then?' she whispered. `We are on the eve of another break-out?'

`No, it is not planned for some months yet; not until the autumn, sometime in November.'

The silence lasted for at least a minute, and then he moved and put his hands on her shoulders. With a sigh she turned and moved inside his arms. They leaned one against the other in silence, a calm moment of love without passion, and she relaxed in the solidity of their love and forgot the uncertain future ahead ... summer had not yet reached its zenith, and autumn was a long way off.

*

Two weeks later, on the evening of Sunday 24th July, a number of breathless young men running at speed arrived in the vicinity of Imaal. One was John O'Niell, who had moved to open his own dairy business in Dublin after marrying Michael's sister Cathy. Dark night had fallen when they were brought to a harbourer's house at Rostyduff, and gave Michael the news.

`Emmet was betrayed! All our plans are broken! The whole business erupted months before time and Dublin was in chaos last night. But it's clear Emmet had traitors in his camp. Now it's all over bar the shouting and the manhunts.'

`Where is Emmet now?' Michael asked. `Do you know?'

`Aye, he's where the most of us are now – on the run.'

The next few days found Michael constantly out on the hills with his principal men, keeping a sharp look-out for the arrival of news from Dublin, and news of Emmet, who was still in the country.

In the long silences on the sun-shadowed hills, Michael found himself thinking a great deal about Robert Emmet, a young aristo, polite and trusting, who believed fervently in the words that his fellow Protestant, Theobald Wolfe Tone, had spoken only five years earlier at his trial; that the aims of the United Irishmen were: `To assert the independence of our country, to unite the whole people of Ireland, to abolish the memory of past dissensions and to substitute the common name of Irishmen in place of the denominations of Protestant and Catholic.'

Emmet had passionately believed that was possible. And Michael too had dreamed of being a part of it when it came to pass. Dreams of young men, dreams on wings, chasing the mythical phoenix of victory, the phoenix rising in glory from the embers of defeat, the symbol of the United Irishmen.

Now Emmet, too, was just another bird in flight, fleeing from the hawks, and Michael was hoping that he would fly to the hills of Imaal, and to the protection of himself and his men.

But Emmet never came; then events took a turn that had Michael Dwyer looking out for no one but himself and his Wicklow comrades; and Mary knew that all her worst fears were about to be realised.

*

The alarm created in Dublin Castle by Emmet's exposed conspiracy was great, especially when it was revealed that seventeen counties had been prepared to join him in rebellion. The powers of government went into action immediately. Martial law was proclaimed; the Act of Habeas

Corpus suspended, and hundreds randomly arrested and imprisoned without charge.

Then the Castle turned its attention from Dublin to Wicklow. They knew that by some accident or default, Michael Dwyer had been in Wicklow and taken no part in the trouble in Dublin, but they also knew that he must have been privy to Emmet's conspiracy and encouraged him. Their biggest fear now was an invasion by the French who had promised to support Emmet, and if a French force were to land, and Michael Dwyer was still at liberty, they decided he could constitute a threat to the whole country. They became convinced of this when an officer of the 38th Regiment wrote to Under-Secretary Marsden.

> `Wicklow is quiet for the present, although it is well know to the best informed that Dwyer could, at half an hour's warning, draw to his standard nineteen out of every twenty of the inhabitants.'

The Chief Secretary William Wickham also read the letter, and then placed it before the Viceroy, Lord Hardwicke.

`The capture of Michael Dwyer alone would make the difference of an army to us,' Wickham said.

Lord Hardwicke agreed. `If this man were to remain in the fastness of Wicklow at the time of a French landing, there is no doubt that a formidable insurrection requiring a powerful force to put it down will instantly break out there.'

'He has to be captured and brought in,' Wickham said. 'It's now imperative.'

Lord Hardwicke agreed. 'I am also still very uneasy about Cork, Limerick, and Kerry, but Michael Dwyer is my nightmare. From the information we have received, there is no doubt that if things had gone to plan, he would have raised his gun and his men to assist Emmet.'

Three days later, Lord Hardwicke issued a Government Proclamation, which stated that:

Michael Dwyer stands charged with repeated acts of High Treason and with furthering the Rebellion that lately broke out in Ireland.

Five Hundred pounds was offered for his apprehension and a further five hundred for information leading thereto. One hundred pounds was offered for information in respect of those aiding, abetting, harbouring or concealing the said Michael Dwyer, and all were warned of the dire results that would follow any attempts to aid or conceal him.

A general order was sent out to all officers commanding the military forces in Wicklow to *'punish according to martial law not only Dwyer himself but anyone assisting or sheltering him.'*

Lord Hardwicke then sent a copy of the Proclamation to the Home Secretary in London.

> `I beg leave to send you enclosed the copy of the Proclamation issued on Tuesday offering large rewards for apprehending Michael Dwyer the noted rebel, who still maintains himself in the fastness of the County of Wicklow, and has acquired an extraordinary ascendancy over the inhabitants of those parts.
>
> I am in great hopes that if neither the rewards offered in the Proclamation, nor the threats by which they are accompanied, should achieve success, that some more active measures which I have concerted with the Commander of His Majesty's Forces will tend ultimately to secure this man and enable me to bring him to punishment.'

*

When, after a month, the proclamation brought no results or information, a military offensive against Dwyer was put into action.

Large detachments of soldiers and spies were sent to the mountains to try and trap him. Soldiers in twos and threes were free-quartered all over Wicklow in the houses of suspected harbourers, and every member of the house subjected to close scrutiny. They could not take out a vessel for water, nor go any distance from the house without being watched.

When this offensive also brought no results, the Castle put their final plan into action.

Michael's mother was feeding hens in the yard when the hammering of hooves made her turn and look towards the bohereen that led to the home fields.

`God in Heaven...' she whispered.

Within minutes the farmhouse at Eadstown was surrounded by soldiers on horse and foot and every member of the family arrested, including Michael's mother. She was sent, accompanied by Maíre and Etty, under military escort to Dublin and all three were confined in the women's section of Kilmainham Gaol.

Michael's three brothers, James, Peter, and John, were sent to the hold of a prison ship lying in Dublin Bay. His father was sent to the prison at New Geneva, near Passage, in Waterford.

At the same time the Doyle's house at Knockandarragh was also being surrounded.

By that evening every relative of Michael Dwyer, and several of his neighbours, had been arrested and sent to prison. But the one person who eluded the search – the one person they had hoped to arrest and use as their main hostage and weapon against Dwyer – was his wife.

From dawn to dawn the soldiers searched every habitation, no matter how isolated, even John Cullen's house at Knockgorragh, but Mary Dwyer could not be found.

In the days that followed, the military officers had no option but to report to the Castle that she was proving as elusive as Dwyer himself. Wherever he had her concealed, it was beyond their reach.

The Castle was disappointed, but not without hope. They waited eagerly for Dwyer's response to the arrest of his family and relatives. But the only response they received was from his twenty-five-year old brother James, imprisoned in a little sloop of war in Dublin Bay, who sent a communication to the government, challenging them to bring his mother to trial – for the heinous crime for which she had been arrested and imprisoned – that of being the mother of a son who would not surrender or allow himself to be arrested.

The challenge went unheeded.

Chapter Fifteen

Winter came early to Wicklow. By the end of November the country lay under deep snow, making travel for the military parties almost impossible.

The soldiers remained free-quartered in the houses, wrapped up against the cold as they doggedly followed the inhabitants in and out; but a halt had been forced on the searches through the valleys and mountains bound by snow.

Lord Hardwicke was getting desperate. On November 22nd the House of Commons had debated the recent trouble in Ireland, and the opposition party did not hesitate to scathingly point out the logic of a government that dismissed Emmet's rebellion as nothing more than a contemptible riot, yet needed the powers of martial law to keep the country under control.

In France, Napoleon made no secret of his sympathy for the Irish, declaring that his heart was deeply grieved by the stories that were reaching him from Ireland. Persecution was widespread, but the spirit of the Irish people was unyielding.

He announced in Paris that he would never make peace with England until the independence of Ireland was recognised.

The French journalists took up the theme, and made great satire of a British government that had shouted their horror at the executions on the guillotine during the French Revolution – yet considered the recent public executions of young Irishmen in Dublin's Thomas Street to be quite civilised and found no horror in the fact that the city's dogs had been seen lapping up the blood.

The words of the radical Englishman Thomas Paine were repeated for the benefit of all.

> `The heads stuck upon pikes which remained for years upon Temple Bar in London, differed nothing in horror to the scene from those carried about on pikes in Paris: yet this was done by the English government. Lay then the axe to the root

– and first teach GOVERNMENTS humanity!'

The cobblestones of Thomas Street in Dublin truly had been soaked in blood. Lord Hardwicke's *conciliatory* administration in Ireland had lost all credibility; he realised his administration needed a propaganda victory to restore it.

To this political end, he looked again towards Wicklow and the intractable rebel who would not allow himself to be arrested.

A relative of Dwyer's, an aunt, was released from Kilmainham and given a letter for Michael Dwyer bearing his Excellency's seal. The letter urged him to throw himself upon the *mercy* of the government, and surrender. The terms of surrender offered were a safe retreat out of Ireland with his immediate family.

Lord Hardwicke waited, as the letter was no doubt passed from hand to hand along the mysterious trail that led to Dwyer. He was willing to rid Ireland of Michael Dwyer at any price. He wrote to the Home Secretary in London, explaining the reasons for his offer of surrender terms.

> `I offered him a retreat from the Kingdom with his family, a measure which I thought right to take, on account of the little hope I have been advised to entertain of apprehending him by any ordinary means. And the fact of him having taken an active part in the late Insurrection seemed to present a fair pretext for removing from the country a very dangerous rebel, by an act of leniency.*
>
> *He thought proper, however, to reject my offer, trusting, as I have reason to believe, to his being able to make a new effort on the landing of the French, an event which he is taught to consider as very near, and represents to his associates as certainly to take place before the close of winter.'*

*

The falling snow was Michael's greatest ally. While it

continued to fall he was able to move swiftly across the mountains. When it lay on the ground smooth and ordered he was forced to take the precaution of defacing his footsteps as he went.

He had spent a long time turning over in his mind Hardwicke's terms of surrender. For Mary's sake he felt he should have considered it even longer, but he knew that he could never accept the offer, for it made no provision for his principal men. How could he make terms for himself alone, and desert the men who had faithfully stood by him throughout? Men like Hugh Vesty, John Mernagh, and Martin Burke.

The imprisonment of his family and relatives had shaken him badly. For a time he had descended into utter despair at the thought of his mother in prison. Then his sister Cathy, who now lived in Dublin and had not been arrested, sent a message to say his mother did not want him to play the Castle's game on her account. Maíre and Etty had given Cathy the same message.

He was torn by his responsibility to them as well as to his men, and although he showed no outward signs of it, the whole situation left him depressed and confused, torn in all directions between emotional ties to his family and his friends. The only thing he was certain of was that no redcoat would ever lay hands on his wife and children, and no redcoat would take him.

His friends in the villages knew how difficult his situation had become, but to his surprise it was his Protestant acquaintances who offered to do anything they could to help him, risking imprisonment as they did so.

He had accepted Billy the Rock's offer to harbour Mary and the children, for no soldier would ever think of looking for her in the house of a staunch Protestant yeoman like William Jackson. She had stayed with Billy throughout the weeks the military had searched for her, and Billy had shielded her well, but now that the search was off, she was back in the wilderness with John Cullen at Knockgorragh.

Michael himself withdrew to the most inaccessible parts of the mountains with his friends, determined to avoid capture at all costs by refusing to sleep in any house, not even Cullen's. The weather was severe and the snow deep; but the cold, he told himself, would do no more than harden his determination to beat his enemy, every man jack of them.

As always in winter, the rebels had separated to make the best they could for themselves, but ten men remained in hiding with Michael in a cave near Oakwood. Eight of them lay deep in the heart of the cave, quite warm as they slept around the heat of a brazier, while Michael and Hugh Vesty were out in the cold dawn fishing for breakfast.

There had been a snowstorm in the night, piling the snow in great heaps on the banks. They crouched at the edge of a small lake which was frozen over but for the large hole they broke in it with the butts of their rifles.

`It's a good thing fish are notoriously deaf,' Michael said, and Hugh Vesty laughed; and once the activity under the water had settled down again, both set to the task, and after an hour five fish lay on the ice.

`That'll do,' Hugh said, shivering. `They're big enough to give a decent- sized half apiece to every man.'

Late in the afternoon Michael set off to see Mary and his children. Hugh Vesty advised against it, but he was shrugged aside.

`Sure look at him!' Laurence O'Keefe shook his head as Michael trudged away through the snow. `The man is crazy. Why does he have to keep checking on them all the time?'

`It's easy for you to talk,' Hugh Vesty snapped. `You have neither chick nor child to worry about. You have only yourself.'

`Well you have three children too, Hugh Vesty,' argued O'Keefe, `but I don't see you venturing across the mountains at all times of the day and night to check on them like he does.'

`Because, you bloody fool, I'm not the man the military are bent on catching. My wife and children are safe enough, but Michael's mother and father and brothers and sisters are all now in prison. Mary's family too. All hostages. But the Castle knows – and Michael knows – that if they were to get his wife or even one of his children, then they have him!'

*

Wrapped up well against the cold, Michael trudged through the white wilderness and green pine forests in the direction of Knockgorragh. His black greatcoat, woollen scarf around his face, and hat pulled low over his brow, all helped to keep the bitter cold from cutting into him, as well as obscuring his identity; although there was not another soul to be seen across the panorama of white mountains. As he slid down the slopes he glanced up at the fleecy sky, darkening in the east, and knew it would be snowing again before nightfall.

He travelled southwest past the Three Lakes, round Table Mountain and into the Glen of Imaal.

At the ridge above Cullen's house he paused, and stared in surprise at a hunched figure shuffling away from the house, muffled against the cold. He stood in silence, and was even more surprised to see the figure making tracks not down to the lowlands and habitations, but up towards the uninhabited mountains.

`Father...'

The parish priest of Imaal glanced up, and then sang out his usual greeting. `Musha, Michael, are you alive yet?'

`I am, Father,' Michael responded in kind. `Are you?'

`More or less,' the priest replied. `More than tomorrow and less than yesterday.'

`What are you doing here?'

`Come down and I will tell you,' the priest called.

Michael made the jump down on the soft snow, glancing over the priest's shoulder towards the house. `Is all well inside?'

The priest nodded. `As well as can be expected.' Clouds of breath issued from his mouth in the chill air. `But now, it's glad I am that Providence sent you down here, for I was on my way up to find you.'

Michael pulled down the wool of his scarf. `Up the mountains?' His voice was incredulous.

`Up the mountains?' the priest confirmed. `And no doubt climbing on my knees before I found you.'

198

'You would never have found me,' Michael informed him. 'But why did you want to?'

The priest glanced back at the house and saw old man Cullen peering through the window. 'Come over to the barn,' he said urgently. 'What I have to say is for your ears alone.'

Michael blinked, half nodded, then found himself following the old priest over to the barn. As he neared the house he looked at Cullen by the window and shrugged his bafflement. Cullen shrugged back, then quickly made the sign of the cross over himself with one hand by way of warning, and Michael instantly knew that despite his warm greeting, the priest was on the warpath.

Inside the barn the priest sat down on a bale of straw and Michael stood watching him as he loosened his muffler.

'So,' Michael said warily, 'why were you prepared to tramp through all the snow and miles to find me?'

'To persuade you to surrender.'

Again Michael looked at him incredulously. 'You must be having another brainstorm, I'm thinking.'

'Surrender, Michael,' the priest urged. 'It is the best thing now.'

'You must be crazy! Do you think I've spent over five years holding out against the army and the yeomanry just to surrender because you think I should? Go home, Father, before you catch your death of cold.'

The priest looked at his angry face with tired eyes, then clasped his hands on his lap and spoke slowly and deliberately.

'I did not come to argue with you, Michael, I came to reason with you. It was last week that John Cullen told me about Lord Hardwicke's offer, and I thanked God for it. No man could be as lucky as you, I thought to myself. Whether you make your own luck, or you are charmed as the people say, I do not know. All I know is that at the close of summer the government were obliged to enter into a system of example by the brutal execution of young Robert Emmet in order to convince the world the Irish could be controlled under their Imperial hand. But now that the blood of the sacrificial lamb has been spilled, they need another example, this time of their *mercy*. And so they have chosen you as their scapegoat.'

The priest nodded. `Yes, yes, the sacrificial lamb and the scapegoat, both have their uses. The scapegoat, in case you didn't know, was named after the goat which, in ancient Jewish religious custom, was allowed to escape into the wilderness after the high priest had symbolically laid all the sins of the people upon it.'

`But I'm no goat, scape or otherwise,' Michael said coldly. `I'm a man, and as a man I shall continue to do what I think is right. And neither you nor the Castle will persuade me different.'

`But a man must always be ready to consider the necessity of change if he wishes to survive,' the priest continued reasonably. `And you are a survivor. You have proved that time and time again. The Castle know you are a survivor, and so for their own purposes they offer you certain survival.'

`I've survived well enough with their hindrance,' Michael said dismissively. `I'll continue to survive without their help.'

The priest continued reasonably. `It would be wrong for me or anyone to ascribe your attitude to the mere wantonness of youth or the intoxication of vanity. In the first instant, you are no longer a youth, you are twenty-nine years old, almost thirty, a father or three children. In the latter instant, you have been known to be intoxicated by the beauty of a woman and the imbibing of spirits during a celebratory frolic, but never by your own esteem. So, deprived of the wantonness of youth or the intoxication of vanity, the only reason left for your refusal to surrender is downright bloody-mindedness!'

`Wait a minute,' Michael said. `I don't believe this. When atrocities were committed on the people of Wicklow during the Rebellion and the years following it, who did they look to for protection? When the militia sallied out to give you one more flogging for the hell of it, who stopped them? *We did!* Who gave the people a small sense of self-respect because some of their own were still holding out a resistance against all the odds? *We did!*'

'Yes, Michael, you have served your cause well. You fought gallantly in the Rebellion of 1798, and throughout the aftermath you and your comrades were the only safeguard the local people had in the face of such terrible acts of savagery – and now you are regarded as a hero. Your exploits are already part of local legend. You have become a heroic symbol of bravery and defiance – but the time has come to stop being a hero -- and be the *man* that you say you are.'

Michael studied the pale and aged face of the priest. 'I'd not be much of a man if I let them beat me now, and humbly surrendered.'

'For God's sake, what can you possibly hope to achieve by staying out?'

'Freedom.'

'Indeed. Your own freedom? Or your country's freedom?'

'I have the first, the second will come.'

'The devil it will – not in my lifetime and not in yours. The men in ninety-eight tried it, Emmet tried it, but generation after generation of men will keep trying and dying before the Bell of Freedom ever rings in Ireland.'

'Defeat is not always wrong!' Michael cried. 'Even by trying we achieve a measure of victory. All I have ever fought for is the natural and basic rights of man. The right to own our own farms. The right to live in peace and be able to provide a decent living for our families, not hand the greatest measure of our crops over to an English landlord who will then invest that money in England and leave Ireland impoverished. The right to consume our own beef and corn – not meekly stand by and see it shipped to England while the Irish live on potatoes. The right to make the English people see that they are *not* the chosen people. And it is *not* the fair hand of God that allows an Irish child to die of famine at the same moment an English child sits at a full table and consumes Irish beef! It is *not* the fair hand of God that wills that – it is the thieving hand of the British government!'

Michael stared at the priest a bit wild-eyed. He was rising into a fury and he did not want that. He wanted to see his wife and children. He turned to walk out of the barn.

`Wait!' the priest called. `Wait!'

He jumped up and snatched Michael's arm. `Look at me, man! Look at me and tell me how long you think you can live like this. How long you think you can keep up a resistance against an Empire with only a small army of men? How long? How long?'

`How long?' Michael snapped angrily. `I'll tell you how long I can hold out. One day the future children of Wicklow will see a very old man wandering over those mountains with a gaming-gun in his hand – and it will most likely be me!'

`All right.' The priest nodded and passed a hand tiredly across his eyes. `I have tried reason, now I must resort to rage.'

Michael looked at him, wryly; but the priest's voice thundered through the barn in genuine black anger.

`There is more in life to consider than the rights of man! The *rights* of man, indeed! What about the *duties* of man? No rights were ever given that were not accompanied by duty. A man who adheres to his duties is far more honourable, far more admirable, than the man who insists on his rights! You are an Irish Catholic, boy, and you have no rights, not in Ireland. But you do have duties.'

The priest waved a hand towards the land beyond the open barn door. `Forget the great dream of reform in Ireland and look to your own locality of Wicklow. Look at the poor people now placed under an intolerable burden supporting so much soldiery. No recompense do they get from the government for feeding the soldiers free-quartered in their houses and must be fed before even their own children. And without complaint they are suffering this – because of you!'

Michael took the verbal blow with no words and no reaction.

`But if you care not about your duty to them – think of your duty to your parents, to your brothers and sisters, all confined in prison – because of you! Think of your relatives, removed from their farms and families and confined in the wet and stinking hold of prison ships – because of you!'

Michael was unable to cover his reaction this time. `By God,' he said harshly, `it is not only the Castle that wants to turn me into the scapegoat and heap the suffering of Wicklow on my back – you do also.'

`I am reminding you of your duty to these people because, as your pastor, it is *my* duty to do so. I am a priest, I too have taken an oath. And my duty is to the care and situation of my whole flock, not just one. If you must know, Michael, there have been many times when I have heard of your escapes and clapped my hands in glee. The rebel in me cheered you all the way. But I can no longer cheer you, not anymore. My respect and admiration for you ended the moment I heard that you had turned down Lord Hardwicke's very generous offer.'

Michael's dark stare went right through the priest. `To hell with your respect, to hell with your admiration, I have never asked nor looked for either – but I once gave you both – as a priest and as a man. Now I would not give you the touch of my hat. I've listened to you long enough, but I'll never listen to you again. From this day on you are no longer a priest to me – you are a traitor!'

He turned to go, then flashed back in anger. `Every bit as much a traitor as the Catholic Archbishop of Dublin who purchased his own secure position by selling us out for the Union, and now preaches English supremacy and decrees it as the Will of God – let him shake hands with Cromwell in hell!'

`I am not a traitor,' the priest whispered whitely, `And neither is Bishop Troy.'

`No? Then explain why Troy sent out a letter to be read in all Catholic chapels reminding the Irish Catholics of their *religious* obligation of loyalty to the King, and their *religious* obligation to give respect and obedience to all those constituted by Divine Providence to govern us? Religious obligation, indeed. Divine Providence, indeed. I say he is a big fat traitor! And as you read out his sickening letter, you too are a traitor.'

`I did not read out the letter, I could not.' The priest sagged down onto the bale of straw, too old and too cold and too tired to take much more. A verbal whipping could rip sharper than any cat o' nine tails.

`Bishop Troy knew nothing of Emmet's conspiracy,' he said, `but the oligarchy at the Castle are now saying that the Catholic Bishops not only backed it, but organised it.'

`So the letter was to save his own skin?'

`In part, yes, but not entirely. You cannot judge a man or a nation without knowing their history. Troy and myself were both priests during the Penal Days. To have lived through them is to have lived through a nightmare more horrific than Dante's visions of Hell. But like a man who is given a morsel of food after a long famine, some of our priests think we now enjoy a feast of British blessings. They see our present condition as a great sign of British benevolence and government conciliation, because, although we are not one dead body nearer to emancipation, it is no longer a crime of death to practice our faith.'

`The priest at Rathdangan read out the letter. As did all the other priests in Wicklow.'

`Well I did not and could not. How could I tell my people that it was their *religious* obligation to give respect to an oppressive regime that rules them.'

`So by not reading out the letter, you have disobeyed your Archbishop.'

`Yes.'

`He will threaten you with eternal damnation,' Michael warned. `He may even defrock you.'

The priest shrugged. `Then I will borrow a pair of your breeches that Mary makes and sews so well and carry on as before. Once a priest, always a priest. But at the end of the day, I am subject to a higher power than the Archbishop.'

The priest smiled wearily, and Michael felt a flash of shame. `I apologise,' he murmured. `I shouldn't have called you a traitor.'

`I have been called worse.'

Michael looked narrowly at the priest. `Why did you

really come here?'

`To ask you to surrender.'

`Then I'll give it to you straight,' Michael said impatiently, `one last and final time – I will never surrender.'

`What about your wife?'

Michael was halfway out of the barn. He turned and stared at the priest. `What about my wife?'

The priest stood up and walked towards him, drawing in his breath as if preparing for one last attack with the weapon of reason.

`Your wife brings me back to the original point of my reasoning with you, before you confused me with other argumentative issues. You have obviously abandoned your duty to your parents and relatives, but are you also going to abandon your duty to Mary? Is your love of your lofty ideal so much greater than your love for her? I think it must be. Is your affection and duty to your comrades so much more important than your duty to her? I think it must be. And in that case, you should never have married her and vowed to forsake all others for her. In truth, Michael, you have forsaken nothing or no one for her. The vows you made at your wedding have turned out to be lies.'

`That's unfair,' Michael burst out. `I have always put my wife's welfare and protection before my own. I love my wife... in a way that you couldn't possibly understand.'

`A strange love it is, then. A selfish love it is, then. That girl has given you as much as any woman could ever give, and what have you given her in return? Nights of pleasure from time to time obviously, but no days of happiness, no days of contentment free of worry. In the past five years she has borne you three children and lived every day the life of a fugitive.'

`You make it sound wretched,' Michael said quietly. `It was never like that. We have known much happiness, despite the hardship. We have known great happiness, in each other, and in our children.'

The priest snorted. `I'll wager the happiness was all on your side, the hardship on hers. So well for you to live amongst the companionship of your men while she is left alone with your babies in the back room of some harbourer's house. And however kind and friendly the harbourer's may be, a woman with children needs the stability of a permanent place to live. A permanent nest to settle her young at night. A permanent place to hang her pots and pans. Good God, even the travelling gypsy women who settle nowhere still have their own little permanent wagons to live in by day and by night.'

Michael opened his mouth to speak, but no words came, for suddenly he understood. Suddenly it all became clear to him why the priest had been ready to search the mountains to find him. And having found him so close to the house, had embarked on his long rigmarole about rights and duty without coming straight to the truth of it.

`Mary asked you,` he said at last. `It was Mary who asked you to ask me to surrender, wasn't it?'

The priest sighed, as if a great weight had been lifted from his shoulders. `Yes, it was Mary. She could not ask you herself. It seems she made a vow to you in the days after Derrynamuck and she has never broken it.'

He could only stare at the priest, trying to remember what the vow had been ... and then it came back to him. She had vowed never to ask for more than he could possibly give her, and now she was asking him to give up the very principles of his existence, and surrender to the Castle.

`You must know how grieved she is to ask this of you,' the priest said, `for she has always taken great pride in your defiance and bravery. She too defied her father when she ran away and married you, and she has never regretted her choice. Her love for you then was like a rushing river that has now swelled into an ocean. She has tried very hard to be a fit mate for you, but she has three small children and she is tired of her nomadic life. And now that the Viceroy is being so magnanimous by offering you a safe retreat from the kingdom with your immediate family to a country of your choice, she sees a chance of her dream coming true – a life of peace and freedom waiting for you all in the friendly land of America – and she cannot understand why you won't take it.'

His lack of response, the paleness of his face, gave the priest hope. He put a gentle hand on his shoulder and spoke softly.

`For over five years she has been true to you. Now it is your turn to be true to her. You have told me how much you love her, and she has told me how much you love your children, and now is your chance to prove it. Now is your chance to prove which means most to you – being a hero of the people, being a faithful comrade, or being a protective husband and father.'

The priest moved to leave, pulling his muffler around him. `Now I must go. I have done what I see as my duty, done what I promised faithfully to Mary that I would do. Cullen knows nothing of this, by the way. Mary and I spoke in private in the bedroom. I will leave you to your decision. But whatever you decide, I would remind you of the words of St. Paul to the Corinthians: "Take heed, lest this liberty of yours becomes a stumbling-block to them that are weaker than you."'

Michael still made no response, and the priest moved out of the barn. He had only been gone a few seconds when he reappeared again in the doorway, pulling down his muffler.

`There is something else you should know,' he said, his voice flat. `Because you love your wife ... in a way that you say I could not possibly understand ... she is expecting another child.'

*

It was maybe half an hour later when Mary walked into the barn without the cover of even a shawl over her dress. She had made a guess at his response when he had stayed in the barn. He was always reluctant to face her when he was angry. He was standing where the priest had left him, leaning against the wall. She stared at him, white-faced and shivering. He looked back at her in silence.

Silence, that dark silence that Mary had come to know so well. No words were needed, for suddenly she knew it was the end, the final and bitter end. The life had gone out of his face and she could see his soul dying in his eyes.

A pang of pain and a sense of her own betrayal assailed her. A maelstrom of memory flashed back of their life gone by, a memory of that golden summer years ago, the summer of 1798, when he had regularly travelled over nine miles of difficult and deserted mountains from the rebel camp in Glenmalure just to see her, a sash of green around his waist denoting his rank as a field officer, smiling defiance in his eyes and careless of the dangers that surrounded him.

A memory of that same year when she had first lain with him as his bride in a candle-lit bedroom and his rapturous eyes had moved over her, and how he had looked at his baby daughter with such transparent love on his face, such smiling pride as he watched his first-born son grow from a baby into a boy, then another son, chubby and contented, the drowser of the family.

Days, months, years of running together, living together in the spaces between that hunted life up in the distance of the mountains where men primed their rifles and refused to face defeat. Day, months, years, all leading up to this awful moment.

She wound her arms around his neck and kissed his face sadly. He pulled her shivering body into the shelter of his own and returned her embrace, in silence.

*

They eventually spoke to each other, briefly and quietly. He spent only a few minutes in the house, just long enough to take his children in his arms and grip them tight to his body. First Mary-Anne, who at sight of him had jumped up excitedly and run to cling to his legs. He reached down and lifted her up, tousled her mop of black curls and smiled into her liquid black eyes. She laughed her excited laugh and he saw love in her eyes, love for him, simply because he was her daddy. She was too young to understand that he was a hero.

Three-year old John was the next to be hauled up until he stood with a child on each arm and looked at the wooden object John proudly held up.

`Dada, look ... Uncle Cullen whittled me a whistle,' the small boy cried, pushing the wooden whistle between his father's lips. Michael blew it and Mary-Anne screamed when the sound blasted into her face. John thought her discomfort hilarious and let out a gleeful laugh until the room was filled with their noise.

Then he felt a tugging at his legs and looked down to see fourteen-month old Peter balancing and swaying on his chubby legs like a drunken little man, gurgling and clawing for some of the attention.

He set the other two down and swung Peter high in the air above his head, and he chuckled down at him. He brought the boy down and laid him across his shoulder, and then slowly he turned and looked across the room at Mary.

`What did the priest say?' Cullen asked, puzzled at the silent stare that was passing between husband and wife. `What's going on. Michael?'

Michael did not answer Cullen, he couldn't. He was unable even to look at his old friend. When Cullen spoke to him again he barely heard the words. He hastily restored Peter to his mother then turned and quickly left the house without a word of farewell to anyone.

Mary rushed to the door and watched him go. He went quickly, running and skidding over the snow as if fearing he might change his mind if he allowed himself to think about it a second longer.

It was the end, and now it had come she felt only a terrible sorrow for him, for he would never believe that it was hopeless, had always been hopeless. The fight for this heartbreaking, tragic country had been fought and lost and would never be won. But he would never believe that, not to his dying day, not even if God himself decreed it.

She stood at the door crying uncontrollably, her bewildered children looking at her in frightened silence, but Cullen was at the end of his patience.

`What ails you?' Cullen demanded. `Crying like that. And where's himself gone in such a hurry – slipping and sliding over the snow without even a glance or a word to myself?'

`He's gone to see Billy Jackson,' Mary murmured. `To

tell him that he's prepared to surrender.'

When she finally glanced round, Cullen's face was as white as his hair.

`It is the best thing now,' she whispered.

`But ... but,' the old man seemed short of breath, then disbelieving, `but he's always said that he would not desert his comrades. I've heard him saying that so often, heard him with my own two hearing ears.'

`And he'll not desert his comrades,' she assured him. `He'll agree to a peaceable surrender on the terms the Viceroy has offered, but on the condition that Hugh Vesty, John Mernagh, Martin Burke, and their wives and children are also included in the terms.'

Cullen was all of a fluster. His hands moved over his face. He stepped outside and looked all around him, his eyes bewildered as he tried to imagine the Wicklow Mountains without Michael Dwyer. Since boyhood he had hunted and wandered up there, and for five and a half years the silent hills had seemed alive with his presence, aflame with his defiance. Even without seeing him, Cullen always knew he was up there, somewhere.

Of a sudden, in the imagery of Cullen's mind, the mountains were no longer white and cold, but green and lush with spring, covered in yellow gorse and purple heather. Lambs bleated lazily, herons cried over the lakes, and larks and thrushes disturbed the peaceful solitude with their melodious chatter. Everything was wild and tangled and familiar, and Cullen remembered how Michael had always loved this green and tangled land, loved it with the passion that never cools.

Michael had always believed he would live here and die here; he had never yearned to make his home and fortune some place else. He had never truly been anywhere outside Wicklow, except once to Wexford and thrice to Dublin. He had never even seen the County Clare. How would he ever survive out in the alien world? A world where the Irish luck given to him long ago would lose its magic.

Cullen turned back to Mary, his eyes and voice brooding. `And if the Viceroy agrees about the other lads, treasure, where will youse all be going to?'

`There is only place an Irish person will choose to go outside Ireland,' Mary answered softly. `And don't you know that well, old man. If the Viceroy agrees, we shall go to North America.'

Chapter Sixteen

No one answered him, for no one could quite take in what he had just told them. The men in the cave all looked at each other, and then back at him. He sat staring in front of him, eyes stilled on the flames of the fire.

`What about us?' Laurence O'Keefe asked. `What are we to do?'

`You must do the best you can for yourselves,' Michael replied quietly. `I have to consider my father, my mother, my brothers and sisters, my relatives and in-laws, my wife and children, and my comrades who have been with me since the beginning. But I cannot be every man's friend and keeper.'

O'Keefe and the others looked from Dwyer to Hugh Vesty, John Mernagh, and Martin Burke – the unbreakable foursome. All at some time or another had risked their lives for each other, and even now, at the end, were not to part.

`If it's any consolation,' Michael said, `Billy the Rock assures me that the present military operations will be suspended once the four of us surrender. The heat will be drawn off Wicklow. He is convinced that many of you will be able to slip back to your homes and carry on with life without any Imaal yeoman bothering you. Most will choose to forget that you were ever rebels. Very few of the Wicklow yeomanry feel any allegiance to this government, except the old rancorous true-blues at Rathdrum, Baltinglass, and Hacketstown, of course. You will have to take your chances with them, but so you would if you were not rebels. Some things never change.'

The rest of men drew away from the foursome into their own group and held a council on the subject of what they should do. In the end all agreed they could not blame the captain, who had other responsibilities beyond them. Most decided to stay where they were until after the proposed surrender had actually taken place, for few truly believed that Dwyer would be able to do it at the last. But if he did, they would wait until the military activities in Wicklow had ceased, then head back to their homes and take their chances.

Only one man decided to leave the camp there and then, and to everyone's surprise it was one of the unbreakable foursome – John Mernagh. He had not uttered one word since Dwyer's return, and now he looked at him as if waking up out of a trance, his eyes dull with contempt.

`You make whatever arrangements for surrender you want, Captain, but leave me out of it. You forget that I have no wife or child, and need not surrender to emotional involvement or the damned and bloody Castle. If I have to, I'll keep up the fight on my own. In other words, Captain, you can take my name off your surrender terms, *and go to hell!*'

The whole cave fell into a silence that centred on the captain, who breathed softly to himself then closed his eyes for a moment.

`You must do what you think fit,' he said tonelessly.

`Too right I will!' yelled Mernagh, and then grabbed up his things, turned and flung himself out of the cave.

`Maybe I should go with him,' O'Keefe said somewhat sadly. `It wouldn't be right to let the poor bastard fight the whole British Empire on his own.'

`What about you two?' Michael murmured to Hugh Vesty and Martin Burke when O'Keefe had run after Mernagh. `I made provision for you only because I felt I could not secure terms only for myself and desert you. But you are men with minds of your own, and can go your own roads if you wish.'

`And let you have all the fun in America?' Hugh Vesty shrugged. `Don't be crazy, boy.'

Martin Burke smiled quietly, `Don't fret, Michael. Mernagh will be back at your side soon enough. How many dark nights in the past has he upped and left us to go and form his own army, but he was always back for breakfast.'

`It only happened once,' Hugh Vesty said in all fairness, `and then only because John got furiously drunk. But once common sense returned, he returned.' Hugh Vesty grinned. `Aye, Martin, you have the right of it. Mernagh will soon be back.'

213

Michael hoped they were right. He cared deeply for John Mernagh and would have liked to have gone after him and talk it over. In the past five and half years they had been good comrades and Mernagh had proved himself as loyal as Hugh Vesty. But everything had changed now, and in the last extremity, every man had the right to choose his own way.

*

Billy `The Rock' Jackson was already at William Hume's house at Humewood. Billy was still in shock at Dwyer's sudden and dramatic capitulation, but he managed to hold up the paper and read out the terms proposed.

`In response to Lord Hardwicke's offer that he will be given a safe passage out of the kingdom in return for his peaceable surrender,' Billy said, `he agrees to such surrender on the condition that his parents, brothers and sisters, and all those presently confined in prison for no other reason than being related to him, are released. Also that Hugh Vesty Byrne and Martin Burke, together with their wives and children, as well as John Mernagh and his cousin Arthur Devlin, are included in the terms of his surrender. And the country of their exile to be the United States of North America.'

William Hume was very excited; the fact that Michael Dwyer had chosen to surrender only to him would elevate his standing with the peasants and farmers and people of his own Wicklow. It was a declaration of trust, for according to the practice of the time, whoever accepted a man in surrender was then responsible for his fate until the agreed terms of surrender were carried out. By this act, Hume knew that Michael Dwyer was entrusting his life to him, and Hume was determined that such faith would not be in vain.

`There is one other condition,' Billy said. `From the moment of his surrender he asks that his wife and children be allowed to lodge with him and on no account are they to be separated.'

`A strange request,' Hume said.

Billy shrugged. `I suspect it was made by her. I doubt she

would allow him to go as far as Dublin without some guarantee that she will be allowed to join him soon after.'

`Well,' Hume said thoughtfully, `if the Castle agree to the rest of the terms, I can't see why they would not agree to that also. Some of the United leaders in 1798 had their wives with them while awaiting deportation.'

Within the hour Hume had set off in his carriage for Dublin Castle where he discussed the matter with Lord Hardwicke, and two days later he hastened to Brusselstown to give Billy The Rock the news that Lord Hardwicke had agreed to the terms. By the mercy of government, Michael Dwyer and his four named associates would be allowed a safe retreat from the kingdom with wives and children on condition of their peaceable surrender to William Hume, Member of Parliament for Wicklow.

So on the black and cold night of 16th December, at a place called the Three Bridges, Michael Dwyer met William Hume in secret and alone, handed over his gun in surrender, and the two walked back together to the estate at Humewood, where hot food and warm red wine were waiting to be served to both of them.

Neither of them slept. They spent the long night in reflective conversation, and by grey dawnlight the two, if not friends, had developed a certain respect for each other.

By mid-morning a cavalcade of mounted yeomen were ready to escort him on the forty mile journey to Dublin Castle, and Michael was amused to see that nearly all were yeomen who, at one time or another, had been accused, not unjustly, of befriending him. William Hume was obviously determined that he should reach his Dublin destination safely.

William Hume remained behind at Humewood to await the surrender of the others. He assured Michael that as soon as his own surrender at the Castle was completed, he would personally arrange for Mary and the children to join him in Dublin. Then Hume gave him one of his very best horses, and surrounded by his servants, stood by the high iron gates of Humewood and watched the rebel captain and his escort ride off.

*

His face was calm and without expression as they rode through the snow towards Donard. It was his last journey through his own Imaal; and, like his life, the mountains of his beloved Wicklow were shrouded in dark mist.

The news of his surrender had spread like wildfire. Every mile along the route people came out and stared up at him as he rode by. To them it was the end of an era. But it was not the end they had expected. Surrender was not a fitting end for a hero. And to them, he was the greatest hero that had ever lived in Wicklow.

or over five years Michael Dwyer had been what every Wicklow youth dreamed of being – a man that owns no master, a man that refused to bend the servile knee. And they had thought he would die as undaunted as he had lived. No, surrender was not the end they had expected, nor the end that great stories and great ballads were made of.

Riding by, he looked in silence at the faces of all the people he knew, and he knew every one, every face a part of his life that was now over. They shouted up to him, words of gratitude, words of encouragement, words of farewell, words that trailed off like the last few notes of a sad song . . .

At Blessington he yearned to look back, turn and take one last look at the wild mountains that had been his playground, his battleground, and had sheltered him so well. But he kept his eyes fixed on the road ahead. There was no point in looking back at the man he had once been.

PART THREE

She took and kissed the first flower once,
And sweetly said to me:
`This flower comes from the Wicklow Hills,
dew wet, and pure,' said she.
`It's name is Michael Dwyer –
The strongest flower of all;
But I'll keep it fresh beside my breast,
Though all the world shall fall.'

`The Three Flowers' by Norman G. Reddin.

Chapter Seventeen

Shortly after his arrival at Dublin Castle he was given a brief interview before members of the Privy Council, then Under-Secretary Marsden informed him that he was to be transferred to Kilmainham Gaol – on a charge of high treason.

Michael stared at Marsden in disbelief, and then his eyes turned as cold as ice. `You forget one thing, Mr Marsden – all Wicklow knows about my surrender terms. All Wicklow knows that Lord Hardwicke made the offer and I accepted and submitted in good faith. If you persist in this treachery, you will be responsible for bringing danger and disgrace to the name of William Hume.'

`The terms of your surrender as agreed with William Hume will be honoured,' Marsden said, as if faintly shocked at the accusation of a double-cross. `The official charge of high treason is simply for public reassurance that even rebels like you can eventually see the futile error of your ways. Wicklow may know you entered into secret terms with the government, but the world does not. And when we speak about the world, we mean, of course, England.'

`Give me back six minutes,' Michael said angrily, `and all the soldiers in the Empire will not take me in six years.'

`We will give you a clean and well-furnished cell in Kilmainham Gaol,' Marsden said in bland tones, `where you will be given the political status and privileges of a first class State prisoner, and not those of a criminal. You will also be allowed to enjoy the company of your wife and children there, until a ship is available to take you out of the kingdom.'

`And my relatives?'

`Will be liberated within a very short time,' Marsden said dismissively. `We have no further need of them.'

Michael breathed softly to himself. He was still angry, very angry that the Castle were going to use him in their usual propaganda to show the world how decent they were in their handling of the Irish savages. But he was also very relieved that his surrender terms would be met and his family liberated. The fact that scores of men and women had been arrested and thrown into prison merely for being *relatives* of a rebel would not be told to the world, for then the world might think the Irish had a true grievance against those who governed them after all. So it had always been in the war between the two islands, while the government silenced free speech and controlled the newspapers and thereby the ears of the world, the British story suffered no contradiction and would always be believed.

`How long can I expect to be confined in Kilmainham Gaol?' he asked.

`Not too long, hopefully, for we are very anxious to get you out of Ireland.' Marsden's grey eyes glazed over until their expression was hard to read. `But however long you remain in Kilmainham, I think you will find that we shall treat you well.'

*

And they did. Within days of being transferred to Kilmainham Gaol, Mary and the children joined him in his large and well-furnished cell and for the first time in six years they spent the entire festival of Christmas together, albeit behind bars. But both had the satisfaction of knowing that all their Wicklow relatives had been set free and were now back in the comfort of their homes, including Michael's father who had been released from New Geneva in Waterford.

On New Year's Day, 1804, Mary began to wonder about the life that awaited them in America.

`Did Mr Hume say which part of America we would be sent?' she asked. `Did he say New York?'

Michael shook his head vaguely as he placed more logs on the fire in the corner of the cell. `I think he mentioned a place called Baltimore, wherever that may be.'

`Baltimore,' Mary repeated, then her face broke into a sunburst of a smile. `It sounds Irish, doesn't it? Baltimore.'

`Aye,' he smiled back at her. `I suppose it does. There's a

220

Baltimore in Cork.'

It was still dark, not yet dawn, the room lit only by the flames of fire that had to be kept alive in defence of the winter chill permanently in the air.

Mary sat on the side of bed, relieved and happy in herself as she looked over at the small curly heads of her three children asleep in a bed along the opposite wall. This was how they would live from now on, all together, day in and day out. And when they reached the land of the free she would have him all to herself, just him and the children all to herself in some little thatched cottage in Baltimore in America. No harbourers in the next room, no soldiers on the hills, no comrades looking for their leader.

She bit her lip thoughtfully. Were the houses in America thatched, she suddenly wondered, or were they mansions with long windows that required a great deal of lace for curtaining?

Ach, no matter, she would settle for either. By all accounts it didn't take long for a hard-working man to get rich in America.

Her eyes rested on the dark hair and sleeping innocent face of Mary-Anne, Michael's favourite child, and Mary wondered if maybe their daughter would end up a very rich and grand lady by marrying one of the Boston Irish? A gentleman prisoner on the floor above, a wealthy young lawyer named St. John Mason, had told her that the Boston Irish were some of the richest people in the world.

`Is Boston anywhere near Baltimore, do you know?' she asked Michael.

Michael didn't know the answer to her question, and didn't query the point of it either. He sat down on the bed beside her, his eyes looking up to the barred window of their cell at the sky beyond.

After a life so long and free on the mountains he found the stone walls of the prison crushing. But the unease that had followed his interview at the Castle was dropping away, the unease of not knowing whether they were planning a double-cross or not. So far, Marsden had not been lying – they had treated him well, providing him with the company of his family, adequate fuel for the fire, adequate food and drink, and no reason for complaint.

Except that he was not allowed access to the joint cell of Hugh Vesty and Martin Burke who had not been quite so well-treated, given the status of *second class* political prisoners and placed in a narrow cell with sparse comfort and sparse diet. His only consolation on their behalf was that things would improve for them once they were all out of this prison.

`What are you thinking?' Mary asked.

`How long it will take for our ship to come in,' he murmured.

*

Time passed – weeks, months. He became very uneasy at their long detention and demanded to know why the conditions of his surrender had not yet been fulfilled. His enquiries were set aside with one plausible explanation after another.

Summer came, warm and humid; and with it the birth of Mary's child, a delicate little girl born in the infirmary of Kilmainham. They named her Esther.

Again Michael demanded to know why the terms of his surrender had not yet been fulfilled. The response as always was negative, but he attacked and pressed for an answer on all occasions. He requested an explanation from Dr Trevor, the Superintendent of the Gaol.

`I know nothing about it,' Dr Trevor snapped, `other than the Castle are trying to engage a ship.'

`Ships are going to America all the time.'

`Trading ships that have room for three or four passengers and no more. Very few have enough space to accommodate five men, three women, and seven children. The Castle are trying very hard to engage the right ship, I can assure you of that.'

Dr Trevor hurried away from him, and avoided him henceforth.

*

Harvest time came, cool and dry; and Dr Trevor spent part of each day watching Michael Dwyer from behind the thick drapes of his office window, watching and waiting for some little sign that his patience was ready to break. He watched every day without fail, for every day Dwyer and his companions took a good deal of exercise at ball playing and the like in the yard below.

The Governor of Kilmainham Gaol was John Dunne, but Dr Trevor was the Inquisitor-General and the Castle's chief spy. Trevor had given good service to the government over the years, and in return had received not only large sums from the secret service funds, but a variety of well-paid offices:

He was Superintendent of Kilmainham Gaol; physician of Kilmainham Gaol; a justice of the peace; agent of transport ships; recruiting agent for army and navy, and in this latter office he regularly toured the prisons persuading prisoners that a life on the high seas or marching across the world carrying a musket in His Majesty's service would be far more enjoyable than a high hanging.

And a `high hanging' was what Dr Trevor dreamed of whenever he looked down at Michael Dwyer. He hated the rebel with undiluted venom. Since Dwyer's arrival at Kilmainham he had disrupted the very life of the prison. For years Dr Trevor had maintained the natural order of what prison life should be – misery, degradation, dull eyes in dull faces, men brought so low that complaint and lament was their natural conversation – but Dwyer had changed all that, for despite the frustration of his long wait, the rapscallion still enjoyed a sense of humour and a bit of fun.

He watched Dwyer in the yard below, grinning broadly as he gave orders to a gentleman prisoner named John Patten, then ran down the other end of the yard to confer with John Mernagh, another Wicklow rebel who had speedily joined his leader in Kilmainham after Christmas.

Dr Trevor jerked round as the governor, John Dunne, entered the room. `Is it our rebel chief you are watching again?' the governor asked wryly.

`Look at him!' Trevor cried. `He's at it again – these

games of his cannot be allowed to continue! This is the seventh or eighth match at ball he has organised amongst the men in the past month. His effect on the second-class prisoners is deplorable.'

`In what way?'

`In what way, sir? In the most unsatisfactory way. According to the turnkeys, these men at night are as tired as ploughboys at harvest time, falling down on their mats in sleep before the doors are even locked.'

The Governor, a Lancashire man, looked down to the recreation ground at Dwyer and his companions, all active fellows, playing a match with sixteen others while the rest of the yard looked on with great interest and pleasure.

Such enjoyment, the governor knew, was anathema to a man like Dr Trevor who had been described by one suffering prisoner as `a monster in human shape'. Another had stated that Dr Trevor had treated him `with such cold- blooded cruelty it nearly brought my life to its termination.'

And John Dunne, as Governor, knew both had been speaking the truth, indeed Dr Trevor has become known as the `Tyrant of Kilmainham'. He too despised Dr. Trevor, but he was powerless to act against him, for Trevor was answerable only to the Castle, who continually ignored the complaints sent to them about his brutality, especially against the women prisoners.

And now it seemed that the superintendent's venom was to be sprayed in full force at Michael Dwyer. And John Dunne knew why. It was not only Dwyer's ball games that infuriated Dr. Trevor, it was his wit against the turnkeys that he used in such a manner that no one ever knew if he was serious or not.

Then there was also the business of Trevor's ring of informers that Dwyer had effectively broken – men sent out to the recreation ground under guise of being political prisoners, but in truth planted there for the purpose of picking other prisoners' brains in the hope of discovering the names of rebels still at liberty.

These informers – Trevor's men – were suspected by the real prisoners and all had been pointed out to Dwyer. And according to gossip, when the informers went out and mixed with the men watching the ball game, cheering with them, Dwyer had seemingly selected one at a time for friendly attention at the end of each match, sidling up to him and asking in pretended earnest, `Do you know any of the informers, avic? I'm told there are some of the reptiles skulking amongst us. If you know who they are, will you point them out to me?'

And so terrific was the reputation of Michael Dwyer that now not one of Trevor's men would set foot on the recreation ground while he and his friends were on it, and the rest of the prisoners had enjoyed seeing the rebel chief sending the informers sneaking away in a hurry.

`He's a tyrant!' Trevor snapped, `A damned tyrant and no less!'

The Governor turned his eyes from the men in the yard and stared at Dr Trevor. `Oh come, Dr Trevor,' he said coldly, `I cannot support your charge. Apart from Dwyer's enthusiasm for the ball games, I find him, on the whole, a rather quiet and peaceable man.'

`Do you indeed? I find his manner rather pert! And why should he not be quiet and peaceable when he has his woman and brats to keep him company in his cell? Is it not a pretty thing that this rebel received the privileges usually only accorded to *gentlemen* prisoners.'

`He is not technically a prisoner,' the Governor said by way of reminder. `The government made surrender terms with him and he remains here while awaiting deportation.'

`I know nothing of his surrender,' Trevor snapped, `except that he made it when he could hold out no longer.'

Trevor moved away from the window then, but he was back standing by it the following day, his eyes piercing and dangerous as they watched Dwyer playing with a five year old female brat in the yard.

One false move from you, my boyo,' Trevor whispered, `just one false move, one act of insubordination is all I need, then I will have you.'

*

A few days a later, during their recreation period in the yard, a gentlemen from the first-class spoke quietly to Michael, and showed him a written memorial complaining about the system of cruelty and abuse that was being carried on inside Kilmainham Gaol by Dr Trevor, and the deplorable conditions.

Michael looked at the names at the bottom of the paper, many were gentlemen of first-class status: St. John Mason, a lawyer and cousin of Robert Emmet, John Patten, brother-in-law of Robert Emmet, Philip Long, banker to Robert Emmet – Fourteen from the first-class in all, and forty-one from the second-class – all from the wing that housed the political prisoners, otherwise known as *State* prisoners.

The memorial stated that `a system of avaricious and malignant severity is practised in this prison which calls aloud for, and might be sufficiently demonstrated, by a fair and impartial investigation.'

`St John Mason,' said the prisoner to Michael, is going to try and get one of his barrister friends to slip it to a judge on the bench. And once the barrister gets it into the judge's hand, the judge is obliged by law to do something about it.'

So what do you want me to do about it?' Michael whispered.

`Sign it.'

`I can't do that.'

`Why not? Can't you write?'

`I can write well enough, but that's not the problem. Each man on that list is complaining about his treatment here in Kilmainham, but as far as it is possible inside a prison, I have been treated well.'

`And how long do you think that will last?'

`Until I board my ship.'

`You must be stupid or crazy, man, to trust the Castle. There won't be any ship. Can't you see – you were a big fish they finally baited in their net, and they'll make you pay, Dwyer. Somehow and someway, they will have their revenge on you.'

Michael looked around the men in the yard, then at the

guards, then up to the windows while he spoke. `I have William Hume's oath of honour that my surrender terms will not be violated,' he said firmly. `But my surrender is not the issue here. I have been treated well so far, and therefore I cannot sign that paper.'

`Look at the three names at the end.'

Michael glanced down at the three names: Hugh Vesty Byrne, John Mernagh, and Martin Burke.'

`While you have been enjoying first-class privileges, they have been living in deplorable conditions.'

`They tell me so,' Michael answered softly, `and they are the reason I cannot add my name to the list.'

`I don't understand you.'

`Then I'll explain it to you, avic. If that memorial is to have any effect with men of influence on the outside, it has to be seen as a genuine and truthful account of life in here. But if my name is on it, enjoying the privileges that I do, my wife and children allowed to lodge with me and so on, then it will be disbelieved and seen as nothing more than a list of complaints from a bunch of ungrateful malcontents. It will not receive the attention it deserves.'

'Ah ... now I understand you.'

`I'm glad that you do,' Michael said, and then strolled away.

*

The yard was empty, being so early in the morning, but Michael Dwyer was already out in the air as usual, as if the confines of his cell were something he could not bear in daytime.

And Dr Trevor was watching as usual. He had no knowledge of the prisoners' memorial that contained not only complaints about the severity of the prison, but a personal indictment against him. A memorial that Michael Dwyer had declined to sign.

Dr Trevor watched him playing with his female brat again, saw him chase her down the yard, heard her excited screams.

As his eyes followed them, Trevor saw something else

which made his blood boil – down the far end of the yard a small boy with black curly hair was feeding bits of bread to a cluster of tame pigeons. Now wasn't that a pretty thing – government bread being wasted by one of Dwyer's brats!

Then he saw the boy running towards Dwyer on his four-year-old legs, saw Dwyer swinging him up onto his shoulders, saw the two of them smiling, the girl also, as the three stood watching the birds happily eating away.

Trevor sent for a turnkey who came at the double. Trevor beckoned him over to the window.

`Do you see those pigeons down there?'

`Oh yes, sir,' replied the turnkey. `They belong to a prisoner who's been training them for months.'

`Kill them,' Trevor said.

`Beg pardon, sir?'

`You heard me!' Trevor fiercely retorted. `Collect four guards with four guns and tell them to go out to that yard and shoot those birds immediately.'

Trevor watched as the guards entered the yard, aimed their guns and killed the tame pigeons while Dwyer's brats stood bawling their eyes out.

Trevor nodded to himself, smiling as he watched Dwyer stare in disgust at the guards, utter a few words to them, then take his wailing children back inside.

The turnkey returned, and spoke to Dr Trevor's back.

`The guards want to know what they should do with the pigeons, sir. Should they take them to the kitchen?'

`No. Tell the guards to leave the dead birds where they lie. They must not be removed from the yard, not under any circumstances. Understand?'

`No, sir ... I mean, yes, sir.'

`What did Dwyer say to the guards? Was it a complaint?'

`It was, sir. He said if they were forced to kill the birds, they might at least have given him time to remove the children before they did it.'

`Remove the children indeed! From my prison they should be removed.' Dr Trevor frowned. `But I'll need a better complaint from Dwyer than that.'

He looked at the turnkey. `What other weaknesses has

he? Apart from his children?'

`He's developing a bad need for liquor, sir. And not ale. He's beginning to need spirits.'

`And are we supplying his need?'

`Oh yes, sir. Just like you ordered. He can't seem to sleep at night without a noggin of whiskey to help him.'

`And when he wakes up? Does he need whiskey then?'

`Not yet, sir. But if word of his ship doesn't come soon, then I reckon it won't be long before he'll need it to face another day within these walls.'

`How long before he is totally dependent on it?'

`Hard to say, sir. He's a quiet enough fellow, for all his wild reputation, but I reckon it's his wife who's keeping him calm, her and the liquor.'

'Her and the liquor? And if we denied him both at a stroke – 'Trevor turned to face the turnkey and smiled cunningly. `What have you learned about the wife?' he asked.

`She's queer in the head, sir. A tasty wench, but not quite the full shilling. She thinks this place is one of Dublin's luxury hotels.

`Does she indeed?' Dr. Trevor's wide eyes invited the turnkey to elaborate on his opinion, and the turnkey obliged with a shrug.

`I knew she was a bit loony after her first day in here. For a start, she brought her own soap but requested a bowl. When I brought it, she asks if we could supply her with a full bucket of water every morning to warm up for washing. Then after breakfast she asked for more water to wash up the plates, and when I told her to use the water they'd washed themselves in, she refused and asked for fresh. So I asked her if she thought this was a luxury hotel and I was a bleeding chambermaid, but she turned to himself, and he said nothing, but the look he gave went right through me. And ever since she's had water for washing and fresh water for washing the plates. The governor said she could.'

`The governor –'

`Allowed her more soap when her own ran out, and now she gets a regular supply as well as being provided with a broom to sweep out their room. All the turnkeys laugh at her, not when himself's around, of course, but I reckon she's more to be pitied than laughed at. Mind, she aggravated me something sorely last week when she took her broom and viciously pushed out a turnkey who did me a favour by carrying in her bucket of water – she said he had lice crawling on his hair and she didn't want him near her children or baby. Then I asks her if it was maybe a nursemaid in white starches she would prefer as a turnkey, but she starts sobbing and wailing and says all she wants is to go to Baltimore or back to the mountains of Wicklow.'

Dr. Trevor was smiling; the turnkey had given him an idea.

`It's not decent, sir, having women in a male prison, women that can't be treated as prisoners, if you understand.'

`I understand perfectly,' Trevor murmured.

`I mean ...' the turnkey scratched his head, `if she were a real bona fide woman prisoner, I could just give her a punch or a kick and life would be easy. But I can't very well do that with him around. He can see no fault in her queer and fancy ways, but then he gets the pleasure of her in his bed at night but all I get is tears and complaints and requests for more bleeding water.'

`How much daily food rations is Dwyer allowed?' Trevor asked, his mind working furiously.

`Same rations as all the other first-class prisoners,' the turnkey shrugged, `except Dwyer has to share his with his family. Every day I give his wife one pound of bread, half an ounce of tea, three ounces of sugar, half pint of milk, and one pound of beef or pork.'

Divided between two adults and three children and a baby, it provided no more than a cup of tea and a meat sandwich daily, but Trevor considered it far too generous, especially when the brats could save enough of the bread to feed to birds.

He hmmned to himself. The total cost of such an allowance was three shillings a day, three shillings a day that could go into his own pocket, if his idea went as planned.

`Has Mrs Dwyer had her rations today?'

`Yes, sir, first thing this morning. Just after I humped in her bleeding bucket of water. A nice thing it is that rebel prisoners can wash and shave before I get a chance to even scratch meself after my breakfast.'

Trevor scowled. Lord Hardwicke may insist that Dwyer's conditions should not be interfered with while awaiting his ship, but Mr Marsden was not such a lily as His Excellency. Mr Marsden was still a formidable power at the Castle. He knew the amount of every bribe that had been paid to government officials to secure the Union, for he had been the Castle's pay-clerk. He knew every trick, every secret of every one, and apart from His Excellency, very few would dare to stand or speak against the Under-Secretary. Very few could manage to even look him in the eye, and as long as they kept their eyes averted, Marsden remained the real power at Dublin Castle. And Marsden was Trevor's employer.

`Take the water in as usual tomorrow,' Trevor told the turnkey, `but leave the business of the food rations to me.'

*

The following morning a new attendant carried the Dwyer's' food rations in to their cell; a convicted prisoner from the felon's side. He was no more than a filthy bundle of rags with lice crawling all over him.

With horrified eyes Mary stared at the crust of grime on his hands and face as he set down the tray of rations, but before she could utter a word, he suddenly grabbed the portion of cooked meat in his filthy hands and tore off a piece, shoved it hungrily into his mouth, then scurried out.

His foul smell lingered, but as Michael stared at the meat he had left, he saw it was putrid. The smell of it almost made him sick as he carried it to the door and called for the turnkey.

The turnkey rushed to report the matter to the Tyrant of Kilmainham.

`Dwyer has made an official complaint, sir.'

`A complaint? An *official* complaint?' Dr Trevor looked shocked. `And what could he have to complain about, may I ask?'

`About the food, sir. He says it was served in an offensive manner as well as being rotten and foul-smelling.'

`Served in an *offensive* manner? Oh you are right, my good man, these savages think this is a ruddy hotel. I run the best prison in the western world and my meat is as fine as that served in the Castle. Did he eat the meat?'

`No, sir. He just handed it back to me.'

`Was he abusive?'

`No, sir. Just asked for it to be removed. He suggested it might be given to the rats, as a way of killing a few of them off.'

Dr Trevor almost collapsed with frustration and fury. `That is not good enough! I need a better complaint than that!'

`Why not just invent one, sir?'

`Invent one? With that turnip of a governor on my back! John Dunne is just waiting for an opportunity to expose me to Lord Hardwicke. The man is overburdened with notions of morality and humanity. He should not be in the prison service. He should have stayed in Lancashire and tended docile sheep instead of hardened men. No ... when Dwyer finally loses his temper and breaks the rules, I want the governor either to see it, or hear of it from men he trusts, men he relies on to tell him the truth.'

`What about Dwyer, sir?'

`Oh, get out!' Trevor fiercely retorted. `I'll think about Dwyer tonight. In the meantime, tell him he must do without meat today, but he should find everything satisfactory tomorrow.'

When the turnkey had gone, Dr. Trevor mustered his humour and marched down the corridors. There were more prisoners than Dwyer who needed his attention.

His face was soft and gentle when he entered the solitary cell of a fifty-year-old man with long black hair rapidly turning grey all over. The man sat on the stone ledge under the high barred window, as still and silent as if he were in a trance.

`And how are we today, Mr. Devlin?' Trevor said kindly.

Brian Devlin made no answer.

`I have some news for you,' Trevor said kindly. `I performed an autopsy on your son's head at the time of his death, to discover the cause, but it is only now that the Castle have given me permission to tell you the result.'

Brian Devlin moved his head and looked at Dr Trevor with staring eyes of hatred.

`You killed my nine-year old boy!' he rasped. `You made him walk and walk in the pouring rain even though you knew he was half-blind and suffering with gaol fever. To call yourself a doctor is an obscene joke – and now you tell me that you did an autopsy on my son's head!'

Brian Devlin sprang at Dr. Trevor, but was brought down to his knees by the pull of the chains and irons around his ankles.

`I did an autopsy,' Trevor confirmed, his voice still kindly. `And the verdict has been accepted officially as Death by Visitation from God – in lay terms, natural causes.'

After a very long time, Brian Devlin crawled off his knees and resumed his seat on the stone ledge.

`Oh, Devlin,' Trevor exclaimed, `this hostility is getting us nowhere. It upsets you and it hurts me for I was deeply grieved at the death of your boy. But I would like to make it up to you. I would like to become a friend to you and the rest of your family. I would like to help you all. What say you – shall we bury the hatchet and let bygones be bygones?'

When Devlin made no answer, Dr Trevor took a wad of money out of his pocket and held it before the prisoner.

You are an uncle to Michael Dwyer. Tell us everything you know about him and agree to testify against him in court. You needn't tell everything. All you need describe is details of all the innocent people you saw him kill in cold blood and before your very eyes. In return we shall give you freedom and protection and make you rich. A wise man would know what to do. Only a fool would refuse it.

Brian Devlin met Trevor's eyes. `A pox on you and your money. I would rather die than lie under oath.'

Dr Trevor's face split into a wide grin. `Then, in that case, you shall be hanged!'

He strutted out of the cell and down the corridor, unaware of the figure of John Dunne standing in the shadows.

The governor motioned to the turnkey who relocked the cell, then turned and nodded.

`You heard every word Trevor said?' the governor whispered.

`I did, sir. And a nice state of affairs it is when a prison doctor spends his days going round the cells telling prisoners they're going to be hanged.'

`None of these men have yet been charged with any crime,' John Dunne said, `and if they are charged and brought to trial, it will be a judge and jury and the rule of law that decides if they will be hanged, not Dr Trevor.'

`Trouble is, sir, while they're in here, Dr. Trevor is the rule and law.'

The governor nodded; that was true. But somehow the man had to be stopped. Not only was he starving prisoners and pocketing the money allowed for their food, he solicited, threatened, starved, and bribed uncharged prisoners to become soldiers and enlist in the army or the fleet. But it was his treatment of some of the prisoners on the women's side that was totally inhuman. To allow Trevor to attend them as a doctor was an obscenity. And the Under-Secretary of State allowed it.

*

St John Mason, barrister-at-law and cousin of Robert Emmet, wrote to Richard Brinsley Sheridan in London, in the hope of publishing an indictment against Dr Trevor's personal conduct and administration of Kilmainham Gaol, which he hoped would be brought up in the Parliament at Westminster.

St John Mason described Trevor very charitably as `One whose sleepless hours are consumed in plotting against

234

human happiness and human life'.

And in Kilmainham, Dr Trevor lay awake; plotting against the human happiness of Michael and Mary Dwyer. By dawn he had come up with another idea to spoil their temper and appetites.

*

After the turnkey had brought in the water, another new attendant brought in their food rations. This time he was fairly clean, and the meat was fresh, a succulent joint of roasted beef from which their portion had not yet been sliced off.

Michael was sitting on the bed endeavouring to get Peter's chubby two-year-old legs into a pair of breeches. Mary sat at the table holding baby Esther. Mary-Anne and John sat each side of her, their eyes wide with awe as they stared at the giant who had brought in their food.

`I'll slice a nice big piece for you, shall I, ma'am?' the attendant said pleasantly to Mary, taking up a huge, very long-bladed knife.

This time it was Michael who froze and paled as he stared at the massive man, a man who had been pointed out to him on the first occasion he had seen him walking with Dr Trevor along the corridors of Kilmainham Gaol. He was Tom Galvin, the public executioner and hangman.

`Hello, me young hearties,' Galvin said brightly to Mary-Anne and John. `Yez are a bit young to be in prison, ain't yez? You ain't rebels I hope?'

Both stared back at him, too young to have learned what rebels were, although they had often heard people say their daddy was a rebel.

Galvin smiled at John and held up the huge knife. `Do you like my knife, boy? Ain't it a beauty?'

John nodded nervously at the giant. `It's a big one.'

`Aye, and a famous one. This is the knife that hacked off a rebel's head on Thomas Street.'

Peter yelled in fright when he was suddenly flung down on the bed and Michael sprang at the hangman.

Seconds later the guards rushed in on cue, and all the

235

children were screaming as the guards pounced and seemed to need all their strength to pinion Michael to the wall.

Dr Trevor entered the cell and pretended to look shocked and appalled. `This is not the kind of behaviour we expect from first-class prisoners, Dwyer. Good gracious, no! If you wish to create ructions then I am afraid you will have to be removed from the first-class to more appropriate accommodation elsewhere.'

`I demand the fulfilment of my terms!' Michael said with rage. `I did not surrender to William Hume for the privilege of spending my life caged in a prison! I demand that the government either fulfil my terms or admit it was all a double-cross.'

`Terms?' Dr Trevor looked at each of the guards with a disbelieving smirk, and then scornfully at Dwyer. `The government made terms – with you? I know nothing about your terms.'

`You damn well *do* know about my terms!'

`*Your terms! Your terms!*' Trevor screamed back, his eyes popping out of his head. `I know what your terms are better than you do yourself – you have no terms at all! There is no robber or highwayman could make better possible terms than saving his life, and the Capital Offence is where a rebel like you should be!'

And a devil like you should be back with your horn-headed father in hell!'

`Remove him to the felon's side and have him double-bolted,' Trevor ordered.

`No! No!' Mary screamed, throwing herself at the guards, who coldly pulled back the fingers gripping her husband's arm and pushed her aside. Her screams and those of the children brought Michael back to his senses.

`I'll go quietly,' he said in a low voice to Trevor. `Tell them to unhand me and I'll go quietly.'

Trevor was startled by his sudden change of demeanour. `Why should I allow you to go quietly?'

`Because my children are watching,' Michael hissed.

After a moment's consideration, the sides of his mouth turned down, Trevor nodded to the guards. `Let him come quietly.'

The guards were grinning at their victory over the noted rebel. `I will be back soon,' Michael said brightly to the children, flashing a message with his eyes to Mary, asking her to play the game. `We are all friends again, see?' He looked at the grinning guards. `And I will be back soon.'

Mary-Anne and John clung sobbing to his legs, but he restored them to their mother and firmly told them there was nothing to cry about, nothing at all.

Then he moved out of the cell and walked quietly down the corridor with guards before and behind and each side of him, and Dr. Trevor strutting like the ex-army man that he was, five paces behind.

`Dr Trevor, sir!'

The Superintendent spun round to face Tom Galvin, who was still very sour at being attacked by Dwyer and not getting the opportunity of using his knife before the guards came. But then, on reflection, Galvin was glad the guards had come in on signal, for he was not really a fighter, he was only used to dealing with men whose hands were chained.

`What shall I do with this now?' the hangman asked, holding up the tray of beef.

`What you have been paid to do with it, Mr Galvin,' Trevor retorted. `Serve it to the rest of the first-class prisoners.'

`Yes, sirrah!'

Galvin threw back his head and roared with laughter as he visualised the stunned faces of the prisoners when the public hangman walked into their cells. He laughed all the way down the corridor, for the whole situation delighted his gallows-style humour.

*

When Dr Trevor returned to the corridor an hour later, little Mary-Anne was still standing by the cell door, staring down the dark passage where her daddy had gone, hiccupping sobs to herself as she waited vigilantly for his return.

Trevor paused, stood for a moment looking down at the child who stared back at him from under her mop of curls in terror, and then he passed on and looked calmly at Mary as he entered the cell.

When she looked up, he bowed. `Madam,' he said reverently.

`Yes?' Mary whispered.

`I would be deeply grateful,' he said in a languid voice, `if you would kindly do me the pleasure of removing yourself and your brats from this prison within the hour.'

For a few seconds Mary said nothing, then her voice very quiet. `I' will not go anywhere without my husband. It was agreed that I could stay with him,' Mary's gaze was bitter. `Where I belong.'

Trevor's smile was mocking, almost pitying. `No, Madam, you belong back in Wicklow, but he belongs on the scaffold.'

`He'll die of suffocation anyway,' Mary cried savagely, `if he's kept caged in this prison much longer!'

`Then you must pray for him,' Trevor said with gentle scorn.

*

By that evening, Mary had been turned out of the prison with her children, Michael was securely bolted on the felon's side, and Dr. Trevor ended the day in blissful contentment as he smoked his long-pipe and pondered on the day's work.

It had taken longer than expected to get Michael Dwyer where he wanted him, and where he should have been from the day he entered Kilmainham eleven months ago; on the felon's side, in the company of murderers, highwaymen, and pimps.

And Dwyer's health would suffer in a very bad way for a time – deprived of the liquor he had come to need so badly to help him sleep. Just the thought of Dwyer shaking with his craving made Trevor almost swoon with pleasure.

The pity was that he would not be able to keep him there for long, not for more than a few weeks. The bastard had the status of a political prisoner and would eventually have to be sent back to the rebel wing – 'but not to the first class. His status would be reduced to second-class, and although deprived of the liquor and the company of his beloved wife, he would be consoled by the company of his dear comrades, Byrne, Burke and Mernagh, all back together with their leader in one cell. And then the next stage of the plan could be put into operation ... *Ley fuga*.

Dr Trevor smiled. In stalemate situations of this kind, *ley fuga* was the best solution – prisoner shot in the act of escape. It had worked many times before, and it was the easiest way to get rid of the four rebels in one swift move – plan their escape for them, and shoot them as they attempted it.

But every coin had two sides, and within minutes Trevor was frowning. Of course, Lord Hardwicke had every intention of putting Dwyer on a ship, as soon as he could procure one.

Trevor sat back and took a long reflective chew on his pipe, and then he inhaled deeply and blew out the smoke with a slow smile.

Still, Lord Hardwicke would be spared the trouble and have no further need to procure a ship... if his plan of *ley fuga* succeeded.

Chapter Eighteen

Since the day of Michael Dwyer's imprisonment fifteen months previously, Lord Hardwicke had been pressing the Home Office in London for a ship. And now, at last, in the spring of 1805, he had received word from Lord Hawkesbury that a ship had been engaged and would leave England within two months.

Everyone in the Castle breathed a huge sigh of relief; and Alexander Marsden sent for Dr Trevor.

`Inform the prisoner,' Marsden said, `that a ship has been engaged and will soon be on its way.'

Trevor looked crestfallen. `How soon?'

`The ship is called the *Tellicherry*,' Marsden said. `It will hold one hundred and eighty passengers, including Dwyer and his associates. We have hopes of it docking at Cork sometime at the beginning of June. So, with any luck, we should be rid of the rebel captain by the end of summer.'

*

Dr Trevor had the sly look of a cunning old fox when he stepped into Michael Dwyer's cell, a cell he shared with Hugh Vesty. It was a hellhole containing nothing but a pile of straw for sleeping, the window was unglazed, making the night temperature sub-zero in winter, and the door was always locked.

A hellhole the other prisoners had complained about in a signed memorial of protest, which had not included the name of Michael Dwyer. He had signed the second memorial to be sneaked out, but their complaints were largely ignored as a list of `gross exaggerations.' And so they were continually served with food that was uneatable; the meat putrid and vegetables rotten.

A hell-hole in which Michael's treatment at the hands of Dr Trevor had got worse and worse as the days passed, until it became a mental battle of wills between the two of them. The Inquisitor-General had even concocted a plan to provide an excuse to have him and his three comrades shot while attempting to escape.

As soon as the escape plan had been whispered to him, Michael had jumped at the chance, and had even succeeded, with Hugh Vesty and the others, to get as far as the governor's empty office and were about to escape down the coal hole beneath, when the simple easiness of it all suddenly made him suspicious. He scrambled up to the window and saw a large guard of soldiers with fixed bayonets outside the prison wall; some were simply waiting, others were priming and loading ... *ley fuga.*

It was an old prison trick, and in their desperation they had almost fallen for it; and for weeks afterwards Dr Trevor had stalked Kilmainham in a black rage of frustration. He was a lot calmer now as he looked down at the two rebels sitting on their straw and playing cards.

`Well, Dwyer,' Dr Trevor said brightly, `it seems your ship is about to come in.'

Michael did not lift up his head but turned a wry face to Hugh Vesty. `What do you say, avic? Should we believe him?'

Hugh Vesty shook his head. `No, sir, we should not. The man is incapable of telling the truth. You only have to look at his eyes to see they've gone crooked with his roguery.'

`Very funny, very funny,' Trevor declared, quite used to their sarcasm. `You boys will never lose your dry tongues and humour, will you? But maybe a long dose of the salty sea-air will dry them up completely.'

Trevor held up the sheet of paper bearing the government seal. `This is the official notice which orders me to inform one Michael Dwyer, Hugh Vesty Byrne, John Mernagh, Martin Burke, and Arthur Devlin, to prepare themselves to sail out of the kingdom – in accordance with the surrender terms agreed by the aforementioned Michael Dwyer.'

Trevor hefted a defeated sigh. `As you know, Dwyer, I have always been of the opinion that the whole lot of you should be hanged, but what can I do now but accept the situation and pray the ship will sink. The same ship that has been arranged by Lord Hardwicke himself. A ship called...' Trevor looked down at the paper...`the *Tellicherry.*'

Michael leaned forward and peered at the paper, which was undoubtedly genuine. He could hardly believe it. `America...' He looked at Hugh Vesty, his voice full of wonder. `Do you hear that, avic? As long as it has taken, our ship is truly coming in at last, to take us to America.'

`America?' Dr Trevor could no longer contain his laughter at the joke it.

`You will never see America, Dwyer. Do you think the government are such damned fools as to send you to the rebel states of America from which you might come back when you please to rise another rebellion?'

Michael looked at Trevor stunned.

`But William Hume – '

`William Hume took too much upon himself when he promised you America,' Trevor said contemptuously. `He over-estimated his influence with the Castle. Lord Hardwicke did agree to spare your life and give you a passage out of the kingdom in return for your peaceable surrender, but the day after you obliged, his Excellency wrote to London requesting a convict ship for Botany Bay – and that is where you are going – to the penal colony of Botany Bay. You and your comrades and one hundred and seventy-five more along with you. And seeing as the ship will be overcrowded, your wives and children, of course, will not be going with you.'

Trevor laughed again at the disbelief on their faces.

It was Hugh Vesty who finally spoke.

`If what you say be the true intention of your government, then they are what we always took them to be, a corrupt and perfidious set, and they have a ready and willing tool in you!'

`All Ireland knows the terms agreed on my surrender,' Michael said, coming out of his shock, `and the blatant violation of those terms by the government will be published to the world. Have no doubt on that.'

`The government,' Trevor said, `has asked me to present you with an ultimatum, Dwyer. Either publicly declare your willingness to go to New South Wales, or stand trial for high treason.'

`I'll stand my trial,' Michael snapped. `And as every rebel trial is rigged – I'll have my speech in the dock and publicly tell the bastards what I think of them.'

`Oh, they've had enough of that kind of speech,' Trevor said blithely. `You'd be gagged and dragged away after your first sentence. What you should concentrate on now, my boyo, is the event that usually takes place after a trial – the high hanging.'

Michael managed a contemptuous smile. `If you are trying to terrorise me with visions of the noose, Dr Trevor, then you haven't yet learned just how callous I am.'

`Callous enough to allow your precious wife and children to stand and watch you swing in the wind?' Dr Trevor looked deeply shocked. `Oh yes, they would be brought to watch. And every yeoman in Rathdrum and Baltinglass would be cheering as they wept. And as a physician I feel I should tell you that many a young wife has had to be committed to the insane asylum after witnessing such a scene. Now ... how do you think your poor devoted wife would cope?'

As soon as Dwyer sprang to his feet, the waiting guards rushed in. Dr Trevor escaped the rough and tumble and rushed back to the Castle to report the result to Alexander Marsden.

`He'll never agree to go willingly in public,' Trevor opined.

`Then you must persuade him!' the Under-Secretary snapped. `That is what the secret service funds pay you for!'

`Why not just bring him to trial and execution?' Trevor demanded. `It's no more than he deserves. I have threatened him with no less.'

Marsden flopped down in his chair and looked at Dr Trevor with cool grey eyes.

`We cannot bring him to trial and execution without exposing a flagrant breach of his surrender terms. And those terms were his life and a passage out of the country. But never once, in any newspaper article, was it mentioned that the passage was to America. So if we can send him off to Botany Bay with as little trouble as possible, and with his agreement, the whole sorry business and Michael Dwyer himself will be quickly forgotten.'

`Then I have no choice but to continue my efforts to persuade him.'

`Do!' Marsden said. `And remind him that any decision he makes affects not only himself, but the friends he sought fit to include in his surrender terms. Remind him that if he is brought to trial, they will too. If he is hanged, they will too. But if he agrees to go to the sunny climate of Botany Bay, they will too.'

`That's a fair enough argument,' Trevor agreed. `I'll go back now and use my powers of persuasion.'

*

In Kilmainham, Dr Trevor used all his powers of persuasion on Michael Dwyer. He was removed to the worst cell in the dungeons, double-bolted to the wall, and loaded down with four stone of irons. The only window in the cell opened on to the corridor and was kept closed. He was taken off the food allowance and allowed only bread and water and one pint of milk a week. And all to persuade him to agree to be transported to Botany Bay.

After two months, Dr Trevor reported to Marsden that the rebel was still holding out as strong as ever.

`I thought his cell in the dungeons would do the trick,' Trevor said despondently. `There is little air in there as the window is on the corridor wall and is kept locked. For a man that was reared on the fresh air of the mountains it must be sheer torture, but the bastard is every bit as callous as he said he was.'

Marsden looked worried.

`And that's not the worst of it,' Trevor informed him. `Hugh Vesty Byrne, John Mernagh, Martin Burke, and Arthur Devlin have all been double-bolted on the felon's side, but they too are holding out – none will agree to show the public that they are willing to forego the promise of America and go to Botany Bay as a more just and appropriate penance for their crimes.'

`They'll agree to go if their leader does,' Marsden said,

`and we need him to agree soon. The Tellicherry is already at anchor in the Cove of Cork.'

`You'll just have to transport him by force then,' Trevor said. `What else can you do?'

`I'd better bring in the newspapers to help us,' Marsden said. `They can start a campaign against the rebel captain which should bring public opinion to our view. In situations of this kind, the newspapers have never failed us yet.'

`I should think not!' Trevor exclaimed. `Considering the vasts amount of money you pay them. I'm told Cody of the *Post* is receiving a salary of four hundred pounds from the secret service funds – more than myself!'

`And he is worth every penny,' Marsden snapped, and could not help thinking just how essential to any good government was the system of having the newspaper editors in their pay. The editor of the *Dublin Post* in particular, rarely ever published a word without submitting it first to the Under-Secretary of State.

*

William Hume had been away in London attending Parliament. On his return he went immediately to Dublin Castle and furiously demanded to see Lord Hardwicke.

`This places me in a very unpleasant and potentially dangerous position in County Wicklow,' Hume said, `if the terms I promised Michael Dwyer to induce his surrender are not kept. All the newspaper reports have done is make public that the promises I gave have been broken. Do you not understand that I stand in very great danger of being assassinated!'

It was a problem, Lord Hardwicke agreed, but he was determined that Michael Dwyer and his men would sail out of Ireland on the Tellicherry.

`And what about Dwyer's wife?' Hume demanded. `He would never have surrendered only I agreed, as you did, that his wife and children would be allowed to go with him. And I assure you that it will provide no service to the country to leave her in Wicklow after he is gone. She has me tormented over him already. I put it to you plainly, my lord, if Mary Dwyer is left in Wicklow, there will be no shortage of those anxious to carry out her revenge on the man and men she believes have betrayed her husband.'

William Hume's face was the colour of beet, the sweat beginning to glisten on his brow.

`And if I may say so, my lord, it *is* a betrayal. The only reason you offered him surrender terms in the first place, is because you were informed by the military commanders that he would never be taken by other means.'

A compromise was eventually agreed, a compromise that Dwyer might find acceptable, and which would demonstrate to the whole country the *mercy* of its government.

*

Michael was brought into Dr Trevor's parlour to see William Hume. He had lost stones in weight and his hair was an untidy mass of black curls around his shoulders.

`Well damn my eyes,' Michael rasped with a crack of a smile. `Is it Judas or Mr Hume himself?'

`I have not betrayed you, Dwyer,' Hume said with feeling. `I believed you were to be sent to America, but now I am told that I misunderstood, that I made assumptions I had no right to make. It is my belief that we have both been ... misled.'

`I sent you three letters which you chose to ignore,' Michael said. `Three letters written to you in the most respectful terms, asking you to honour the pledges you made to me.'

`And I forwarded those letters directly to the Castle with a note of my own, asking for you to be sent out as soon as possible.'

`And now they intend to send me out, and not to America, but Botany Bay, and the sacred honour of William Hume is set at nought.'

`Not quite at nought,' Hume said quietly. `I have been to see Lord Hardwicke on your behalf and he has now agreed to a compromise ... You and your comrades will go to New South Wales, not as convicts, but as free men. On arrival in Sydney you will each be given a land grant of one hundred acres each. Think of it, man! – a new life for you all, with land of your own, land that will belong to no man but you – one hundred acres of it.'

Dr Trevor, standing quietly in the corner, almost fainted, and had to slump down in a chair when William Hume added:

'And in view of your long detention in prison, which is another breach of the surrender terms, the government has agreed that we should compensate you with the sum of two hundred pounds to help you purchase the farming implements you will need to begin your life in New South Wales. Your comrades will each receive one hundred for the same breach, and for the same purpose. I think it is a very fair compromise, and a wonderful opportunity for you.'

'One hundred acres of my own land is indeed a like a dream come true,' Michael admitted, 'but the wonder fades when I remember that land would be in a British colony, ruled by the British Parliament and its administrators, and ruled by redcoats. How can I be sure that as soon as I land there, I will not be double-crossed again and immediately linked to a chain-gang?'

'Here are the papers,' William Hume showed them to him. 'All are signed and sealed by His Excellency and show that the five of you are to be admitted into the colony as free men. New South Wales has plenty of convicts – it is free men willing to work hard for their fortune and turn the settlement into a country that New South Wales needs.'

'And our wives can come with us?'

'Certainly.'

Michael looked long at William Hume. 'They will never agree to let us go to the free states of America, will they?'

'No,' Hume said emphatically. 'But you have to admit, this is a very good second-best.'

Michael shrugged realistically. 'I reckon it's the best I can hope for.'

After a silence, he said tiredly to Hume: 'Will you advise Mary of this so-called compromise, and ask her to prepare herself and the children for our departure.'

William Hume paled. 'My dear fellow ... I don't think you

understand ... although you will be transported as free men, the Tellicherry is a *convict* ship. It is overcrowded already. Your wife may go with you ... but not your children.'

Michael blinked a number of times, as if he couldn't quite take the last in. `We will not go without them,' he said incredulously. `Are you crazy? How could Mary and I have any kind of new life without the four new lives we have created?'

`You must understand,' Hume said in flustered tones, `it would not be safe for them to go on a convict ship that might break out in fever. Convict ships usually do break out in the most terrible fevers, and children catch it the first. They could very well die before they even reached New South Wales. At least here, in the care of your family, they would be safe. When they have grown into young adults they could join you out there. You will have made your fortune by then and be able to send them their passage money.'

`No.' Michael shook his head emphatically. `I'd rather let my children see me hanged than let them think I willingly deserted them. And my father has enough to house and feed without my four as well.'

Dr Trevor sat back and listened, his humour brighter as Hume reasoned, then argued, and then almost lost his temper as the battle of words became more angry and more heated.

`No!' Michael cried. `I can forfeit my country but never my children!'

`Perhaps I had better speak to your wife,' Hume said wearily.

`Well if I won't agree, she is even less likely to agree.'

William Hume flopped his arms in defeat. `I have done everything I can. I can do no more. I will convey the Castle's offer to your wife and the wives of Hugh Vesty Byrne and Martin Burke. After that, the people of Wicklow will know I have achieved the best I could for you; a passage out of the country as a free man.'

As soon as William Hume had left the room, Dr Trevor summoned the waiting guards and the prisoner was returned to the cell in the dungeon where he was double-bolted again, loaded down with irons and continued on his starvation diet.

A week later Dr Trevor visited him again. `Hugh Vesty Byrne has agreed to go to New South Wales under the government's new terms,' he informed him. `So have Burke, Mernagh and your cousin Arthur Devlin.'

`Good luck to them so,' Michael answered.

`Don't be a fool, Dwyer! They can agree to nothing without you. If the government is forced to send you out as a convict they will be sent as convicts also. The only reason they have not been brought to trial is because they were included in your surrender terms. It is up to you, Dwyer? Are you going to deny your faithful comrades a chance of a new life as free men?'

`I'll not agree to go without my children,' Michael said, stubbornly. `So bugger off!'

Dr Trevor had no alternative but to report his intractable attitude to Alexander Marsden.

`Tell him he can take his blasted children then!' Marsden snapped. `The other prisoners are already being loaded onto the Tellicherry at Cork and yet Dwyer and his men remain in Kilmainham. We are running out of time, Dr Trevor, and we do not wish Dwyer to force our hand. This administration is in enough trouble as it is.'

`What?' Trevor stared at Marsden open-mouthed. `Dwyer can take his children?'

`He can take his children,' Marsden repeated. `I no longer care who he takes as long as he goes and is seen to go willingly.'

Marsden looked coldly at Trevor. `And you can take that look off your face – Dwyer is the least of your problems now. While you have been concentrating on the Wicklow rebels, St John Mason, the cousin of Robert Emmet, has been gathering evidence which he hopes to get published, exposing the suffering of political prisoners in Kilmainham Gaol.'

`Huh!' Trevor was not in the least alarmed. `Mason may have been a talented young barrister-at-law before he became a rebel, but he holds no clout in this city anymore. In response to his last signed memorial, Judge Day examined the prison and found it very satisfactory.'

`Only because you were given a week's warning and had time with your underlings to put on a show and send out for the best food the city could provide – a fact that is now known in all the wrong quarters.'

Marsden's grey eyes were glittering. `Mason is relentless in his determination to bring you down. With his lawyer's hand he has written down every abuse, every act of violence, every act of obscenity. And he has finally succeeded in getting his message to men of influence on the outside. Now one of the noisiest lawyers in Ireland, Mr. Daniel O'Connell, has threatened to lay the conditions of the State prisoners in Kilmainham before people in authority and have the matter brought up in Parliament. A baseless threat, you may say, but now there is also a rumour that over in England, Richard Brinsley Sheridan, a most respected member of the Westminster Parliament, is seeking to raise the subject of prison abuses in Ireland before the Commons – in particular – Kilmainham Gaol.'

Dr Trevor was struck speechless, and remained so when Marsden gave him the worst news of all.

`Also, an allegation has been made that both you and I own the bakery that supplies food to Kilmainham Gaol. Do you see the headlines that could make: the Under-Secretary of State and the Prison Superintendent own the bakery that receives large amounts of government money for supplying food to the starving prisoners in Kilmainham Gaol! They will say we are worse criminals than the inmates!'

Marsden looked as if he was going to be sick, his face as pale as a sheet. `The allegation shall be denied as a slanderous lie, of course.'

`But ... surely you can deal with them, Marsden? You have great power here in Ireland.'

`But *not* in England! Not since the Emmet affair. Why else, despite my years as Under-Secretary, was I not promoted to Chief Secretary when Wickham resigned with all that nonsense of not wishing to dip his hands in any more Irish blood. I should have been given the post as Chief Secretary, I *earned* the post as Chief Secretary – but they sent Evan Nepean over instead. No, Dr Trevor, I cannot, as you say, deal with them. Not very easily, anyway.'

And in that moment Dr Trevor knew that Alexander Marsden would not hesitate to send the Superintendent of Kilmainham to the wall, if the situation and his own reputation required it.

*

When Mary arrived at Kilmainham, Dr Trevor greeted her in a very subdued and contrite manner.

`Mrs Dwyer,' he said respectfully, `I have done wrong to you in the past, and now feel compelled to ask your pardon and forgiveness.'

Mary spoke softly. `I don't think I could ever forgive you.'

`I understand,' Trevor replied wearily. `Yes, I do. But could you, perhaps, find it in your heart to at least try?'

`Why should I?'

Trevor shrugged. `Because I once thought you and your husband and your kind were despicable. Now I realise it is the men in high places who are truly the despicable ones. They use men like me to do their dirty work, and then throw us to the wall when we are of no further use. Now it is them I despise. Now it is you I would like to help, by making amends, and doing something decent for a change.'

Mary's confusion showed on her face. `How can you help me now?'

`In a very practical way.'

*

Dr Trevor was at his most gentle when he personally came to bring Michael Dwyer up to his parlour and give him the wonderful news that he could take his children with him to New South Wales.

Michael was so relieved he smiled in genuine gratitude at the infamous tyrant, and even accepted the glass of whiskey Trevor shoved into his hand.

A different Michael, full of strength, might have taken the

opportunity to throw the whiskey in Trevor's face, but weakened and wearied by his starvation diet and long confinement, he no longer cared enough. All he wanted was to get out into the fresh air with his wife and children and start a new life.

`Drink up,' Trevor urged gently. `I know how you must need it; but believe me, it was the Castle who ordered me to double-bolt you and load you with irons. Yes, yes, they are a savage set and I'm suddenly sick to the heart of doing their dirty work.'

Michael looked at Trevor first in shock, then suspiciously. Then he took a drink of the whiskey which burned down to his empty stomach, then went dizzily to his head.

`I remonstrated very hotly with the Castle on your behalf,' Trevor explained, topping up the glass. `I told them that any man – any man – who had seen you with your children – as I did here in Kilmainham, could not possibly expect you to leave without them.'

Michael narrowed his eyes. `What little game are you playing this time?'

`No game, no game,' Trevor said quietly and tiredly. `It happens to men, you know, to the most unlikely of men too. One morning they wake up and take a good look at their life, at themselves, and they don't like what they see ... and I suddenly don't like the man that Dublin Castle and Kilmainham Gaol have made me.'

`An overnight conversion, eh? An old devil like you?' Michael chuckled, then laughed outright.

Dr Trevor accepted the insult meekly. `It has happened to better and worse men than me. It happened to St Paul on the road to Damascus. Yet before that day he was violent in the extreme against the Christians. Was it not he that ordered the stoning of Stephen, the first Christian martyr. And yet, after Damascus, when he saw the badness of his ways, he became a Christian martyr himself.'

Michael stared at him, listening to the bizarre words and unable to believe or make sense of them. Trevor talked on in a low contrite voice, but Michael had stopped listening. He looked around the room, which appeared, very cluttered and colourful after his bare cell, and then he turned his eyes to the window and sat staring, his mind going blank.

He was only vaguely aware of Trevor moving to his feet and going to the door. Then a hand touched his face and he heard her voice.

He came back to life at once, turned, and slowly stood up and stared at her; still the loveliest thing he ever saw. And then she was in his arms, kissing him in full view of Dr Trevor, and he didn't care.

Dr Trevor found the loving reunion quite unbearable. `I think, my dear girl,' he said finally, `that we should give the poor man time to breathe and recollect his strength. We are very short of time, and we have to discuss the subject of your children.'

He carried over a chair and placed it beside Mary. The two sat down again, but Mary would not let go of Michael's hand. She was suddenly nervous, and very unsure of herself.'

`I have brought you a new set of clothes,' she told him. `I made them myself.'

`You have heard that we can all go together?' Michael said to her. `As they originally agreed.'

`Aye. Dr Trevor told me yesterday.'

`Yesterday.' Michael looked from one to the other. `So why was I not told until today?'

`Because I have been seeking a way to help you both,' Trevor said gently, and then looked at Mary. `Perhaps you will explain.'

It was only then he noticed how thin she had become, how black her eyes looked against her pale skin, and there was a continual trembling about her mouth as she spoke.

Mr Hume, she explained, had told her about the government's compromise that did not include the children. At first she had been in an agony of confusion, for she would not let him go without her, but neither could she leave her children. But then, the more she thought about the danger of the convict ship, the fever and contagion that killed many adults on board those ships, she knew she could never agree to let her babies travel on such a vessel whether the government agreed or not. What was she to do? She thought she might die with the suffering of her mind. She could see no answer to it, until she came to the prison yesterday after receiving word from Dr Trevor, and he now had come up with a solution.

Michael turned his eyes to the reformed tyrant who suddenly looked very tired and old.

`It is the only solution to your wife's dilemma,' Trevor said softly. `As you know, I am the agent of transport in Ireland. There is another vessel leaving for New South Wales three months after the Tellicherry. A trading ship containing cargo and supplies needed in the colony. Passengers such as military men and their families will be travelling on it. I can arrange for your children to be sent out after you on board that ship, accompanied by one of your relatives as chaperon.'

Mary turned huge black eyes to Michael. `It's a wonderful solution,' she said breathlessly. `The only acceptable solution. Don't you see, Michael, I *cannot* allow the children to travel on a convict ship full of prostitutes and men and women riddled with all kind of diseases. But a trading ship with officers and their families would be free of all sickness.'

He looked at her as if she had been uttering the same sort of bizarre words as Trevor had done earlier.

`Then ... why could you not wait and travel with the children later in the trading vessel?'

`I can't,' she said, tears in her voice and eyes. `The Castle insist I must go with you. Mr Hume insists I must go with you. And Michael ... I *want* to go with you!'

He wanted her to go with him too. But he was so confused, so bewildered, it was all too much to take in his weary and weakened state. He was unable to cope with the confusion of it all. After holding out in his irons long enough for the Castle to agree about the children, now Mary was asking him to go without them. He turned his eyes to window, not knowing what to do.'

`I'll not risk my children dying,' she said vehemently. `And Dr Trevor has given his solemn word that he will make sure the children travel on the trading vessel. He has

254

given his oath on the Bible.'

Again Michael looked at Trevor suspiciously. `Why are you doing this? You have done your best to abuse and torture and starve me, even hoped to have me shot dead in the act of escape. Why should you now want to help me or mine?'

`I understand your lack of faith,' Trevor replied softly. `I can hardly blame you for it. But I assure you, I will do as I say. Even Mr Marsden agrees that your children should be allowed to go, but not on a convict ship, that would be too uncaring of such small children. So now you must make your decision. It is something only the two of you can worry over and decide. I shall not try to influence you in any way. And now I will leave you alone for a short while.'

He stood up, nodded his head at Mary. `The cutter engaged to take the five men to Cork is leaving Dublin Bay tomorrow. If you want to make any last final arrangements about your children, you will have to leave here fairly soon, and then make your own way to Cork. The *Tellicherry* will soon be leaving Ireland, and the government is determined that your husband will be on it.'

`When?' she asked. `When will the ship be leaving?'

`In a matter of days.'

When the door had closed, both looked at each other in helpless anguish and impotence as they considered the decision before them. Their children ranged from six years to ten months. How could they leave them? But could they expose them to the dangers of a long voyage on a convict ship? Could they take even the smallest risk on their children's lives when Dr Trevor had promised to send them on only a few months later in the care of one of their relatives?

Some short minutes after his departure, Dr Trevor returned. `Well?' he asked, looking at them both. `Have you decided?'

Michael had enough sense to remain silent. He knew that if he was forced to say the words he would weep. Mary answered for him, then sat looking around her in tear-drenched puzzlement, every part of her shaking, as if suddenly wondering why the bottom had fallen from her world.

What had happened? It had all seemed so simple when she had asked him to surrender. Why had it all gone so terribly wrong?

Her mind was still in turmoil when she finally left the prison to make her arrangements and say a last tearful farewell to her parents and her children. She knew she would never see her parents again; and yet, as painful as that was, it was nowhere near the pain she felt when she thought of the eleven months that she would be parted from her babies, eight months on the sea and three months following. Eleven long months and twelve thousand miles between them.

Her father and mother travelled with her to the farmhouse at Eadstown where she handed her children into the care of Michael's mother. Everyone tried to be cheerful and said encouraging words to Mary as she whispered lilting little phrases of love to one child then the next, then stood crushing her handkerchief between her palms as she stared at her baby daughter sleeping in her own mother's arms.

Michael's mother dealt with the situation as she always did, employing herself busily and efficiently with the numerous things that had to be done in a house where four little ones had come to stay. But when she finally paused to take a sip of the tea she had poured out for everyone, she suddenly made a choking sound in her throat and the cup crashed down onto the table. For a moment tears glistened in her eyes, but before anyone could notice them, she moved hastily over to the sink and began pummelling away at the washing, her brows contracted, as if nothing on earth was more important than the job she had in hand.

The rest of the family stood around the kitchen but no one spoke. Even William Doyle was lost for a sentence as he sat in moping silence, dressed in his finest coat and holding a new hat. He would not allow anyone else to take his daughter all the way to Cork harbour, and he intended that when she took her last look on him as she sailed into exile, she would remember him at his best.

`Where is himself?' he said suddenly, looking around for Michael's father, who he had only just noticed was not present.

`He's gone to Dublin,' Mrs Dwyer murmured, without turning round. `Gone with a hope and a prayer of being allowed to say a last goodbye to our son.'

*

His prayer was answered. John Dwyer stood in a corner of the empty yard of Kilmainham Gaol, a helpless look on his face as he looked at his son.

Michael closed his eyes for a brief moment. His head ached and the yard still tilted at a sickening angle.

`I know one day I will look back and say it was worth it,' he said shakily. `The day my children join me in Botany Bay. But truth to tell, Daddy, at this minute I feel a high hanging would have been easier.'

John Dwyer stared at his first and favourite son, saw the tears in his eyes, and the pain in his own heart swelled so much he had to turn away.

`Aye,' he said bitterly. `It is not always those who die on the battlefield or on the gallows that suffer the most. But who would ever believe that?'

A guard stepped into the yard and called out. It was time to go, to the cutter waiting in Dublin Bay.

Both men ignored him.

John Dwyer looked up at the August sun. It was promising to be a very warm day and he was already hot in his Sunday suit. The misery in his heart, the ache of parting was no less than bereavement, for he knew he would never see Michael again after this day. He looked at the sky again, hugging his sorrow tightly, frightened it would escape him. He dare not weaken; the first thing that Michael had asked of him when he arrived, was that he should not weaken and make it harder for both of them.

`I have no money left and nothing to give you,' he said finally, `except these...' He took from his pocket a small piece of whitewashed stone from the wall of the house in Eadstown, and a small lump of turf from the fields around it.'

`Two small pieces of home to take with you,' he whispered.

Michael nodded and took the mementoes of Imaal. He was silent for a moment, and then said in a soft voice. `I was thinking last night of the time on the high meadows when we hunted the dog-fox together. Do you remember that, Daddy, the night we finally caught that vicious old chicken-killer?'

`The fox that ran across the moon?' John Dwyer smiled. `You were my hero that night, boy.'

They stood in silence, miserably conscious that their life together was almost finished forever.

Then Michael started as another memory struck him. `I nearly forgot ... I have something for you.' He reached into his pocket and withdrew a fold of money and pressed it into his father's hand.

John Dwyer was struck speechless as he stared at the money.

`One hundred pounds,' Michael said, `to help with the expense of the care of my children until they can join us.'

`Where ... where did you get this money?'

`William Hume and the government decided to compensate me for my two years imprisonment and the breach of my surrender terms with two hundred pounds. It seems I will need to purchase farming implements and other goods for my new life in New South Wales.'

His father shook his head. `Take it back so. I don't want any money for the care of my own grandchildren.'

`I want you to have it,' Michael insisted, turning away as the guard called again, less politely this time. His father had no choice but to follow him across the yard.

The guard held the door open for them and again spoke urgently about the carriages that were waiting to convey him and his comrades to the docks. John Dwyer muttered an apologetic response, but Michael did not condescend to exchange a word with any of his guardians who attempted to speak to him as he returned to the dark interior of Kilmainham Gaol.

They came out into the bright sunlight again a short time later, but this time Michael was in the company of his three comrades and the waiting crowd outside the gates roared their cheers and calls of support. A few seconds later Arthur Devlin was brought out to join them, and the five walked towards the waiting carriages which had armed guards front and back and either side of them.

Again Michael tried not to look back as he moved to climb inside the carriage, but the yearning was just too great. He turned and looked back, his eyes searching over the heads of the blur of people until his eyes rested on the lonely figure of his father standing by the inner gate of Kilmainham Gaol.

His father nodded, his mouth doing its best to smile.

Michael grinned bravely, then waved as the carriage pulled away. And that was the last memory of him that his father cherished through every day and month and year of his life that followed.

Chapter Nineteen

In Cork harbour, the *Tellicherry* was almost ready to set sail.

A number of communications were sent to the Castle informing Mr Marsden that 166 convicts were securely on board; 130 men and 36 women. The convict list should have been more, but as the fever which was reigning in the *Renown* lying alongside had now crept into the *Tellicherry* it was decided to put no more on, especially as enough space had to be allocated to Michael Dwyer and his associates, a space which would keep them separate from the convicts and still in security.

Among the communications was a report from Dr Harding who had inspected the *Tellicherry* and found the men's prison not sufficiently ventilated. He also found the women's prison very small, but decided that –

> '...*as most generally sleep in other parts of the ship, it is of no consequence, but for the danger of spreading the fever. On the Tellicherry I saw a soldier (who informed me he was ill for two days) lying in the berths with the other soldiers and women. If they are not more circumspect and cautious about contagion the consequences must be very bad'.*

Then Marsden received a communication that made him smile with satisfaction and relief. Michael Dwyer and his associates had been received on board. So far they had behaved very well, except with the barber who had been denied his earnings of sixpence a head; Dwyer had slapped the barber's face when he attempted to touch his hair, saying the government had agreed that they would not be shaved or put with the convicts or put in irons or treated in any way as convicts.

For their accommodation they had been given one of the Hospitals on the Tellicherry, a space big enough to accommodate them adequately, which they acknowledged.

Marsden's face showed no expression when he read the last few lines:

> `I shall request Captain Cuzens not to put them in irons at present. When he is at sea he will of course do what he considers most proper.'

The Tellicherry lay far out in the waters of Cork harbour. Up and down its decks the crew were preparing to weigh anchor and set sail. Mary stood in a nightmare of anxiety beside Michael on the deck, both staring silently towards the distant shore, both thinking the same thoughts. Neither was yet capable of speaking calmly or intelligently about their children to the other.

Consumed as she was by her own worries, Mary cast pitiful eyes at the dejected faces of Hugh Vesty and Martin Burke standing each side of them; neither of their wives had come to Cork to sail into exile with them.

Mary was not too surprised that Rachel Burke had not come, for she had seemingly lost interest in Martin after his first few months in prison. But Sarah Byrne ... Mary could not believe that Sarah, her dear friend Sarah who had shared and cared with her in the days gone by, had now turned her back on Hugh Vesty. She had always believed that Sarah was as faithful and devoted to her man as she was.

Hugh Vesty had always believed that too. He stared towards the harbour in the far distance like a man in a trance. Michael put a hand on his shoulder with the intention of giving comfort, but suddenly his hand gripped Hugh Vesty's shoulder hard as his keen eyesight detected a small boat rowing towards the *Tellicherry* with a female in it. The boat was almost half a mile away, but he could clearly see the bonnet of a female.

`Hugh...' he whispered, pointing to the boat.

Hugh jerked alert and stared and stared, then in a fever of excitement shouted up to the captain on the bridge. `It's my wife! You can't sail yet! She has government permission to sail with us!'

Captain Cuzens was well aware of that, and being a

261

conscientious and good-natured man, agreed to let the *Tellicherry* lie while waiting for its final passenger.

Mary was delighted, not only for Hugh Vesty, but herself. Now she would have her dear friend for female company and solace when they reached the alien new land on the other side of the world. She stood with palms pressed at each side of her smiling face, but as the boat drew near, and the quarter-master ordered the chair to be lowered over the side, the smile slowly faded from Mary's face, her eyes widening; then a sound like a choking cry escaped her lips.

Michael also stared at the occupants of the boat, just managing to catch Mary who suddenly slumped against him as Sarah stepped on board with her children.

`I couldn't leave them!' Sarah cried, seeing their reaction. `I couldn't leave my children, not for the eight months of the voyage nor the three months in following. I couldn't leave them for that long – not for eleven hours, never mind eleven months!' She turned to her husband with a look of desperation. `I had to do it, Hugh, risk the fever and the dangers. I couldn't leave them behind.'

Hugh Vesty could only smile at her with love and relief. But the sight of the children had reduced Mary to an agony of breathing. She looked wildly at them with dilated nostrils, her bosom heaving. How could she endure the length of the voyage with these children to remind her of the four she had left behind?

As the slow swelling pain became unbearable she broke down completely, emitting great grinding heaving sobs that echoed over the ship, evoking deep pity in everyone that heard her.

Grief and frustration struggling violently within him, Michael looked up at the captain, although he knew it was futile even to think it, let alone ask. The journey to Wicklow and back would take too long, too many days.

The small-boat was rowing away. Captain Cuzens gave signal to the ships of the East India fleet waiting to escort the *Tellicherry* as far as Madeira.

The convict ship sailed out of Cork on the evening tide. And it was then, that Sarah moved with the others to the ship's rail and reached to take Mary's hand in her own. Mary gripped it tightly, her other hand clasped in Michael's as the Wicklow group stood in sombre silence and stared at the land shrinking away. They were sailing southward, at six knots an hour; out of sight of land after the ship had cleared the headlands of the bay.

Ireland of the Sorrows was no more. They were no longer citizens of their homeland, but then they had never been. Each in their own silent way said farewell to the land all had loved and most had fought for. Each in their own silent way said goodbye to Ireland.

Mary was not even aware that Sarah's hand had slipped away as one by one the others left the breezy deck and the Dwyers alone.

They stood together, watching the rise and fall of the sea, but thinking of the land, the solid dry land of the Glen of Imaal.

In Imaal the sun would be setting behind the hills. In the farmhouse at Eadstown four little children would be feeling sleepy now, maybe still wondering where their mammy had gone.

Gone with their daddy.

And as the wind sung around the rigging of the three-masted ship and the sky darkened over the sea, Mary-Anne's familiar little questioning voice floated over the waves to Mary ... asking the same questions she had asked night after night in the months after they have been forced out of Kilmainham Gaol and back to Wicklow . . . `And where has Daddy gone? Is it far, far away? Is it somewhere down the dark passage in Kilmainham Gaol in Dublin town?'

And Michael's mother would no doubt hush and pet and give the answer always given to Irish children who asked where their daddies had gone.

`He's gone to find the crock of gold at the end of the rainbow. And when he finds it, darling, he will send for you.'

And the answer would satisfy, as it always did at sleepy evening-time when the hills were draped in blue shadows and the stars began to twinkle in the sky. But in the harsh light of morning the questions would be asked again.

Where had their daddy gone? Was it far, far away? Was it somewhere down the dark passage in Kilmainham Gaol in Dublin town?

*

From the bridge, the Captain of the ship watched the couple standing alone on the deck, wrapped into each other, like one person and not two. It was clear they were fond of each other, very fond indeed.

Good luck to them, Captain Cuzens thought, unaware that he was the most humane captain ever to master a convict ship. Good luck to them, they would need it where they were going.

But he puzzled over the rebel's frantic assurances to his sobbing wife earlier – that their children would be following in three months on a trading vessel. Three months? Trading vessel? No trading vessels ever left Ireland for New South Wales. Any goods the colony needed were shipped direct from England. And from what he had been told, there would be no more convict ships leaving Ireland for at least five years, maybe even longer. It had taken over two years to engage the *Tellicherry*. Most of Britain's ships were needed in the war with France.

The woman began to cry again, her head falling on the rebel's shoulder. His hand moved over her dark hair as he spoke, soothing her with words that could not be heard against the swish of the sea. Unlike her he had masterly control over his emotions and would not readily break down. Perhaps he would though, Captain Cuzens thought, if he knew the truth of it. Someone in that Dublin Castle had played a very cruel trick on him.

He obviously loved the woman, his wife, and it was well that he did, for it would be up to him to supply the strength they would both need in the time ahead. That's if the two of them even made it to New South Wales. No convict ship ever made it to the Antipodes with a full cargo. There were always a number of deaths on the way, no matter how well runs the ship.

As the ship rolled on its course towards the other side of the world, with nothing for the eye to see but waves cutting their crests and the fine spray of foam, Captain Cuzens saw the couple again often, standing together on deck and gazing beyond the ocean. There had been no need to put any of the rebels in irons or restrict them to their quarters, so good was their behaviour so far.

The Wicklow group spent hours all together on deck during the day, the men often improvising a hurling game with old pieces of wood and a ball made of knotted hemp; a number of times they had cheekily fired the ball towards the captain, but it was always a crew member who raised a deck-scrub or a brush and sprang to send it rebounding back to a tumultuous cheer of approval. The crew, who had viewed the rebels suspiciously at first, were now quite civil and pleasant to them.

The two women were not so active, the captain observed. Hugh Byrne's wife looked quite ill at times, often lying under the awning while Dwyer's wife sat nearby and cared for the children. And so determined was Captain Cuzens that his ship would have the lowest mortality rate of any convict ship, he occasionally sent the sickly woman nutritious food from his own table.

But it was the couple – the rebel chief and his wife, who interested him the most. Especially at night, for at night they always came up on deck alone. Sometimes they would stand together in their usual position, but mostly they would sit closely on one of the rope coils, their eyes on the sky, as if carefully watching the stars.

*

They were watching the North Star. Night after night they watched it sinking lower and lower until the night finally came when it was gone, never to be seen again. After that they looked to the sky no more. Soon there would be new stars in the heavens, the stars of the Southern Cross. But however beautiful the stars of the Southern Cross, they were not the same stars that twinkled and gleamed and could be seen by four little children in the Glen of Imaal in Wicklow.

PART FOUR

I wished you slept where your kin are sleeping –
The green green valley is sweet;
And the holy mountains their strange watch keeping
Would love you lying still at their feet,
The soft grass for your winding sheet.
You would sleep sweet with you lips smiling,
Dreaming and hearing still
The bonny blackbird with songs beguiling,
The rain's light feet on the hill,
The children's laughter merry and shrill.

`Ballad for Michael Dwyer', by Katherine Tynan.

Chapter Twenty

Twenty years later, in 1825, two dark-haired young Irishmen stood on the deck of the *Marquis of Huntley* and cheered with the rest of the passengers when a small sliver of land was seen on the horizon. After almost seven months at sea, even the smallest glimpse of land was a truly beautiful sight to land-lovers.

The land swelled into high dark cliffs as they skimmed through the Bass Straits. John and Peter Dwyer were becoming restless with excitement at the prospect of seeing their father again. Neither could even remember what he looked like, but they had grown up in Wicklow listening to his legend. The Insurgent Captain of the Wicklow Mountains. Even if he had not been their own daddy, the tales and ballads would have still made their blood race, their hearts thump with pride as they listened to the accounts of his bravery remembered in song.

More cliffs appeared in the distance; someone announced they were the headlands of Botany Bay. All morning they coasted along the high dark cliffs which suddenly terminated in a precipice, called the South Head, on which stood the lighthouse and signal station. The North Head in the distance was a similar cliff, and between the two the ship entered the deep blue waters of Port Jackson, one of the most beautiful harbours in the world.

As they passed the North Head, one of the crew pointed out the Quarantine Ground where a fever ship was moored. John and Peter Dwyer stared at it full of pity for the passengers who had finally reached their destination after such a long voyage, only to be imprisoned indefinitely in the hold of the fever ship. Above the Quarantine Ground they saw a hill of tombstones marking the burial places of those who had come this far, but had been destined never to set foot alive on land again.

But excitement came back on their faces as they looked again towards the harbour of Sydney, their eyes roving the many bays and inlets of the estuary and the pure white sand that formed the beach, looking almost silver against the deep blue of the water. It was nothing like they had imagined, it was far more pleasing to the eye than they had ever hoped, this foreign country in which their parents had lived for over twenty years, and which now was to be their home too.

Their excitement turned to impatience when the *Marquis of Huntly* dropped anchor and lay for a time within sight of the quays, but too far away to disembark. A small group of people were gathered on the quayside waiting, but as both lads no longer knew what their parents looked liked, it was impossible to pick out any familiar figure. Presently the harbour-master came on board to examine their papers, followed by a doctor who examined their bodies. Then, at last, passed as fit and healthy, and being fare-paying passengers, they were part of the first few to climb into the boat that took them ashore.

It was the woman on the quayside that John Dwyer saw first. Instantly he knew she was his mother. A tall and dark-haired, still-beautiful woman who stared at him as if he were a ghost come to haunt her. Suddenly her eyes lit up with a strange wild gleam and a delighted cry escaped her lips as she moved towards him.

`Michael,' she said breathlessly. `Oh Michae...'

John turned to Peter, and saw the same stunned look on his brother's face that stiffened his own. They knew of their mother's obsession for their father, and both had often been told of John's physical resemblance to his father, and now she had confused the two, both knew at once that their father must be dead.

`Mary...' A man came forward and caught her arm. A tall man with fair hair. A priest. He spoke to her gently.

`Your sons are here at last,' he said. `Your sons, John and Peter.'

She came back to herself and stared at them, an apologetic smile moving her lips. Like a woman in a dream she put a hand to each of their faces, then stared again at the young man with black hair who looked just like her husband had looked on the day she had married him all those years ago.

`Welcome to Sydney,' the priest said brightly, taking control of the situation. `I am Father Therry, a friend of your parents. But come; come, meet your brother and sisters. They have been wild with impatience for days waiting here in Sydney for your ship to come in.'

John and Peter turned towards the three young people standing a few feet away. All smiled uneasily as they looked at the brothers and sisters they had never met. Father Therry introduced the Australians: eighteen-year-old James, seventeen-year-old Bridget, and thirteen year old Eliza.

Of all the three, James seemed over the moon at finally meeting his two Irish brothers, but Bridget and Eliza shrieked with joy at the news that their Irish sisters Mary-Anne and Esther were following, would already have set sail, and should arrive in New South Wales in about six months.

Mary-Anne – the thought of his sister made John's face stiffen again. Mary-Anne had spent her life dreaming of the day she would go to New South Wales. But John knew she was not interested in sisters or brothers or even her mother. Mary-Anne was coming here in search of the man she had always loved above all others.

`Daddy?' John finally said to his mother. `Why is daddy not here?'

His mother lost her smile as she looked at him. Never had he seen eyes that looked so sad; huge brown eyes that misted over like the Wicklow Mountains at dusk.

`I thought he would live forever,' she whispered. `He was that strong, stronger in heart and mind and body than all his comrades. But his comrades are alive and well, and he is dead.' She nodded her head and looked around her with a vacant air as if she still could not believe it. `Yes, yes. My Michael is dead.'

`When?' Peter cried, the realisation that their journey had been in vain suddenly rendering him heart-broken. `When did he die?'

Mary couldn't remember. To her it seemed an eternity

ago. James, Bridget and Eliza moved around her like a comforting blanket while Father Therry answered for her, his voice subdued.

`Your daddy never forgot his children in Ireland. His greatest sorrow was the mistake of leaving you behind, and his greatest dream was to see you all again, bring you here to live with him. He would have done it from the first day he landed if he could. But it was not to be. This is not the time or place to tell you of his fortunes here in New South Wales. But at least I can tell you that he died a natural death in his home, just a few months ago.'

Just a few months ago. John and Peter were close to tears. After all these years, they had come just a few months too late.

`A natural death? A natural death!' Mary glared at the priest, her voice harsh. `You never saw the weals of the lash on every inch of his back. You were not even in the colony then! And as long as I live, Father Therry, and as much as you preach to me about forgiveness, I will never forgive William Bligh, that *Bully of the Bounty* who persecuted not only Fletcher Christian but also my husband!'

*

Six months later it was two dark-haired young women that stood in excited anticipation on the deck and stared around the beautiful harbour as their ship entered Port Jackson. They were bonneted and gloved and had changed into their finest dresses. Mary-Anne wore green plaid, which suited her attractive dark looks. Esther wore blue and looked a timid young thing next to her imposing and volatile sister.

Mary-Anne peered towards the quays and, for a moment, thought she saw her long-lost and long-loved daddy. But then she realised the man standing alone could not be him. He was too young. And then she let out her usual excited laugh and waved a hand as the small-boat drew nearer to the shore and she recognised the familiar features of her brother John.

It was a happy and noisy reunion. Other people on the quayside turned to look at the two young women laughing and jumping up and down and knew at once who they were.

Irish!

Only the Irish could laugh and joke and jump up and down after one of the most hazardous and lengthy sea journeys in the world. The English, at least, had the decency and good manners to land in respectable and sallow exhaustion.

In answer to his sisters' babble of questions, John told them the family were all anxiously waiting for them at the house at Cabramatta. It was impossible for them all to come, never knowing for certain the actual day or week that an expected ship would come in.

`Yes, yes, we know!' Mary-Anne laughed. `It's all in the wind, all in the wind. If I had a shilling for the number of times we were told that on our journey I'd be rich now.'

The three walked along the quays. `Everything is different here,' John said. `There are English and Irish and Scots, and the place is mainly Protestant. But it's not like back home ... here there is no national or religious hatred. It's a new country in a new world, and although the inhabitants will never forget their original homelands, most are now beginning to think of themselves as a new race. As Australians.'

Mary-Anne looked sharply at her brother, and saw he had already fallen in love with New South Wales. `So it is not the hellhole they say it is?' she said.

`Only if you are a convict.'

Esther finally managed to get a word in as John led them up to a waiting horse and trap. `What are the brother and two sisters like?' she asked curiously.

John smiled. `Oh they're grand, just grand. James is a very fine young man, and clever too. You will like them, Essie, especially the girls.'

Mary-Anne's face turned dark with resentment as she thought of the two daughters who had grown up with her daddy when she had been left behind with relatives. All she had known of him in that time was the number of letters he had written to her over the years, and they had been few and far between, since it could take three or four years for a

273

letter to reach Ireland from New South Wales and vice versa. Even so ... whenever a ship did come, there was always a letter on it, a letter full of love and promises, but no money for a sailing ticket.

Reading her expression, and guessing her thoughts, and not wanting to be the one to tell her, John hastily bustled her up to the bench of the trap, and then spent the journey informing his sisters of some of the things he had learned about New South Wales.

`Everything is topsy-turvy here,' he told them with a smile. `Instead of the falling of the leaves in autumn, here we have the stripping of the bark which peels off the gum trees in long ribbons at certain seasons.'

`Is it always this hot?' Mary-Anne tugged at the bodice of her thick plaid dress.

`This is quite cool,' John replied. `When we arrived it was summer and hot beyond endurance. Peter and I spent the first few weeks flaked in continual exhaustion. And the rains are not the soft mists of Ireland, but great battering rains that drench you to the skin in seconds.'

Mary-Anne looked around her curiously as they drove along and saw a few one-storey houses dotted here and there. It was twenty miles from Sydney to the family home near the banks of George's Creek at Cabramatta.

Deprived of the sea breeze, the road inland to Cabramatta was several degrees warmer than Sydney and John pointed out a number of orange groves and vineyards as they rode along. Peaches were very cheap and almost abundant, he told them, as were all kinds of melons, but apples were very expensive as they mostly had to be imported from Van Diemen's Land.

The noise, which had been in the air from shortly after they started their journey, began to grate on Mary-Anne's nerves.

`What is that noise?' she demanded.

`Grasshoppers,' John said, now quite used to the chirruping, creaking, and whirring of the varmints. `Millions of them, and all invisible. Their sound used to drive me crazy but in all my searches I've never managed to

274

see one of them. I'm told they are more like dust-hoppers and live beneath the dust on the road. Now I no longer notice their noise.'

`Look!' Esther smiled with delight as they turned a bend and to her right she caught a glimpse of the Blue Mountains in the distance. Mary-Anne also smiled at the nicest view she had seen so far ... mountains covered from base to peak in forests of tall trees.

In reply to their questions, John told them that no one had yet managed to discover what was on the other side of the mountain range, so dense was the bush, but many believed China was on the other side. John then told a famous tale, which made the two girls roar with laughter; and as she listened and laughed, Mary-Anne wondered if it was one of her daddy's humorous tales.

`There was a convict,' John said, `an Irish convict, who managed to escape into the bush. Someone had told him that if he made his way over the Blue Mountains it was only then a fair walk to China. So off he set, deciding he could fare no worse in China where he would be free at last of redcoats. He had been assured that there were definitely, most definitely, no redcoats in China.

He walked for days, cutting his way through the bush; until at last, in the vast tangled wilderness, he descended down a hill into a clearing and saw a number of strange-looking habitations and knew he had reached China. He approached the first building cheerily, and got the shock of his life when out stepped an officer from the New South Wales Corps from Sydney. The convict greeted him without rancour, for he was free now. `A long life to you, colonel,' he said curiously, `but what brought your honour to China all the way?'

John smiled. `The poor devil ended up back as a convict-servant in the barracks, insisting he'd been short off his mark; just another day of walking would have taken him to China all the way.'

Esther twisted sideways to see completely into his face. Never having known her father, being only ten months old when he had left Ireland, she loved her eldest brother John very much and was pleased to see how much he liked this new land.

`Not being a convict yourself,' she said, 'is there anything about New South Wales that you *don't* like?'

`There is, Essie, there is. I hate the dust, the flies, the ants, and the intense heat of summer. And then there are the locusts – in summer they cling in swarms to the bark of trees, and the noise they make... rattle, rattle rattle. But even that you get used to after a while.'

`What about the people?'

`The people are like most people, good and bad, and bad and good. The people on the whole are friendly enough, but the entire country seems to be permanently drunk.' He looked at Esther gravely and nodded. `Ireland is temperance in comparison. And the women have bigger thirsts than the men!'

`The women?' Mary-Anne laughed in disbelief but John told another story to prove his point.

`Our brother James was born a year after Mammy and Daddy arrived in the colony. Mammy was weak and not in good spirits after the birth, so to help her, Daddy got a female convict assigned to them as a nurse-maid, and also bought Mammy a bottle of her favourite lavender-water to cheer her, even though it cost more than a gallon of rum would have cost. The following morning Mammy looked for her lavender-water and found the convict-maid gulping it. Aye, they'd drink anything that looks like liquor, and if its not liquor, they drink it anyway. Daddy thought it amusing, but Mammy dismissed her there and then, so grieved was she at losing her precious luxury of lavender water.'

Mary-Anne could well believe it. If there was one thing she had never forgotten about her mother, it was her smell of lavender-water.

They had driven for miles along a country road with nothing to see each side but the monotonous scenery of rows and rows of gum trees. Awful they were, for they had very little foliage, and even that was a dull and sapless-looking green.

At last, they reached Cabramatta. The girls jerked alert

when in the distance they saw a house.

`This is it,' John said as they approached a long low white-painted building of ten windows with a spacious veranda in front of it and a small neat garden at each side. The door and all the window shutters were painted green, as was the wooden railings each side of the drive leading up to the house.

Mary-Anne had intended to be suitably superior whenever she met her younger Australian sisters. After all, she was the eldest, was twenty-six years old, had been married, and was now a widow, a *young* widow. Oh yes, twenty-six was old for a maiden but young for a widow. And now she had come to claim the only beloved man in her life, to live out her days making up for lost time with him, and if her Australian sisters thought to prevent her from taking first place in his paternal affections – then they had another think coming! By the hand of St Patrick they did!

But when Bridget and Eliza came running out of the house, Mary-Anne sat looking coolly at them only for a second, then leaped from the trap and was squealing and jumping up and down with excitement and laughter every bit as much as Esther, Bridget and Eliza.

Two parrots sitting on the branch of a nearby tree fluttered their splendid colours and squawked in unison with the girls.

Then Mary-Anne saw her mother standing silently by the door.

`*Mammy!*'

The parrots squawked again and began to move in an excited side-step along the branch of the tree, pausing to look at the emotional scene below, inspecting the newcomers first with one eye, then with the other.

`Why, Mammy, you have hardly changed at all!' Mary-Anne said through her tears when the hugging had eased. `Hardly at all!'

`Such flattery is irresistible,' her mother said with a laugh, tears spilling down her face also when Mary-Anne insisted it was true.

`This is a great day for me, Mary-Anne,' she said softly,

`having all my children with me again ... all my children...'

`And Daddy?' Mary-Anne cried in cheerful indignation, looking beyond her mother to the large comfortably-furnished but empty living room behind her. `Where is he now that he's not here to greet his first and favourite daughter?'

Mary didn't answer, just stood staring at her daughter, the colour fading from her face. Then slowly she turned agonised dark eyes to her son John, who had promised to relieve her of this.

John stood with head bowed, fingers twisting the brim of the felt hat in his hands and looking as if he would like to shrink inside his clothes. He had broken his promise to his mother, had been unable to prepare the way and lighten the burden for her. But then – his mother didn't know Mary-Anne as well as he did. His mother didn't know anything of the years of childhood and youth that Mary-Anne had spent sitting on hills, under sun and under stars, talking of the past and dreaming of the future, of the sea, and of a land far, far away. His mother didn't know that Mary-Anne had come twelve thousand miles to see her daddy, and nobody else.

In the thick silence Mary-Anne also looked at her brother John, then at the faces of her other brothers and sisters, new and old; only Esther looked as perplexed as she herself felt.

Suddenly Mary-Anne knew – knew the first dull ache of failed ambition, then the splintering pain of shattered dreams.

She stood staring at her mother with eyes gleaming. Her bosom and breath heaved as if someone was choking her. A slow whining sound moved from the pit of her stomach and crawled up to her heaving throat, then erupted in a high-pitched sound that sent the parrots fluttering and flying under and over the branch of the tree, chattering and screaming as Mary-Anne lunged screaming at her mother, the mother who had left her four children behind when she sailed into exile with their father, the mother that Mary-Anne had always blamed for the desertion, and no one else.

`You *bitch*!' she screamed. `You let me cross three oceans

and twelve thousand miles to come here knowing there was nothing and no one to come for!'

Her mother staggered back and muttered something incoherent. Then she gasped with pain. James moved sharply and caught her about the body, shoving Mary-Anne roughly aside as he did so, for their mother had fainted.

Holding her slumped body securely in his arms, James turned his head over his shoulder and glared with angry hazel eyes at Mary-Anne.

`If you ever dare speak to my mother like that again,' he warned in a cold voice, `I will kill you stone dead.'

Mary-Anne's throat contorted violently, but she was speechless. She stared at the eighteen-year old young man they had said was named James, a stranger she had met only minutes before, a stranger who had referred to her mother as *his* mother.

And then a great wave of despair engulfed her as she realised that it was she who was the stranger. A stranger who had once been a child sobbing by a cell door and watching her daddy walking down a long dark passage in Kilmainham Gaol in Dublin town, and she had waited and waited, all through that day and all through the years, to see him smiling at her again as he came back to her out of the long darkness, but he never did, and now he never would.

`John!' she gasped, needing the comfort and protection of someone she knew well, the comfort of family against the sudden loneliness of this strange place and these strangers.

`John' she gasped again; and John was at her side immediately, as was Peter and Esther, until the four Irish children who had been left behind, stood in a small group and watched Bridget and Eliza follow their brother James as he carried their mother into the house, the house in Cabramatta which the three had grown up in, with their parents, Michael and Mary Dwyer.

*

The four were still standing in a group outside on the veranda when the three came out of the house again.

Mary-Anne stood within John's arms, her head against

279

his shoulder. For a minute or so the two sides stood looking at each other silently, then James shrugged, still angry.

`This was not how Daddy would have wished it,' he said quietly. `This would have grieved him sorely.'

`You don't understand,' Mary-Anne cried harshly. `You don't understand because you don't know about Ireland. *We* were their children in Ireland. *We* lived on the run with them, in harbourer's houses all over the Wicklow hills. *We* lived in Kilmainham Gaol with them. Esther was born in Kilmainham Gaol. Anything we didn't know about our parents, things that happened when we were too young, or before we were born, was told to us later, by those who were there ... Michael Kearns of Baltinglass who made it to Dublin but not America; John Cullen before he died; Thomas Morris and John Jackson; Billy the Rock; scores of others; all had their own tales to tell us about our parents – Michael and Mary Dwyer – who said they would send for us a few months later, but nearly twenty years passed before they did.'

As Mary-Anne spoke, the expression on the three Australians' faces slowly changed from anger to sadness. James looked steadily at his sister.

`And for that, you blamed mother?'

`Not only for that,' she said with quiet honesty. `The thing I blamed her for most of all, was the surrender. Only for that we would have all stayed together in Wicklow. They would never have caught him. And you three – '

`Would still have been born,' James told her. `If not here, then there. You may look at us like some distantly related strangers, Mary-Anne, or possibly even half-brother and half-sisters. But we are not, we all have the same mother and father, and they would have been our parents too, regardless of where we had been born.'

`You three were the lucky ones,' Mary-Anne said bitterly.

`And you four were the beloved ones,' James said. `The ones they always pined for. We had our moments, too, of feeling second-best.'

`Mary-Anne... Essie...'

All turned to look at their mother standing in the

doorway, her face pale and pinched – and smiling.

`Mary-Anne ... Essie, this is a great day for me, having all my children with me again ... all our seven children together ... it was what we often talked of, and always dreamed of, and now here you all are.'

Still smiling, as if all memory of Mary-Anne's attack had been lost in her faint, she opened her arms to her two daughters from Ireland, and it was Mary-Anne who reached them first.

`Oh, Mammy,' she wept. `I blamed you. Every day I blamed you.'

`So did I,' her mother said, patting her weeping daughter's head on her shoulder. `So did I, Mary-Anne.'

Then Mary released a hand and held it out in welcome to Esther, who was standing in timid silence, `And I was never able to forget any of you, and God knows, sometimes for the sake of my sanity, I did try.'

*

It took weeks for Mary-Anne to find out the full story of her parents early life in New South Wales. And not from their mother, who seemed reluctant to talk about her husband at all, but on the rare occasions that she did, always seemed to lapse into a world of her own private visions, until the length of her silences became unendurable.

`Hugh Vesty is the man,' James said one evening to Mary-Anne. `Himself and Sarah will tell you anything you want to know. Just as they always told us anything we wanted to know about Ireland.'

Mary-Anne looked at him in surprise. `What did they tell you about Ireland?'

James smiled. `Everything.'

*

Hugh Vesty Byrne's farm was a wide and rambling building surrounded by outhouses and cattle-pens and acres and acres of land – land that belonged to Hugh Vesty.

`We have to keep the calves locked securely in the byre at night,' Hugh Vesty said, `because of the danger of the

281

dingoes.'

Mary-Anne shuddered as they walked back towards the house. Dingoes were the native dogs and very numerous in number. She had soon learned that dingoes didn't bark but howled, and at night the sound of their howling from the neighbouring forests had a most eerie tone.

`I used to hate foxes,' Hugh Vesty said, `but now I often long for a glimpse of one. There are no foxes here. You know that of course. No cunning red foxes to pit your wits against, just wiry old sandy-coloured dingoes. Old Reynard is a gentleman in comparison to those savages.'

He paused and stared over the land into the distance, a trace of a distant smile on his face, as if seeing again the red brush of a fox lolloping through the luxuriant green grass of the Wicklow hills on a cold and frosty morning.

Mary-Anne's gaze wandered over Hugh Vesty's face. A lean-faced man, fair hair turned grey at the sides. A man who had loved history. A man who had been a part of Ireland's history.

`Tell me, Hugh ... Tell me ...'

His mind preoccupied, Hugh misunderstood, for those were the words young James Dwyer always used when he wanted to know about the past. `Tell me, Hugh, tell me ...'

`About Ireland?' Hugh Vesty shrugged. `That was all in the long-ago. All part of another time and another world. A world that ended for me on the day our ship sailed away from the Cove of Cork...'

She hesitated as Hugh Vesty paused to stroke a bay colt standing by the paddock fence, but then she asked: `Were you on Spike Island, Hugh? In the prison on Spike Island in the bay of Cork?'

Hugh Vesty furrowed his brow. `The prison on Spike Island in the bay of Cork? No... but I was in the prison on Norfolk Island in the Pacific Ocean, about a thousand miles away from here. Myself and Michael were there for six months, before they sent us to Van Diemen's Land.'

`Michael ...?' Mary-Anne prompted, for Hugh Vesty had proved as reluctant to speak about the early days in New South Wales as was her mother.

`Michael was my cousin, do you know.' Hugh absently stroked the colt's neck in a slow motion, his mind already back in the long-ago. `My cousin and my comrade. It was on Norfolk Island that he showed them what kind of a man he was. A man that would never bend the knee. The monsters in charge of us were man-killers, and they only liked creatures that grovelled at their feet for easy kicking. Many did in the end, of course. But not myself ... and not my cousin...

`One day they had him, my cousin Michael, tied to the flogging frame, and all of us made to watch. Two of the man-killers stood at a distance with whips ready, one on each side of him, so they could thrash from right to left.

`Then with a shout they went to work, thrashing his naked back with their flails, first one then the other, as hard and as regular as any two farmers threshing in the fields at harvest-time. The count got to thirty and blood and flesh were flying off the steel ends of their cats into our faces. Some of the lads were moaning as if they themselves were being whipped, others were shouting with rage and abuse, for Michael was a popular kind of fellow with them all. But Michael himself never made a sound, never uttered a moan, although we could see him flinching from the blows.

`The man-killers set to work again on the twenty still to go, and you could see the beasts they were by the enjoyment on their faces, for only the cruellest animals enjoy torturing their prey. On they thrashed with their whips until his shoulders were ripped to shreds, and no doctor present, for a doctor only had to be present when the count was over fifty.

`At fifty he had still not uttered a sound, not even a whimper, so the bastards broke the rules and flayed on, seething with evil frustration, for as much as they enjoy the flogging, their true moment of ecstasy is when they hear the screams. At sixty they paused for a breather, and it was then Michael turned his head and looked at them with a look as cool and defiant as ever I saw on him in Wicklow.

`"Thrash away until doomsday, avics," he told them, "but you will never make me sing."'

283

Hugh Vesty paused in his stroking of the colt's neck. He looked vacantly around him at his acres of land. `There was another time,' he said, and then broke off, and tears formed.

*

A bright log fire was crackling and blazing merrily on the white painted hearth. A leg of ham was smoking over the fire, for ham and eggs seemed to be the continual diet in New South Wales. On a hot plate to the side of the hearth was an iron dish filled to overflowing with hot mealy potatoes peeping through their cracked and peeling skins.

`He gets carried away and forgets who he is talking to,' Sarah Byrne said apologetically to Mary-Anne. `Hugh's mind has always dwelt in the past. Truth be known, he probably thought he was back on the Wicklow hills talking to his comrades. I ask your pardon for him, Mary-Anne, for I am sure Hugh forgot that he was telling that horrible tale to Michael's daughter.'

Mary-Anne nodded, convinced that Hugh Vesty had not even been aware of her hasty departure. `I'm fine now, Sarah. Truly I am.'

When Hugh Vesty wandered in some minutes later, Sarah rushed to greet him and Mary-Anne could hear her admonishing him in hushed tones.

`Crying and shaking she was, mortally upset at what you told her. Tis one thing telling the lads those kind of things, Hugh, but not womenfolk. Do as her own family do and speak no more of it.'

`Oh no,' Mary-Anne cried, `I want you to speak of it Hugh. I want you to tell me ... tell me everything ...'

But Sarah would not allow any more conversation about the early days until after supper was eaten. She moved to the back door and rang a large brass bell that clanged over the fields and brought her tribe of children in to the house. Mary-Anne counted eight from Catherine who was about eighteen, down to three-year old Sylvester. But two of the elder children that had been born in Ireland, Michael and Rose, were missing. `Helping out over at John Mernagh's place,' Hugh said.

Later, much later, when all had gone to bed, Mary-Anne was disappointed when Hugh Vesty said goodnight also and retired. He had to be up at dawn and the land was a hard taskmaster.

Mary-Anne looked in appeal at Sarah who had settled herself near the lamp on the table, her knitting in her hand. `I always sit up by myself for an hour or so at night,' Sarah said softly. `Helps me to wind down before sleep.'

Mary-Anne then realised that Sarah must have ordered Hugh Vesty off to bed and allow any further reminiscences to be a gentle matter between women.

`What happened on the ship?' Mary-Anne asked. `Word came back to Ireland that Michael Dwyer had staged a mutiny on the *Tellicherry* at San Salvador and the captain and all the crew were killed. It was brought back by an Irish seaman and for a time no one could be sure if the rumour was true or not.'

`A mutiny? On the *Tellicherry?*' Sarah looked amazed. `Oh my, but that Irish seaman must have been dishing out truth from a bowl of wishful thinking.'

She shook her head. `No, there was no trouble whatsoever on the *Tellicherry*, not from Cork to Sydney, and not from any of us. We had the best captain ever sailed the seven seas, Captain Cuzens. He treated us fair and well, and we did not repay him with anything other than respect.

`We were not classed as convicts,' Sarah went on, `but free-settlers destined for Botany Bay, and so we were housed in clean comfort in the ship's hospital quarters, away from the convicts. It was a well-run ship and we lost only six convicts from fever, five men and one woman, and that was the lowest loss any ship ever had on reaching Sydney. Captain Cuzens was very pleased, of course, but the smooth passage only served to sadden your mammy and daddy even more, added to their regrets, for they knew then that ye four would have suffered no ill effects if you had sailed with us. Oh, how they regretted leaving you behind... Only for that they would have been happy on reaching Sydney and facing the prospect of starting a new life, for we were treated well on our arrival.'

`You were?' Mary-Anne said, surprised.

`Oh yes, we were,' Sarah said, and as she sat back and gazed into the past, Mary-Anne let her talk on and on without interruption.

`At the time we arrived in Sydney in 1806, Philip Gidley King was the Governor of New South Wales. He ordered the five United Irishmen to go and see him at Government House at Paramatta, and there gave them a long lecture on his knowledge of the capricious disposition and turbulent nature of the Irish, followed by his encouragement that they would settle down and work hard as free-settlers in New South Wales and become worthy British subjects. He then gave each of them a government land grant of one hundred uncultivated acres at Cabramatta; and each grant of land was situated next door to the other, which pleased the men greatly.

`You see, we didn't know it then, although we know it now, that Britain wanted the settlement to grow into a self-sufficient country, and for that to happen, New South Wales needed married men with children and the prospect of more children. In hindsight, I am sure that is why the Castle reneged on the surrender terms first offered to Michael and sent us all here instead of America, so bad was the need here and few would come voluntarily.

`The convicts sent out were all single and mostly male, and they provided the free labour needed to build roads and buildings and so on. But married men who arrived with their wives were the ones who would have the children and be more likely to work hard on the land in order to provide a decent standard of living for their families – families that would, as I say, help the settlement to grow into a country.

`Well now, they were not disappointed in us, for no people worked harder in that first year than we did. Although we arrived in the month of February, it was summertime here. We lived in tents for the few months while the men built the houses on each grant of land, all helping each other. Each house was made entirely of timber, the boards cut evenly and lapped one over the other and nailed to upright posts which came from the bole of gum trees which, as you know, are available in plenty. Often we sighed for the pine trees of Wicklow, but however, the houses were finished and lathed and plastered within, then whitewashed within all over.

`With some of the money the Castle had paid us for their breach of faith and with which to buy farm implements to work the new land, Mary had bought some lovely coloured material when we moored at St Salvador – one of the crew got it for her – and she made curtains for each house. Then a bright fire crackling in the white hearth and, begor, at night you could pretend you were back in Wicklow.

`We were proud of our little houses then, but even moreso later on when we took the time to travel beyond our own land and see the land of others. Begor, but the industry was poor and lazy, especially those owned by single men who had come out as convicts and earned their ticket-of-leave. Wretched huts or hovels built of heaps of turf, or slats of wood nailed haphazardly together and plastered with mud to keep them weatherproof, and the window no more than a gaping hole. Oh aye, whoever said it did say it right – a man with children will work hard to make the world a better place, but a man without children sees only his own future, and many, God help us, are very short-sighted.'

Mary-Anne shifted restlessly. It was all very interesting, but not what she wanted to hear.

`I want to know what happened to my Daddy,' she said softly.

Sarah gave a half smile. `Sure I know that you do, darling. Shall we have some tea?'

Mary-Anne nodded in a resigned sort of way, for she had soon discovered that tea at every opportunity was the colonial beverage amongst the women of New South Wales.

The tea made and poured, Sarah placed her elbows on the table, and over the rim of her cup, stared into the glow of the lamp and continued. `Hard as we tried, not one of us could fault the British system in New South Wales insofar as their treatment of settlers went. Because as settlers, we were entitled to draw free provisions from the Government storehouse for the first eighteen months in order to help us get established. That was very fair, we thought. And despite Governor King's long lecture about knowing all about the Wicklow men and their rebel activities in the past, the fact that he did not separate them to different parts of the colony, but allotted them land grants next to each other, showed that he had faith in them and no real misgivings. No, for all his talk about the capricious Irish, Gidley King knew that when it came to crop-growing and horse-rearing they were the best in the world.'

Sarah chewed her lip. `Although he was not too pleased when he learned that Michael had quickly discovered a way of turning peaches into cider and cider into brandy. But he left him off with a warning. Peaches are so abundant here, we discovered that if a peach-stone is thrown into the ground, a large quantity of fruit may be gathered from the tree that shortly shoots up without any subsequent culture. Michael still made the cider, but he never again broke the rules and made the brandy – not that I know of anyway. In truth, I am sure he did not, for his intentions were truly to become a peaceable and prosperous citizen of the land he had been banished to, for the term of his natural life.

`However, it was Michael who was the one who went into Sydney on any business that needed doing, for he never lost his love of rambling for miles as was his habit in Wicklow. Even at the end, when something was on his mind, he would ramble almost as far as the Hawkesbury. But in the early days into Sydney he would go, and bedad, he became good friends with a number of the English soldiers in the New South Wales Corps. But then, in Ireland he had many a friend in the English and Scottish camps too. He was that kind of man. And it is still hard to figure it all out, for no one really knew, except him, who his friends were.

`I remember Hugh Vesty once telling me about the time in Wicklow that himself and Michael were down near the Three Bridges when around the bend came four Highlanders from the Duke of York Regiment. Hugh nearly had heart failure at the sight of them so close, but they passed by without recognising who the two were – or so Hugh thought – until one of them turned his head and called back, "Make sure you are nowhere near Glenmalure tonight or the next few days, Dwyer, for we shall be going there in search of you." And Michael calls back, "I wasn't planning to go anywhere near Glenmalure, Cameron, but thanks for warning me anyway."'

Sarah smiled. `Oh, the tales I could tell about the happenings in Wicklow... Another unlikely friend of his turned out to be a captain in the Somerset Fencibles – '

`The New South Wales Corps...' Mary-Anne said, turning the conversation back to the land they were in. `What about them?'

`Good men some of them. And I'll tell you for why. At the end of the first year Michael had managed to clear forty acres of his uncultivated land, so determined was he to succeed and make his land profitable, for only then would he be able to send for his children in Ireland. It was a dream that spurred him to work from dawn to dusk, for Captain Cuzens had told him during the voyage that Dr Trevor had tricked him, and not to live in hopes of seeing another ship from Ireland for at least three to five years.

`Months later Michael and Hugh had a fair number of acres planted with maize and wheat and the early crops were looking good. Michael drove us all mad doing his arithmetic, but no matter which way he did his figures, he reckoned it would take him at least five years of hard work before he would have enough money to send for his children. But each day was a day less, and on he worked, as they all worked. But then a terrible thing happened in New South Wales. Governor King announced that his term in the colony was over, and a new Governor was already on the seas. And when he arrived, the new Governor of New South Wales turned out to be none other than William Bligh, the former Captain of the *Bounty*.

`Bligh was not long in the colony when he showed signs of unbalanced hatred for two groups of people – the soldiers of the New South Wales Corps – and the five Wicklowmen that lived at Cabramatta. You see, in 1800, Bligh had been sent to Dublin by the British Admiralty for the purpose of making surveys of Dun Laoighre harbour and the surrounding coasts – he was a great man for drawing maps apparently. But while in Dublin he saw the proclamation and knew all the gossip about the *Insurgent Captain of the Wicklow Mountains.*

`Next thing we knew, Michael, Hugh Vesty, Mernagh, Burke, Arthur Devlin, and two English convicts were arrested and charged with planning to raise a rebellion in New South Wales as a reprisal for the defeat on Vinegar Hill in 1798.'

Sarah looked into the astonished eyes of Mary-Anne and nodded. `Aye, it would have been laughable but for the ugly fact that the men faced death if found guilty.'

`But... the English convicts,' Mary-Anne said. `How could they have been accused of planning a rebellion in return for Vinegar Hill?'

`They were accused because Bligh wanted them accused. You see, the *Bounty* was not the only mutiny that Bligh had suffered. Some years later there was a second mutiny at the Nore. The crew were caught and tried, some hanged, some transported to Botany Bay, and these two English convicts were mutineers from the Nore. Captain William Bligh was obviously a man who could never write `*paid*' against a crime or a grudge.'

The silence that followed was so long, the faraway look in Sarah's eyes so dark, that Mary-Anne got to her feet and made more tea. When she placed the steaming cup in front of Sarah, Sarah did not seem to notice.

`Whenever I think back to that time,' she said quietly, `the time of that trial in May 1807, I think not of our men, but myself and Mary. She had not long given birth to James then, her first child born in the new land. The arrests of our men was a savage blow to us, made worse because we could not even begin to understand the why of it.

`However, in Sydney the evidence against them was being gathered, and two convicted murderers who were serving their time as *lifers* were brought forward by Bligh as the two main prosecution witnesses, and he later gave them both a free pardon for their testimony at the trial. It was held in the Criminal Court before Judge Atkins and six military officers.

'Well, first the charge was read out*," Instigating many people to revolt from their allegiance and to rise in open rebellion".'*

Sarah sighed and eyed her teacup morosely. 'Cons and ex-cons by the score were marched in to give their evidence. All claimed they had heard the Wicklowmen rousing other Irish in the taverns to make ready for a rising and steal the guns of their masters. The two convicted *lifers* admitted they were turning King's evidence and had planned to take part in the rebellion, stimulated as they had been by the persuasive powers of Michael Dwyer, whose plan, they said, was to seize the barracks, kill all the leading gentry and start a general massacre.

'There was a terrible commotion when that was said. By that evening members of the leading gentry had arrived in Sydney and all were clamouring for the immediate hangings of the Wicklow men.'

Sarah shuddered at the memory. 'Then, it came, the time for the defence. Michael represented himself. But Mary and myself had not been lazy, indeed not! No two women were as relentless as us, and poor Mary carrying little James everywhere with her. I also found it hard because I was fair advanced in pregnancy myself. But Mary and I lost no time in going to see all our landholding neighbours who had known us since our arrival, not the hovel-dwellers, but the decent ones. And strange as it may seem to some, it was our English neighbours that travelled into Sydney and the court and gave firm evidence in the Wicklowmen's defence.

'One by one the Englishmen stepped forward and testified to the peaceable nature and hard work of the Wicklowmen. Then Michael, who acted in his own defence, as did the others, recalled a number of the prosecution witnesses and questioned them carefully on their testimony. Hugh questioned a number of them too, only he asked the questions in a different way, and that's when the cracks in their testimonies began to show. All the witnesses, including the Englishmen, were questioned by the officers on the bench. Then they retired from Friday to Monday to consider their verdict.

`Five days the trial lasted, but that break from Friday to Monday was the longest time I ever knew, and Mary was almost unbalanced in her terror. I had more trouble calming her down than could be imagined. She was shaking like a leaf on a tree in autumn when the court resumed and the officers and Judge Atkins gave the verdict.

`"Michael Dwyer – Not guilty.
`"Hugh Byrne   – Not guilty.
`"Martin Burke   – Not guilty.
`"John Mernagh   – Not guilty.

`I stopped listening after that, so gushing with floods of tears were myself and Mary, and never did I like six military officers so much as those sitting in judgement at that trial. Fair men, good men, Englishmen, who had the courage to be just and lawful. Which goes to prove that men should be judged solely on their characters and not their nationality.'

Mary-Anne was all of a fluster. It was not the verdict that she had expected. `But the flogging on Norfolk Island! Van Diemen's Land! When did that happen?'

Sarah looked at her coldly. `Didn't I tell you that William Bligh could never write `paid' against a grudge! As soon as the men stepped out of the court he had them re-arrested and refused to set them free. He refused to accept the verdict of the court. He accused Judge Atkins of being drunk throughout the trial of the Irish State prisoners. Well, by God, there was a terrible commotion. Michael told Bligh that he was not an Irish *State prisoner*, that he had come to the colony without conviction, that he still had not been convicted of any crime, and therefore was still a free-settler and a free man under the law!'

`"The law!" Bligh shouted. "Damn the law! My will is the only law in New South Wales!"'

`The next day they were taken before a bench of civic magistrates and tried again on the same charge. We knew what the verdict would be even before it came, because according to Mr Blaxland, a very decent and fair English gentleman, Bligh selected only those magistrates who did his will; and so the Wicklowmen were found guilty, along with the two English convicts who had been charged with them.

'It was Lieutenant Minchin, one of the officers who sat in judgement at the first trial, that came and sadly gave us the news – hard labour in a penal prison for as long as Governor Bligh decreed. Two were to be transported to Norfolk Island, two to the Derwent, and the others to Port Dalrymple. Michael was also sentenced to receive a thousand lashes, to be inflicted in stages, as was Thomas McCann, one of the Nore mutineers.'

Sarah put a hand to her brow and smoothed it wearily, as if the memories were tiring her badly.

'I could not take it in. I lay in a trance for days, and indeed, only a week later I gave premature birth to Catherine. But Mary ... poor Mary ... she never strayed from her position down at the harbour where they had Michael imprisoned on Bligh's own ship, the *Porpoise*, begging and crying to see him, but she was denied any sympathy or consideration.

'We later learned through Mr Blackland, who travelled to and from England, that Alexander Marsden's brother, William Marsden, who had lived for some time in Wicklow but was at that time Secretary to the Admiralty in London, had said – even to Mrs Bligh in England – that although others had been appalled and outraged at the news of a projected massacre by the Wicklowmen, he considered it nonsense and that the informers were the people he distrusted most. Hugh Vesty Byrne, he said. he would believe nothing against.'

Sarah sighed. 'A fairer man than his brother it would seem. But transported in chains our husbands were ... and how Mary and I managed after that was something like a nightmare, our families broken up, our cultivated land left to smother under weeds. We would not have managed at all only for the kindness of our English neighbours. But no one in the whole wide world could console Mary ... poor Mary ... her devotion to Michael had always been a matter for comment...

'But then, after about nine months, when she heard that

he had been moved from Norfolk Island to Van Diemen's Land – what did she do? She did what no other woman in her right mind would do. She took up her little son James and somehow managed to get herself on a trading vessel destined for Hobart and followed Michael all the way to Van Diemen's Land.'

Chapter Twenty-One

They talked until almost dawn. At least, Sarah Byrne did.

Mary-Anne listened without interruption, staring wide-eyed at the yellow bowl of the lamp on the table, a bowl of bitter visions. She could imagine it all vividly, but not objectively, for the people suffering in this piece of human history were not characters in a story or a song, but her parents, Michael and Mary Dwyer.

`Went to find her husband in Van Diemen's Land,' Sarah said. `And for a time I never knew what had happened to her. Did she ever make it there? Did she ever find him? Did tragedy befall the ship she was on? All I could do was pray. The last was my biggest fear, for ships were always going down in the waters to Van Diemen's Land. Some due to pirates, some due to a host of other reasons.

`But here in New South Wales things were getting worse and worse under Governor Bligh. Some would say they got better. It depended on who you were and where you were. He was a demon to the convicts and the small landholders, but he was adored by the gentry and leading landowners on the Hawkesbury, which was the very best area in the colony. Bligh was a man who favoured only one side of a community, a divisive man, a man who had a temper and a tongue on him that would raise a blister on a brick.

`In the end it was the soldiers and officers of the New South Wales Corps that he raised – to mutiny. Led by their officers they marched to Government House, and there Major Johnstone – one of the officers who sat on the bench at our husbands' first trial – read out a document informing Governor Bligh that he had been judged unfit to rule the colony, and that the military were assuming command until a new Governor could be sent out from England. Bligh was put under house arrest and the whole of Sydney seemed to be cheering; but the Hawkesbury, of course, was glumly silent.

`When the news finally sank in, I went to Major Johnstone, who had assumed the role of acting-Governor, and requested that the convictions of Bligh's kangaroo court on our husbands be quashed.

'He agreed, and Colonel Patterson who was then embarking for Van Diemen's Land was ordered to inform the Wicklowmen that they could return. You see, although they were originally separated and sent to Norfolk Island, the Derwent, and the Coal Mines, after six months or so they all ended up together in Van Diemen's Land.

'Well, back they came. First my Hugh Vesty, who saw for the first time our daughter Catherine born some eighteen months previously. Then back came John Mernagh and Martin Burke, then Arthur Devlin; but not Michael, and not Mary who had reached there safely and found who she went looking for.'

'Why did they not come back?'

'Why? Because Mary was so terrified of Governor Bligh, she would not allow Michael to return to New South Wales until Bligh had left not only Government House, but also the colony itself. And so they stayed in Hobart, where Colonel Patterson who was the commanding officer there, gave Mary new accommodation and Michael government work. And it was while they were in Hobart that Mary gave birth to Bridget.

'Bridget was born in Van Diemen's Land?'

'Aye, she went off with one little child in her arms and fourteen months later came back with two.' Sarah sniffed. 'But then, you being a widow and all, Mary-Anne, you'll not blush when I say that Michael and Mary were always that way inclined with each other.'

Mary-Anne blushed, but Sarah did not notice. 'And knowing Mary as I do, I can imagine how she must have near smothered him with her embraces first opportunity she got him alone, and well, as you know, being inclined as they were, need I say more ...'

Sarah sniffed again, and Mary-Anne could not help thinking that as inclined as her daddy and mammy had been, they had not produced as many children as Hugh Vesty and Sarah – eight she had counted, and two were away, and Sarah was pregnant at this minute.

`So then,' Sarah said, a new light beginning to shine in her eyes, `in that year of 1810, the great man himself came to New South Wales as Bligh's replacement. Oh! Mary-Anne, it would take me another night and a day to extol the virtues of Lachlan Macquarie. An army officer he was, in his late forties, and 'tis said that his family once owned a castle in Scotland before their fortunes changed and he was reared on an impoverished farm in the Hebrides. He brought with him his lady wife, and his own 73rd Regiment who had fought with him in India, and some of them, would you believe, were Irish.

`So Bligh was sent home to England, and poor Major Johnstone was also sent home for court-martial for leading the mutiny – although he got off lightly and was soon back in the colony with his friends again.

`But it was in that year of 1810 that the reign of Governor Lachlan Macquarie began. A man who was everything that Bligh was not. A man with a great deal of common sense and humanity. A *gentleman*. But with none of the pompous pretensions of the gentry who liked to think of themselves as the `elite' and thought all convicts should remain convicts for life.

`But Lachlan Macquarie was not of their ilk. He believed in giving a man a fair chance. And that included the convicts. When he announced his new policy to the colony, he said that in his view, good conduct had to be recognised and rewarded. For if good conduct produced no benefit to a man and did not lead him back to his place in society, then why should he ever abandon bad conduct?'

Sarah sat back, eyes glowing with admiration. `Oh aye, Lachlan Macquarie was not only a man fit to rule a colony, he was a man fit to rule a nation.'

`Is that when my parents came back to New South Wales?'

Sarah nodded. `Governor Macquarie sent for them. And when they returned he summoned the five Wicklowmen to Government House at Parammata, and after a long discussion, gave them all confirmation of their pardons, as well as the official papers for their land grants at

Cabramatta, and even assigned them two convicts each to help them restore their land.

`And so for a few months life was good again for your Daddy who was back hoeing and sowing his land and doing his arithmetic. But then Michael got a summons to go to Government House and Mary was sure that ill fortune was about to descend upon them again. She could never forget the night when the summons had come from Governor Bligh and Michael had ended up in chains. So you can imagine her shock when Michael returned and told her that he had been asked to become one of Macquarie's newly reorganised police force.

Sarah smiled.

`Well, I tell you, Michael was near sick at the thought of being a policeman. To him it was like becoming a militiaman. Especially as he would have to wear the dark blue uniform when on duty. He had been given time to think about it, and he declared to us all that he would never do it. If he had not worn the green uniform that Emmet had sent down to him in Wicklow, he would not wear Macquarie's blue uniform in New South Wales.

`We all disagreed with him, especially Hugh Vesty, who pointed out that we need never fear the law kicking in our doors again, not if the local lawman was our own cousin and comrade. Mary too, encouraged him to accept the offer, if only to remove her constant fear of his sudden arrest. She was also very proud, because one of the reasons put forward in the offer was Michael's ability to read and write, which a great number in the colony still cannot do, myself included.

`And so it was that Michael became a policeman. I think he always knew that he would have to, if only to prove to Macquarie that his rebel days were truly over. And he did the job well, treating the Irish convicts with great humanity and kindness, as you can imagine. And only a year later Macquarie made Michael the Chief of Police of the George's River and Liverpool district.

`John Mernagh, his comrade from Wicklow, also became a policeman, so did Martin Burke. And Lachlan Macquarie never had a day's trouble with the Irish in this area during his whole twelve years in New South Wales, not when the men in charge of policing the district were ex-rebels who had been part of the sharp-shooting force on Vinegar Hill.'

Sarah smiled at Mary-Anne. `A clever man, that Lachlan Macquarie, wouldn't you say?'

`From an outlaw to a policeman,' Mary-Anne could not help smiling at the irony of her daddy's life. `But to me,' she said, `growing up as I did with only his legend, he will always be the rebel on the Wicklow Mountains.'

`Because he had no other choice on the Wicklow Mountains,' Sarah said. `But Governor Macquarie wanted to shape this colony and make it a good place for people to live and build their futures.'

Sarah's eyes were glowing again, as they always did whenever she thought or spoke of Lachlan Macquarie.

`In that first year after Michael became part of his police force,' she said, `Governor Macquarie himself twice dropped into the Dwyer homestead at Cabramatta for refreshment. On the first occasion he explained that himself and his guide had been out inspecting the farms around George's River and Harris Creek and had got lost in the forest for three hours before riding onto Dwyer's land.

`On the second occasion, he said that he had been inspecting the outlying area of George's River with the intention of creating a town. That second time he was accompanied by Mrs Macquarie and Captain Antill.

`Elizabeth Macquarie was a lovely lady. Although in her first year here she shocked the mock-gentry greatly, by giving a party on St Patrick's Day for all the Irish convicts in her husband's service. A lovely lady, as I say, and she seemed quite relaxed in Mary's home at Cabramatta. Mary in turn lost some of her nervousness and spoke to Governor Macquarie about a matter that had been troubling her. You see, whatever happened to Mary during her time in Van Diemen's Land, when she returned she had become very religious. And so, as Governor Macquarie was at his most convivial and charming, she mentioned to him that there was a large number of Catholics in New South Wales, and not one Catholic Church or priest to serve them.

`Lachlan Macquarie very gently assured her that she need not worry about the large number of Catholics in New South Wales, because it was his intention that by the time he had finished his term as Governor, he would have turned them all into Protestants.'

Sarah chuckled. `And Mary believed him! Not knowing that the reason Lachlan Macquarie was in the area that afternoon was because himself and Captain Antill had been marking out a square for the Catholic Church he intended to build in his newly created town of Liverpool.

`He sounds indeed like a good man,' Mary-Anne said.

`Aye, a man like General John Moore. Two of a kind. Both soldiers and both great men. Although in the end it was in Sydney that the first Catholic Church was built.'

`And my parents were happy from then on?'

`With each other they were always happy,' Sarah said quietly, a sad expression on her face. `As you know, or must have been told, it was a love story with them two from start to finish, from the first day they met in Wicklow until they parted at your daddy's grave in Sydney. Have you been there yet?'

`Not yet,' Mary-Anne said. `I want to know about his life first, before I go and face his death.'

`Well yes, as you ask, they were happy enough in those years after coming back from Van Diemen's Land. But they still had their problems, financial problems, like every other farmer in New South Wales. Despite being a policeman Michael still depended on the land as his main source of income, but the soil was not good fertile soil and repeated cropping only seemed to tire it and not rejuvenate it. Then in 1813 there was a terrible drought which parched and killed the land, as well as killing thousands of sheep and cattle. Water! Blessed water! Not man nor animal nor land can survive without it.

`Well, the drought lasted for almost three years, and when the rains finally came in 1815 it was glorious! Everyone was running and dancing and laughing in the rain until they were soaked to the skin.

`But then the laughing stopped, because the rain didn't

stop, and the floods from the Blue Mountains destroyed all the new crops and stock and drowned a number of the settlers... Such hard days for the people of New South Wales, lean and hard days... Your daddy was despairing of ever saving enough money to send for you four... But all we could was face it like Christians and start again when the weather stabilised, which it did in 1818, and that's when Michael decided he could wait no longer and worked so hard, brutally hard, so he could save every penny to send for his children in Ireland.'

Mary-Anne lifted her dark eyes from the lamp on the table and looked at Sarah directly.

`What made my daddy die?' she said.

`He just got sick, Mary-Anne. After being out in the bush a few days he got sick, and was sick for a week or so, and then he just closed his eyes and drifted away, back to the hills of Wicklow I've always believed.

`Mary won't have it that it was as simple as that. She still claims that it was his years in the prisons in the Pacific Ocean that put him in an early grave, and maybe she is right too, because even Hugh Vesty still says that he cannot believe how Michael survived after all the slaughter his body took from the man-killers in Norfolk Island.'

Sarah sighed sadly again, a tear slipping down. `But nothing Mary says will ever bring him back to her, and that is her continual heartbreak. For although she is now forty-five years old, in her heart she is still the same girl that ran away from home that October night in 1798 to marry him, the same girl who followed him all the way to Van Diemen's Land.'

Sarah reached out across the table and lifted Mary-Anne's hand in both of hers and clasped it tight. `Understand this, daughter of Mary Dwyer. Whatever you may learn about your daddy, good or bad, bad or good, and however you may think you loved him, the one who truly loved him was his wife Mary. And always at the back of her mind was the fear that he would die, and she would be left in this world without him. And now that has come to pass. So I am asking you, Mary-Anne, daughter of Michael Dwyer, to be gentle with your mother, be good to her, be kind to her, because ... because I don't think Mary will live for very much longer.'

Chapter Twenty-Two

Mary lived to see her children's children. She lived for thirty more years. She lived to see her daughter Mary-Anne married in New South Wales to a Wicklow man named Patrick Grace and give birth to four children.

She lived to see John and Peter married before they both moved to Bungedore and settled down on their own land with their families. She saw Bridget married to a bank manager named John O'Sullivan.

Esther married another Wicklow man named Owen Byrne, and both set up their own business, the Lake George Hotel, and were now prosperous members of the New South Wales community. James married a girl called Jane and moved to the district of Lachlan. The youngest, Eliza, ran away from home at fifteen in a fit of romance and she too was now married and a mother.

Her family scattered all over New South Wales, Mary was left alone in the house her husband had built at Cabramatta, which he had extended over the years to twelve rooms. A lonely empty house surrounded by forests where the dingoes howled at night, and memories of another time and another place came to life again in the flames of a crackling fire.

Each of her children wanted her to go and live with them; the choice was hard, but in the end she chose to go and live in Goulbourn with her third daughter, Bridget, the daughter she had conceived and given birth to in Van Diemen's Land.

*

The O'Sullivans' house in Goulbourn was spacious and comfortably furnished, as would be fitting for a banker. The lace curtains on the open long windows hung limply in the heat of summer, the air outside full of the noise of bees, and exquisitely coloured butterflies flitting everywhere.

Mary sat by the open window staring wide-eyed over her life. She knew the end was near, and was glad of it. Looking back, she had not done very much of note in her allotted time, except leave her beloved Ireland, and give seven children to Australia. And they in turn were giving more children to Australia, young men and women who were helping to shape a colony into a country. Yes, it would be to these early settlers that Australia would one day look back, as a piece of history, and wonder how it had been.

They would look back and try to imagine themselves into a world of convicts, and think how terrible these early days in Australia were; yet the convicts in Australia always had more hope than the oppressed people of Ireland, because the convicts always knew there would be an end to their bondage, seven years, fourteen years, even the lifers could earn their ticket of leave with good conduct; but for the people of Ireland there seemed no end to their agony.

There had been a terrible famine there ten years before, in 1846, a famine in which over one million Irish had died; corpses on the roadsides, dead children with green lips from eating grass; mass famine graves.

And yet – in that year of the potato failure and terrible famine, enough corn and beef to feed the whole of Ireland three times over, had been exported as usual to England; while emigrant ships left Ireland weekly, packed with over two million skeletal hopefuls on their way to food in America.

`They are going, going, going' the London Post had written cheerfully, `And very soon the Irish will be as scarce on the banks of the Shannon as the American Indians are on the banks of the Potomac.'

And Jesus said – `Love thy neighbour! Her eyes moved down to the missal on her lap. She still could not read more than a word here and there, although she pretended to Michael that she could read now, and he was very pleased with her progress, not knowing that she was learning the pages of her missal by memorising his words and not by reading them.

In the distance she heard the sound of a horse's hoofs hammering away and she looked up, a sunburst of a smile breaking on her face as she saw the distant and dark figure of a young man riding towards the house. He was still quite far off, but she knew it was him. She grabbed up her stick and moved out to meet him, not shuffling or hobbled, but slowly and sedately; she didn't truly need the brass-topped stick, but it had been given to her a year before by Bridget, and she felt obliged to use it, and now was fond of its company.

She stepped out to the veranda and watched him for a moment. No hat on his head as usual, black curls flying in the breeze of his horse's speed.

`Michael!' she cried joyously, waving her stick like an Irish child with a hawthorn branch.

He slowed to a canter as he approached, then drew rein and grinned down at her, before leaping from his saddle and tying the horse to the veranda rail.

`Michael,' she said, `have you have come to escort me to Mass?'

`I have indeed,' he said, smiling. He bent and kissed her cheek, and she looked up at him adoringly.

`Michael,' she said, `why is it that you always make me feel young again?'

`My natural charm,' he said seductively.

She frowned at that, but then she smiled again, for she knew it was a manner he used only with her, and no other female. From as far back as she could remember he had always had a special kind of love for her. And oh! how she had loved him! Of all the children of her children, this one had always been her favourite grandchild – Michael, now twenty-five years old, son of her own son John, and the first young man to be ordained a priest into the new Benedictine order in Australia.

He paused, and looked up at the sky for a moment, and she saw that his face was very tanned. But then it would be, for he spent most of his time riding all over New South Wales to tend the scattered population of Catholics who lived too far away to attend church for their marriages, baptisms, and requiems.

`I see you are ready and waiting,' he said, glancing from her bonnet and shawl to the missal clutched in her hand. `Did Bridget leave the trap?'

`No,' Mary answered. `She took the trap and left the chaise.'

John and Bridget O'Sullivan were away from home with their children, visiting James in Lachlan, and were expected back late that night. But two kind and faithful servants were in residence in the house to see to all Mary's needs. One of them, Teresa, now came out on to the veranda and greeted Michael with a delighted smile.

`Good morning, Father, is it to Mass you'll be taking your grandmother now?'

`And not only my grandmother, Teresa, but yourself and Molly as well.'

`Good gracious, Father, but ye'll be turning us all into saints yet!'

And with that Teresa skipped away and returned in less than a minute with Molly, both of them bonneted and wreathed in smiles, for they took great pride in being the only two Catholic servant girls who were regularly escorted to Mass by the priest himself. And himself a fine young specimen of a priest at that!

`I'll return to share breakfast with you,' he told Mary as he helped her into the chaise, `but after that I must leave. I have to ride over to Bungendore this afternoon.'

Mary nodded, for he spent his life riding here and there from dawn to dusk and never showed any sign of fatigue whatever. `And what hymn have you planned for me today, Michael,' she asked, never managing to call her grandson `Father'.

`A special hymn, Grandmother,' he said with a smile. `One that will please you greatly.

`The twenty-third psalm?'

`No,'

`O Glorious Redeemer?'

`No.'

`Hail Queen of Heaven?'

`No.'

`Oh, Michael!' she said indignantly, banging her stick on the floor of the chaise. `Stop teasing me now!'

He threw back his head and laughed. `Wait and see,' he

said, climbing up to bench and lifting the reins. `Wait and see.'

*

Mary sat in the front row of St Mary's Church, Teresa and Molly each side of her, all eyes on young Father Dwyer as he said Mass; and it was a very different young man that stood before the altar, to the one that had ridden up to the house like a wild and carefree horsemen earlier that morning. He looked slowly and reverently around at his congregation then stood with arms open, palms forward, in a gesture of welcome.

`*Dominus Vobiscum,*' he said. `The Lord be with you.'

`*Et cum spirit tu tuo,*' the people answered, `And with you.'

`*Sursum corda,*' the priest smiled. `Lift up your hearts!'

Memories, memories. Mary's mind drifted back to another time and another place, and a young French priest in a secret penal chapel on the Quays of Dublin. Memories, memories, ghosts that had haunted her for thirty years moved through the mist before her eyes as in the background she could dimly hear voices saying the Pater Noster and the Credo. Then she heard music, beautiful music that touched her very soul and quickened her breathing.

`The hymn, Ma'am.' Teresa nudged, knowing how much Mrs Dwyer loved her hymns and always joined in the singing of them, however quietly.

Mary turned her eyes towards the choir, but then sat silently as a young boy of about ten years old rose to his feet at the pulsing sound of the organ. She knew him to be the son of a convict-servant from Wexford, the son of man who had died in Ireland's famine and whose mother, ten years ago, had been transported, although pregnant, for stealing corn. A ten-year-old boy that her grandson had taken under his wing, as if he were his own son, the only kind of adoptive son a priest could have.

The boy now stood alone and sang with a voice so full of beautiful and innocent purity that Mary closed her eyes and

307

felt her heart race with the mixed emotions of agony and ecstasy.

> `Hail, glorious Saint Patrick,*
> *Dear saint of our isle,*
> *On us thy poor children*
> *Bestow a sweet smile;*
> *And now thou art high*
> *In the mansions above,*
> *On Erin's green valleys*
> *Look down in thy love.'*

The Choir rose for the chorus:

> *On Erin's green valleys,*
> *On Erin's green valleys,*
> *On Erin's green valleys*
> *Look down in thy love.*

As the organ played and the boy prepared to sing again, Mary looked towards the young priest at the altar, and saw her grandson smiling at her, a smile that took her right back to the Glen of Imaal in Wicklow, her eyes misty with mourning for the hills and vales that she would never see again.

> Thy people, now exiles
> On many a shore,
> Shall love and revere thee
> Till time be no more;
> And the fire thou hast kindled
> Shall ever burn bright.
> Its warmth undiminished,
> Undying its light.'

Mary leaned on her stick and tried to stand as the choir and the entire congregation rose to its feet and joined in the chorus that rose up to the dim arches and wooden rafters of the church.

> *On Erin's green valleys,*
> *On Erin's green valleys,*

On Erin's green valleys
Look down in thy love.

`Well, Grandmother,' the young priest said with a smile as he came out of the vestry and walked towards the front row of chairs when the Mass was over. `Did you approve of the hymn today?'

Mary had not managed to rise to her feet to join in the chorus. Teresa and Molly were standing in front of her.

`Oh, Father Michael...' Teresa turned a tear-stained face to the priest, then herself and Molly moved aside from the woman who sat as if she was sleeping, but as her grandson stared at her, he knew that Mary Doyle Dwyer had heard her last hymn.

*

Three days later Father Michael Dwyer officiated at his grandmother's Requiem Mass; then at the funeral which was led by the Bishop of Sydney's carriage and attended by large numbers who followed the cortege into Devonshire Street Cemetery where Mary Dwyer was finally laid to rest in the same grave as her husband.

The people stood in a large silent crowd and watched as one by one the children and grandchildren of Michael and Mary Dwyer stepped forward and sprinkled holy water into the grave. They were all there, those who should and could have been there – all the old and elderly friends who had come to this land from Wicklow under the surrender terms offered to their captain.

And perhaps it was for them, that the priest ended the burial service with the hymn that Michael Dwyer, in his last dying moments in the house at Cabramatta, had requested be sung at his own burial, but which was not, because no one in the colony had known the words.

But the young Benedictine priest had learned them long ago. And so, with a quiet but resonant voice, Michael's grandson stood by the grave in Devonshire Street Cemetery, and sang the Corpus Christi.

Come then, good Shepherd, bread divine,

Still show to us thy mercy sign;
Oh, feed us still, keep us thine;
So we may see thy glories shine
In the fields of immortality...'

After a silence, the priest then held up his hand over the mutual grave of his Wicklow-born grandparents, and said the farewell.

`The body lies in the dust of the earth, but the spirit is free again. May God, who has called you, bid you welcome, into that place where Lazarus is poor no longer. May his angels greet you, and lead you home to Paradise, and establish you in that bliss which knows no ending.'

Epilogue

Some thirty years later again, when he was no longer the youngest, but the most famous Benedictine priest in New South Wales, Father Dwyer who had become Dean Dwyer, attended a celebration in Sydney held in honour of his grandfather. The events were reported in the Sydney *Freeman's Journal*, copies of which were sent back to the people of Ireland, and many a flush of pride mantled a Wicklowman's brow as he read the words from Australia.

> Sixty years ago there passed away in our city one who, in his own sphere, had led a life as adventurous, heroic, and full of romance as any recorded in the history of struggling nationalities. Michael Dwyer, the insurgent chief of the Wicklow Mountains, was exiled to this colony in 1805, and now sleeps his last long sleep in Devonshire Street Cemetery – far from the hills of his own Imaal. But still the patriot captain cannot be said to occupy a grave in the land of the stranger. His descendants are still amongst us, and by them, as well as his countrymen, the memory of the dead patriot is kept green and fresh as in his own shamrock land; and many years will pass away ere this gallant Kosciusko of Irish history is forgotten.
> *

In Ireland a number of monuments were erected to Michael Dwyer in the County of Wicklow, but in Australia, in 1898, on the centenary of the 1798 Rebellion, over 100,000 Irish who travelled from all over Australasia attended a procession which started at Devonshire Street Cemetery, where the coffins of Michael and Mary Dwyer were removed into a hearse and taken to Waverley Cemetery where they were reburied beneath a beautiful white marble and bronze monument topped by a Celtic Cross, draped with the Green flag of Ireland and the Blue and White flag of Australia.

At the graveside stood the grandchildren, great

311

grandchildren, and great great grandchildren of Michael and Mary Dwyer, and 100,000 others. But the monument was not only a tribute to Michael and Mary Dwyer, and all those others who had been transported after the 1798 Rebellion, it was a tribute to all the young Irish men and women who had left their own oppressed country, and helped to build a nation, in return for the chance they had been given, and the freedom they had found, in the new land of Australia.

* Tadeusz Kosciuszko--Leader of Rebellion for the freedom of Poland in 1794.

Short Bibliography

Diary of Sir John Moore, edited by Major-General Sir J.F. Maurice. 1904

Charles Cornwallis, Memoirs and Correspondence.

The Viceroy's Postbag: Whitehall Papers and Correspondence of the Earl of Hardwicke. Michael MacDonagh. 1904

Luke Cullen Paper and Manuscript, National Library of Ireland.

Memoirs of Miles Byrne, edited by his widow. Paris, 1863.

Memoirs of Joseph Holt, edited by T. Crofton Croker. 1838

Michael Dwyer, by Charles Dickson.

Life of Robert Emmet, by R.R. Madden. 1856

Vice-Admiral William Bligh, by George Mackaness. 1931.

Irish in Australia, by James Hogan. 1887

Lachlan Macquarie, by M. H. Ellis.

Historical Records of Australia.

Newspapers:
Saunders Newsletter – 15th August 1798.
Freeman's Journal – 30th June 1798.
Wicklow People – various dates, 1938
Sydney Gazette – various dates, 1807 and 1810.

Also by Gretta Curran Browne

(The Liberty Trilogy)

TREAD SOFTLY ON MY DREAMS

FIRE ON THE HILL

A WORLD APART

*

(The Macquarie Series)
BY EASTERN WINDOWS

THE FAR HORIZON

JARVISFIELD

THE WAYWARD SON

*

GHOSTS IN SUNLIGHT
(Contemporary Thriller)

RELATIVE STRANGERS
(TV Series Tie-in starring Brenda Fricker)

ORDINARY DECENT CRIMINAL
(Novel of Film starring Kevin Spacey)

www.grettacurranbrowne.com

CPSIA information can be obtained at www.ICGtesting.com
Printed in the USA
LVOW04s1511230615

443536LV00017B/689/P